I BRAKE FOR
BAD BOYS

I BRAKE FOR BAD BOYS

Lori Foster
Janelle Denison
Shannon McKenna

BRAVA

KENSINGTON PUBLISHING CORP.
http://www.kensingtonbooks.com

BRAVA BOOKS are published by

Kensington Publishing Corp.
119 West 40th Street
New York, NY 10018

All Kensington Titles, Imprints and Distributed Lines are available at special quantity discounts for bulk purchases for sales
promotion, premiums, fund-raising, and educational or institu-
tional use.

Special book excerpts or customized printings can also be created to fit specific needs. For details, write or phone the office of
the Kensington special sales manager: Kensington Publishing
Corp., 119 West 40th Street, New York, NY, 10018, attn: Special Sales Department, Phone: 1-800-221-2647.

Brava Books and the B logo Reg. U.S. Pat. & TM Off.

ISBN-13: 978-0-7582-0418-9
ISBN-10: 0-7582-0418-3

First trade paperback printing: November, 2002
First mass market printing: February 2013

10 9 8 7 6 5 4 3 2 1

Printed in the United States of America

CONTENTS

Drive Me Wild

Lori Foster

Chapter One

She'd gotten herself into a pickle this time.

Too distracted to work, Erica Lee slouched back in her office chair and blew her bangs out of her face. Who would have thought that uptight Asia and ultra-shy Becky would have followed through on the dares? Erica sure hadn't. But with only a little prodding both of them had traipsed right over there and done the un-expected.

It boggled the mind, it surely did.

Now her turn had rolled around and hey, it wasn't that she had anything against porn shops or fantasies or the like. But where the hell did they expect her to find a man who wouldn't be a pain in the patoot?

Of course, for them it had turned out great. That is, if one considered marriage great. Erica was still unde-cided on that particular point. Then again, footloose and fancy-free wasn't really working for her either.

She winced over that sad truth.

In the next second her office door slammed open with startling force. She jumped a foot and almost fell out of her rolling chair. She was alone in the office, and in fact, the entire floor was deserted while employees attended some meeting that she'd managed to opt out of. She'd been so lost in thought she hadn't even heard anyone approaching.

Holding a hand to her heart and ready to blast the noisy offender, Erica looked up—and up some more until she fell headlong into the mesmerizing midnight gaze of none other than Ian Conrad.

Oh, boy. Her heartbeat didn't calm with recognition. Nope. If anything, it tripped even faster. Ian was just so . . . so male.

Hot around the collar and sweaty, clad in blue jeans, a dirty cambric work shirt, and scuffed lace-up black boots, Ian epitomized all that was man. He wasn't particularly handsome, at least not in the classical sense, but that didn't lessen his impact one bit.

His features were bold with a strong, straight high-bridged nose, a powerful chin, and high, harshly carved cheekbones. His eyes were the darkest blue and piercing in intensity—the type of eyes that froze a woman to the spot whenever he directed his attention on her. His dark brown hair was more straight than not, a little shaggy and unkempt.

Bracing his long thick legs apart, he filled the doorway—and then some.

Well, well. Quiet, masterful, impossible-to-ignore Ian. Erica raised a brow, wondering what had put him in such a temper when in the past she'd never seen him so much as frown—even when she'd deliberately provoked him.

Unlike most of the men she knew, Ian was always calm and always firmly in control—of himself and everyone around him.

Not that she'd ever let him control *her.* "I've witnessed more polite entries."

She'd meant to be a smart-ass, of course, but her attitude got snagged in her throat when Ian took two long heavy strides to her desk, braced strong, lean hands flat on the surface, and bent down—way down—until his nose nearly touched hers.

Good Lord, she could see every eyelash surrounding those mesmerizing eyes, feel his warm breath against her lips, and smell his raw, potent scent.

"I know exactly what you're up to, Erica."

Her eyes widened over that gravel-deep voice that seemed to sink right into her bones. Combined with the heat of his gaze, his rough tone was impossible to misunderstand. It was that man to woman tone, and sexual awareness rolled over her. Feeling helpless, she asked, "You do?"

"Damn right." His mouth appeared tight with annoyance, but still sexy. "Your buddy George was more than willing to spell it out."

Her gaze snapped back to his. "George spoke to you?" With Becky as a best friend, and George as Becky's fiancé, she supposed he could be considered a buddy. That is, unless he'd done something to irk her—and given Ian's unusual mood, it sounded like he might have.

In that case, Erica would have George's hide.

"No, he didn't speak to *me.* And that's most of the problem right there."

Ian's disgruntled scowl was dark enough to make grown men tremble. No wonder he kept it under wraps in polite company. Not that Erica intended to tremble in front of him. Later, when she was away from him and remembering how close he'd gotten and how delicious he smelled, she might shake a little. But no way would she let him know he affected her that much.

"Well, if George didn't speak to you, then . . . ?" She let the sentence hang, waiting for him to explain.

"He didn't. But he did tell a couple of other guys what you have planned at that damn porn shop."

Erica's mouth fell open. It took a lot to shock her, and this definitely qualified. She sputtered a moment before finding her voice. "Why, that miserable rat!"

Ian straightened, studied her a second more, and then waved away her indignation. "Forget that. Hell, the whole factory knows what you and Asia and Becky have been up to so it's hardly a secret."

She'd just gotten her mouth shut when it dropped open again. "They don't!"

"You're not naive, Erica. You know something like that can't be kept quiet. Hell, I'd be surprised if all of Cuther doesn't know about it."

Erica shot out of her chair to pace. She, Asia, and Becky had made a deal when the new porn shop, Wild Honey, had opened up in their miserably quiet hometown of Cuther, Indiana. They were each to visit the somewhat titillating establishment with a specific fantasy in mind. As soon as they spotted a man shopping for wares that indicated a similar interest, they had to ask him out.

Asia had gotten off easy when Cameron overheard the initial discussion as well as the fantasy she'd claimed. Without letting on, he'd visited the shop on the right day at the right time and he'd specifically purchased items that would draw Asia to him, as per the dare. Since Cameron had already been half in love with Asia, one thing had led to another and they'd quickly advanced from making love to making wedding plans.

Then Cameron had played big brother and helped

set Becky up so she got exactly what she was looking for too—in both her fantasy and her choice of man. George had been something of a surprise, but Erica liked him. Or at least she had before he let the cat out of the bag. Now she wasn't so sure.

Becky and George were currently shopping for engagement rings while Asia and Cameron had just tied the knot. As the only unattached female still in their circle, that left Erica out in the cold. Not that she wanted to be married, because she didn't. No, sir. Huh-uh.

It didn't matter that George and Cameron made it look so damn appealing with the way they catered to Becky and Asia and kept them both smiling like lovesick saps. Hell, these days it was downright nauseating to be around any of them, they all walked around in such a vacuous fog of romantic bliss.

Fuming, Erica whirled around to face Ian. "Who did George tell it to?"

"I don't know and I don't care."

"What do you mean, you don't know?" She didn't exactly mean to screech, but there were only around two hundred workers at the factory and everyone pretty much recognized everyone else. "What department do they work in?"

He narrowed his eyes. "I didn't see them, Erica. I was in the ceiling wiring the lights when they walked in. They didn't even know I was there and I didn't care to announce myself."

"Never mind, then." She started to go around him. "I'll find out." And when she did, she'd . . .

Blocking the door, Ian crossed his massive arms over his wide chest and glared at her. "It doesn't matter who they are because you're not meeting up with either one of them."

Erica drew to an indignant halt. She hadn't planned

to go anywhere with either of the men but, oh, boy, Ian's tone was guaranteed to get her back up. She knew him well enough since they worked in the same company and their paths often crossed. They chatted regularly, too, especially when he'd rewired her office, but then, she chatted with all the men.

Unfortunately, she was more aware of Ian than the others. She couldn't put her finger on it, but something about him just really got to her—and she didn't like that. She didn't want to be drawn to him, but how could she not? When Ian was around, his personality was so quietly dominant that every other guy faded into the woodwork.

Regardless of all that, there was no way in hell she'd let Ian or any other man dictate to her.

Holding his steady gaze, she stalked closer toward him, her stride as long as her leather miniskirt would allow. "I'll see them, and a dozen other men, if that's what I want to do."

"No." He stared down at her from his lofty height. "You'll see *me*."

That drew her up short in mingled shock and affront. He'd sounded so . . . certain, so in charge and imperious . . . Luckily, she managed to laugh over her reaction. "You?" Her sneering tone sounded just right. "Gee, Ian, I didn't know you were interested."

His expression turned cynical; he even went so far as to shake his head in an indulgent way. "Erica, you assume every guy is interested."

Insults? Now just what did he think that would accomplish?

"This time," he conceded in that deep voice that felt like a tactile rub and sent shivers down her spine, "you're right."

He admitted it? And why did *that* give her such a thrill? She started to deny him, but he didn't give her the chance.

"I think you're interested as well, which is why we need to bypass this foolishness with the porn shop."

Foolishness? Okay, so now that it was her turn to visit the place, it did seem a tad foolish. Unlike Becky and Asia, she didn't need encouragement to date. Heck, her calendar stayed booked. She considered herself the quintessential party girl.

Her only problem was finding a man who could keep her interest, because so far no one had. Most were selfish and shallow and set in their ways—meaning they had no room to adjust to a woman who was also set in *her* own ways.

But she'd devised the plan and it had worked brilliantly to bring Asia out of her self-imposed celibacy, and to help Becky shed her unfounded insecurities.

So how dare Ian call her plan foolish?

She needed to bring Ian Conrad down a peg, and fast—before his dynamic manner started to turn her on. Sheesh, sometimes she was such a female, enjoying all that macho arrogance. "Did George, perchance, mention what kind of man I was looking for?"

Ian's eyes darkened a bit more, until they appeared more black than blue. He stared at her, his gaze so probing Erica felt pinned in place. She couldn't look away, and he wouldn't look away. "Yeah, something about sex slaves."

Despite herself, Erica's face heated. Becky was liable to be a widow even before she tied the damn knot, because Erica seriously considered killing George. She hid her turbulent thoughts from Ian, unwilling to let him know how the conversation disconcerted her.

Instead, she shook back her hair, propped her hands on her hips, and slowly smiled. "Should I presume you're here because you're willing to fill that role?"

"As a sex slave?" He grunted. "I'm here because I want you to stop dodging me."

"I don't." Her reply was fast and automatic. How dare he suggest such a thing? She didn't dodge anyone—not even big buff men who were a little too tempting and a lot too overwhelming.

"Bull. You'll flirt and tease with every timid weak-kneed jerk in the factory, but you're always cautious with me, never quite letting loose."

"That's not true." She didn't let loose with anyone.

"And no matter how many times I manage to corner you long enough to have a conversation, you're still jumpy as hell."

"Ha!"

"You're jumpy right now, Erica." With one finger, he touched the racing pulse at her throat. His voice gentled. "I know I intimidate some people, but—"

He'd noticed her uneasiness? And here she thought she'd concealed that with plenty of sarcasm. Ian Conrad was just too damn astute for his own good.

Through her surprise, she managed a credible laugh. "You, intimidating? Be real, Ian. So, you're big? So what." *So,* Erica reminded herself, *he was big and calmly autocratic in a way that would make any sane woman think twice about getting too close.*

Unlike many of the men she'd dated from the factory, Ian wasn't in a managerial position. His work was physical—and suited his large, hard frame. Compared to the guys in suits, he looked deliciously rugged and capable in his work clothes. Very capable. Very manly. Maybe *too* manly.

Halfway through the day he'd be all hot and sweaty,

his brown hair damp against his nape and forehead, his shirtsleeves rolled up to show off thick forearms. And his jeans were always well worn, snug on his tight butt and long muscular thighs and a heavy . . .

She nearly shuddered, just thinking about it, then covered that innate reaction by checking her nails and striving for a look of indifference. She *did* have to do that around him a lot, it seemed. But it wasn't her fault he exuded such raw, powerful appeal. "Ya know, Ian, it's hard for you to intimidate anyone when you're always quiet as a church mouse."

"Until I have something to say. And Erica, I have plenty to say to you."

That sounded like a warning, causing her heart to lurch and regaining her attention. He could be so damn intense, and yes, intimidating. She'd never admit it out loud, but it was a little thrilling. If she'd been truthful about her fantasy and what really turned her on, then . . . but no, she'd claimed to want a sex slave, and damn it, she'd stick with that story. "Yeah, all right, big boy. So speak up."

Trying her best to be casual, Erica propped her hip on the edge of her desk and crossed her legs. To her annoyance, though she had a lot of leg showing Ian never looked away from her face.

But oh so slowly, the corners of his mouth curled and wow, that gradual smile had a devastating effect on her equilibrium. It was wicked and sensual and suggestive, just hinting at what outrageous things he might do.

And then he did it, again with a distinct lack of haste that had Erica near to bursting with anticipation. By the time he stepped up, firmly clasped her knees in his big hands and drew her legs apart so he could stand between them, Erica was ready to swoon when she'd never considered herself a swooning type of woman.

Stunned by his daring, more than a little breathless, she stared up at him. He wedged himself closer—and in the process spread her legs more. She felt the rough denim of his jeans rubbing the tender insides of her thighs, felt the tensed steal of his muscles, his carefully restrained power.

"Listen up, Erica." He was again so close that if she leaned forward one measly inch she'd be kissing him. "I want you. I've wanted you since I first saw you months ago."

One breath, two . . . "That right?" Damn, her voice still sounded like a squeak.

"Mmm. You're bossy as hell, gutsy, a little too outspoken and risqué, but all in all, I like it."

Some of her sensual haze dissipated, replaced by annoyance. "What's with all the insults?"

"Just telling it like it is. You flirt too damn much, tease without regard to consequences, and avoid any man who might come close to matching you. But you won't avoid me. Not anymore." His midnight eyes glittered dangerously. "Isn't that right?"

Annoyed by her own desire to submit, Erica pushed away from him, only he didn't let go of her knees and he was such a solid hulk he sure as hell didn't budge. Instead, she almost fell flat on her desk, sending papers scattering to the floor. She caught herself on her elbows but it was still an ignominious position, and Ian in an aggressive mood wasn't a man to be taken lightly.

Straightening seemed a high priority but before she could manage it, he lowered himself over her. With the impact of an electric jolt, she felt his hard abdomen press against her soft belly, his groin nestle against hers. *Oh, wow.*

Her legs, literally hanging over the end of her desk, sprawled wide apart to accommodate his muscular hips.

If anyone walked into her office right now, she'd have a lot of explaining to do—that is, if she could find any breath to speak, which was doubtful given how she panted.

When she realized just how quickly and easily he'd aroused her, she stiffened in alarm.

Ian snuggled closer and murmured, "Shhh, relax," and none of the flustered anxiety she suffered sounded in his tone. "Everyone's gone to a meeting. We're all alone."

And that was supposed to reassure her when all she could think about was wrapping her legs around his waist? So unlike her! So . . . submissive.

He cupped her face and smoothed her chin with his thumbs. His touch was sexual, but also tender, and Erica got flustered all over again. "Now tell me you'll forget this sex slave business and give me a chance to show you how good it'll be between us."

He oozed so much confidence, she couldn't help but believe him. And she wanted to agree, she really did. But old habits were hard to break, so she raised her chin, narrowed her eyes, and smiled her most taunting smile.

"You want a chance, Ian? Then meet me at Wild Honey after work, and plan on playing. Because I'm not about to back out of my deal with Asia and Becky and that means I need a sex slave. It can either be you—or it can be someone else. You decide."

A taut stillness settled over him, but his eyes remained bright, turbulent. "You're pushing me," he accused, still stroking her chin with an incredible gentleness in direct contrast to his tone. "I have to wonder if it's because you really expect me to back off, or because you're hoping I'll push back."

Erica gulped. "Just . . . just telling you the rules."

Damn it, she'd stammered so she quickly tried to compensate. "You do know how to follow rules, don't you, Ian?"

She waited for him to lurch away. She waited for a dose of masculine anger, or at least annoyance. She waited for the typical male response.

What she got instead was a soft sigh and a butterfly kiss that came and went before she could even appreciate it. Resigned, he growled, "Have it your way, lady," and to Erica's astute ears it sounded like another warning, which had her heart beating double time.

In excitement and challenge.

She was still contemplating all the things he made her feel when he straightened, caught her elbows and pulled her upright so fast her head swam.

"I'll be there," he said, and chucked her chin. "But just remember, turnabout is fair play."

Now *that* was a warning, no two ways about it.

He released her and Erica almost slid off the side of the desk into a molten puddle. He left much more quietly than he had entered.

Lord have mercy. What had she gotten herself into?

Ian smiled once his back was turned. Sexy, sultry Erica had looked so stunned, so confused, maybe even annoyed.

And definitely intrigued.

For months now he'd been studying her, getting closer to her though she didn't seem to realize it and she sure as hell didn't cooperate. But finally, he knew just how to get her where he wanted her—which for starters was in his bed, under him, her body open and willing and hot.

He'd seen the subtle signs, the prickly temper, the contempt she veiled behind sharp teasing, and he knew Erica Lee was a woman in need of a good, long ride. Not some half-baked quickie, which seemed to be the speed most men preferred these days. He liked things longer, deeper, more intense. When he made love, he liked to take his time, to appreciate every nuance, to wallow in the sensations.

And so did Erica. He'd bet his eyeteeth on that.

From the very first glance she'd turned him on, and he spent a lot of time contemplating what a perfect match she'd be, in more ways than one. Sexually she'd be ideal. He thought of the different ways he'd take her, how he'd make her muscles burn, her skin sweat, her body melt. Once he got inside Erica, he wouldn't stop pleasuring her until she throbbed in satisfaction from her ears down to her dainty little toes. He'd leave her every nerve ending tingling and begging for more.

From him.

But Erica liked to play games and he'd never been a player. He did things his way and only his way. So he'd dredged up patience and watched for the right opportunity.

In the meantime, he'd gotten to know her better and he liked what he'd learned. He liked her. A lot.

She was a hard worker, always on time, rarely calling in sick. And she was loyal. No one could question her dedication to her friends. Ian knew she truly cared about Asia and Becky. They were a trio.

On top of those fine qualities, it had only taken him moments to recognize her intelligence, which gratified him since he had no tolerance for stupidity. Erica had a quick wit, a sharp sense of humor, and a massive chip on her shoulder that should have weighed down her slender body, but instead kept her backbone rigid and her shoulders stiff in cocky defiance.

Once he got her naked, though, he'd rid her of that rebellion. She'd bend to him—and enjoy doing it. He'd see to it.

"Hey, how'd it go?"

Ian stopped, startled to see George and Cameron standing just inside his basement office. Management rarely ventured into the gloomy bowels of the building, as they liked to call it. Ian preferred to call it quiet and private.

Whenever one of the suits wanted to see you, you were summoned upstairs.

Yet there they both stood, expectant, impatient. Hell, he hadn't even been aware of taking the elevator down, he'd been so engrossed in his plans for seduction.

Ian shouldered his way around George and dropped into the enormous leather chair behind his sturdy metal desk. "I hope you two don't expect a blow by blow report?"

George scowled. "No, of course not. But we don't want her unhappy either."

Cameron leaned against the wall. "If you manage to piss Erica off, she'll tell Asia and Becky and—"

"And ruin your marital bliss, yeah I know." Ian leaned back and surveyed the two men who, due to short association, couldn't quite be called friends yet, but were certainly on their way there.

The fact that they actually cared about Erica helped a lot in gaining his respect. "Everything's fine. I'm not going to make her mad or unhappy. Just the opposite. But you know Erica. She's bound to do some blustering before she settles down."

"But it will be just bluster? You're sure of that?"

Ian shrugged. He wasn't about to tell them that Erica's grumbling would turn to soft moans soon enough. "I'm meeting her at the shop after work tonight. Just avoid her till then and you should be in the clear."

George turned to Cameron. "He's awfully damn confident, don't you think?"

"Yeah." And then, with a dose of suspicion to Ian, "Just how well do you know Erica?"

Ian almost laughed. They honestly expected her to chew him up and spit him out. Neither of them had understood Erica's subtle signals, but because the sexual chemistry Ian shared with her was enough to choke a horse, he'd recognized her silent pleas for satisfaction on a gut level.

She was a complex woman, more so than most. She intrigued him, amused him, and made him hot enough to burn. He looked forward to discovering all the facets to her personality. He looked forward to calling her his own.

He needed to reassure Cameron and George, and he tried to do that without telling them things that would be private between him and the woman under discussion. "I know what Erica hides, and what she wants exposed."

Judging by their expressions, they didn't believe him.

Cameron's brows rose and he almost laughed. "God, she's going to hang you by your balls."

Groaning, George said, "I should never have gotten involved in this. When you told me you wanted Erica, I really thought you'd use a little more finesse."

"She's not a cactus that has to be approached carefully," Ian said.

George gave him an incredulous look before turning

away. "I should have called a halt the second you told me this harebrained plan." Hands deep in his pockets, he began to pace. "Becky is going to be so upset."

Ian could clue him in on a way to get around Becky's temper, but George didn't look open to coaching. And anyway, a man in love could be very prickly about hearing his woman's name mentioned—especially by another man.

Then George chuckled and said, "I guess I'll be doing some making up." He rubbed his hands together. "I do love how sweetly Becky forgives me."

Ian grinned. Maybe old George knew just what he was doing after all.

Cameron pushed away from the wall. "It's not that I don't find this fascinating, but I need to get back to work. So just tell me if things went according to plan."

"Perfectly. I told her George here had spilled the beans to two men—"

George whirled around. *"Two?"*

"—but that I didn't know who they were."

"Shit, shit, shit."

Ian barely hid his grin over George's distress. "She wouldn't admit it, but she's embarrassed."

"Erica?" Cameron asked with a fat dose of incredulity.

"We're talking about Erica Lee, right?" George seconded, just to make sure there was no confusion.

"One and the same." Ian frowned at both men. "She's first and foremost a woman, you know."

"Gotcha."

"Whatever you say."

If he hadn't needed their help, Ian never would have confided so much to them. What he did with Erica, the way their relationship evolved, was nobody's business. But she was skittish at the idea of giving herself to him,

so after he'd heard the gossip of how the other two cou-
ples had met at the porn shop, he'd cornered George
and Cameron before things could progress without
him, and he'd insisted he be included—for Erica.
"Being embarrassed makes her more likely to accept
me before either of the two imaginary guys can make a
move."

At least with George and Cameron, he knew they
cared about Erica without being romantically involved
with her. Not only were they both already in solid relationships, but they spoke about Erica with the fond ex-
asperation they might have doled out to a pesky younger
sister.

Cameron chuckled, but he could barely be heard
over George's grumbling about ending up in the dog-
house.

"Hey, I'm all for making the little witch squirm,"
Cameron said. "It's only fair."

She'd squirm all right, Ian thought, but not the way
they meant.

"Amen," George added. "God knows she loves to
dish out the barbs, and I've got the holes in my hide to
prove it. It'll do her good to get knocked off her high
horse."

Ian had no intention of bringing Erica down, but he
did expect to get all that energy and attitude normally
used for sarcasm funneled into a new direction. When
he thought of Erica concentrating fully on him, his
muscles clenched in anticipation.

"Just don't hurt her," George tacked on. "I mean
that. She rubs me the wrong way sometimes, but deep
down I like her."

Ian eyed him. "Deep down, huh?"

"Same here," Cameron added. "Erica can be a little
hard-edged, but she has a good heart."

"When I'm done," Ian promised with a smile, "she'll be thanking you both."

Neither of them appeared convinced, given the way they rolled their eyes and snickered. But they did finally leave his office, giving Ian the opportunity to plan. He tilted back in his chair and propped his booted feet on the desk. He was semi-hard and had been since first walking into Erica's office. She'd looked downright edible in her miniskirt, her glossy black hair loose, that taunting smile. And those slanted green eyes . . . His hands curled tight. Damn, he could just imagine how sexy she'd look in the middle of a screaming climax.

He closed his eyes and concentrated on breathing.

Afterward, he thought, once Erica was softened up and more relaxed with the release of sexual tension, they'd talk. Her guards would be down and she'd be open to him, emotionally vulnerable. The image of Erica curled beside him, all womanly warm, was almost more satisfying than the idea of taking her sexually.

It was definitely as big a turn-on.

He'd never get rid of his boner thinking like that. To distract himself, Ian pulled out a pen and paper and started jotting down notes. He'd need to make a few purchases at Wild Honey and he wanted things that would give the most impact, items that would rock her feminist foundation.

He put body oil at the top of the list, and worked his way down from that—and all the while, he smiled in anticipation.

Chapter Two

Erica was in the lounge waiting when Becky and Asia finally strolled in. They took one look at her and balked. Becky even tried to turn around to sneak back out but Asia snagged her arm and dragged her to the table.

"My, my, my," Erica quipped. She hadn't been able to locate George, so Becky and Asia would become the recipients of her discontent. "Don't you two look apprehensive. Now why would that be, I wonder?"

Asia plopped down into her seat and even rolled her eyes. "Knock it off, Erica. You're terrorizing Becky with all that nasty sarcasm."

Wide-eyed Becky showed a lot more caution in seating herself. "Are you mad?"

Erica shot her a look. "Now Becky, why would I be mad? Just because your honey manipulated things a bit for me?"

Becky nodded, making her dark blond curls bounce. "George told me that he was trying to help you out by telling someone about the plan, but—"

"Do you know who he spoke to?" Though Erica asked the question casually, curiosity burned inside her. Who besides Becky, Asia, Cameron, and George knew about her risqué plans?

According to Ian, all of Cuther. Erica bit back a groan at that possibility.

"He didn't say," Becky ventured carefully. "And I didn't think to ask, not after he told me that Ian Conrad had overheard it all and that now you and Ian are . . . well . . ."

Suddenly Asia leaned forward. "George and Cameron said you're going to play sex slave with Ian."

There was a priceless look of scandalized trepidation on her friends' faces. Trying not to laugh, Erica said, "That's right," and she was proud of how cool she sounded—as if the idea didn't give her a little apprehension herself.

"But with *Ian Conrad*?"

Erica's reaction had been the same as Asia's, but she shrugged. "Yeah, so? What's wrong with Ian?"

With a worried look, Becky said, "Nothing's *wrong* with him, exactly."

Asia agreed. "Nope. Not a thing."

Fidgeting, glancing at Asia, Becky said, "Except that he's, well . . ."

"Enormous," Asia supplied.

Becky nodded. "Yes, enormous. Perfect description. And maybe . . ." She searched for the new word.

"Forceful."

"Exactly. *Very* forceful." Becky looked quite concerned by that fact.

Maintaining her lazy pose, Erica looked first at Asia, then Becky. "He's so quiet, how do you know he's forceful?"

Asia pushed back her long brown hair and propped her chin on a fist. "Maybe it's because he's so quiet, and still everything gets done. He'll have some guys start working on wiring something and if they don't get it right, he doesn't say a word, he just has this . . . look."

"He does have a look," Becky said.

Asia shivered. "All the new guys stammer around him."

"So do the women," Becky confided. "I've heard them asking him out, coming on to him. And you know what he does?"

Despite herself, Erica was fascinated. "No, what does he do?"

"He gets this little smile and this real gentle look in his eyes and, oh, man, it's . . ."

"Devastating." Asia sighed.

"And then . . ." Becky bit her bottom lip, building the suspense.

"Then?" Erica prompted her.

"He says no."

"No?"

"That's right, no. He turns all the women down."

Erica snorted. Ian Conrad was not a monk, and he sure didn't strike her as the type who favored celibacy. The man oozed sexuality out of every pore. "Like I'm supposed to believe that?"

"It's true. Ask them. Yesterday in the ladies' room they were speculating about whether or not he's gay."

After a disgruntled huff, Asia rolled her eyes. "Wounded vanity. Just because a guy's selective . . ."

Erica started laughing. Sometimes her friends were downright nuts. "I had no idea you two had taken so much notice of him. And here you're both supposed to be happily involved women."

"We noticed you noticing," Becky explained, "so naturally we paid closer attention."

Erica studied her two best friends—her two *guilty* best friends. "And then you sicced Cameron and George on Ian to set me up because you thought I'd need help with that?"

Asia flattened back in her chair. "No way! We told you that was an accident. George was just talking about it—"

"About *me.*"

"Yeah." Asia grinned. "But you give them both such a hard time, you know they're dying to see how this turns out for you."

"They're dying to see me get my comeuppance, you mean."

"Not true." Becky appeared affronted by such an idea. "George is actually a little worried about you."

"Worried? Why?"

Becky's voice dropped to a whisper. "Ian makes everyone nervous. He wouldn't have been my choice for you."

Damn, if they kept this up, *she* was going to get more nervous. And she was plenty anxious enough already without any added help.

Hoping to convince herself as well as her two friends, Erica boasted, "I can handle Ian, don't you worry about that. He might seem like the big, quiet, intimidating type, but he's still just a man, and like all men, he'll—"

Becky suddenly looked beyond her, and her face blanched. She elbowed Asia, who followed Becky's gaze and then immediately slid lower into her seat. Her cheeks turned red.

No, Erica thought. No, no, no . . .

Warm breath touched the back of her ear, along with

the hot scent of a big man who'd been hard at work. "Just a few more hours, Erica, and you can see just how well I handle."

Erica stared at Becky and Asia, willing either of them to lend a calming influence to help even out her tripping heartbeat. But they weren't looking at her. No, their panicked gazes were directed over her shoulder.

At Ian.

Now how in the hell had he gotten behind her?

Becky and Asia were horrified enough for all three of them, so Erica refused to join in. Instead she fashioned a snide smile, slowly twisted her head around to face him, and met his oh-so-close piercing blue eyes dead on. "Hey, Ian. Skulking around the break room, are you?"

"Repairing a busted circuit, actually." He surprised her by crouching down next to her seat, which put him slightly below her. In her experience, a man always chose a position of power, choosing to tower over a woman in an effort to intimidate her with his size. That Ian should lower himself beside her, giving her the advantage of looking down on him, was curiously touching.

But even with him practically kneeling, he was so big she still felt surrounded—by his strength, his scent, his blazing intent, which one and all could easily see given the way he devoured her with his eyes.

He braced one hand on the back of her chair so that his hot wrist touched her nape, sending tingles down her spine. His biceps, already impressive enough, bulged even more. His other hand clasped the edge of her seat, causing his fingertips to brush up against her hip.

She started to lean back to escape some of that overwhelming masculinity. The smile that Becky and Asia had just warned her about suddenly tilted his sensual mouth. Erica halted, then forced herself to relax. Or at least, pretend to relax. With him practically in her lap, his face level with her breasts, she felt so wired she couldn't draw a breath.

He swiveled his head toward her friends, finally releasing Erica from that piercing gaze. Everything inside her went liquid with relief, even her backbone. She had a hell of a time staying upright in her seat.

"Ladies," he murmured by way of greeting.

And her friends, both mute ninnies, just gaped back at him.

His smile widened, looking more like a crooked grin. "Now don't be embarrassed," he chastised in a gravel-rough voice. "It's okay that you were talking about me. I'm sure you just wanted to reassure Erica, right?"

After a moment's hesitation, their heads bobbed comically.

"Yeah. That's what I thought." He pinned Erica in place again. "Not that you need reassurance, do you, Erica?"

Where *had* her voice gone? It took her a painful three seconds to find it, and that annoyed her enough that her natural self-confidence returned. "Of course not. As my personal slave, you'll do anything and everything I say. Isn't that right?"

Very gently, he asked, "Do you really think so?"

Her back stiffened, in alarm, in dread—maybe a little in relief. "Are you telling me you've changed your mind? Are you backing out now?"

He looked at her mouth . . . and looked some more. A little unsettled, Erica squirmed. They were all so quiet, she thought she could hear Becky and Asia breathing; she knew she could hear the erratic knocking of her heartbeat against her breastbone.

Finally, Ian broke the nerve-stretching tension. "Naturally not." He came to his feet with an amazing fluid grace considering his size. Then he touched her chin. "One warning, though. Be very careful what you instigate because you never know how it might turn against you."

Damn him! Insults and more threats. She would not put up with it.

Erica surged to her feet too—a ludicrous affectation since she only reached his shoulder. But she did poke him in the chest, and found out he was so hard she nearly broke her finger. Wincing, she said, "Quit trying to intimidate me, Ian Conrad, or I'm liable to just call the whole thing off."

He grinned, caught her finger, and cradled it to his chest in a manner that felt oddly protective. "But I don't intimidate you, isn't that right?"

Still staring at her slender hand caught up against that broad granite chest, she blinked. "What?"

He took a step closer to her, forcing her to tilt her head back to maintain eye contact. "I refuse to believe you'd back out on me now just because of a little uncertainty. After all, Asia and Becky went through with it and survived just fine."

After holding silent for the whole damn visit, her friends started sputtering over having their sorry butts dragged into the conversation. Ian spared them an apologetic glance, saying, "Ladies, it's hardly a secret," then continued to Erica, "Trust me, you're woman enough, and you're definitely ballsy and brazen enough, to do what they've done. Isn't that right?"

He'd challenged her, the rat. Erica slanted her eyes and gifted him with her own small secret smile. "You betcha. I wouldn't miss this for the world."

He didn't seem the least put off by her inference. He even nodded in satisfaction. "Perfect." He glanced at the silver watch on his thick wrist. "Four more hours, then I'll see you at Wild Honey. We'll pick up a few things before we head to my place."

"Your place?" She raised a brow, a little amazed at his authoritative manner considering he'd agreed to be her slave. "Did I say I wanted to go to your place, Ian?"

"No, but you did specify that we'd meet right after work and since one thing after another has broken down today, I'm sweatier than usual. I'll have to shower."

"Maybe I'll let you shower at my place."

He smiled at her taunting way of saying maybe. "I'm not going to wallow in my own sweat all day, not even for you, so forget it. Besides, if we're at my place you can walk out whenever you decide you've . . . had enough."

Another challenge, as if she'd be the one to cry uncle. Her teeth clicked together even as she managed another not-so-sweet smile. "I can always just order you to leave."

That actually made him laugh and the sound of his humor was so unexpected, so deep and masculine, it gave her a small thrill. Her toes curled inside her shoes, but not by so much as a twitch did she give herself away.

When he saw her facade of disgruntlement, he laughed some more. Erica tapped her foot on the floor, waiting for him to get over his chuckles. Finally he wiped his eyes, but his grin remained as he said, "Order me to leave, huh?" and then, with a touch to the tip of her nose, "I suppose you can always try. In fact, I think I'd enjoy that."

And once again, he turned his back on her.

Erica stood there while he saluted Becky and Asia, who mumbled farewells, then she watched him leave the lounge. Every woman he passed visually noted his progress with sly, covetous intent. The men just got out of his way.

"Oh, my."

"Good Lord."

Erica didn't want to look at her friends because she knew what they were thinking, even before their muttered exclamations. She was thinking it, too. The difference was that her heart pounded and her body felt tight and hot, and it wasn't all because of apprehension. Ian's forceful nature scared her a little—and excited her a lot.

"Erica, sit down before you drop."

Becky added in a whisper, "She does look dazed, doesn't she?"

Erica shook herself. She had a reputation to maintain. "Dazed? Don't be silly. He's just a man." She sank into her seat and pretended her knees weren't shaking and her skin wasn't flushed.

"There's no *just* to it," Asia said. "Whatever he's got, he's got it in spades. I'd be very, very careful if I were you."

Becky mumbled, "If I were her, I'd hide."

Laughing, Erica propped her head on her hand and considered the situation. She'd be walking a fine line between maintaining control and enjoying him for the man he was and what he made her feel. Eventually, she'd let him drive her wild with his dictatorial ways. But first, she'd show him a thing or two about control, about women, and about Erica Lee.

For a man like Ian, being a slave could prove a formidable task. Already she imagined the things she'd tell him to do, things that would excite him—but keep him from satisfaction. It'd be frustrating for her too, but at least she'd prove her point.

Who she'd be proving it to, she wasn't sure yet.

* * *

Thanks to a last minute snafu with an ancient air-conditioning unit, Ian found himself behind schedule. Only five minutes late, but he'd been looking forward to this all day, and he just knew Erica would try to give him hell about it. Thinking of the way her eyes burned green fire whenever she got riled, he grinned.

A few seconds later he strode into Wild Honey. He maintained a steady pace, but he didn't allow himself to rush. Given half a chance, Erica would have him wrapped around her little finger and no way would he allow that. He barely glanced up as he passed the checkout counter and the tables of books and magazines.

Erica wouldn't be loitering in the front of the store. No, the little witch would be in one of the fetish sections—and he knew exactly which one.

He found her standing in front of an aisle of domination wear, fingering a heavy leather dog collar with silver studs. Knowing her thoughts, he stepped up silently behind her and growled low, "Unless you want to end up wearing that thing, I'd suggest you put it back down."

She'd been so lost in thought her whole body jerked with his first words. "Damn it," she snapped even before whirling around to face him. The leather collar was gripped tight in her hand. "Can't you ever make a normal entrance?"

In contrast to her near shout, Ian's words were calm and quiet. "Into a porn shop? What would you consider normal?"

She scowled, then mumbled, "For such a big guy, you're awfully good at sneaking around."

"Next time I'll clear my throat." He deliberately

made his tone patronizing enough that she couldn't possibly let it pass.

She didn't. Her brows drew down, her eyes glittered with annoyance, her mouth opened—and Ian leaned down and kissed her.

They were in the middle of a porn shop with a few customers milling around, but that didn't stop him. At the moment, a tornado couldn't have stopped him.

He'd thought about tasting her all day.

On the most basic level, her innate sexuality called out to him. Because he was a big man and could easily cause harm with his physical strength, he'd learned early on to control his reactions in all things. He kept an iron grip on his anger with men, and he tempered his sexual drive with women.

But with Erica, he had a feeling he could let loose in every way and she'd handle it—and him—just fine.

Focused on that fact, he curved his hands around her neck and used his thumbs to tip up her chin. Her eyes widened just before he took her mouth the way he'd wanted to take it since first meeting her.

A small, very feminine sound escaped her and a heartbeat later she went soft and warm. He watched her thick black lashes drift shut, felt her hands curve against his chest. The hard leather of the collar she still held dug into his left pectoral muscle.

Her lips were full and soft and opened more to allow the slide of his tongue. There was no gentle prelude, no tentative exploration. In so many ways, he'd been thinking of Erica as his since the moment he'd learned what she and her friends had planned. The reality of having her here now, soon to be his in fact as well as fantasy, was almost more than he could survive.

He kissed her deeply, loving the hot, damp taste of

her mouth, the way she kissed him back, her expertise. The sound of their accelerated breathing echoed in his ears. Damn, he was a hair away from losing it.

He pulled back the tiniest bit, saw the excitement and reciprocal urgency on her face, and kissed her again.

The collar dropped to the floor.

Because they weren't alone and he didn't want her to suffer any regrets, he eased away, releasing her slowly, pressing small damp kisses to her chin, her cheek, her throat. "This way," he murmured, and carefully stepped her around the forgotten collar.

With a naturalness that normally came from long association, she nestled into his side. He kept his arm around her, his hand curving over her shoulder. In his opinion, she fit against him perfectly.

For the moment, she seemed docile enough.

A smile tugged at his mouth, but he resisted it. If he laughed now, Erica would not only go back for the collar, but probably a leash as well.

"What are we doing?" she asked when he stepped up to the back counter where an array of oils, exotic scents, and lotions were displayed.

"Making a few purchases."

"But I haven't decided what I want yet."

He knew what *he* wanted, so again, he smothered his satisfied grin. "It's your day, right?"

Wearing a suspicious frown, she nodded.

"So I figured I should pamper you."

One brow rose. "Pamper me how exactly?"

"How's dinner, a massage, and a long bubble bath sound?"

"Like heaven, but what's that got to do with sex?"

He almost said, *You're kidding, right?* but then he saw she was serious. Damn, but she must have been with a bunch of losers if she didn't understand the pleasure in setting the mood and indulging in extensive foreplay.

He gave her his own frown while carefully deciding how to word his answer. "Sex is best when both people are totally into it. I want you to be as comfortable and satisfied as possible. We're getting together during dinnertime, so I want to feed you. You've worked hard all day, so I want to relax you. Anything sexual you want, anywhere along the way, you just say so and believe me I'll be more than happy to oblige."

"You think so, do you?"

More bluster. He'd taken her by surprise, so naturally she got defensive. It was odd, but as often as not, Erica touched his heart as much as his libido.

He stroked his hands over her glossy black hair and lowered his voice more. "Erica, there isn't anything you can ask me to do to you or for you that I won't enjoy. I thought you already knew how much I want you."

The signs of arousal were easy to see on her face; the color in her cheeks, her expanded pupils, her parted lips. Still, the words from her mouth weren't encouraging.

"And if I want to watch you squirm? If I want to see how you deal with waiting?"

If he didn't know her so well, Ian might have been duped. But he did know her and the little darling wanted him, she just wanted to see how far she could push. Well, two could play that game—but only one would win, and he already knew when the night was over, Erica would be his.

He touched her mouth with his thumb. "I've been waiting months already. I can survive a few more days." Turning away, he picked up a small decorative bottle of massage oil. The label claimed properties that would leave your skin tingling and your nerve endings alive. Erica was such a sexy little thing, he doubted he'd need the oil, but maybe . . .

Erica snatched it out of his hand. "What do you mean you've been waiting months?"

Except for one quick, questioning glance, he kept his back to her. "The day I first saw you, I wanted you. There hasn't been a minute since that I *haven't* wanted you." He fingered a massage mitt—some fuzzy contraption far too small for his hand—then moved on to the bubble bath. He could feel Erica standing just behind him, befuddled, annoyed, brimming with nervous uncertainty that she'd do her best to hide.

He gave her half a minute to mentally chew on what he'd said before facing her again. When he stared down at her, she met and held his gaze by sheer force of will. She had guts, his Erica, and he admired her more every moment he spent with her. "Sometimes I wonder if I'll ever stop."

She swallowed. "Stop?"

"Wanting you." Then he shrugged, dismissing the moment of heavy sexual tension and again turning back to the products. "But we'll work that out this weekend." He handed her the bubble bath.

She accepted it automatically. "Work what out?"

"How we really feel about each other."

"Bu-but that's absurd!"

"Stammering?" He draped his arm around her again and headed them both toward the checkout. "Not at all. I like you a lot, but it's hard to say how much when all I can usually think about is getting inside you."

She stumbled and would have fallen if he hadn't caught her.

"Wait a minute." Annoyed, she tried digging in her heels.

He kept walking, sweeping her along with him. "I have only so much patience, honey."

"But . . . what is this about a weekend? We're getting together for one night and one night only."

He snorted, but otherwise kept his thoughts to himself. She sounded panicked enough without him telling her why he needed a whole weekend. One way or another, he'd convince her, once he got her alone.

"Damn it, Ian, I am not committing the whole weekend to you."

She could really dent his ego if he let her. Not that he would. He said only, "Why not? I figure it'll take me at least that long just to get used to seeing you in my place."

"Yeah?" Like a dog on a bone, she jumped on that. "Well if you don't want me there, then . . ."

"Oh, I want you there all right."

"Blast it, Ian." She jerked to a halt, forcing him to do the same.

"What's wrong now?"

In typical Erica fashion, she tossed her head, sending her silky mane of hair to fall behind her shoulders. "You keep throwing out these obscure comments in between insulting me and threatening me." Her nose lifted. "I don't know that I want to spend a whole weekend with you."

Ian took in the sight of her, from the determined tilt of her head to the bold fighter's stance. "Look at it this way," he whispered, "there's a whole lot of bossing around you can do in two and half days. We both know you'll enjoy that."

"But you won't."

"Wanna bet?" He had her flustered, not that he minded. Gently, he relieved her of the oil and bubble bath. She stayed there in the center aisle while he paid for their purchases. With the bagged items in one hand, he again drew her close and led her out the door.

The late afternoon sunshine glinted off her hair, highlighting the blue-black depths. When he started to lead her to his car, she again balked. "I have my car with me."

"I thought we'd ride together."

"No way. You said it yourself—I should be able to leave when I want to."

She had him there. "All right. Would you like to follow me to my place, then?"

"Do you need to stop for groceries?"

Shaking his head, Ian said, "No. I have everything I need already at my apartment."

She looked skeptical, but didn't cavil. "All right. I am curious to try out these culinary skills of yours."

"I promise you won't be disappointed—in anything." Silently, they walked to her car across the scorching pavement. Ian waited while she unlocked the door and rolled down the window to let in fresh air, then he said, "Erica?"

She dug her keys out of her purse, pretending to ignore him, which was absurd considering every line of her body bespoke her awareness. "Hmmm?"

"You're going to enjoy yourself, you know."

He'd meant to reassure her, but apparently he hit a hot button. She slanted a narrow-eyed look at him over her shoulder, then slowly turned to him in full battle mode. Her voice was low and mean and sarcastic. "Oh, I'll enjoy myself all right. After all, I'll have you at my beck and call, tending to my every whim . . . right?"

He loved her like this, all prickly like a hedgehog, full of feminine challenge. Because he couldn't help himself, he smiled the tiniest bit. "Okay."

His easy agreement only annoyed her more. Her

mouth flattened and her brow beetled. "If I stay the whole weekend—"

She was staying, all right. One way or another, he'd make sure she did.

"—then prepare yourself, because you'll be seeing the real me."

Curiosity rose in tandem with anticipation. "Meaning?"

"Meaning I don't always look like this." She indicated her face, hair, and chic clothing. "When I'm at home relaxing—my home or yours—I like to be comfortable. That means no makeup, no polite work manners. No frills."

No clothes, he silently added. *And even better than that, no inhibitions.*

Ian's smile widened though his voice remained infinitely gentle. "I have a very strong constitution, Erica. I think I can handle it."

She glared at him a moment more, then dropped into her car and slammed the door. Through the open window, she growled, "Maybe you can and maybe you can't. But make no mistake: you can not handle *me.*"

Chapter Three

He had a nice home. His apartment was on the third floor with an impressive balcony that looked out over a wooded back lot. A creek ran the length of the apartment complex, softly churning, housing a duck or two and surrounded by a multitude of flowers and birds and butterflies.

"That's my favorite part," he mentioned when she went straight across the living room, past the kitchen to look out the double glass doors on the far end of his dining nook. He detoured into the kitchen, opened a few cabinets, ran a little water, and seconds later Erica felt him come up close behind her. His breath touched her ear. "I always wanted to make love on the balcony, late at night so no one would see. You can hear the creek and see the stars."

Peeved at the idea of him sexually entwined with another woman, she said, "Yeah? So have you?"

"Nope."

"Why not?"

"I never had the right woman here before."

Erica's brain froze. *Right woman?* Surely, he wasn't suggesting that *she* was the right woman? Never in her life had any man labeled her such.

But she had to admit, the idea of climbing atop that big muscular body with the fresh air surrounding them and the sounds of nature just beyond appealed to her too.

She shook herself. "Show me around your apartment."

"All right." His hand, like a burning brand, pressed at the small of her back. "Let's start in the kitchen."

Erica's eyes glazed over at the expanse of tall cabinets, the enormous refrigerator, and high-tech stove. She wasn't much of a cook herself, but she appreciated how functional a kitchen like his would be.

He'd set out two thick pork chops, a fat zucchini, and a plump ripe tomato. Her stomach rumbled; she might not enjoy cooking, but she definitely enjoyed eating, especially after a long day at work.

"It's a hobby," he explained. "Would you like something to drink?"

"Tea?" Erica found it somewhat amusing to watch a man as large as Ian move with such economic grace. He still wore his ragged jeans and sweaty work shirt, but he looked elegant in the kitchen, waiting on her.

He took a glass from the cabinet, filled it with ice from the automatic ice maker, and poured in a dark brewed tea. "Sugar or lemon?"

She shook her head and accepted the tea. He was full of surprises, she found. She couldn't help but comment on the neatness of his home. "You have a cleaning lady?"

"It's just me so I don't need one." He handed her a napkin and resumed the tour. "There's only the living room and the little dining room here."

Only, didn't quite describe it. The room was large, with heavy masculine furniture and very little decoration other than a few framed prints on the wall and a scattering of family photos on a mantel over an electric fireplace. But still it looked very put together, and somehow homey and warm.

He flipped a switch and the fireplace lit up. "It doesn't give off heat," he explained, then continued down the hall. "My bathroom."

Erica peeked into the wholly masculine domain. Done all in cream with a glass tub enclosure rather than a curtain, it was spotless at best, near barren at worst. Other than a toothbrush in the holder and an electric razor plugged in, there were no personal items about.

It smelled of Ian, of his aftershave and soap, and his own unique, earthy scent. Her heart did a little flip as she breathed in and accepted the now familiar reaction in her body. She loved his smell, so masculine and raw and . . . Ian.

She was still a little goggled when he took her hand, otherwise she might have protested. Having her hand engulfed in his much larger one made her feel small and weak—and she hated that. She made a habit of not letting men feel superior in any way. But Ian tugged her only as far as the next door.

"My spare room. I use it as an office since it isn't really big enough for a bedroom."

"You work at home?"

"No, but I prefer to keep things organized and this way they are. I grew up with my father spreading the bills across the dining room table." He shrugged. "I didn't like that."

Fascinated by this glimpse into Ian as a child, she turned to him. "I saw a bunch of pictures on your fireplace. Brothers and sisters?"

"Six. Three brothers, three sisters." His grin went crooked, a little self-deprecating. "It's not easy to make ends meet with that many mouths to feed, so my dad was forever fretting over the bills. It's not easy to find your own space either. My brothers are slobs despite the way my mother kept at them. And my sisters have always collected knickknacks, so—"

"So you now relish your own place, which you can keep as you like it." Erica hadn't expected such an out-pouring of personal confidences. Most of the men she knew clammed up if you asked anything even remotely private.

Ian proved to be very different from any other man she knew.

"That's about it," he said, and moved her farther down the hall. "This is my bedroom." He pushed the door open and ushered her inside.

While Erica took in the king-size mattress, tall armoire, and long dresser, Ian crossed his arms and leaned against the door frame.

"What about you?"

She stepped farther into the room to explore. There was another set of glass doors that also opened onto the balcony. "What about me?"

"Any brothers and sisters?"

She halted in the process of smoothing her fingers across the plush, dark blue coverlet neatly spread over his bed. Ian's hot gaze could be felt on her spine, in her heart. He was so intense sometimes that every fiber of her being was aware of his attention.

Fashioning a cavalier smile, she turned. "Naw, no siblings at all. Just me and my mother and whichever man she was with at the time."

His brow rose. "Your mother's boyfriends lived with you?"

Erica rolled her shoulder in a negligent shrug. Damn it, she hadn't meant to say so much, but now that she had, she found talking about it more difficult than it should have been. "Mom often trusted the wrong guy, that's all."

He hadn't moved. He still stood casually in the doorway, thick arms folded, ankles crossed. But suddenly he appeared more tense, more alert. "Wrong in what way?"

Feeling like a coward and blaming Ian for it, Erica strode to the glass doors. She tried to open them but they were locked and her fingers fumbled without success.

Big hands settled on her shoulders and a soft kiss touched her temple, setting her heart to a furious gallop.

They were in his bedroom, alone, and he'd just kissed her . . .

Without a word, Ian reached past her and opened the lock, then slid the door open. As soon as that was done, he again settled at her back, holding her loosely.

Erica didn't move. Part of her immobility was caused by sheer enjoyment; she liked being this close to Ian. Her body liked it too, warming and softening in all the right places just because he touched her, because his scent surrounded her.

But she held still too, because she felt foolish. So far, Ian had managed to drag every unwanted emotion from her with little effort. She wouldn't keep allowing that to happen. She *couldn't* allow that to happen.

She reclosed the door. "Wrong, in that she thought each of them was the love of her life."

As if there'd been no awkward break in the conversation at all, Ian nodded. "Some people find that special person early in life, and others have to wait."

She forced herself to move away from him. Keeping her gait casual, she retraced her steps to the kitchen. Ian followed. "What about you? Ever found that special someone?"

"No. You?"

She laughed. "I'm not at all convinced special people exist, at least not in a one-on-one-forever kind of way."

"So cynical." He pulled out a stool for her. "What about Becky and Asia? They're your friends and I know they're happily involved. You expect them to crash and burn?"

Why did he push her? She flipped her hair back and shrugged. "I don't know. Their relationships are too new to tell."

"George and Cameron would be crushed."

She grinned. "No, they'd just give me hell and harass me and tell me to mind my own business."

"You like them?"

"Sure. They're good to Becky and Asia." She felt compelled to add, "So far."

Ian studied her a moment longer before shaking his head in an indulgent manner. "You want to keep me company while I cook?"

Erica had really expected him to jump her bones the minute they were alone in his apartment. She was mildly put out that he didn't, and yet fascinated with all he shared. Hoping he'd share even more, she opted to stay close rather than set the tone by leaving him alone.

"Sure." She started to seat herself, but was taken by surprise when he relieved her of her tea, set it on the counter, and then hefted her up to the bar stool.

Standing far too close, his hands still at her waist, he gave her a small grin and asked, "Comfy?"

His strength constantly amazed her—and turned her on. He'd lifted her as easily as he might have lifted a child. She cleared her throat. "Yeah."

He continued to look down at her, to hold her and smile. Then he leaned down for a kiss.

Erica knew she should tell him no, that she should deny him or at least reprimand him for not following the dictate of their agreement, which meant she was the boss and he was the slave. She should pull back right now. Or better yet, if she waited until he almost kissed her, then he'd really . . . *Wow.* He tasted so incredibly good.

Without conscious volition, her hands crept to his wide, hard shoulders. His cotton work shirt was soft, and she could feel the flex and play of muscle and bone beneath. Her fingers dug in with an effort to get him closer. She opened her mouth and felt the brief foray of his damp, velvet tongue, and . . .

"Damn." He straightened over her. "I forgot, I need to shower."

Erica blinked, trying to bring herself back around. She'd been so lost in that hot, devouring kiss. All she really wanted at the moment was more—of that kiss, of him, of how he made her feel, and his delicious, clean-sweat scent. She reached for him, but he shook his head.

"Sorry, honey. Shower first, then we can play all you want." He turned to the stove—*turned his back on her*—and set a pot full of water on to boil.

Erica went rigid.

"I'm going to go ahead and get the food started, then jump in the shower. I promise I won't be more than five minutes. That is"—he glanced over his shoulder and caught her fuming—"unless you want me to shave?"

Erica eyed the beard shadowing on his jaw, which made him look like a dark rogue. "No." Damn it, her voice sounded like a croak again. She cleared her throat and squared her shoulders. "You can shave later while I watch."

Both his brows lifted. "A voyeur, huh?" He sounded vastly amused by that. "I'm game."

"Of course you are," she said through her teeth, "because I'm the boss, so whatever I say is okay with you."

"Right."

Within seconds he had the thick chops sizzling on the range-top griddle, set on low, and he started out of the room with the admonition, "Be good—at least until I get back."

Annoyed more with herself than him, Erica snatched up her drink and went to the glass doors. At least this time she knew how to open them, so she sauntered outside, dropped into a padded chaise, and stretched out her legs.

The blazing sun had disappeared behind gray clouds without her realizing it, and the air smelled of an impending storm. She loved storms, found them sexy and energizing, and at the moment, they certainly matched her turbulent mood.

How could she teach Ian a lesson when all he had to do was look at her and she got tongue-tied?

The aroma of cooking pork drifted out to her, but she wasn't about to tend to dinner, too. That wasn't the deal, and she had to keep at least some part of the original bargain pure. She checked her wristwatch and saw it was six thirty-six. She'd give him the requisite five minutes he'd claimed, then she was leaving. And she'd have a legitimate excuse for walking out, too, given how he'd started things out.

A humid wind blew in, tangling her hair. Not that she cared. She turned her face up, closed her eyes, and tried to relax.

Not more than three minutes after that she heard Ian whistling in the kitchen. Ha. She wouldn't move. Let him come outside and find her. She waited, but all she got was the sounds of food being diced and dishes being rattled.

She stubbornly kept her eyes closed and maintained her feigned position of comfort. In truth, she felt as wired as a ticking bomb waiting to go off.

Then gentle fingers touched her head, smoothed her windblown hair behind her ears, and drifted down her neck. She was aware of Ian crouching beside her, fresh from his shower, big and powerful and imposing.

He leaned closer to her, brushing his mouth over her cheekbone, her ear, down her throat. "Tired?" he asked, in a voice low and rough and gentle.

Erica slanted her eyes open—and found herself face-to-naked-chest with him. Stunned, she quickly straightened and looked at the rest of his body, but he had on jeans. Just jeans. Butter soft, well worn jeans that weren't properly buttoned, likely due to his haste in getting back to the food. His bare feet were big and lean.

God, she was lusting over his feet.

She looked back at his body, at that strong abdomen, the impressive, muscular chest lightly covered in dark hair, and she wasn't sure if she should be relieved or disappointed that he'd grabbed the damn jeans.

No words came. Ian shirtless was a sight to enjoy. He remained balanced on the balls of his feet, his arms

draped loosely over his bent knees, his eyes direct, un-
flinching, watchful. His brown hair was damp, brushed
straight back from his forehead, and he still had those
sexy whiskers on his cheeks and chin. His eyes seemed
bluer than ever, and as she absorbed his presence, he
again came forward to kiss her.

She again let him.

It seemed she had no willpower around this one
hunk of man. Somehow, she ended up lounged back
with him caging her in, his mouth eating at hers, slow
and deep and oh, so thorough. His whiskers rasped her
delicate skin, but gently, as if he knew exactly what he
was doing.

Tentatively, she touched his chest and felt his astounding heat, the heavy beat of his heart, the taut silk
of his shoulders, the crisp hair over his chest. Her
hands flattened on him, her fingers spreading wide.
"Ian?"

He groaned as if in pain, then levered himself away.
"Damn, you are a temptation."

He said it like an accusation, confounding her.

"My chops are burning." His crooked grin was
back, more endearing—and frustrating—than ever.
"Stay put, relax while I finish dinner, okay?" With that,
he touched the end of her nose, straightened with a grimace that eased once he readjusted himself, and
strolled into the kitchen, again whistling.

Erica flopped back in her seat, utterly speechless.
She was losing and she knew it. And even worse, he
knew it. Using almost no effort at all, he had her panting after him and she couldn't let that continue. Somehow, some way, she had to get control so that he was
the one panting.

She had to turn the tables on him.

* * *

Ian tried but failed to ignore his straining boner as he diced tomatoes, sliced zucchini, and seasoned the light sauce for the linguine. Having Erica alone in his apartment was enough to tempt a saint, and God knew he wasn't a candidate for sainthood. She'd surprised and aroused him with her quick capitulation each and every time he touched her. Of course, he'd known they'd be great together, a fact that had driven him nuts for the past few months. But now that he had her where he wanted her, he'd expected to have to work for it.

Apparently, Erica had expected the same. Grinning, Ian peeked out the glass doors at her, saw her frown and mulish expression.

She was conniving something, he could feel it.

And his anticipation grew.

Seconds later she strode in, all saucy and in control once more. She perched on the stool while sizing him up. Or admiring him. With Erica, it was hard to tell.

He glanced at her over his shoulder. "You should get more comfortable." Pretending to be struck by his own words, he shook his head. "No, I said that wrong, didn't I? I'm your slave for the weekend, so I should get you more comfortable."

As he spoke, he wiped his hands off on a dishcloth.

Erica's smile was slow and wicked, just the way he liked it. "All right. What do you suggest?"

"When you get home from work, what's the first thing you do?"

"Kick off my shoes."

"We'll start there, then." Without hesitation, Ian went to one knee in front of her and lifted one slim leg. Her shoes were leather wedges that tied around her ankles. Very sexy. He propped her foot on his thigh and loosened the lace, then slipped the shoe off.

She wore stockings, and for a moment, he enjoyed the silky feel of them against his palms.

He was involved in imagining her legs around his waist when she offered him the other foot.

Ian took his time removing this shoe, while noticing that his lowered position and the way her leg bent gave him a peek at her iridescent peach panties. She knew it too, the little witch.

"It's warm today," he murmured, most thoroughly distracted. "Why don't we take these stockings off too?"

Erica stood, again placed her foot on his thigh, and said, "All right. They're thigh-highs, not panty hose."

"I noticed."

"Do it slow."

Ian's heartbeat quickened. She was in full boss mode now, and damn, it was exciting. Without looking away from her, he took quick note of the food, using his nose to determine how much more time he had.

The scents of sautéed veggies joined the other aromas in the room. The chops were almost done, and the pasta wouldn't last more than another minute without being overcooked.

He leaned in to reach beneath her skirt, putting his face even with her belly. Eventually he'd have her in this exact same position again—but she'd be naked.

As if she'd heard his thoughts, she inhaled. Moving as slowly as he could manage given the trembling in his hands and the thundering of his heart, Ian trailed his fingers up her right leg until he encountered the warm, firm flesh of her bare thigh. He'd love to feel that flesh on his jaw while he tasted her. He'd hold her naked bottom in his hands and control her while she bucked and cried out a climax . . .

"Ian?" Her shaky voice drew him back.

"Just making it slow—the way you said." He allowed his fingertips to graze the crotch of her panties—and his heart almost stopped when he realized they were damp.

His control snapped and his muscles went slack. He leaned into her, his jaw against her pelvis while he inhaled the spicy scent of her sex.

"Ian?"

She sounded as breathless as he felt. Disregarding her orders, he quickly rolled the stocking down her leg and removed it, tucking it into her shoe.

Bracing her hands on his shoulders, she offered her left leg and he went through the routine again. But he only touched her thigh this time, not wanting things to progress so fast that he ruined his plans. When the second stocking joined the first, he didn't stand. Instead, he looked up at her, met her heavy, darkened eyes, and wrapped his arms around her hips.

Keeping his eyes locked on hers, he leaned forward until he could kiss her belly through her soft cotton shirt above the waistband of her skirt. Her lips parted on an indrawn breath. Nostrils flaring, he opened his mouth and gently bit. She was soft, just as a woman should be. Very edible. He'd enjoy nibbling on her everywhere once he got her complete acceptance of him as her man.

The kitchen filled with the sounds of their accelerated breathing. Suggestively, easing her into his command, Ian nibbled his way lower.

Her eyes closed and her hands on his shoulders clamped tight, stinging in force.

The leather skirt felt slick and impenetrable, drawing him to a halt. "You know what I think?" he rasped while noting the way her breasts rose and fell and her legs were braced apart. "I think you should be dessert."

Her eyes snapped open. For one long moment, she looked disoriented, and then she shoved away from him with a flushed face and a noticeable dose of annoyance.

Giving her room to collect herself, Ian went to the stove. He removed the browned chops, arranging them on two plates on a tray. He lifted the pot of linguine from the burner and emptied it into a strainer. While steam rose in his face, adding to his inner heat, Erica approached. Without her shoes, her petite stature was more obvious than ever. At least, she was petite next to him. He supposed she stood around five-feet-six, an average height for most women.

Her fingertips skated along his naked spine, making his stomach clench. "Speaking of dessert, I'm wondering if you shouldn't be naked while you do all this."

He almost snorted. Once again, she'd taken him by surprise. While water ran over the pasta, rinsing it, he faced her with a smile and his hands on his fly. "Want me to shuck the jeans? Just say the word."

Her eyes widened, but quickly narrowed. "Not just yet. I'm afraid you'll be a distraction and I am hungry."

"For food?"

"That too."

Giving her her due, he saluted. "You're the boss."

Under her breath, but not quite under enough, he heard her mutter, "Now if we could both only remember that."

"You want to eat on the balcony?" He seasoned the pasta, mixing in the sauce and zucchini and topping it off with diced tomatoes and freshly grated Parmesan cheese. "It's cooling off a little, so it won't be too uncomfortable."

"I think it might rain."

He looked her in the eyes and said, "You won't mind getting a little wet, will you?"

Her nose lifted into the air. "I'll wait outside. You can serve me." And off she went, her hips swaying, leaving Ian to grin behind her.

Twenty minutes later, when she was halfway through her meal and he was almost done, she gave him a genuine compliment. "This is absolutely delicious." Up until then, she'd been quietly eating, and he'd been quietly watching her.

Because he'd just taken his last bite of pork, he merely nodded in acknowledgment of her praise.

During the meal, the sky had darkened considerably but Ian hadn't bothered with the outside light. He'd considered getting a candle, but the breeze had picked up so there didn't seem to be much point. Besides, the dim evening suited Erica and her exotic looks. In the deepening shadows, her eyes were more luminescent, her skin softer. And the charged, humid air repeatedly stirred her scent, keeping him on the keen edge of awareness.

A heavier gust of wind brought the promise of an energetic storm. Erica held her hair away from her face and studied him. "I had no idea you were such a good cook."

"I'm good at a lot of things."

She swirled linguine around her fork and asked, "Such as?"

Ian leaned back, getting comfortable while she finished. Just watching her mouth as she chewed, her throat when she swallowed, turned him on, proving he was in dire straits. He liked the way her lips closed around her fork, how he got the occasional peek of her tongue . . . "I'm the best electrician around."

She waggled her fork at him. "And modest, too."

He shrugged. "Modesty is overrated. Did you know I've considered setting up my own shop a time or two?"

"So why haven't you?"

Because I like working with you. He shook his head. "The timing isn't right yet. Maybe soon."

She looked a little downcast by the idea that he might leave the factory, which encouraged him. "What else are you good at?"

"Building things. Someday I want to build my own house."

"All by yourself?"

"With subcontractors, but using my designs and direction. I'd like a place isolated away from neighbors. In the woods maybe, with a pond or a creek nearby."

"Wow. That sounds wonderful." At that moment, Erica looked softer than he'd ever seen her. She wasn't bristling, wasn't erecting barriers to keep him away. She looked almost . . . dreamy. "I like my privacy too."

He sent her a look. "Really?"

The dreamy expression faded, replaced by teasing. "Hey, even us party girls like our downtime."

"So you wouldn't be averse to living quietly?" He hadn't expected that. In fact, he'd thought the living arrangements might be his biggest obstacle.

"Someday. So when do you plan to build this dream home?"

Ian pushed his plate away and crossed his arms over the table. He saw Erica's gaze skirt to his chest and then, with marked determination, come back to his face. Since her body fascinated him, he was glad for some reciprocal interest. "When I marry and settle down."

She, too, pushed her plate away. "Got a woman in mind for that?"

Before he could think it through, he said, "Oh, yeah." *A beautiful, intelligent, stubborn woman*—who suddenly looked ready to strangle him.

Well, hell. He'd certainly set himself up now.

Chapter Four

Erica drew up straight, making Ian regret his hasty admission. In a flash, she was on her feet, pacing to the railing behind him, her every step filled with barely restrained anger. "Strange." She looked out over the back lot. "I can't imagine a woman fitting into your life."

Ian twisted to see the rigid line of her back. She looked cute standing there in her short skirt, her legs bare, her hair dancing in the wind. "No? Why not?"

She huffed. "Just look at how you live. All neat and orderly with things just so. Men your age are very set in their ways."

"A truism? Is this from experience or supposition?" Or from watching her mother? A string of boyfriends, she'd said, all of them wrong . . .

"Men don't like to change just for a woman."

She hadn't bothered to look at him when she made that ludicrous accusation. "Maybe a woman would be the one changing."

Whipping around, she glared at him. "Typical male

attitude," she all but spat. "The woman is always the one who needs to adjust."

Ian stood. With every minute he spent near her, he better understood her. "I just said maybe, Erica. No reason to bite my face off." He moved closer to her until she braced her hands behind her on the railing, but couldn't lean any farther away. His eyes on hers, his hips nestled close to her pelvis, he said, "Seems to me if two people are in love and ready to build a life to-gether, they both ought to do some adjusting."

"Ha! What adjusting are you willing to do?"

She flung the words at him, as if she expected him to be totally inflexible. How could he be inflexible when she already had him wrapped around her little finger?

She didn't know that though, and part of his plan was not to tell her. She needed a man to match her, and love her, otherwise she'd grind him under.

He stroked her cheek, bent till his mouth touched hers. "For the right woman, I'd do whatever I need to." His words were an explanation she couldn't yet under-stand, only because she didn't know *she* was the right woman. But before the weekend was over, she'd figure it out and she'd know he had done whatever he needed to—including duping her, with George and Cameron's help.

Erica flattened her hands on his chest to keep him from kissing her. He allowed her to put a small space between them.

"Who's the woman?"

"What?" He'd been so close to taking her mouth, so lost in the best part of his duping, *mainly getting her in bed,* that his thoughts were scattered.

"This paragon you hope to marry and settle into the woods with. Who is she? Someone we work with?"

A slow smile took him by surprise. Why, she sounded jealous. "It doesn't matter. She doesn't want me that way. Yet."

"So I'm here to fill the time?"

Damn it, how had he gotten into this exchange? Ian locked his jaw, measured his words in his mind, then mentally shrugged. He'd give her some truths and see what she did with them. "You're here because we're sexually attracted to each other."

He half expected her to deny it, but she only pursed her mouth. "You want me enough to risk alienating this other woman? What if she finds out about this weekend?"

"She'll know because I don't keep secrets." He lowered his voice to a growled whisper. "And yeah, I want you more than enough."

"For a weekend."

He couldn't very well tell her he wanted her for a week, a month, a hundred years. "So what about you? Are you always honest?"

"Brutally."

That made him laugh.

"It's not funny, Ian. A lot of guys expect women to sugarcoat things, to always cater to their macho egos. But honesty is important to me."

"Yeah?" Damn. What would she think when she found out he'd finagled their weekend from the start?

"If I don't like something I'm going to say so, and if a guy can't take it, tough."

"I'm not exactly fragile, Erica."

"Not your body, no. But male egos are far more delicate than—"

On behalf of males everywhere, he felt he had to interrupt. "You can be as honest with me as you want.

Feel free to tell me exactly what pleases you, what you like and don't like." She looked skeptical, so he added, "I want to hear it."

She gave a sharp nod. "Fine. I don't want anyone to try to change me. And I definitely don't want anyone to try to control me."

Ian sighed. If he took her words to heart, all of his plans would be wasted. But he didn't want to change her. He just wanted her to stop trying to be so tough, to accept him and how he made her feel. As to controlling her, well, only in a few sexual situations where he knew she'd enjoy herself.

He cupped his hand over her shoulder and trailed it down her arm until he could lace his fingers in hers. "Speaking of control . . . I promised you some service, remember?"

Just that easily, she went breathless. "Of course I remember. It's . . . it's our deal."

"So you want to soak in the tub while I put away the dishes? When I'm finished I could help you with your bath."

A little more color bloomed in her cheeks. Embarrassment, or excitement?

"Help me how?"

"However you want. It's your show." He started backing up into the apartment, tugging her along with him. The idea of having his hands on her naked, wet body damn near took his knees out from under him. If there was any justice in the world, he'd have her tonight because waiting any longer than that would be torture. "I'll wash your back, your feet, your hair."

"I just washed my hair."

Such an inane comment for Erica. He loved it. He loved her. "Then we'll skip that part. You're in charge, so what you say goes."

They reached his bedroom and Ian opened the closet. "Help yourself to a robe or a shirt or whatever you'll feel most comfortable in. I'll get the bath water ready."

She stood in the middle of his floor and bit her lip.

Ian wanted to hold her, to coddle her, to lay her atop the mattress and make slow, heated love to her. But more than that he wanted her trust. "I'll be right back."

He wasn't gone for more than a minute. Once the temperature of the water was adjusted and the tub began to fill with bubbles, he went back to her. She'd pulled out his old terry cloth robe and had it clutched in her hands.

"Erica?"

"Hmmm?"

"You're not shy about getting naked are you?" He approached her slowly, more because he had to hold himself back than because he was afraid of rushing her. "Remember, no matter how damned tempting you are—and believe me, you're plenty tempting—I won't do anything that you don't want me to do."

She nodded. "Right." And then with a frown, she said, "I want to ask you something first."

"Shoot." They stood five feet apart and *not* touching seemed almost impossible.

Slowly her head lifted until their gazes connected. "Why me?"

His brain went blank. What could he tell her that wouldn't blow his whole plan? That lust at first sight had morphed into love rather quickly? That wasn't the way to handle Erica. "What do you mean?" he asked, stalling for time.

"I know you keep talking about sexual chemistry and all that. But there's more to it. Why focus all this energy on me? You know, Becky tells me that a lot of the women at work try to get your attention."

"Yeah?"

Nodding, she said, "They think you're gay because you ignore them."

He grinned at that.

"You think that's amusing?" She looked more confused than ever.

"Am I supposed to be insulted over someone else's assumptions? Let them think what they want."

"But . . . why aren't you interested in any of them?"

He drew a long, deep breath. Time for a few more truths. "You want me to bare my soul? All right." He held out his arms. "I'm a big man."

Her gaze dropped to his lap, making him laugh. "I didn't mean that, although everything about me is . . . proportionate."

Judging by the way her eyes widened, she understood his meaning. He *was* a big man, from his feet to his intelligence and everywhere in between. "I meant that my size intimidates people, especially women."

"The women at work?"

He waved a hand. "They're silly, hiding in the bathroom and gossiping. So, yeah, they'd probably be the type to jump over a look. Ever since I've been a teenager, I've had to hold back. My temper, my attention. And my sexual drive."

"But you figure I'm different?" She sounded a little awed by that.

"From the moment I saw you flirting and taunting and driving all the guys nuts, I knew I could let loose with you and you wouldn't turn tail and run."

Touching her became a necessity so he took one long stride and closed the space between them. He caught her shoulders and brought her to her tiptoes, close to his chest. "I know if I grumbled, you wouldn't get afraid. You'd just grumble back."

"Damn right, so don't try it."

"Yes ma'am." He kissed the end of her nose. "But I am just a man, so if I forget or lose my temper, you won't quail, will you?"

She snorted, but asked with a scowl, "Just how violent do you get when you lose your temper?"

"I get loud, not violent. And that's enough to send most women running."

The very idea set her off. "I don't run from anyone!"

"And I don't hurt women. Ever. I'd sooner break my own arm. I swear it."

She nodded. "I believe you. But don't think you can get away with yelling at me either."

The things she said made his heart full to bursting. Gently, he said, "If I did, I wouldn't mean anything by it. Besides, you'd just yell louder."

"And longer."

He laughed. "When I have you under me, small and vulnerable, you'll love it. You'll take what I give you and want more and you won't ever feel overpowered."

Her lips quivered and a pulse raced in her throat, but she thrust up her chin. "I'll demand my turn on top."

"Yeah." His voice went low and hoarse. "That's what I figured." She started to lean up to kiss him, and Ian said, "The bath is probably ready to overflow."

He hustled her out of the room and down the hall. The tub was full, but he caught it in time. Kneeling, he shut off the water, set a thick towel on the ceramic floor just outside the tub, and turned—in time to see Erica unbuttoning her shirt.

Apparently, their exchange had emboldened her. Ian dropped back onto his ass with a thump and watched, spellbound. She smiled as she slipped each button free, knowing she drove him crazy and enjoying it.

"I told you that I take my shoes off when I get home, but know what else I like to take off?"

"Your clothes?" Damn, he sounded hopeful.

"Sometimes. But my shoes and my bra are always the first to go. Both are so constrictive. You won't mind if I spend the weekend barefoot and braless, will you?"

He shook his head, rendered mute by the sight of pale flesh visible through the gaping shirt. Any second now he'd see her breasts. Be strong, he told himself. Do not start groveling. Or drooling. Drooling would be bad, too.

And here he'd thought this would be the easy part.

She shrugged the shirt off her shoulders and tossed it at his face. "Fold that for me."

"Right." He dropped it to his lap, unwilling to look away for even a second.

She reached behind herself and dragged down the zipper on her skirt. "Ian?"

"Mmm?"

"I need you to help me. Tug this down my hips, okay, so I can step out of it."

Oh, good Lord. He moved forward on his knees and reached for the skirt. But that close to her, his hands automatically went to bare flesh. He shaped her waist, loving the fine texture of her skin in contrast to his rough palms. Her belly was gently rounded, smooth and pale, and her navel made only the slightest indent. He had to kiss it.

"Ian? The skirt."

He cleared his throat and gathered what meager control he had left. He just hadn't counted on the effect of her nudity. He felt like a ravening beast, hungry, in heat, ready to conquer. He wanted her under him—now.

The skirt was tight and had to be worked down. Her

panties almost came with it, tripping his heart and freezing his breath in his lungs, but at the last second she caught the waistband and kept them on her hips.

Her bra matched her panties, and the shiny peach shade did interesting things to her rich black hair and ivory skin. It also did interesting things to his dick, making him swell to a full, demanding erection.

Through the thin material of her underclothes, he could see the darker circles of her nipples and a neat triangle of pubic hair between her legs. Still on his knees—a position now somewhat familiar with Erica—he reached up for the front clasp of her bra, then waited.

"Go ahead," she whispered.

Ian had been in his teens when he'd mastered getting a female's clothes off her. He sure as hell didn't fumble now. The bra clasp opened and he drew the material apart. She lowered her arms and the straps slid down, then off so that the bra landed on the floor.

Her nipples, not pink but a deep mauve, were tightly puckered, making him groan. She didn't have large breasts but they were soft and round and this was Erica. He'd wanted her for so long, he almost couldn't remember ever *not* wanting her.

Erica curved her hand around his neck. "I want you to kiss me."

His gaze snapped to hers but he didn't need more encouragement than that. Oh, he knew what she intended: to make him hot, then make him stop.

She wanted some payback.

But hell, he was already hot, and stopping wouldn't be easy for her, either. Eventually she wouldn't want to stop. He knew he was right about that.

He lifted himself a little higher until his face was level with her torso. Wrapping his arms around her he tugged her close, tilted his head, and drew her left nipple deep into the wet warmth of his mouth. He sucked, not hard, but he wasn't the least bit timid about it either. His nose pressed into her plump breast and she smelled so good he was already breathing hard.

Her body arched and her hands knotted in his hair. Ian tugged, using his tongue to tease, to flick and lick. Then he sucked some more until they were both shaking.

"That's enough," she whispered, but without much insistence.

"Not yet." He moved to the other breast. "Gotta be fair."

"To you?" she asked on a sigh.

"To these." And he kissed her right breast with the same enthusiasm. Within moments, Erica moved against him, her belly nudging his chest, her legs shifting with the need to get nearer. He stroked her shoulders, down to the small of her back, and finally over her firm cheeks, kneading and plying the resilient flesh, helping to grind her against his body.

When she was all but lost, he hooked his thumbs in her panties and pulled them down her legs. Leaning back, he looked at her. Her green eyes were smoky with desire, her nipples wet from his mouth, her whole body quivering. With one finger, he stroked the silky black curls on her mound, up, down, pressing in just the tiniest bit until he felt her small, taut clitoris. She groaned.

Jesus, she was the most appealing woman he'd ever seen.

And she was his.

He stood and scooped her into his arms; at the same time, Erica hugged him, pressing her face into his throat. "Where are we going?" Her voice was deep, affected by sexual need.

Regret stung him, but he didn't head for the bedroom. Not yet, he told himself, not just yet. "You're going into the tub and I'm heading to the kitchen." His voice was unusually gruff.

She jerked her head back. "What?"

Lowering her into the now tepid water, he said, "Relax. Soak. When I'm done with the dishes I'll help you wash then dry you off and give you a massage."

The water level was high, all but covering her except for her breasts and rosy nipples. He turned away, ignoring her slack-jawed surprise while struggling to contain himself. He would have liked to whistle, but his mouth wasn't working right at the moment and no way could he pucker.

Just as he reached the hall, he heard a furious splash, followed by a soft moan of dismay. He had her right where he wanted her.

Unfortunately, she had him in the same position.

Only she didn't know it, and he did.

Erica scrubbed herself with a vengeance. Let him help? Ha. She'd let him rot, that's what she'd do. He'd had his chance and he'd walked away. She'd been willing, damn it. Willing and needing and . . .

The problem, at least to her mind, was that when he got near, she couldn't seem to remember that she was the boss. She just went all soft and female. She hated going soft and female.

It made a woman weak and left her open to misuse.

She didn't have enough fingers and toes to count the men who had used and discarded her mother. Her mother would give a man everything—her heart, her home, often even her paycheck. And eventually he'd leave her, devastated and financially broke. They'd had to struggle so many times because of the scoundrels that her mother had grown fond of.

Erica prided herself on being different. Unable to accept her mother's lifestyle, she'd gained her independence early on and she protected that above all else. She said and did exactly as she pleased and never would she let a man dictate to her.

Yet Ian had only to touch her and she lost herself.

She needed to rethink this whole thing. Really, what was it she wanted? She lifted one finger: Ian naked. That would be very sweet on the eyes, not to mention how much her hands—and her mouth—would love it.

She lifted another finger: Ian making love to her. Yes, that would be heavenly.

A third finger went up: Ian at her mercy.

As if a lightbulb went on, Erica suddenly realized she could have all that with only one simple ground rule. Before he touched her again, she'd spell it out to him, then it'd be on him to maintain control, rather than on her.

Now why hadn't she thought of that sooner?

She sat up in the tub and sluiced off the clinging bubbles. She wasn't going to get any cleaner and no way could she relax. She'd just stepped out of the tub when Ian came back in.

He stopped in the doorway, his blue eyes nearly incandescent as they tracked every inch of her body. Subtly, the muscles in his chest and shoulders grew tight until the strength in his upper body was clearly defined. His hands curled into fists.

"Damn, you look good."

The bottom dropped out of her stomach at the way he said that and how he looked at her. She lifted a hand. "Don't come any closer."

His back straightened. "What?"

"I mean it, Ian. We have to talk first."

He looked troubled, and aroused. "Let me help you dry off, then we'll talk."

"No! I'm the boss, right? Well I say we talk first." Gaining a little momentum on her attitude, Erica crossed her arms beneath her breasts and waited.

Slumping back against the door frame, Ian cupped one big hand over his crotch and winced. "I'll wait, but I don't know if John Henry will. Jesus, Erica, I'm about to explode here."

Caught between a laugh of triumph and overwhelming excitement, Erica looked at the straining erection beneath his jeans. Yep, he was plenty in proportion. She gulped. "You walked away from me."

"No easy feat, I don't mind telling you. But you're the one who set up the rules—that I'd wait on you. I'm trying to do that."

She wouldn't let him fool her again. "I want you to make love to me."

He jerked straight. "Yes."

"What do you mean, yes?"

"I mean, yes. Hell, yes. I'm more than willing."

This time she did laugh. "But I have some stipulations."

His biceps bulged. "Name them."

Oh, Erica could easily see why women got nervous around Ian Conrad. In his hunger, he looked savage and hard and ready to conquer. Only he'd never conquer her. "It has to be just sex."

His eyes narrowed, intense and bright. "Come again?"

Well, damn, now he was starting to make her nervous. "I don't want you muddying the waters with too much talk, unless it's sex talk. And no more playing games."

"Games?"

She sighed. Well, she could admit a little, and then he'd have to do the same. "We've both been doing it and you know it. This business of one-upmanship has to stop. We'll both be naked, and if you have any skill at all, we'll both enjoy ourselves. Period."

For three seconds he looked ready to erupt. His jaw was locked tight, his body tensed as if for attack, and anger practically vibrated off him. Then he let loose with a string of stinging curses that made Erica's heart leap in shock. "Ian!"

He turned away, paced two steps and came back. "No."

That drew her up. "What do you mean, no?"

"I mean no." He stared at her hard. "I want more than just sex."

Her jaw worked several times before she could get the word out. "More?"

He advanced and she—damn it—backed up. Her naked fanny smacked into the ceramic tile wall and in the next heartbeat Ian pressed into her front. "I want *everything* from you, Erica Lee. Everything you have to give."

Because she didn't understand him, she went on the defensive. "You want to control me."

"I want your trust." He pressed a finger to her mouth, halting her denial. "Before you say it, they are not the same thing. I know you keep men at a distance for a reason. I suppose some of what you told me about your mother is to blame for that."

She tried to speak, but he leaned down and briefly kissed her, silencing her with the warm press of his mouth, the gentle sweep of his tongue. "I want your body, your humor, your cocky sarcasm. I want *you,* Erica. Right now, but tomorrow too."

Her mouth touching his, she asked, "And the day after that?"

"Always."

She jerked back so fast her head cracked on the wall, making her wince. "Damn it."

With a huff of annoyance, Ian's hand opened over the back of her head and rubbed. "Don't be nervous with me."

"You do not make me nervous."

"Not physically, no. You want me too, I can tell that much." He settled his hips into the notch of her legs. "But you're nervous because you're not sure if I'm for real. You're afraid you'll start to like me, to trust me, and I'll walk away."

"Your ego is massive."

"Erica." He pressed his forehead to hers. "Can't you let go just a little?"

She wanted to so badly that it scared her. Then a thought occurred to her and she glared. "What about this woman at work who you want to marry and carry off to the woods?"

By small degrees, he gathered her tightly to him. Erica couldn't draw a breath without feeling some part of Ian, without inhaling his scent. She couldn't move a millimeter without her lips touching his, her body rubbing into him. Once he had her locked close, he whispered, "That's you."

"Me?" She barely squeaked the word out.

He nodded, bumping his nose into hers.

"But I thought . . ."

"Shhh. Drop your defenses just until tomorrow morning, and then we'll talk about it again. I promise. I'll explain everything."

"And until then?"

"I'm going to make love to you." He kissed her softly. "And I'm going to fuck you." The kiss turned raw and demanding, almost frightening in intensity.

He wrapped one arm beneath her bottom, one across her back, and lifted her. "I'm going to drive you wild, sweetheart, which is what you deserve considering how wild you've made me."

It all sounded wonderful to her, savage and gentle, raunchy and sweet. Everything she'd ever wanted, and too much to resist. She laced her fingers in his hair and managed a smile. "Okay."

Relief darkened his face, wrought a groan from deep inside him. "I'll prove to you that you can be yourself with me and I'll love it."

She almost believed him.

Without thinking about it, Erica wrapped her legs around his waist and returned his kiss. He started walking them to his bedroom and the friction of his rough denim between her open legs inflamed her. He kept kissing her, deep and long, and then she felt her feet touch the floor.

Within seconds, Ian had the coverlet stripped off the bed. He opened a night table drawer and removed a whole box of condoms.

How considerate, Erica thought, wondering how many of them they'd use, but glad they wouldn't have to worry about running out.

"Ian?"

He lifted her onto the bed, stretching her out crosswise, then stepped back to strip off his jeans. Erica rose to one elbow to watch, her breath suspended, her fingers curled into the sheet. He pushed the denim down his long legs and stepped free, then stood there a moment to let her look.

His pelvis was a shade lighter than the rest of his

body. His legs were long and muscled, and his big, narrow feet were braced apart. Her gaze slowly rose again until she stared at his erection. He was long and thick and she swallowed hard. "My, my."

Naked, macho, and to her mind, perfect, Ian climbed onto the bed beside her. Erica wanted to spend at least five minutes just looking at him, absorbing the sight of him, but he didn't give her the chance. He tangled his hand in her hair, took her mouth in a ravaging kiss, then didn't stop kissing her. Not that she wanted him to stop.

If she were honest with herself, she'd admit that she loved his caveman approach, loved the feel of his big hands now roaming her body, gripping her behind, kneading her breasts. She even enjoyed the rasp of his whiskers. From the first, his bold, assertive manner had drawn her. She didn't like wimpy men, but she did like Ian. A lot.

Maybe too much.

She'd wanted him for a long time, she just hadn't wanted to acknowledge it. Now that she had, she felt free—free to indulge her secrets, her desires.

Maybe on Monday she'd thank Cameron and George for speaking out of turn. If they hadn't, who knew what type of guy she might have ended up with? But because of them, she had Ian. And with Ian kissing his way down her throat to her breasts, she knew she was lucky indeed.

Chapter Five

Ian knew he should slow down a little, but he couldn't. He cupped one soft breast, thumbed her nipple, then drew her into his mouth for a soft suckle.

Erica squirmed, trying to get closer to him. Putting one leg over hers and pinning her hands above her head, he held her still. When he expected to hear her complaints over the restraint, he got a surprisingly hot moan instead.

Ian lifted his head to look at her.

Why, the little sneak. She liked being controlled sexually. And he liked taking his turn at control, at least in bed. Out of bed, well, Erica's independent nature was part of what he loved.

After transferring both her hands into one of his, he used the other hand to stroke down her body to her belly. "Can I reverse the order?"

She gave him a blank, anxious look.

"Seeing you like this . . . I want to fuck you first, and make love to you after."

"Yes."

He was so hard it hurt. "Let's see if you're wet enough yet." Holding her gaze, he pressed his fingers lower, through her dark curls and over slick flesh. Her body arched.

"Open up for me, Erica."

Her throat worked as she swallowed, then slowly her legs parted.

He looked down to where his large hand completely covered her. "Bend your knees. I want to see you."

Without hesitation, she did, opening herself fully to him. He took in the sight of her pale thighs laid open, her damp curls, and her glistening vulva. He pressed his middle finger deep. She groaned hard, her hips lifting, her eyes squeezing shut.

"Nice and wet," he murmured, pleased with how her muscles squeezed his finger. "God, the things I want to do to you . . ."

He pushed another finger in, testing her, filling her. She was aroused enough, wet enough, that there would be no discomfort for her. He pulled out and found her clitoris again, at the same time bending to catch a nipple in his teeth. Her moans turned raw, her body moving with his hand, and suddenly it was too much. He'd waited for this moment, for this woman, too long to hold himself back.

Ian sat up, startling a groan of protest from Erica though he didn't take time to explain. He caught her knees in his hands, spread her legs wider until he could see every glistening pink inch of her sex. He heard her gasp even as he bent, tasting her with his tongue, licking and finally sucking. Erica became frenzied.

He hooked her legs over his shoulders and caught her hips in his hands to keep her still. She tasted hot, sweet, like a woman should. Her fingers locked in his hair, holding him closer to her as she cried out and twisted, as the sensations built and expanded.

"Ian."

With utmost care, he held her swollen clitoris in his teeth for the concentrated rasp of his rough tongue.

Erica came. She cried out in a nearly soundless scream, her legs stiff, her heels digging into his shoulder blades. Before her last shuddering breath had subsided, he was reaching for a condom.

Erica lay there, limp, a little sweaty. Smiling.

Damn, he loved her. In record time he had the condom on and had settled between her thighs. "You'll take me deep, won't you sweetheart?"

Her smile of contentment faded as he again hooked her legs and held them high. He outweighed her by a hundred pounds easy, was big and hard where she was slim and delicate, and still he settled against her.

"Tell me, Erica." His cock nudged against her sensitive lips, swollen from her climax. In this position, she was completely vulnerable—and they both knew it. "Tell me you want all of me."

She lifted her hands to his chest, a futile effort to hold him back. Her nails bit into his pectoral muscles as he began pressing inward.

"Tell me."

She panted. "Yes."

Her compliance, combined with the wet velvet grasp of her body on the head of his dick nearly forced him into an early release. He gritted his teeth. "Then relax for me."

She gave a choked laugh. "Can't."

He pushed in another inch and heard her inhalation of discomfort. Biting off a groan, he said, "You're gonna have to, babe." He felt himself sweating, felt his every muscle quivering with the effort it took to hold back. "You're clenching. Relax and let me in."

She took three shallow breaths, then one long, deep one. She closed her eyes, loosened her grasp on his chest, and nodded.

Through his intense concentration, Ian summoned a smile for her. "I love you, Erica."

Her eyes popped open again, huge and stunned, and he thrust in hard, filling her up and obliterating his last trace of control. He was so deep, a part of her—*his woman*—that holding back became impossible.

Alive with acute, burning pleasure, he stroked in and out and just when he felt his stomach coil, felt his balls tighten and knew he was about to lose it, Erica began countering his thrusts. He heard her raspy breathing, saw the heated rise of pleasure on her face, and he came, aware of Erica joining him, of her body milking his. Aware of the perfection of the moment.

He slumped on top of her, replete, boneless. His weight wrought a moan from her, reminding him of her position. "Sorry," he murmured, then carefully lowered her legs. Turning his face inward so he could taste the salty warmth of her neck, he rumbled, "You okay?"

She grunted, making him smile again. Damn, from the day he'd met her she'd amused him even while setting him on fire. They were both damp, sticking together, and he never wanted to move.

"Give me a second," he said, "and I'll make love to you."

This time she choked, but the sound turned into a low laugh. Her limp arms came around his neck and she contrived a halfhearted hug. "You're something else, Ian Conrad."

That perked him up. "Something better than what you've known," he agreed. "Someone you can trust."

"Maybe."

He lifted his head to growl at her. "Your second's up."

"What?"

"It's time to make love to you." She started to protest, to laugh some more, and Ian kissed her quiet— then went on kissing her for a long, long time. When she tried to wiggle out from under him, he flipped her onto her stomach and kissed her spine, the small of her back, her dimpled bottom.

By the time he finished with that, Erica was again squirming with need. He turned her over, cradled her gently, and this time he took her slow, cherishing her body and showing her that she not only made him crazed with lust, she overwhelmed him with love and tenderness too.

After nearly two days of uninhibited debauchery, Erica was badly rumpled, lazy, and still so sexy Ian wasn't sure he'd ever stop wanting her. It was nearing ten o'clock on Sunday morning, and he still couldn't glance at her without feeling a rise of sexual awareness. He couldn't hear her breathe without wanting her. And her laughs, her taunts, drove him to the very edge of lust.

Every single thing they'd done had felt like foreplay. He'd showered with her, wanting only to let the hot water ease her sore muscles. Instead, he'd taken her against the wet tile wall with the enthusiasm of a schoolboy on prom night.

He'd pulled out the massage oil, intent on fulfilling his end of the bargain. But Erica lying on her stomach with her beautiful back and shapely ass showing proved more than he could take. The oil got set aside while he kissed her all over, occasionally shocking her, definitely thrilling her. He'd drawn her to her knees to take her from the back, holding her breasts in his hands with his thrusts so deep he hadn't lasted more than five minutes—which was fine since Erica had started coming in half that time.

In the midst of steamy sensuality, there'd been very little personal grooming. Ian let her use his toothbrush and he remembered brushing her long silky hair once, only to muss it again when he carried her out to the balcony to fondle her under the moonlight. He liked having her outside.

Late Friday night, the storm had rolled in, spraying rain on them, leaving them both damp and windblown. Erica had tasted especially fine with her skin dewy.

Thinking of it made him want to taste her again. *Down boy,* he told his overenthusiastic cock. *Enough already. Let her rest.*

Saturday morning everything had been fresh from the rain, sparkling clean, and they'd lingered in bed beneath a ray of sunshine slanting in through the open window. Seeing Erica lit by the sun made him more determined than ever to get her to that house in the country, where privacy would allow them to make love outdoors as often as they liked.

Ian was amazed at his stamina. He'd always had a strong sexual appetite, but he'd never been so insatiable that he couldn't seem to stop. Of course, he'd never been with Erica. And he'd never been in love.

She hadn't bothered with makeup at all, but her slanted green eyes looked sexier than ever, especially when they were soft from a recent climax, as they were now. He knew he should get up and cook her breakfast. They hadn't had a full meal since Friday night; Saturday they'd only snacked so neither of them had to leave the bed for long. She had to be getting hungry. He was starved.

But then Erica tucked her head into his shoulder and hugged him, and Ian knew he wasn't ready to move yet.

"I am so exhausted," she teased.

Touched by a modicum of guilt because he'd awakened her from a sound slumber a few hours earlier by sliding into her from behind, Ian asked, "Are you glad now that you stayed?"

"Yes." She tilted her face up to see him. "You are imposing, intimidating, insatiable, and very sweet."

Most of that he couldn't deny, but . . . . "Sweet, huh?"

"Surprisingly so."

Perhaps now would be a good time to come clean, while she was still calling him *sweet.* He knew she'd want to go home tonight since they both had to work in the morning. But damned if he was ready to let her go. "There are still a few things we need to talk about."

She yawned and nestled back into his side. "What kind of things?"

He didn't want to start a fight, not when she seemed so peaceful and trusting. But he wanted to start their new relationship with a clean slate. Feeling possessive, he cupped her breast and said, "About why you keep men at arm's length."

She laughed. "I dunno about that. You're pretty close." She reached down and encircled his penis, which was thankfully at ease for the moment.

"Physically." He bit the bullet and added, "But you know I want more."

She again looked up at him. "Really?" At his nod, she

looked very satisfied—and a little shy. "You think there's something about that porn shop that brings people together? I mean, look at Asia and Cameron, and then Becky and George."

"And me and you?"

"I do like you, Ian. Everything about you. Most especially your honesty."

His stomach twisted with dread. "My honesty?"

"That's right. You told me up front what you wanted and why. If it wasn't for you being so honest about the whole thing, I think I would have bailed out on you."

He couldn't bear the thought that he might have missed this special time with her. "Erica, honey . . ."

"I suppose I should be honest too, huh?"

His admission died in his throat. "I'd love for you to trust me enough to tell me about yourself."

She nodded, causing the silky weight of her hair to glide against his ribs. "You were right about why I don't open up to men. I've never told this to anyone before. Not even Becky or Asia. But my mom . . . well, she was confused. And weak. She always thought she needed a man around and there was always one willing to hang on her. They used her. For sex, for money. She took care of them, playing house and pampering them—until they walked away."

Ian rubbed her scalp, kissed her forehead. "I'm sorry. But you have to know I'm not like that."

"I do know it." Again, she twisted to look up at him. "I kind of think you're the type who would resent relying on a woman for anything."

"Not true. I'm relying on you to keep me happy." He caught her chin on his fist and lifted her face more. "You're fast becoming a requirement in my life."

She grinned, but didn't look like she believed him.

"I grew up with men hanging around the house. I hated it. When they were there, my mother thought she had to be perfect. She'd get up early to put on her makeup and fix her hair because otherwise she'd get complaints and insults. It made me so damn mad, but the more I tried to convince her that we didn't need them, the more distant we got with each other. She never relaxed, never let herself just kick back and enjoy life." Erica shook her head. "She tried to get me to do the same, but I fought her every inch of the way."

"You're your own person, Erica, not a replica of your mother." He kissed her temple, hoping to reassure her. "She made her choices and you make yours. That's how it should be."

Erica lowered her face and hugged Ian. "There was another reason why I refused to primp for them." She took a deep breath. "When I was about sixteen, the men started looking at me differently."

Ian stiffened with a mix of disgust and rage. "They didn't—"

"No." She gave him a teasing pinch, deliberately lightening the mood. "I wouldn't have allowed that and you know it."

Ian squeezed her so tight she gasped. Erica just didn't realize how susceptible she was as a woman. She considered herself tough, but from her toes to her eyebrows, she was feminine and soft and certainly weaker than the majority of men.

She'd spent more of her life building bravado than any female should ever have to. "You're sure no one ever . . ."

"I'm sure. When I was seventeen I moved out."

Startled, Ian tipped her chin up. "Seventeen?" She'd been so damn young.

Erica shrugged as if it was no big deal. "I spent a year working, staying with friends, moving around a lot. I eventually landed here, and after working my way through a two-year technical college, I started at the factory as an office assistant."

Ian gave a mental salute to the divine hand of fate for delivering her into his path. He'd always be thankful for that. "How are things with your mom now?"

She was silent for a long moment. Her fingers teased at his chest hair, and Ian felt her press a soft kiss to his side. "She died when I was twenty-two. Ovarian cancer. I hadn't seen her for a long time, and I didn't know she was sick until it was too late."

"Jesus, Erica, I'm so damn sorry."

She crawled on top of him, kissed his chin, the bridge of his nose, then his mouth. "You have nothing to be sorry for. But thanks."

"Do you ever see your dad?"

"Never met him. Mom told me he didn't know she was pregnant, and by the time she was showing, he was long gone. Soon after I was born, she'd moved on to a new man."

"And so you've always been fiercely independent."

"It's not just that, you know." She propped her pointy elbows on his chest and put her head in her hands. "Guys in general are pigs."

"Is that so?"

"Yep. They work hard at pretending they care just so they can get you into bed, but then spend the mere two minutes they need there to get off."

"Not always true."

She grinned. "So I'm learning."

He hated to think about it, but he said, "You've picked some losers, haven't you?"

Instead of getting angry at that observation, she nodded. "Yeah, and I was beginning to think I was like my mom, that all I could pick were losers."

"Wanna hear my theory?"

"I don't know. Do I?"

He swatted her delectable behind. "Yeah, you do." Both hands now holding her bottom, he said, "Because of your mother's choices, you've always thought you had to control everything to prove you were different, independent and able to do your own thing. That naturally meant you chose guys who'd let you have control."

Her eyes narrowed. "I still have control."

"Over yourself." He squeezed her butt. "That's all anyone should want to control. I don't want to control you, and you don't need to control me."

"Because you're not going to use me?"

He nodded. "And because I love you, I don't ever want to see you hurt."

She went still. "That's the second time you've said it."

"Keeping count?"

"Maybe."

"Want me to say it about a dozen more times?" With Erica lying naked atop him, it was getting difficult to carry the conversation. He could feel her pubic hair on his belly, the soft cushion of her breasts on his abdomen. "It's true, you know. And I think you care about me too."

She didn't admit it, which bugged Ian, but he knew she needed time. "You're a strong, intelligent woman, Erica. You need a strong man, not a weak-kneed ass."

Her shoulders started shaking, and seconds later she burst out laughing. Ian rolled her beneath him, spread her legs, and settled against her. Her laughter died.

"You know I'm right."

Breathless, she said, "I'm willing to admit it's possible."

"Because you care about me too?" Damn it, he was pushing her after all.

"Because you drive me wild." She grabbed his ears and took his mouth. Her kiss was meant to get him off track, and it damn near did. But he was used to her tactics and he wanted to clear the air once and for all.

"Shh. Erica, wait." He stroked his fingers through her hair, spreading it out over his pillow. "Let's finish talking first, okay?"

"Talk?" She sent him a mock look of surprise. "Did I finally wear you out?"

He couldn't resist kissing her. "Never. I could make love to you for a lifetime and not be done. But this is the first time we've really talked about personal stuff, and there are things I want to tell you."

She sighed theatrically. "All right. Spill your guts and I'll try to be attentive."

"You're such a generous woman."

She laughed. "Quit stalling."

He *was* stalling, but Erica's reactions were unpredictable. She was as likely to walk out on him as she was to understand. But damn it, he did love her. That had to count for something. And he knew she cared for him too, even if she hadn't admitted it.

Somehow, he'd get her to tell him. She could get mad, but before she left his apartment, they'd have an understanding.

Ian drew a deep breath, and said, "I set the whole thing up."

She didn't explode, but only because she didn't yet understand. "Set what up?"

"Our meeting at the porn shop."

"I know. You overheard George and Cameron and . . ."

"No, sweetheart." He rubbed her arms, trying to prepare her. "Like I told you, almost everyone at the factory knows about the deal you three ladies had. I knew you'd be next and there was no way in hell I could stand the thought of you playing sex games with some other man. I wanted it to be my turn."

She stiffened beneath him. "Your turn?"

"You kept shying away from me," he growled. "I wanted a chance to prove to you how good we'd be together."

"What did you do?"

The time for truth. "I approached George and Cameron and they agreed to help me." She didn't comment on that, so he continued. "I knew just showing up at the right time wouldn't work with you, Erica, not the way it had with Becky and Asia. You wouldn't have a single qualm about ignoring me or telling me to get lost so that you could choose some spineless jerk to play with instead. So I challenged you."

Erica didn't speak, but like a volcano ready to erupt, he felt the tension building in her.

Damn, her silence hurt almost as much as the lethal look in her eyes. He held her shoulders and gave her one firm shake. "I lied about overhearing George and Cameron. I confronted them, convinced them to go along with my plan, and they . . . well, they did."

"I see."

Ian didn't trust her soft tone. "Don't be mad at them, Erica. They made me swear I wouldn't hurt you. Hell, they dogged my heels like two mother hens, worrying about you."

"What a lovely image."

"Your sarcasm is misplaced. I told you I love you—"

"And you told me you lied, and that my friends all know it. One big joke on Erica. I bet they thought you'd teach me a lesson, huh? That you'd turn the tables on me—and you did. Did they laugh about it?"

"No." He hadn't expected her to be hurt, but judging by her tone and the dampness of her eyes, she was exactly that. It made him feel sick and helpless.

"Have you been giving them blow-by-blow reports on your progress?"

Ian's own temper started. "You know better."

Her eyes were solemn, her gaze direct. "Right before you confessed, I was thinking how little I knew. About men, about myself. Now I'm doubly sure that I'm an idiot."

"The hell you are! You're an intelligent woman, damn it."

"Would you mind getting off me?"

Ian drew a breath and reached for control. "Yes, I would mind. I want you to understand. I want you to tell me that you care about me."

Erica opened her mouth, but a furious pounding on the front door interrupted what she might have said. Ian twisted to stare out toward the hall, cursed, and refused to budge.

"Aren't you going to answer that?"

"No."

"Then I will." She tried to slide out from under him.

"No." If he let her get away now, she'd go back to avoiding him. He just knew it. "Erica—"

The pounding on the door increased. It sounded like there were a dozen fists hitting it. "God damn it!" Ian exploded, and then to Erica, "I don't suppose you'd stay put while I go see who's trying to break down my door?"

"Yeah, right."

Sounding very put upon, he muttered, "That's what I thought." He pushed himself away and watched as Erica scrambled to her feet. In a show of temper, she snatched up the sheet and wrapped it around herself.

Ian sighed, opened a drawer to pull out boxers, and stepped into them.

Erica hustled up beside him when he started out of the bedroom. "You're going to answer the door in your underwear?"

They went through the hall and into the living room. "No, I'm going to tell whoever it is to get lost in my underwear."

And then he heard George call out, "Better open up, Ian, before the female battalion knocks it down."

Ian and Erica looked at each other in surprise.

"Erica! It's me, Asia. Becky's with me. Let us in."

Erica slugged Ian in the stomach, making him grunt. "You told them all we'd be here?"

He scowled right back at her. "Of course I didn't. They probably figured if you weren't at home, you must be here. We did have a detailed discussion in the break room, if you'll recall."

Looking sheepish, she said, "Oh, yeah."

Ian jerked the door open. "Did someone plan a party and not tell me?"

Asia gawked at him, her gaze moving over his naked chest and down his body until Cameron cleared his throat. Becky started to look too, but George quickly covered her eyes. He glared at Ian. "Good God, man, put some clothes on."

"Why? You're not staying."

Somewhat flustered, Asia shoved her way past him.

"Erica, we had nothing to do with this. George and Cameron didn't tell us. I can't believe Ian had them lying to us."

Ian rolled his eyes while Cameron barked, "I did not lie to you, damn it. I just didn't tell you about it."

"A lie of omission!"

Ian gestured to George, who still had Becky's eyes covered. "Looks like you might as well come in too. I'd like to shut the door to spare my neighbors all this drama."

George, still blinding Becky, hustled her in and kicked the door shut.

"George?" Becky asked.

"Yeah, sweetheart?"

"What am I missing?"

He kissed her temple. "Just Ian in his underwear."

She tried to pull his hand from her eyes.

Erica had gone back into the bedroom, Ian assumed to get dressed. Instead, she returned with a pair of his jeans and a T-shirt. "Try for a little decency, okay?" She tossed them to him.

"You wouldn't like me decent." She scowled, but when he winked at her, she actually flushed. Maybe, just maybe this would prove a timely interruption. God knew he'd been floundering on his own.

Ian stepped into his jeans just as Becky got George to turn her loose. "Well, heck. I miss everything."

"I'll get naked for you just as soon as we finish this misguided mission."

Becky turned to George, smiled, and said, "Promise?"

Asia cleared her throat. "Can we all remember why we're here?"

"I know why I'm here," Erica said, keeping the sheet tight around herself. "But no one told me we were planning an orgy."

"Damn," Cameron said to George, "I don't think we're dressed for an orgy."

Asia elbowed him. "Becky and I were worried all along about you getting tangled up with *him*." She glared toward Ian. "And it looks like we were right."

"You were?"

Asia leaned closer, and in a stage whisper said, "Erica, he set the whole thing up."

"Yeah, I know." Erica crossed her arms over her chest and nodded. "He told me."

Asia drew back. "He did?"

Ian threw up his hands. "What do you have against me?"

Very matter-of-factly, Becky said, "You're big."

George choked, making Becky blush and swat at him. "George! I didn't mean *that*."

Rubbing his eyes, Ian asked, "God knows I probably shouldn't ask, but what's wrong with being big?"

"You're dictatorial too," Asia claimed.

They were worried about him being heavy-handed with Erica? He shook his head. "Yeah, so is Erica and you like her."

Cameron nodded. "He's got ya there, honey."

"People are nervous around you," she insisted.

"Not Erica." Ian turned to her. "Are you, sweetheart?"

"Certainly not." Erica sat down on the edge of the sofa, making certain the sheet covered what it should. "I don't see why you and Becky are all up in arms. It's not like this is anything new. Cameron lied to hook up with you, pretending he hadn't overheard your fantasy about spanking."

Ian's head jerked around so fast, he almost knocked himself over. Spanking? Asia and Cameron?

He stared, fascinated. The newlyweds both flushed, and said almost in unison, "That was a misunderstanding."

"And Asia, you hand-picked George when you found out Becky was into bondage."

Bondage! Ian eyed Becky with new insight. And here he'd always thought her to be shy and innocent. Maybe he needed to reevaluate.

"Erica," George growled while shoving a giggling Becky behind his back. "One of these days . . ."

"Oh, give up, George. Becky's not fine china. You're perfect for her, just as Cameron is perfect for Asia."

Ian stood right in front of Erica. "And I'm perfect for you."

She peered up at him. "You lied to me."

Frowning, Asia sat down beside her. She no longer looked so certain in her mission. "But as you said, Cameron lied to me, and I still love him."

"Yeah. I'm working that part of it out in my head."

Becky sat on her other side. "George lied to me too, but only for a little while. He admitted to me that it was a setup. And you know what? I remember he said he would help set you up with the perfect guy too. I just didn't know he'd think Ian was perfect."

George stepped forward. "I didn't, but Ian did. And why not? He's crazy about her. How much more perfect can it get?"

Cameron added, "We are talking about Erica here, remember. She scares most guys to death."

Erica tossed a throw pillow at him. "I never scared you."

"That's because I knew Asia would protect me."

George nodded.

"It's heartwarming that you're all so concerned

about her. Really." Ian looked at Erica. "But I think we can work things out on our own."

Cameron cleared his throat. "Well, I don't know about that. I feel rather protective."

Asia nodded. "Me, too."

Becky smiled at George. "We all do."

Laughing, Erica said, "Now why would you all feel protective of me?"

Ian knelt down in front of her. "Because they love you as much as I do. And if you're still keeping count, that's three."

Erica looked small and very uncertain sandwiched between her friends with their men crowding close to their sides.

"Three what?" Becky asked.

Erica's eyes went soft and dark. "Three times now that he's told me he loves me."

Asia and Becky were mute. Cameron said, "I believe him. God knows he's worked hard enough to get you here."

"Damn right," George agreed. "And I think Erica loves him too."

Ian raised a brow. "You do?"

"Sure. She's been defending you since we got here. Damned if I've ever heard Erica defend a man before. Usually she's ripping them to shreds."

Slowly, Ian's grin spread until he thought he might burst with satisfaction. Erica had been taking his part, defending him to her best friends. The look she gave him now was part wary, part annoyed. She was such a prickly woman sometimes. "Tell me you love me, Erica."

Cameron and George quickly seated themselves on the arms of the sofa next to their respective women. "I don't want to miss a word," Cameron said, despite the way Asia tried to hush him.

George said, "I wish I had my video camera," and Becky elbowed him hard.

With everyone looking at her, Erica naturally went cocky. "Yeah, sure, I love him."

Four mouths fell open. Ian just continued to smile.

"I mean, what's not to love? On top of being gorgeous, the man's a great cook, a talented electrician, and he plans to build a house off in the woods." She looked at Asia. "I always wanted to live in the woods."

"You did?"

Erica nodded. And then to Becky, "And I've always had a thing for the big macho guys."

"You have?"

"Oh, yeah." She slid off the couch to land in Ian's lap. He toppled onto his rump, but kept her locked in his arms, near to his heart. "I just didn't realize it until Ian came along."

"Does this mean you're getting married?" George wanted to know.

Erica laughed. "That better be what it means."

"Great. Then we're out of here." He pulled Becky to her feet. "Trust me, love. They want privacy."

Asia and Cameron stood too. "We'll go," Asia told her, "but I expect to hear from you soon with all the juicy details."

Erica gave a sly grin. "I'm not sure you're old enough to hear these details, Asia. They're juicier than most."

Cameron laughed. "A challenge!" And to George, "You think he's trying to outdo us?"

"Sounds like. I don't know about you, but I'm heading home to add to my repertoire on sexual deviations. The way these three gossip, you can't protect your manhood closely enough."

Becky snickered.

Asia took Cameron's hand. "A good idea. Cameron and I will do the same."

"Such a grand exodus," Ian noted once the door had closed behind them all. "Should we put out the same effort, you think?"

"I believe you already have." She toyed with his chest hair and asked, "All that stuff you did . . . it really was wonderful. You're wonderful."

"I told you that for the right woman, I'd do whatever I needed to." He gave her a lecherous smile.

"So it was just to wear me down?"

"No, it was to get you ready." He kissed the end of her nose. "They call it foreplay."

"Well, it worked."

Maintaining his hold on Erica, Ian came to his feet and headed for the bedroom. "Shall we see if it'll work again?"

"Am I still in charge?"

"For a little while longer. Then it's my turn." He entered the bedroom and placed her on the bed. Leaning over, being as serious in his declarations as he could be, he said, "That's what marriage is all about, you know. I love you, so I want you to be happy. You love me, so you want me to be happy." Then he asked, "Right?"

A teasing, very sexy grin eased into place. "Yes."

"Yes?"

She laughed. "Yes. I love you."

Ian snatched her up for a strangling hug. Laughing, Erica forced him back a bit, then said, "You know, as long as I'm still in charge, where's the massage oil?"

His expression warmed and his eyes grew dark. "You're ready for more pleasure, are you?"

"Absolutely." Erica shoved him to his back, then straddled his hips. "And I figure getting to rub your big gorgeous body all over is probably as much pleasure as any woman deserves."

"You want to use the oil on me?"

"That's right. And any man as controlling as you, ought to be able to control himself while I do this. So lie quietly . . . and let me love you."

Ian smiled. "Well, when you put it like that . . ."

Something Wilde

Janelle Denison

Chapter One

Jill Richardson had the sweetest ass Eric Wilde ever had the pleasure of admiring. Slightly rounded and toned, her smooth, luscious bottom gave way to long, slender legs encased in sheer stockings and three-inch designer high heels he found equally arousing. There was something about a woman's curvaceous backside that turned him on, and Jill's pert bottom, along with the slow, sexy sway to her hips, never failed to cause a rush of heated lust to flow through his veins.

And it had been a long time since he'd found a woman so sexually appealing. So damn distracting. Or so challenging.

He watched as Jill disappeared into the copy room, which was across the hall and adjacent to his private office at Massey and Associates, and released a long exhale. Dropping his head back against his chair, he closed his eyes and squeezed the blue rubber stress ball in his fist, welcoming the clench and release of tendons and muscles. Unfortunately, the exercise did little to ease the sexual tension thrumming through him.

No, there was only one cure for that particular ailment—having Jill hot and breathless beneath him, taking him hard and deep, and begging him for more.

Oh, yeah, he thought with a slow, lazy smile as he enjoyed the private fantasy filtering through his mind. Of stripping away the conservative peach suit she wore, along with her pragmatic facade, and discovering the sensual woman he sensed beneath the composed exterior.

"Eric, are you sleeping on the job?"

Startled by the sound of Jill's voice so close, he blinked his eyes open and found her standing on the other side of his desk. Amusement glimmered in her green eyes, and a matching smile curved the corners of a mouth so tempting he ached to taste her lips, and deep inside. She wore her auburn hair tucked into a tidy twist at the back of her head, and too many times he'd wondered about the length of those strands—the feel and texture against his fingertips and trailing across his skin. From head to toe she looked every inch the corporate professional and damned if the entire sensible package didn't do it for him in a major way.

Smiling in return, he sat up straighter, kneaded the ball in his hand one last time, then set it next to his computer. "Just taking a rest. It's been a long day." Twelve hours for him, to be exact, filled with budget meetings, a three-hour presentation to a client, and half a dozen contracts pored over and approved.

"And a very productive one for me," she said, her excitement nearly tangible as she slid a glossy color flyer on top of the reports in front of him. "I think I finally nailed the concept and layout design for the Enchanted Cruise Line account."

He picked up the presentation brochure, taking in the impact of her design and identifiable artwork, unique to the cruise line they were representing. The concept was tied together with the catchy slogan they'd brain-stormed together late one night, and he knew without a doubt she'd captured the full effect of what their client was expecting in their final presentation.

She walked around his desk and came to a stop next to his chair. Bracing her hand on the mahogany surface, she bent low to look at the brochure with him, bringing with her the unique but familiar scent of feminine softness and sensuality that wreaked havoc with his mind and body.

"So, what do you think?" she asked, obviously anxious for his approval.

He glanced toward her, witnessing the exuberance reflected in her expression, and felt that jolt of chemistry that was always present between them. Not for the first time he wondered if all that creativity and enthusiasm for her work extended into the bedroom. He wanted to find out in a way that was bordering on obsession.

"I think that mind of yours is absolutely amazing," he said, giving her the compliment she deserved for a job well done.

A huge smile lit up her face. "So, you really like it?"

"I love it," he replied honestly. "And I think our client will, too."

She turned her attention back to the brochure, and his gaze traveled down the smooth expanse of her throat to the conservative overlapping "V" of her suit jacket. Her stance caused the lapel to gap open slightly, giving him a glimpse of the delicate slope of one breast and the peach lace trim of a bra—just enough to tantalize and tease his senses before she straightened again.

"I have to admit that the generous bonus Massey is offering me to bring the campaign in on time and to the client's full satisfaction is a huge incentive in getting this presentation absolutely flawless."

And that bonus was important to her, he knew. Had been from the very beginning, since the promise of that monetary reward had been the deciding factor in her taking on this freelance project. According to her impressive resume, she used to work for an equally large advertising firm, until she'd abruptly quit and started her own small agency. On occasion she did freelance work, and the president of Massey and Associates insisted she come on board as temporary creative director for this potential multimillion dollar contract, at any cost. Thus the bonus. There had even been talk of the partners wanting her on a full-time basis, but so far Jill had turned down their very generous offers.

She shifted beside him and handed him a signoff sheet. "If you'll give me your final approval and signature on the layout of the presentation brochure then both of us can call it a night."

"Only to return tomorrow morning bright and early," he said wryly. Reaching for a pen, he scrawled his signature on the appropriate line of the attached report.

"It's a vicious cycle in this business, you know that," she said as she took back her papers to add to the presentation package. "But look on the bright side. Another week or so and we should have this campaign wrapped up and contracted. I'll be gone, and things can finally return to normal for you and your creative team."

With that, she issued him a final good night and headed for the door.

He sat there as she exited his office, her idle comment a jarring reminder that his time with her was limited. As for things returning to normal, he didn't know what normal was anymore. Not unless it included a daily dose of her, which fueled his erotic nighttime fantasies of them together, in carnal ways that left him hot and bothered and hornier than he could ever remember being. After three months of working side by side, another week and a half and she'd be gone, and already he was mourning the loss.

He shoved his fingers through his hair, then scrubbed a hand down his face and along the late evening stubble lining his jaw. Oh, man, he was in way over his head when it came to Jill, intrigued beyond reason, and so crazed with wanting her that he knew his brothers would laugh their asses off if they knew a woman had him so tied up in knots.

While both Steve and Adrian had attempted committed relationships in the past, neither one of them had ultimately been lucky in love. After being burned, they'd opted for the joys and freedom of bachelorhood, and seemed content with their single status—much to the disappointment of their parents, who wanted their boys happily settled, as they were. Being the youngest, and having witnessed his brothers' misery with the opposite sex, Eric had learned to guard his own emotions. He'd always been the consummate playboy, enjoying all women but never allowing one to get under his skin quite the way Jill had.

She stimulated and inspired him, mentally and physically, and it had been forever since a woman had managed that feat. And while the awareness between them was evident and she took his flirtatious behavior in stride, she never acted on the attraction. In that respect, she was reserved and guarded, and damned if he didn't want to delve deeper and unleash the desire he'd seen in her eyes on more than one occasion.

She was a challenge he couldn't resist.

Never before had he hesitated to go after what he wanted. He'd always been aggressive and impulsive when it came to pursuing the opposite sex, and it was past time he took a chance on Jill. Their business relationship was only temporary, which worked to both of their advantages, and there was no denying an affair between them would be both incendiary, and oh, so satisfying.

There was only one thing for him to do. Issue her a mutually satisfying proposition, and hope she agreed to the same.

After shutting down her office, Jill checked in one last time with two coworkers on her design team intent on putting in a few more hours of work before leaving for the evening. She spent a good twenty minutes approving the start of the Web site layout James was designing, and gave Catherine her input on a direct mail marketing outline. Then she took her briefcase and headed toward the bank of elevators that would release her from the confines of the thirty-sixth floor of the Chicago high-rise. Another day down, and only a few more weeks to go before she collected her bonus check and a newfound freedom and independence was all hers. That extra money would finally put her on solid financial ground, and enable her to devote more time to building her own agency.

With a soft *ping,* an elevator arrived and she stepped inside, pressing the button for the underground parking garage. Just as the steel door began to shut, a big body just barely squeezed his way past and into the elevator.

She gasped in startled surprise, then realized the intruder was none other than her gorgeous boss, Eric Wilde, briefcase in hand and his suit jacket draped over his arm, looking every inch the "Wilde, untamable bad boy" he'd been dubbed by female coworkers. The man had a way of looking completely sexy, at any time, including after a long, tiring day at the office.

His tie was off, presumably stuffed into his brief-case. The first three buttons of his oxford shirt were undone, and the sleeves were rolled up to his elbows, revealing the muscular strength in those forearms. His pitch-black hair was mussed since he had a habit of combing his fingers through the strands when he was deep in thought, and his bright blue eyes had the ability to shift from striking to intense to flirtatious, depending on his mood.

At the moment, there was something about his entire demeanor that seemed a bit aggressive, predatory, and too damned sexual.

Or maybe her exhausted mind was playing tricks on her.

Despite that definite possibility, her stomach fluttered in keen awareness, and she did her best to squash her attraction to him, as she'd managed to do for the past three months that she'd been working for Massey and Associates. And keeping her distance included keeping to her side of the elevator, which seemed to have shrunk in size the moment he'd hopped on board.

It dawned on her that she'd never been alone with him in one of the elevators before—they were always surrounded by other people coming and going to different floors. The air around her turned too warm, his presence too intimate, his gaze too purposeful.

The elevator began its smooth descent toward the parking garage and she regarded him with a small smile. "All you had to do was holler and I would have held the door for you."

A disarming grin full of his normal playful charm curved his lips. "I didn't want to take any chances."

His odd remark confused her, but she refused to

read too much into his comment—like the fact that he was insinuating she might not have held the door for him. "Well, I'm glad to see you took my advice to call it a night."

He shrugged his wide shoulders. "I decided work will be waiting for me when I get in in the morning."

"Unfortunately, it's so true." Needing to distract herself from his compelling stare, and the fact that they were sealed in a small confined space *alone,* she opened her purse and began digging through the contents for her car keys. "Wouldn't it be nice if there was a fairy that came in at night and sprinkled fairy dust on all our outstanding work so that it was all done come the morning?"

He chuckled at her whimsical thought, and then the elevator came to an abrupt, jarring stop.

She sucked in a quick breath and her gaze shot to the numbered panel above the steel door, which confirmed her fear. They were stalled somewhere between the twenty-fourth and twenty-fifth floors. "Oh, my God, we're stuck."

"We're fine," Eric said, his low, deep voice reassuring her. "*I* stopped the elevator."

"You did?" She jerked her gaze back to him, and frowned, unable to comprehend why he'd do such a thing. *"Why?"*

"Well, for one, I now have your full attention." Calmly, he set his briefcase and jacket on the floor, then slowly closed the short distance between the two of them, stopping less than a foot away. "And two, I'm buying myself some extra time alone with you, five minutes max, without the chance of getting interrupted by a coworker, or something business related. This is strictly personal, between you and me."

Her pulse leaped, spreading heat throughout her entire body. Somehow, she managed to keep herself outwardly composed, though her mind tried to predict what he intended to do with the five minutes he'd just brazenly claimed as his own. For some reason he'd chosen tonight to bring their attraction out into the open, to force her to acknowledge the desire they'd both skirted for the past three months.

She inhaled a slow, deep breath. He stood so close, she drew in the warm, masculine scent that clung to his skin, could feel the heat of his tall, lean, hard body that made her feel so soft and feminine in contrast. His eyes were dark and focused completely on her, the irises smoldering with an intense sexual energy she found both fascinating and unsettling.

Oh, Lord, he was so virile, so tempting, so . . . *everything.* Yet there was absolutely nothing intimidating about him, if she didn't count the threat to her hormones, and emotions, too. She had a feeling, given the chance, he could devastate both.

Absently, she ran her tongue over her dry lips, and realized her mistake when his gaze dropped to her mouth. "Eric . . . don't you think that security is going to notice that this elevator isn't moving?" Amazingly, her voice didn't betray her nervousness, and she managed to sound steady and pragmatic.

"There's no reason why they should suspect anything's wrong, not unless someone presses the alarm bell," he said meaningfully. "It's after seven in the evening, there are six other elevators operating, and no one is going to miss this one for a few minutes. And you can release the stop button at any time."

He was giving her that choice to make. Giving her a sense of security and a safety net if she wanted one. But that meant brushing past him to get to the panel of buttons. In the process of her sidestepping him their chests and thighs would touch, and she didn't think she could handle the intimate caress of their bodies when her nipples were already so painfully tight.

She stayed put, out of necessity and partly because she was curious. "So, what's so important that you'd go to such extremes to be alone with me?"

"I would think that would be obvious." Flattening one hand on the mirrored wall at the side of her head, he leaned toward her, increasing the heat and awareness between them. "But if not, I guess I need to be a bit more forward. How about having dinner with me tonight?"

Startled by his invitation, one that tempted her beyond reason, it took her a moment to form an excuse that didn't give away her deeper interest in him. "Thank you for the offer, but I had a late lunch and I'm not hungry."

A grin canted the corner of his mouth, as if he saw beneath her struggle to hang onto her businesslike composure when the air around them fairly crackled with a vibrant, seductive energy. "How about a drink, then?"

"I'm not thirsty." Oh, that was totally lame! She caught herself before she could roll her eyes, and uncertain of what his next request might be, she decided to turn the tables and throw him off guard instead. "Do you know it's common knowledge that you're a womanizer?"

"Really?" He lifted a dark brow, seemingly more amused than offended by her comment. "Says who?"

"A lot of the women in the office." She shrugged, attempting a nonchalance she didn't feel. "You've got a reputation for being a love 'em and leave 'em kind of guy."

"That's an exaggeration. At least the second part of

that statement is." With his free hand, he reached down and uncurled her fingers from the handle of her brief-case, then set the leather portfolio on the floor beside her. He straightened again, trapping her completely be-tween the arm braced near her shoulder and the palm he lightly rested on the curve of her waist.

His touch was gentle, incredibly sensual, and one hundred percent confident male. His striking blue eyes, locked on hers, made her tremble deep inside. She knew she should tell him to stop. At the very least to back away so she didn't feel so scorched by his close proximity. But she was too mesmerized by the seduc-tive, forbidden spell he'd so effortlessly woven be-tween them to speak. It was just the two of them, alone, and despite knowing from personal experience how risky it was to get involved with a man she essentially worked for, she couldn't deny the fact that she'd craved Eric from the very first day she'd met him.

She had to resist him . . .

His thumb feathered along her hip, bringing his gor-geous face, and her predicament, back into focus. The fluorescent lights overhead haloed his dark head, giv-ing her the distinct impression that she was dealing with a fallen angel who knew too much about wicked, sinful pleasures.

"As for that love 'em and leave 'em comment, I *do* love everything about women," he murmured huskily. "The way they smell . . ." He dipped his head, his nose skimming her jaw as he inhaled slowly, deeply, as if she were an irresistible drug he couldn't get enough of.

Her lashes fluttered closed, and she bit her bottom lip to keep from groaning out loud.

"The feel of their soft skin . . ."

Warm fingers strummed along the sensitive flesh at the nape of her neck, and her pulse quickened in her chest, between her thighs. With effort, she lifted her hands and placed them against his rib cage, but couldn't bring herself to push him away.

"And especially the way they taste . . ."

His lips parted against her throat, and his soft, wet tongue lapped at her sensuously, awakening long dormant needs and a rising passion she couldn't contain. Her head fell back, and exquisite sensations curled through her, making her knees weak and her breasts ache for the stroke of his tongue, the heat of his mouth.

His lips traveled back up to her ear. "So, if dinner is out, and so is a drink, how about a kiss?"

Oh, yes, please . . . The shameless plea tumbled through Jill's mind, startling her at just how far she'd allowed herself to go with Eric. And just how much farther she ached to go with him, to fulfill the fantasies she'd taken to bed with her for the past three months and finally experience reality in its purest form.

"I'm not interested," she blurted, out of sheer preservation.

He chuckled, the deep, arousing vibrations rippling along her nerve endings. "You are such a liar, Jill." Amusement laced his voice and flickered in his eyes, which quickly faded to a more serious, sensual mood. "I can smell your desire. I can feel how much you want me. And I tasted the heat of excitement on your skin."

The man was absolutely shameless. Despite knowing all the reasons why she should avoid any involvement with him, she felt her defenses crumbling, her resolve weakening. In its place anticipation stirred her blood, and a hot ache settled low.

"Just one kiss?" He bent his head, slow enough to give her time to protest.

But she couldn't resist him, or the deeper longing to give in to something so spontaneous and impulsive when she'd spent the last year and a half alone, being much too sensible about everything. Including her attraction to this sexy man.

Her lashes fluttered closed as his mouth touched hers, soft and fleeting at first, then gradually he exerted a firmer, more coaxing pressure. Her lips parted on a low moan, one he took as the invitation it was intended to be. The gentle glide of his tongue was slow and lazy, seducing her in degrees. Her fingers curled into tight fists against his chest as the kiss grew deeper, wetter. Giving in to the delicious, heady sensations and the thrill of arousal setting her nerve endings aflame, she returned his kiss with reckless abandon.

The hand resting on her hip slid lower and smoothed over the curve of her derriere. He squeezed her bottom in his palm, groaned deep in his throat, and pulled her closer, until there was no mistaking the hard, impressive length of his erection pulsing against her belly. Her body slickened in a purely feminine response as she imagined how all that aggressive male heat would feel stroking deep inside her.

The erotic hunger and need he incited was instantaneous and explosive, an intimate connection that sent her world spinning out of control. Her physical reaction to him was so powerful and instinctive, all from a bone-melting *kiss,* and she knew, and feared, that this man had the ability to make her forget about the hard lesson she'd learned about mixing business with more intimate pleasures.

She broke the kiss and looked up into his blue eyes, heavy-lidded and smoky with passion. For her. And then a breathtakingly confident smile made an appearance.

"I'd *really* like to see you outside of the office," he murmured.

Panic streaked through her. His big hand still cupped her bottom possessively, and somehow she managed to shore up the fortitude to end this interlude before she gave in to the desire simmering between them. "We can't," she said abruptly, then amended that with a firm, "*I* can't."

He tilted his head, looking adorably boyish, and too damn persuasive. "Why not?"

Easing past him, she released the stop button and put the elevator back into motion before she did something incredibly stupid . . . like change her mind, or worse, let him take her right there in the elevator. Lord knew her body was primed and ready for his.

Feeling more in control with distance between them, she turned to face him again, and answered his direct question. "We're coworkers, Eric, and it's not . . . ethical."

He shoved his hands into the front pockets of his trousers, which served to pull the fabric of his pants tight across his burgeoning erection. "We're more colleagues than coworkers," he pointed out in a practical tone of voice.

"It doesn't matter." She crossed her arms over her chest, and wished her breasts didn't feel so sensitive, so achy. "I make it a rule not to mix business with pleasure, and that means *not* going out with someone I work for. Period."

"Don't you think we already crossed that line of yours with the kiss we just shared?"

Her face warmed at his blunt reminder of her eager participation in their embrace, and since she couldn't come up with a snappy reply, she glanced up at the number panel and mentally counted down the floors. *Twenty . . . nineteen . . . eighteen . . .*

"Look," Eric said, and casually strolled over to where

she stood. "You're at Massey on a temporary basis as a freelance creative director, so it's not as though you'll lose a job if you decide to date me and someone finds out about it."

Lose her job? No. But she wasn't about to jeopardize her standing with the firm in any way, since there was no telling what the future might bring, or if she'd need a reference or another freelance project with Massey.

And that thought was enough to make her think twice about involvement with Eric, no matter how much he tempted her to say *yes*.

"In fact, we both know you only have a few weeks left at the firm," he continued, the first tinges of frustration threading his voice. "So don't you think we could make an exception to that business/pleasure rule of yours?"

The man was relentless and it took all of her strength to refuse him. "No." She kept her eyes glued on the flashing numbers. *Twelve . . . Eleven . . . Ten . . .*

"How about when the Enchanted Cruise Line account is contracted and your part in the project is over?"

She looked his way and sighed softly. Regretfully. "Massey is turning out to be a huge, lucrative account for me and my agency, so any involvement with anyone in the firm, let alone someone in your position who has the power to approve freelance employees for certain projects, just isn't smart."

He narrowed his gaze, seemingly hurt that she'd lump him into such an unsavory category. "You think I'd use a personal relationship against you?"

"It's happened to me before." The words slipped out before she could stop them, but maybe he needed to hear the brutal truth from her. And maybe she needed to remind herself, as well.

He appeared taken aback by her candor, and for the first time ever, speechless.

Nearing her stop for parking garage two, she crossed the elevator and picked up her briefcase, then forced herself to meet his gaze again. "How about we forget that the kiss ever happened?"

"You can do that?" His voice rang with disbelief.

She was certain she'd never forget that soul-stirring kiss, and would most likely relive it every night when she tried to fall asleep. Not that she'd ever tell *him* that.

The elevator came to a smooth stop where her car was parked, and the doors opened silently. "I just think it's the smartest thing for us to do."

He caught her arm before she could exit, his sensual lips tightening with determination. "I think I proved there's something between us worth pursuing," he said, and released her. "Just think about it, Jill."

As if she'd be able to think of anything else.

Chapter Two

He had to have her.

Eric quietly and covertly scaled the stone wall to Jill's backyard, knowing there was no other cure for the surge of lust that had gripped him during and after the kiss he'd shared with Jill. And nothing, absolutely nothing, had taken the edge off the raw sexual energy riding him hard ever since.

He'd spent an hour working out at the gym, and had even met his sports enthusiast brother, Adrian, for a fierce game of racquetball. He'd managed to beat Adrian's ass, just barely, and even that victory hadn't eased the tension thrumming through his veins. Probably because his sibling had accurately guessed that it was a woman who had him all tied up in knots, and Adrian hadn't hesitated to rib him unmercifully about his inability to score with this particular female.

As a last resort, Eric had tried a more conventional method of taming his arousal with a cool shower, all to no avail. Or relief. He was *still* hard with wanting her, he thought in disgust.

He had to have her. It was that possessive, all-consuming thought that had driven Eric to more extreme measures. While pacing across his living room floor to help shake off his agitation, he'd come to the conclusion that the only way to bypass Jill's issue of mixing a working relationship with pleasure was to cater to her fears, and that meant keeping the two totally and completely separate. Business would remain at the office, and pleasure and fun would come after-hours, in a private, intimate setting he planned to establish this evening. No one would ever find out that they were seeing each other outside the office, so there wouldn't be any conflict of interest for Jill to worry about. Or any threat to her standing with Massey and Associates.

All he had to do was convince her to agree to the private affair he had in mind.

Now, after climbing over the stone wall surrounding the front of the Victorian house in which Jill lived on the far end of a quiet residential street, he moved stealthily through her backyard and kept close to the lush foliage clinging to the one-story structure. Dressed in a black T-shirt and jeans, and staying well hidden in the shadows of a few long-limbed trees, he waited patiently for the right opportunity to put his plan into motion. To set the stage for a beguiling seduction beyond anything she'd ever imagined, and one she wouldn't be able to refuse. At least not easily, if the combustible kiss they'd shared in the elevator was any indication.

He caught sight of Jill through a window leading into what appeared to be the kitchen. Adrenaline and anticipation rushed through him, and he continued to watch her as she poured herself a glass of wine, then disappeared down an adjoining hallway.

Keeping to the outer recesses of the yard, he followed her through the length of the house with nothing but moonlight leading his way, until she finally entered a large bedroom with a king-size, four-poster bed dominating the room. The French doors leading to a tiled patio were wide open, giving him an unobstructed view of every move she made.

A brass lamp on the dresser gave off a soft illumination, and he watched as she strolled into the bathroom, set her glass of wine on the rim of the tub and turned on the faucet. She added a generous amount of bubble bath to the churning water before returning to the bedroom, where she stripped off her T-shirt, heedless of anyone's presence.

Eric's mouth went dry when her lacy bra followed, baring to his gaze, her gorgeous breasts, which looked full and firm in contrast to her slim waist. The tips were crowned with raspberry-hued nipples, and it didn't take much to imagine them trembling against his stroking fingers, so sensitive beneath the soft scrape of his teeth, and hard and taut as he suckled her into his hot, hungry mouth.

He bit back a low groan at the lustful thoughts tumbling through his head. His groin throbbed, and he pressed a hand to his aching shaft, doing his best to rearrange and accommodate the erection straining uncomfortably against the fly of his jeans.

Her shorts came off next, sliding down her long, slender legs, leaving her clad in a pair of silky bikini panties that looked insubstantial enough to rip off her in the throes of passion. The thin fabric didn't quite conceal the shadowy cleft between her thighs, and the sight of her standing there half naked and completely uninhibited was enough to bring him to his knees. He could only hope that he'd be fortunate to find himself in such an erotic position with her, to be able to press her thighs wide apart with his hands, inhale her warm female scent, and taste her desire with his lips, and the soft lick of his tongue.

He had to have her . . .

He scrubbed a hand through his thick hair, every nerve in his body strung tight as he waited for her to remove that last scrap of material. Much to his surprise and disappointment, she left her panties on while she dumped her clothes into the hamper, retrieved a pair of underwear and a nightgown from an armoire, then returned to the bathroom and the billow of steam curling from the tub. Setting her change of clothes on the vanity, she switched on a radio to a soft jazz station, turned off the water, and in one smooth motion shimmied out of her panties.

Sweet Jesus. Eric exhaled hard as he was graced with a quick glimpse of the smooth slope of her back and the more enticing curve of her buttocks, before she stepped into the steaming water and sat in the tub, immersing herself up to her neck in frothy bubbles.

He remained outside for another five minutes, just to make sure he had himself under control, and giving Jill time to lose herself in the relaxation of her bath.

Then silently, he made his way up to the house and came to a stop just outside the open double doors. Like the phantom lover he hoped to become, he kept himself blended in with the night shadows . . . and waited for the fantasy to unfold.

Jill finished off the last of her wine and sank deeper into the tub of lukewarm water, wishing that the one guilty pleasure she indulged in when she was feeling uptight would do the trick of subduing the tension thrumming through her body. No such luck. The fragrant heat of the water, mellow music, and sweet wine had relaxed her mind, but her body remained restless and needy. And it was all Eric Wilde's fault for instigating such a thorough, dominating kiss, and for planting provocative, tempting ideas in her mind of the two of them together.

Sexually. Intimately. Carnally.

Her stomach clenched as another rush of desire settled low, beckoning her to finish what Eric had started in the elevator. She'd been excruciatingly aroused ever since she'd felt the hard length of his erection against her belly, and tormented by wicked thoughts of his thick shaft impaling her in a sleek, heavy glide, stretching her, filling her with hard, sure thrusts.

Her head rolled back against the rim of the tub and a low groan escaped her throat. Her sex tingled, pulsed, and she knew exactly how to give herself the satisfaction her body screamed for. Feeling defiant, she curled her fingers into tight fists against her sides, stubbornly refusing to cave in to her body's demands. She was so damned tired of the solo, self-induced orgasms she'd resorted to for the past year and half. She wanted—*needed*—a man. Specifically, Eric. She hungered for his touch, and the warmth and firmness of his big hands branding her flesh. She ached to feel his mouth on her breasts, her belly, between her thighs.

Frustrated and aggravated at the direction of her thoughts, as well as Eric's hold over her even in the solitude of her own home, she pulled the plug on her bath and abruptly stood up, determined to put her mind and restless energy to better use—such as immersing herself in the work she had piling up in her office—until she was too tired to think of anything but *sleep*.

And then maybe, *hopefully,* she wouldn't dream of a certain dark-haired, blue-eyed bad boy who'd starred in her most carnal fantasies for the past three months.

A man who'd made it clear with a kiss and the suggestion of an affair that he wanted her just as much as she craved him.

Water cascaded down the length of her like a lover's caress, and her breasts tightened painfully as beads of liquid trickled over her erect nipples and down her belly. She shivered and, gritting her teeth against another onslaught of feverish sensation unfurling along her nerves, grabbed a towel and methodically patted down her wet skin, careful to keep the terry material away from ultra-sensitive places.

Slipping into her panties and chemise, she cleaned up the bathroom, then padded back into her master bedroom. Plucking the pins from the hair she'd twisted into a tight knot at the back of her head, she tossed the clips onto her dresser and let the long, wavy strands unravel until the ends fell halfway down her back. Separating the thick mass into three sections, she began braiding her hair so it didn't end up tangled around her head by morning.

"Leave your hair down."

Startled by the deep, masculine voice she'd heard, she dropped her unfinished braid and whirled around, her gaze scanning the room in a quick sweep. She caught a subtle movement just outside the open French doors. Heart racing, she tried to make out the shadow, wondering if it, and the sexy male voice she'd heard, were all a product of her overactive imagination.

A summer breeze blew outside, rustling a light sprinkling of leaves across the patio. The sultry warmth swept through the room, fluttering her silk chemise around her thighs. Her skin tightened, and the little hairs on her arms prickled to attention just as a large silhouette moved into the open archway, the unmistakable size and build of a man. Silvery moonlight glinted off his dark hair and gave him a surreal aura.

She gasped and took a step back, ready to brandish the brush in her hand as a weapon, if need be. "Who's there?" she demanded.

The man entered her room, bold as he pleased. But instead of running for the phone to call for help, she stared in stunned disbelief, more intrigued by Eric Wilde's presence than she would have liked. His hair was tousled in wild disarray around his head, and he wore tight black jeans that molded to lean hips and long, muscular legs, and a black T-shirt that stretched taut across his chest. He looked dark and forbidding as original sin, and dangerous in a way that excited her.

She swallowed hard and found her voice again. "What are *you* doing here?"

He moved toward her, a lazy smile curving his sensuous lips. "You've been waiting for me," he stated confidently, his tone as pretentious as his entrance into her private life.

She opened her mouth to deny his claim, and quickly snapped it shut again. Despite whatever game he was playing, she couldn't lie. She'd dreamed of him too many nights to count, a fantasy lover who came to her in the dark of the night to fulfill her desires. She'd just never expected him to appear in the flesh. And she'd never expected him to look so good, so sexually intense.

He strolled past her to her dresser with a pantherlike grace that brought all her feminine senses to keen awareness. There was power beneath that control he exuded—power she sensed that once unleashed would have the ability to consume the woman he was with. She wanted that heat and strength to consume *her*.

She continued to watch him, mesmerized, as he lifted one of her perfume atomizers to his nose and inhaled the fragrance. He closed his eyes as he did so, making it seem like an erotic experience in which she wanted to share. When he lifted his raven lashes again, his eyes were filled with a raw hunger, directed solely at her.

She began to tremble, from the inside out, and struggled to maintain the upper hand in this scenario. "Did you know that breaking and entering is against the law?"

"I didn't break in," he said, his voice low and amused. "You left your doors wide open, which isn't safe, by the way."

She rolled her eyes heavenward. "I've lived in this house all my life and there's never been a problem with prowlers in this neighborhood . . . until tonight," she added meaningfully.

He absently touched the other feminine things on her dresser, his fingers lingering on her personal items. "I'm not a prowler."

She eyed him critically, taking in his choice of clothing, his arrogance, and the way the entire length of him radiated pure, unadulterated sensuality. "At the moment, you look *very* predatory to me."

"And you like it." His gaze slid from her face to her chest, then back up again. "The fast-beating pulse in your throat is a dead giveaway, as are the hard nipples pressing against your nightgown."

She resisted the urge to cover her body's response to him with her hands and deny his too accurate claim.

He slowly circled around her, so close she could feel

the heat of his body, the subtle brush of his hand over her silk-clad bottom. "You're filled with anticipation," he murmured huskily, "wondering what I'm going to do, if I'm going to touch you, or kiss you, or if I plan to strip you naked and have my way with you right here and now."

God, how did he know her so well that he could verbalize her thoughts and know *exactly* what she ached for? "What do you want, Eric?"

He stopped in front of her. In direct contrast to his dark attire, his eyes were a stunning, sultry shade of blue that made her weak in the knees. "There's no sense beating around the bush in terms of what *I* want. I'm here to issue you a proposition."

She was too curious to hear the rest of what he had to say to interrupt him with her own immediate misgivings.

"We both want each other, that much we established earlier in the elevator," he said, brazenly reminding her of her wanton behavior with him. "But since dating is out of the question because of how public it would make our relationship and attraction, and you're nervous about risking your reputation with the company, I'd like to propose a fantasy world, one that stays just between the two of us and is only visited at night."

She frowned, not quite grasping his concept, or precisely what he meant. "A fantasy world?"

He nodded slowly. "In this private, intimate world we create for the sole purpose of satiating our desires, I'll be your phantom lover who comes to you only in the dark of night to fulfill your deepest, most erotic fantasies. In this fantasy world, you can be completely open and uninhibited with me, ask for anything you want, and whatever we say or do will stay in this room and go no further. And when the freelance project at

Massey is done, we'll part amicably and go our separate ways."

The impulse to accept his scintillating offer clashed with a wealth of insecurities, and deeper uncertainties.

She chewed on the inside of her cheek, staring at the enigmatic man in front of her, noticing how he'd taken great pains to transform himself into a fantasy lover, all for her benefit and peace of mind. All because he wanted her badly enough to present her with a non-threatening, anything goes, sexual escapade, along with the assurance that nothing would go beyond what they shared in this bedroom.

She believed him. *This* Eric was so different from the shrewd businessman who balanced his more serious, executive side with a carefree, flirtatious attitude. There was nothing carefree about the lover he'd created solely for her pleasure. No, this man was as mysterious as the night, oozed raw male energy even when he wasn't moving, and was outrageously blatant in his intent and approach.

The provocative fantasy beckoned, stealing her common sense and leaving behind an explicit hunger she felt helpless to deny.

"What do you get out of this?" she asked, before she lost the nerve.

He tilted his head. "I have a few of my own fantasies I'd like to fulfill, as well." Retrieving the brush from her hand, he smacked the flat backside against his palm. "Have you ever been spanked by a lover before?"

"No." She quivered deep inside, admittedly feeling a little breathless at the thoughts invading her mind. Wicked, shameless visions that caused a melting warmth to cascade through her veins. She lifted her gaze back to his face, and found him smiling at her in that devastating way of his. "I'm not into pain."

"Me either. For myself, or my partner."

"I'm relieved," she said, and meant it.

He caressed the smooth, wooden surface of the brush with long, stroking fingers. "But you might find it more pleasurable than you think, with the right man. I would think a light spank on such pale, tender flesh, done in a restrained way, could be very arousing."

He walked behind her, and she braced herself for a stinging slap on her bottom, torn between panic and an inexplicable excitement, but the spanking never came. Instead, he gathered her hair back, unraveled the strands from the unfinished braid, and let the silky mass flow down her spine. She shivered and closed her eyes as he slowly pulled the brush from the crown of her head to the ends of her hair. His fingers joined in on the luxurious treatment, massaging her scalp, the nape of her neck, chasing away the last of her tension and completely relaxing her. Unused to being pampered in such a wondrous way, she couldn't contain the soft groan of pure pleasure that rose up from her chest.

"You have beautiful hair," he murmured near her ear, his voice low, deep, and soothing. As was the palm that trailed down her bare arm in a languid, nerve-tingling stroke. "You always wear it up at work, and I never knew how long it was, how wavy and soft."

Her breasts swelled, her breathing deepened, and she felt completely hypnotized by his beguiling monologue, his tantalizing touch.

"I love long hair," he continued. "The way it feels grazing my naked body, and especially how sexy and erotic it feels having the strands wrapped in my fist so I can be the one in control."

His long fingers tightened around the hair at the nape of her neck, and he gently tugged her head back, giving her no choice but to heed his silent command to rest her head against his shoulder. He brushed his warm, velvet-soft lips along her jaw, and let his teeth graze the side of her throat. Her mind spun, and she moaned.

She felt him smile triumphantly against her neck, felt the hot, damp gust of his breath on her skin. "Do you like the way that feels, too?"

Oh, yes, she *liked.* Her whole body felt alive, heavy and hot, pulling tight and aching for him. Between her legs she could feel her own slick moisture, and the steady, growing throb that preluded an orgasm.

"I also like to be in control during sex, and dominant. Even a bit aggressive. Does that bother you?"

She dampened her bottom lip with her tongue, briefly wondering if his dominant act was solely for the purpose of the fantasy, or if he always liked being in control with women. "No, that doesn't bother me." Oh, God, his aggression *excited* her.

He released her hair, set her brush on the dresser, and turned her around to face him. Tucking a finger beneath her chin, he lifted her gaze to his. She glimpsed the hot fire in his eyes, could sense his barely suppressed restraint, and felt singed by the intimate connection between them.

"I want you to know that I would never hurt you," he said, his tone low and reassuring. "*Ever.* Do you believe me?"

She trusted him and his promise. "Yes."

He nodded succinctly, seemingly satisfied with her answer. "This is all about fulfilling fantasies and desires, playful or dark, but if I get too rough or go too far, all you have to say is stop, and I will."

She didn't miss the underlying warning that he *would* get sexually demanding with her. *Dominant.* She swallowed hard, the possibilities arousing her. Oh, Lord, was she really going to go through with this wild, imaginative idea of his?

"Even right now, the choice is yours," he murmured, letting his fingers drift away from her face. "To end the fantasy, all you have to do is tell me to go. To continue the fantasy, issue me an invitation to stay."

Struggling with those personal ethics of hers playing tug-of-war with the simple words, *stay or go,* she attempted to take a step back from him. But in a move she couldn't have anticipated he pressed her up against the wall next to the dresser. Flattening his hands on either side of her shoulders, he leaned into her, aligning their stomachs and thighs. He nudged his rock-hard erection against her mound, and applied a delicious pressure that heightened the need clawing at her.

"Eric . . ."

His eyes glittered like burnished sapphires, and his jaw clenched tight, making him appear as dark and dangerous as the phantom lover he claimed to be. His hands dropped to her waist and slid possessively over her hips, then slipped around to grab her ass. He lifted her up onto her toes, angled her pelvis, and slowly, sensuously, ground his straining shaft against the swollen folds of her sex.

"I want to fuck you," he growled, his words as explicit and rough as the friction of his coarse jeans rubbing against the wet, slick silk of her panties. "With my fingers, my tongue, my cock. Slow and deep, hard and fast . . . and every way there is."

Her stomach muscles clenched in a forbidden kind of thrill, and her head rolled back against the wall in complete surrender. *Oh, yes, please.*

He buried his face against her neck, and as if he had a direct link to her mind and thoughts, he released her bottom and pushed the straps of her gown off her shoulders and down her arms. The fabric slithered to the ground, leaving her bare except for her panties.

He eased back, quickly yanked his shirt over his head, and tossed the garment to the floor. Her breath hitched at the sight of his wide chest, defined by gorgeous male contours and warm tan skin she tested with her splayed palms. He dipped his head again, his damp lips sliding down her throat, and his hands finding and kneading her full breasts. His calloused thumbs raked over her puckered nipples, and then his hot, wet mouth was there, his tongue flicking over the rigid tips, his teeth nibbling the taut swells of her breasts before he suckled her, hard and strong. With each deep, suctioning pull of his mouth, scorching waves of desire rolled through her.

The pleasure was so acute, so intense, she cried out, her body pulsing for the release she'd denied herself earlier. Twisting her fingers into his thick hair, she arched into him to get closer, so beyond rational thought that she couldn't hold back the begging sounds escaping the back of her throat.

His hand slid from her breast down her torso, heating her flesh everywhere he touched. Kneeing her legs apart, he grasped the side of her panties, and with a fierce tug he ripped the insubstantial scrap of fabric right off her hips. She gasped, both shocked and inflamed by his primitive behavior.

Abruptly lifting his head from her breasts, he slanted his mouth across hers and parted her lips with the persuasive pressure of his own. He kissed her forcefully, plundering her mouth with his tongue at the same time his palm fastened over her mound and his long fingers slipped between her slick folds and penetrated her lush, weeping sex. He buried the pad of his thumb against her clitoris, expertly finessed that hard, sensitive nub of flesh, then stopped just as she was poised on the brink of a shattering climax.

She closed her eyes and shuddered at the loss of pulsing sensation that had promised her a glimpse of paradise.

He dragged his mouth from hers and whispered in her ear, "You're so tight around my fingers. I can feel your inner muscles pulling at me, drawing me deeper. You want to come, don't you, baby?"

More than anything. She could only manage a whimper in response, and with her hands clutching his taut arms, she gyrated her hips rhythmically against his hand, a silent plea to end the sensual torment and let her soar.

He withheld what she wanted, his fingers filling her, but absolutely still. "Stay or go, sweetheart," he drawled as his lips caressed her jaw, the corner of her mouth. "One word is all it takes to get what you want."

Bewildered and frustrated, she opened her heavy-lidded eyes and searched his expression, which was etched with unbridled lust. She could feel the sexual tension vibrating off his body and the deep, heavy rhythm of his breathing that spoke of his own arousal as he waited patiently for her to make the final decision.

Stay or go.

With one word from her, he was offering her the chance to explore raw, earthy, uninhibited sex, something she'd imagined in her mind in the dark of night, but had never had the nerve to instigate with another man. Her last boyfriend, Jeremy, hadn't been at all adventurous, and had been as formal and stuffy in bed as he had been working by her side during the day. But Eric . . . Eric was virile and unwavering in his prowess, and confident of the kind of pleasure he could give her. And he might be playing a dark and dangerous kind of role, but his touch was underscored with a tempered gentleness she trusted.

He wanted her permission, her approval. Her complete acquiescence. And more than anything, she wanted to lose herself in physical sensation. With this forbidden fantasy of his, she wouldn't have to worry about the kind of emotional attachments that had turned so disastrous for her in the past, personally and professionally. And she instinctively knew if she let him go, she'd regret her decision for the rest of her life. She wanted this clandestine and temporary affair, and Eric. But with her consent she knew this night wasn't going to end with her climax. No, that would be just the beginning.

"Stay," she said, accepting her ultimate surrender to this fantasy man, *her phantom lover,* and everything else that came with her submission. "I want you to *stay.*"

A grin of male satisfaction curved his lips and he leaned into her, crushing his chest against the soft cushion of her breasts. Their mouths were inches apart, their panting breaths mingling, but he didn't kiss her. Staring directly into her eyes, he proceeded to take her where she wanted to go.

His long fingers thrust into her, slow and deep, and his thumb plied the knot of nerves between her quivering thighs until the fire inside her blazed into hot, liquid sensation.

"Come," he commanded gruffly, and with his sweet, searing stroke to her cleft she gave herself over to the rippling orgasm in wild abandon and a soft, keening cry.

Somewhere in her mind she heard him groan, *"Oh, yeah,"* as he wrung the last of the tremors from her body, followed by, "Oh, baby, you needed that as much as I do, didn't you?"

She didn't have the energy to answer, not that one was required when it was obvious how deprived she'd been, and how aroused he still was. She sagged against the wall, grateful for the support of his body that kept her upright. He withdrew his fingers, lifted his hand, and slid the soft, wet tip of one finger, slick with her desire, along her bottom lip.

She jerked back in startled surprise.

He didn't relent. Instead, he gently pushed the plump flesh of her lower lip down, forcing her mouth to open. *"Taste,"* he ordered.

She recognized the challenge he issued. Another dark fantasy he wanted to fulfill. She'd come this far, and while what he was asking for was something she'd never done before, she wasn't about to back down from his sexy, bold dare.

Drawing his finger all the way into her mouth, she swirled her tongue along the length, tasting the salt on his skin and her own dewy essence. She groaned and sucked him deeper, watching as his eyes dilated with sexual hunger. His nostrils flared, and she reveled in the momentary power she held over him.

"Christ. I can't wait any longer," he muttered, and withdrawing his finger, he replaced it with the heat of his mouth and the thrust of his tongue, his sudden urgency nearly tangible. With his lips fused to hers, he wrapped a strong arm around her waist and maneuvered her toward the bed.

He followed her up onto the center of the mattress and nudged her legs wide apart so he could kneel in between her splayed thighs, giving her no time to cling to any last semblance of modesty. His eyes branded her, from her breasts to her belly to the glistening folds of her sex as he fumbled with his belt, then tore frantically at the buttons of his jeans. His fly opened, and he shoved the waistband of his pants over his hips, freeing his long, thick shaft to her gaze.

Her breath stalled in her lungs as she took in the size and length of him. The impressive width. His shaft looked as smooth as velvet and hard as steel, and more than she'd ever had before. She couldn't hold back the strangled sound that slipped from her.

A slow, bad-boy grin made an appearance. "You did this to me, sweetheart," he said, his accusation soft and laced with amusement as he reached into the front pocket of his jeans and withdrew a foil packet. Ripping it open, he sheathed his erection in the thin latex. "I can't remember ever being this hard and thick before."

A tiny thrill shot through her, that she'd done that to him. "Is that supposed to be a compliment?"

"You can bet it is." He draped her thighs over his and touched her intimately, making her wetter, hotter, all over again. "I've been hard with wanting you ever since the first moment we met."

All talk ceased as he moved over her and the smooth, broad head of his penis nudged her opening, stretching her, giving her no choice but to accept him, *all* of him, until with one final, forceful thrust he was buried to the hilt.

She sucked in a quick breath and gripped his shoulders, his skin slick and damp against her palms. He was big, hot, and solid inside her, and her back arched in an attempt to accommodate his invasion, which drove him deeper. He groaned like a dying man and completely covered her body with his. His hands tangled in her hair, and his mouth claimed hers in a kiss as erotic as the carnal joining of their flesh. The tempo of his pistoning hips escalated into a wild, primitive coupling, and he ground himself against her mound, creating a near unbearable friction designed to make her come again.

The flame of passion between them burned hotter, higher, brighter, and she wrapped her legs around his waist and rocked against him, urging him toward his own climax. With a low, guttural growl, he wrenched his mouth from hers and tossed his head back, his breath exploding from his lungs in heavy, labored gasps. He drove deep one last time, sending her spiraling into a lush vortex of sensation, then shuddered violently with his own release as she contracted around his fully embedded shaft.

When the storm of passion had passed, he stared into her eyes and brushed tendrils of hair from her flushed face, his gaze awed, and his touch gentle and reverent. With his fingers still caught in her hair, he slowly lowered his head and drifted his mouth along the curve of her neck and shoulder, then kissed her again, his lips sliding softly, leisurely over hers.

There was a sensitivity and caring in his actions that made her feel delicate, sensual, and cherished in the aftermath of such an untamed possession. And that revelation was an odd contradiction to the aggressive man she'd just given her body to. Yet there was no denying that this man embracing her so affectionately inspired the kind of intimacy lacking in her life, and seemed to draw something deeper from her than just sex. She felt as though he was touching a part of her soul that had been empty and lonely for too long.

The sentimental thought shook her, because it went against her need to remain detached and unemotionally involved. "Eric," she whispered, uncertain what was happening between them. Wondering if he felt the subtle shift, too.

"Shhh." He kissed her one last time, and without another word he pulled away, separating their bodies so he could take care of the condom and put his clothes back on.

She immediately felt the loss, missed his warmth and closeness, and berated herself for allowing too much reality to mix in with the fantasy.

Once he was dressed, he put her beneath the covers and brushed his mouth across hers in a sweet, fleeting caress. "Good night, sweetheart," he murmured against her cheek.

He moved soundlessly across the room, a renegade dressed all in black, but before he could slip out the French doors and into the night, she rose up on her arm and blurted, "When will I see you again?" She cringed at the desperation in her voice.

He turned and smiled at her, seemingly pleased with her question and that she *wanted* to see him again. "Soon," he said, the promise a vague one, and disappeared into the shadows.

Chapter Three

Eric glanced around the expensively furnished board-room at Massey and Associates, not at all surprised to see avid interest reflected on the faces of the partners of the firm as they listened to what their freelance creative director had to say in regards to the Enchanted Cruise Line presentation.

He hid a smile, knowing Jill's intelligence and bright, innovative ideas had a way of inspiring that kind of admiration from those she worked with. And even from the man she'd slept with the evening before. Not only did he admire her, but he respected her, too. Personally and professionally.

He'd gone to her house with a hot, forbidden affair in mind to get her out of his system. And while they'd indulged in erotic pleasures that had satiated him physically, he'd ended up craving so much more than sex with her. He'd absolutely hated leaving her after the intimacy they'd shared—and that hesitancy was an unfamiliar feeling for him since he didn't usually linger in a woman's bed. With Jill, he almost had.

But, as her phantom lover, he'd made a promise to keep things purely physical between them during their midnight trysts, which meant no postcoital cuddling, and he refused to break his vow so early in the game. But all the warning signs indicated he was falling hard and fast for Jill.

The urge to stay with her had been strong, nearly overwhelming. More than anything he'd wanted to pull her into his arms and savor the aftermath of such an incredible, mind-blowing experience that had rocked his carefree world and threatened the emotional control he'd prided himself on when it came to women and relationships—especially after watching both of his brothers fall victim to a woman's persuasive charms, only to end up cynical about love and long-term commitment.

Last night, her body had been his for the taking, so warm and lush and responsive, but there had also been a softness and vulnerability about her that contradicted the poised, power-suited woman up at the podium in front of him. He found the two personas intriguing, and though he'd made the personal decision to delve into Jill's psyche and discover deeper secrets, he knew he had to tread carefully between their working relationship and their newly developed intimacy so as not to threaten her emotionally.

Lying in his own bed last night after visiting Jill, he'd analyzed the situation, and their affair, trying to figure out a way to use both to his advantage in terms of nurturing an exclusive relationship with Jill outside of the office. Undoubtedly, she expected him to return tonight for another fantasy, and while his lustful body readily agreed with that plan, he'd decided that he wanted to build her anticipation, the desire between them, and heighten the sexual excitement of when, where, and how. And that meant keeping her guessing about his intentions, doing the unexpected, and seducing her mind and body in gradual degrees.

While his own thoughts had wandered, all eyes and ears in the boardroom remained tuned in on Jill, who stood confidently in front of the room, her voice strong and sure as she continued to pitch a mock presentation to the partners for the Enchanted Cruise Line before the final marketing package was put together for their client. Over the span of two hours, she kept everyone's attention riveted with creative designs, along with suggested media vehicles to promote the campaign, visual placement of ads, Web site and software applications, and market research to back up her multimillion dollar proposal.

Eric watched her, too, despite the fact that her gaze never met his during the course of her presentation. The passion she harbored for her job and original layouts and designs was evident in her speech, mannerisms, and the excitement in her eyes as she sold the partners on her ideas. Now, Eric knew that vibrant passion and energy extended to the bedroom, and he was hooked on her. Addicted. More obsessed than before.

"God, she's good," Gary Tillman, a senior partner in the firm whispered to Eric from the seat next to him. "She's just what we need to bring fresh blood to the firm. We want her on our creative team. Permanently."

Eric knew exactly how the partners felt, because he wanted her, too. And for more than just the short-term basis they'd agreed on last night.

"I want you to do what you can to sway Jill to accept our offer to stay on at Massey after this contract is signed, sealed, and delivered," Gary went on in low, hushed tones, looking every inch the shrewd businessman he was.

What this man didn't realize, and what Eric had just

recently learned himself, was that Jill had a mind of her own. She was stubborn at times, independent, and strong-willed in her views and decisions. Sure, he'd managed to sway her last night to his way of thinking when it came to something they'd both wanted so badly, but Eric highly doubted Jill would be so easily influenced to do something that went against her future goals. With Massey—and with himself, he knew.

"You know she's started up her own agency, Creative Consulting, and already has a client base, right?" Eric felt compelled to remind the older man of Jill's interests outside of the firm.

"She can bring those clients with her." Gary shrugged, obviously willing to work the situation to his advantage. "Money talks, and we're prepared to make her an offer she can't refuse, but we need to know what we're really up against, if you know what I mean."

Eric understood perfectly. The partners wanted to know why she was being so resistant so they could cater to her hesitancy with a promise of financial security and job stability. But Eric honestly cared more for what Jill desired than what the higher-ups at Massey wanted.

Then again, Eric was curious to know more about the woman beneath the conservative suit and pinned-up hair. The incredibly exciting woman who was the vixen he'd bedded the night before. And drawing her into a more personal kind of conversation was the perfect opportunity to scratch beneath the surface of her pragmatic, daytime facade.

"I'll see what I can do," he said to Gary, appeasing his boss—and himself—at the same time. He was very interested in hearing her reasons for turning down their numerous offers, but he wouldn't force her to change her mind.

The presentation ended with a round of enthusiastic applause and complimentary comments. There were a few suggestions offered on how to improve the proposal, but all were minor changes in the scope of the incredible job Jill had done with the entire package.

Eric waited patiently until the room cleared before he approached Jill at the podium, where she was gathering her visual displays. "You did an outstanding job," he said, pushing his hands into the front pockets of his trousers.

She slanted him a quick look, not long enough to let him gauge her expression or emotions as far as he was concerned. She'd been a closed book all morning in that regard, not that he could blame her. "Let's hope our client is as enthusiastic as the partners of this firm."

Resisting the impulse to tuck his fingers beneath her chin to force her to look him straight in the eye for the first time that morning, he instead picked up a storyboard and laid it carefully on top of a demo chart in her pile. "I have no doubt that the Enchanted Cruise Line will be just as impressed with your presentation."

"Thanks. You know that means a lot to me." She folded her pointer stick and tucked it in her expandable file folder. "And as long as the presentation results in a signed contract and my bonus, that's all I care about."

He wanted her to care about much more. Like him. *Them.*

Oh, man, he was in so deep with her. He tried to convince himself it was because she presented such a challenge with that cautious, reserved attitude of hers during working hours. But this possessive feeling she roused in him surpassed the simple need to settle a sexual score with a woman. If that were the case, last night's shameless escapade would have satisfied him—and his libido—plenty.

The need to touch her, to be with her, told him Jill wasn't one of his ordinary conquests. And even after one amazing sexual encounter that should have left him drained and his lust for her completely slaked, she was far from being purged from his system, or out of his mind and thoughts.

He glanced at his watch, noting the time, which matched the grumbling of his stomach. "How about grabbing a bite to eat with me for lunch?"

She tensed, and after taking a brief moment to gather her composure, she opened her mouth to reply. Knowing a refusal was forthcoming, he cut her off before she could turn him down.

"Don't tell me you're not hungry, because I know for a fact that you were in this morning at six to prepare for this presentation, and haven't been out since. I'm guessing you most likely didn't eat breakfast, and it's near twelve o'clock. You're probably running on pure adrenaline."

She ducked her head, but not before he caught a hint of an impish smile on her lips. "And caffeine," she admitted.

He chuckled. "See, there. You need sustenance. Besides, this is a business lunch. There's something work related I need to discuss with you."

Her head snapped up in startled surprised. "Oh. All right." Her green eyes were filled with curiosity, and a deeper worry. "Is everything okay?"

Judging by the sudden anxiety he sensed in her voice, he assumed she was thinking about them and her biggest fear coming to fruition: that their secret affair was jeopardizing her job or commission somehow.

"Everything is fine," he reassured her. Handing her the stack of leftover brochures, she took them from him without letting their fingers touch. "Meet me in front of the elevators in, say, fifteen minutes?"

"Sure." This time, she sounded more confident, less worried. Relieved. "That'll give me time to get all this put away."

"Great. It's a date, then." He turned to go, even as he mentally kicked himself for his choice of words, certain she'd choose to interpret them the wrong way when he'd meant his casual comment figuratively.

"Eric?"

He glanced back at her, a deliberately bland expression in place. "Hmmm?"

There were questions in her eyes, but she didn't voice them. Instead, she searched his features, and seemingly not finding what she was looking for, she shook her head. "Never mind. See you in a few minutes."

"Bring your appetite." He winked at her and exited the room before she could call him on that remark.

Jill relaxed in the butter-soft leather passenger seat of Eric's sporty two-seater car as he drove them to a trendy outdoor café off Michigan Avenue. The intimacy of sharing such a small, confined space with him affected every one of her five senses. She was surrounded by his warmth and male scent, and she couldn't help but notice, and appreciate, that he maneuvered the sports car with as much ease as he'd coaxed her surrender last night.

Thankfully, their conversation in the vehicle consisted of casual, work-related business, and never crossed the line into personal territory. True to his promise, Eric behaved like a business associate and the easygoing man she'd worked with for the past three months. There was nothing in his expression or mannerisms to indicate that they'd shared a night of hot, passionate sex, nor could she find a trace of the lover who'd claimed her so possessively, then left her craving so much more upon his departure. If she didn't know better and didn't ache in certain places, she'd swear it had all been a dream.

She swore she was grateful for his ability to keep their working relationship separate from their affair, especially since the woman in her was more aware of him than she'd been before they'd embarked on a private, dark-of-the-night tryst. Because now she knew what he looked like naked, and it was a magnificent sight that was indelibly etched in her mind. She had intimate knowledge of what those hands of his felt like caressing her, knew the pleasure his fingers and mouth could coax from her body, and how his lips and tongue set her skin and senses on fire.

The memory of their night together distracted her at the most inopportune times. Like during her presentation this morning when she'd felt his hot gaze on her, and her body thrummed to life with anticipation and need. And now she found herself analyzing every look he cast her way, every comment, and wondered how she was going to make it through the day and keep her desire under wraps until he came to visit her again in the dark of night.

She had no choice but to be just as indifferent and poised as he seemed to be, because as much as she wanted him, she wasn't about to discuss their "fantasy world" in the light of day and make their relationship public, even verbally.

They arrived at the restaurant, and he opted for valet parking. As they walked side by side up to the entrance and into the waiting area, Jill couldn't help but notice how many women did a double take at Eric. Nor did she miss how he handled the stares—with a slow, easy grin that was an innate part of his appeal and bad boy image, a natural, effortless charm that had the ability to set hearts racing. Jill discovered she wasn't immune to that flirtatious smile, either, and was shocked at the spurt of jealously she experienced toward those other women glancing his way.

And when had she started thinking of him in such possessive terms? She clenched her teeth and reminded herself that he was a temporary fling, and he wasn't hers to keep. No matter how much she wanted to stake a claim on him so those other women would know that he was taken and his nights belonged to *her*.

They sat down across from each other at a table outdoors and ordered their meals. After the waitress delivered their drinks, Eric jumped right into the business discussion he'd mentioned earlier.

"We both know that the partners are interested in hiring you at Massey full-time," he said candidly, getting right to the point of their lunch together. "But so far you've refused their very generous offers."

"Yes, I have." She stirred lemon and sugar into her iced tea, and slanted him a curious look. "Did they send you to try to sway me?"

He grinned, his blue eyes twinkling with amusement. "I know my powers of persuasion might work in certain areas," he said meaningfully, "but you're a woman with her own mind, and I doubt I could force you to do anything you don't want to."

Oh, he was very astute, and clever, considering his words held a double meaning. "I really do appreciate their offers and extra incentives to stay on permanently, but I'm not interested in going back to work for a large advertising firm."

"Can I ask why not?"

She shrugged, and stated the obvious. "For one, I've got Creative Consulting to think about."

"Which is just getting off the ground. We both know it's a whole lot of work and expense maintaining your own agency."

"True. That's why I've been freelancing." She smoothed her napkin onto her lap. "This bonus will go a long way in helping me to establish myself more firmly in the advertising industry. Right now, I'm working on projects out of the office I have at home and I have a small client base, but within the next six months I should have my own office leased and employees on the payroll."

He tipped his head, regarding her thoughtfully. "You really want all the crap and headache that goes with owning a business when you can make a six-figure salary at Massey without the hassles?"

For her, it wasn't a money issue, but a personal one. "I can deal with those kinds of hassles just fine, especially when *I'm* the boss." There was humor in her tone, but she was dead serious about being able to manage the ups and downs of running her own business compared to working for someone else. "What I can't handle is office politics and all the backstabbing that goes along with climbing the corporate ladder and maintaining your position when you're on top."

His dark brows lifted in surprise at her admission. "Is that personal experience talking?"

She hesitated, then decided there was no reason why she couldn't reveal that bit of truth to him. "As a matter of fact, yes, it is."

His gaze held hers steadily. "Care to enlighten me?"

She sat back in her chair as their lunch orders were served, which gave her a few extra moments to consider his question, and her response. Did she really want to apprise him of her past, one that not only explained the business decisions she'd made for the last year and a half, but also touched on deeper personal issues, like the relationship that had cost her so much, professionally and emotionally?

His interest seemed genuinely sincere, as did the concern reflected in his eyes. While she hated dredging up those painful memories, she figured he'd be better off knowing the reasons why she was so adamant about keeping business and pleasure completely separate, as well as why she wasn't interested in working for anyone but herself.

He took a big bite from his burger, indulged in a long drink of his soda, and continued to patiently wait for her reply.

Picking up her fork, she stabbed it into the potato salad accompanying her turkey sandwich, ate the bite, then started her story from the beginning. "I went to work for my first advertising agency, Ad-Logic, fresh out of college. They hired me in the marketing department, and in five years time I'd worked my way up to creative director."

A grin creased one corner of his mouth. "Have you always been so ambitious?"

"You have to be driven in this industry. You know that." She chewed a bite of her sandwich, and licked a smear of sauce from her finger. "If not, you'll get crushed by the competition."

"True." He dove into his French fries, drenching them in ketchup. "Go on."

"Anyway, one of the associates on the creative team I was supervising started flirting with me. Since Jeremy was a subordinate, I turned down his advances, even though the firm didn't have a no dating coworker rule.

But he was very persistent, and before long I was hooked. We went out on a few dates, one thing led to another, and the next thing I knew, we were an item." She glanced up at Eric, and without thinking, she said, "He was good-looking, and charming, much like you are."

He frowned, seemingly taking offense by the comparison. "Sweetheart, don't make the mistake of comparing me to any other man in your life. Especially when I have a feeling this guy screwed you over in one way or another."

She exhaled a slow breath, amazed by Eric's ability to read her so well. "You're right, and I apologize." The man sitting in front of her was open, honest, and very straightforward in his intentions. Important qualities she realized, belatedly, Jeremy had lacked.

"Tell me what happened," he said, prompting her to go on.

She picked at her lunch, while Eric devoured his. Then again, there was no reason why her tale would ruin *his* appetite. "During this time, a big account came in for the firm, and I was also up for a promotion to senior art director, which left my position open to be filled. Jeremy made it clear he was interested in my job, and taking on the big account. Except, quite honestly, he wasn't the best person for the position, and I gave it to a woman who was better qualified. He wasn't happy about my decision."

Eric cringed. "Oh, man, don't tell me this guy was using you to get the promotion."

"Yeah, he was," she admitted, feeling her stomach cramp at how stupid she'd been to believe his interest had been genuine—and that she hadn't figured out his agenda because she'd been so caught up in his romantic pursuit. At least she realized her affair with Eric for what it was—great sex and pure fantasy.

Uh-huh, that's why you hated that he'd left you last night after giving you the best orgasms of your life.

Pushing those niggling thoughts aside, she continued. "One way or another, Jeremy was determined to get that promotion, and he figured I'd give it to him because we were sleeping together. When I passed him over, he cried sexual harassment and told the partners that I'd promised him my job and the big account in exchange for sexual favors."

Eric gave another grimace of commiseration, though he declined to make any comments.

"It turned into a big, awful mess," she said, and pushed her half-eaten lunch aside. "The partners *said* they believed my side of the story, but instead of facing a lengthy and expensive legal lawsuit, they settled the issue in-house. They made Jeremy an associate creative director, as well, and put him in charge of the account he wanted and claimed I promised him. As for me, I lost the promotion to senior art director to someone else, and because everything in the office was so tense, awkward, and stressful, I ended up resigning."

"Jesus," he said in disgust. "I'm sorry about that."

"Yeah, well, it was a valuable lesson learned in many ways. One of which is that I'm better off on my own." That, at least, had been a decision she'd never regretted. "With my own agency, I call the shots, and the responsibilities are all mine. Best of all, I'm in control, and I depend on no one but myself in terms of my success. I have no desire to plant myself permanently into that kind of dog-eat-dog situation ever again."

While his gaze softened in understanding, his corporate, bargaining expression remained in place. "You know, I'd be remiss if I didn't mention that the position the partners are offering you pretty much puts you at the top of the creative department, which means no dogs to deal with," he said humorously.

"That position is one rung below you, which would technically make you my boss and *top* dog." And she was already sleeping with him, which made the entire situation too controversial for her. Not that she was considering accepting the job.

"I have bigger aspirations and plan to make partner in the next year or two, which will eventually leave my position open for someone as intelligent and creative as yourself."

She ignored his sweet-talking compliment. "And let history repeat itself? No, thank you."

His sensual lips pursed with annoyance, and she knew he wanted to argue her point about history repeating itself with them, but that meant dragging their intimate relationship out into the open in the light of day and breaking the vow he'd made to keep their affair private.

He sighed heavily. "I truly understand your reservations and reasons for being so hesitant, and I'm glad you told me about what happened," he said instead, taking a more sensitive approach to the issue. "A whole lot more makes sense to me now. But I promised Gary that I'd talk to you, and now I can say that I did."

A part of her was shocked that he wasn't pushing her harder to take on the position at Massey, yet she was grateful, too, for his easy acceptance. He seemed to genuinely care about her reasons for declining their offers, and his understanding of the situation touched her in places she didn't want to acknowledge for fear of letting those feelings take on a life of their own—if they hadn't already. This new connection between them was unique and special, and had nothing to do with sex or their fantasy world. It was about a man and a woman talking and relating to one another, and she liked the warm, heartfelt bond they'd established more than was wise.

"Tell him I said thank you for the offers, but I'm not going to change my mind." Her tone was firm.

"Fair enough," he said, conceding defeat without further prodding. "At least I can tell him that I tried my best."

Jill attempted to give the Enchanted advertising package another thorough proofreading and review, making sure all the materials were in place and perfectly coordinated for the client presentation scheduled for Wednesday of that week. She made a few last-minute notations for changes before her mind started to wander to other more personal issues, and the lack of concentration where it should be focused, *on work,* infuriated and frustrated her.

So did Eric's no-show at her place over the weekend. And therein lay the crux of her irritable mood.

Three days had passed since her lunch with Eric Friday afternoon. Granted, she'd been a bit distant after their business conversation because it had encompassed too much of her personal history, but she'd never expected him to forgo their agreed-upon affair . . . for the entire weekend.

And here it was, close to quitting time on Monday, and she was beginning to wonder where she stood with Eric. If maybe her story had turned him off to their affair, or if her final refusal to accept the position at Massey had also contributed to his decision to keep *his* distance. But that would make him no different than

Jeremy, and she knew Eric had more character and integrity. Still, the possibility that he'd changed his mind about her made her chest hurt with an emotion she refused to analyze too closely.

She'd seen him briefly in passing throughout the day, had even consulted with him in regards to the media proposal for the Enchanted account. Yet not once did he mention his absence over the weekend. Not that he owed her an explanation as to his whereabouts or how he'd spent those evenings, but she'd assumed there would be more than just one night of sex with him.

He'd been his normal, amiable self all day long, treating her with the same flirtatious, easy charm as he always did, but he never crossed the line into anything remotely personal. She'd found herself continually searching his eyes and expression, but neither gave away what he was feeling. Or if he planned to visit her ever again. She was dying to ask, but she wasn't about to be the one to break the rule they'd established to never mix their business relationship with their fantasy world.

Closing her eyes, she pressed her fingers to her temples, where the beginning of a headache began a steady throb. Thank goodness the day was nearly over, because she needed fresh air, freedom, and a better perspective on the entire situation.

A half hour later she headed home, and discovered a long, white flat box topped off with a big pink bow on her doorstep. She picked up the gift, unable to stop the warm glow of hope and excitement tingling through her. Once she was inside, she plucked the pink envelope attached to the bow, withdrew the card inside, and read the succinct sentence written in a bold, masculine scrawl: *Wear all these things for me tonight.*

There was no name signed to the note, but she knew who the gift was from. Unraveling the ribbon securing the sides of the box, she lifted the lid, separated the pink tissue paper, and felt her stomach flutter when she discovered the sexy lingerie he'd sent.

Jill would have pegged Eric as a man who would have gone for something black and racy and possibly in leather, but what she found instead caused her breath to catch and her heart to quicken. Her fingers glided over white satin and lace, the color of purity and innocence, which was such an incongruous choice since their illicit affair was neither. He'd selected an ensemble for her which included a demi bra in see-through floral lace with matching *crotchless* panties, and sheer white, lacy banded stockings accompanying a garter belt set.

A flush stained her cheeks and she bit her bottom lip. The outfit was incredibly provocative and decadent, more so than anything she'd ever worn before, and she appreciated his thoughtfulness in providing a pale pink silk wrap for her to wear, too. Not that she'd be wearing the robe for long, she knew, already anticipating the fantasy Eric had in mind.

Another smaller box caught her eye, and she gasped as she revealed the contents. She stared in stunned disbelief at the exquisite double strand of gleaming pearls nestled in a bed of burgundy velvet. Picking up the necklace, she rolled the smooth, polished pearls between her fingers, the texture cool, luxurious, and sensuous to the touch.

She was undeniably aroused by his gifts, no doubt just as he intended. She'd dress up for him tonight and play the part he wanted, but he had a few questions to answer before she let him have the full fantasy.

Chapter Four

Standing in the shadows of Jill's patio that evening, Eric watched as she prepared herself for him, a sweet kind of torture that tested his restraint. She'd taken a fragrant bath, then slowly, methodically, slipped into each sexy piece of lingerie he'd bought for her. Unaware that her lover was spying on her, her movements were sensual and uninhibited as she clasped her bra in place, then shimmied into the panties that would give him direct access to her body when the time came. Sitting on the stool in front of the vanity in her bedroom, she pulled the pale stockings up her slender legs to her thighs, then clasped the lacy band to the garter belt secured low on her hips. She put on a pair of white strappy shoes with a good four-inch spiked heel, adding her own special touch to the tantalizing ensemble.

With her hair a cloud of soft waves around her face and shoulders, and dressed so wantonly, she looked like a centerfold straight out of his fondest teenage fantasies. And he was rock hard with wanting her.

Finally, she secured the pearls around her neck and

absently touched one of the luminescent beads. One gleaming strand draped across the full swell of her breasts, and the longer one dipped into the cleavage in between. The tiniest movement rolled the pearls over her nipples like a fluttering caress, teasing them into hard little points that strained against her sheer lace bra. His cock swelled even more with the wicked thoughts filling his mind. Those pearls were going to be the source of immense pleasure for both of them, as was the single lavender rose he'd brought with him.

Last, she slipped into the silk robe, and as soon as she had herself covered and the sash was tightened around her waist, he stepped out of the shadows and through the French doors.

"Hello, Jill."

She glanced up at him, the instantaneous awareness flickering in her gaze quickly replaced with a cool reserve and a defiant tip of her chin. "I'm glad to see you didn't stand me up tonight."

He blinked lazily, not at all surprised at her rebellious attitude. He'd expected it, actually, and the annoyance simmering off her pleased him immensely. Obviously, she hadn't been able to blow him off as easily as she would have liked, which meant he affected her more deeply than she'd ever admit out loud.

He also knew her haughty disposition wouldn't last long. She wanted this next fantasy, wanted to be kissed and touched and fucked by him, or else she wouldn't have taken such care getting dressed up in the things he'd sent her.

Slowly, he strolled over to the nightstand, set the long-stemmed rose next to the bed, and sauntered the rest of the way into her bedroom. "The note I sent with the outfit insinuated I'd be here tonight."

"After not hearing a word from you all weekend," she stated, crossing her arms over her chest.

He inhaled the floral scent lingering from her steamy bath, and couldn't stop the pleased grin that curved his mouth. "Miss me?"

She gave a dismissive shrug, but the hurt he detected in the depth of her eyes told another story. "After our conversation Friday afternoon, I thought maybe you changed your mind about us."

He came to a stop in front of where she stood, sobered by the fact that he'd caused her any kind of emotional pain. He'd only meant to give her space, but he'd obviously given her too much time to *think*. "There's not a chance I'd change my mind about us, sweetheart."

"Then why didn't you come?" She raised a brow, her gaze searching his for answers.

He owed her an explanation, needed to make her understand his reasons for staying away. And being honest with her was all part of the intimacy and trust he needed to establish between them if he wanted their relationship to last beyond a temporary affair. Because for as much as he enjoyed their fantasies, he craved more than hot sex with her. He wanted to see her whenever the urge struck, wanted make her a part of his life in a way he'd never allowed any other woman.

And after their conversation last Friday, at least now he felt better equipped to deal with her fears and insecurities.

Reaching out, he wrapped a loose curl around his finger to maintain some kind of physical connection between them. "Not coming over this weekend was one of the hardest things I've ever had to do. And if it makes you feel any better, I did miss you, and thought about you every waking minute," he said, all the truth.

"But after you told me about Jeremy and what effect he had on you and your previous job, you were on the defensive and I know you were comparing that relationship to ours, especially after that comment you made about history repeating itself. I just felt as though you needed time to calm down and want *me* again without a past relationship gone bad getting in our way."

Her full lower lip puffed out in an adorable pout, but she didn't argue his point. "You could have said something to me."

"I thought about it, but decided it would have spoiled the anticipation of being together again." He ran his finger along the collar of the silky robe, and down the lapel to where it crisscrossed at her breasts. "You thought about me all weekend, didn't you? About all the things we did together and what I still want to do to you."

"Yes." A tangible shiver coursed through her. "But I don't enjoy feeling like a fool, and that's how I felt waiting up for you every night."

"I'm sorry, and I promise I'll make it up to you." He watched her guard drop and her countenance soften and relax. "I think all that buildup of sexual tension is going to make tonight that much more exciting and intense. Are you ready for the fantasy to begin?"

With her nod of assent, he took her hand and guided her over to the side of the bed near the chaise in the corner. Then he took her mouth with his own and kissed her, more than ready to make up for the time they'd lost over the weekend. Grabbing the tie on her robe, he pulled it off and tossed the sash onto the chair behind him for later. Blindly, he parted the silky material, pushed the sleeves down her arms, and let the fabric fall to the floor at her feet. Lifting his head, he looked his fill of her in the sexy outfit he'd bought for her, and when she reached out to grab the hem of his black T-shirt to help him pull it up and off, he caught her wrist and stopped her.

"Turn around and widen your stance," he told her in a low, rough tone, which was all part of tonight's fantasy. When she did as he instructed and he was looking at the smooth slope of her back and her widespread legs, he added, "Now bend forward and put your arms on the bed."

She glanced over her shoulder at him, and probably realizing how exposed the position would make her, a glimmer of uncertainty flickered in her gaze. "Eric—"

"Do it, Jill," he ordered, forcing her past that initial twinge of modesty. "Or the fantasy ends."

He'd warned her that he liked to be in control when it came to sex, which served him well as a defense mechanism in keeping a tight rein on his emotional restraint when it came to women. But he'd come to realize that somewhere along the way he'd allowed Jill to threaten that physical discipline of his, which took their affair to a whole new level of desire and passion.

While he'd continue to play those dominant, aggressive games with her, he'd told her their first night together that he'd never hurt her—and meant it. If she truly felt uncomfortable with anything happening between them, he'd given her the security of knowing a simple "no" or "stop" would put an end to the fantasy.

Tonight, she obviously wasn't willing to forgo whatever pleasures he had in mind. She bent at the waist and propped her forearms on the mattress, which thrust her bottom up in carnal invitation. The peekaboo panties she wore framed the glistening folds of her sex, and it took every ounce of his willpower not to drop to his knees and use his tongue to take her to a shattering climax in that provocative position.

Gathering his control, he passed his palm over one rounded cheek and squeezed the firm flesh, which brought him just as much pleasure. "God, you have such a great ass," he murmured, and heard her moan in response. Positioning himself behind her, he pressed the huge bulge of his erection against her bottom. He could feel her heat and dampness, even through his jeans, and groaned at the perfect fit of their bodies due to the spiked heels she wore.

He splayed his hand low on her spine, and she automatically arched into him to get closer, to feel more heat and friction. "I've dreamed of taking you just like this," he said, and gyrated his hips against her, knowing the fly of his jeans was grazing her tender flesh, heightening her arousal. "Even right now, I'm so ready for you, and all it would take is unzipping my pants, releasing my cock, and pushing inside you, slow and deep. You wouldn't even have to take off your panties."

Her deep breathing turned into a fast pant, and her fingers gripped the bedspread in tight fists.

In one smooth motion, he stripped off his T-shirt, then leaned over her, completely covering her from behind with his naked chest and keeping their thighs aligned and her hips pinned to the side of the bed with the weight of his body. He pushed her wavy hair away from the side of her face and glided his lips along her jaw and up to the shell of her ear while his hands slid around her waist in search of more bare flesh. His fingers dipped inside the lace cups of her bra and pulled the stretchy material down, freeing her breasts. He filled his palms with the warm plump flesh, heard her quick intake of breath, and smiled in satisfaction. He could feel the wild beating of her heart, and reveled in her eager response.

"In this position, I could fondle your breasts just

like this," he rasped into her ear as his rolled her tight nipples between his fingers and gently pinched them. "And I can touch your clit at the same time while I pump inside you." He slid a hand between her legs and followed the lace-edged slit of her panties, knowing even before he touched her she'd be hot and wet. He wasn't disappointed, and easily found that hard kernel of flesh already pulsing with need. "It would only take a few strokes inside your tight body to make me come."

She tossed her head back, pressed her hips harder against his hand and shuddered, on the verge of her own climax. "Oh, God, *yes.*"

"But that's not what I have in mind for tonight." He straightened and turned her around to face him again, amused by the dazed, confused look in her eyes. Taking advantage of her compliant state, he pushed her back until she was sitting up on the bed and her legs were draped over the edge. Grasping one ankle, he bent her knee and wedged the spiked heel into the wooden ledge of the bed frame supporting the mattress, then did the same to her other shoe, leaving her in a very wanton, erotic position for him to enjoy.

She frowned up at him, appearing miffed at him again. "You can't leave me like this."

He laughed, low and deep, since there were many ways to interpret her comment. "Like *how*?"

Her breasts, still bared by the bra bunched beneath the firm swells, quivered as she inhaled an indignant breath. "I was on the edge of an orgasm when you stopped."

The heady, arousing scent of her warm, female flesh slipped through his senses, tempting him greatly. "Then finish what I started. Touch yourself. Do whatever feels good. Come for me while I watch."

She thought about that for a few seconds, her gaze lowering to the erection still confined beneath the zipper of his jeans. Then a slow, shameless smile spread across her face. "Only if you'll do the same," she challenged huskily.

Oh, yeah, he liked that bit of boldness and the unexpected dare she'd tossed right back at him. His blood warmed in his veins, pooled low in his belly, and thickened his groin to the point of pain. It was about time he met a woman who was his match not only intellectually, but sexually as well. And it appeared that Jill knew how to use aggression to her own advantage.

He took in her mussed hair, so soft and crushable, and her skin, flushed with desire. The straps of her bra had fallen down both arms, and she'd braced her hands behind her on the bed, causing her full breasts to thrust forward. Her spread legs, the sexy garter belt, and sinful panties drove him crazy. The silk stockings with the lacy band, the fuck-me shoes . . . hell, the entire package was a man's wet dream come to life.

He knew if he watched her touch herself he'd never make it without giving his body the fierce release it craved. And she'd just presented him with the perfect opportunity to take the initial edge off his own lust in order to make tonight last, because this was just the beginning of his personal fantasy.

"You're on, sweetheart."

She dampened her bottom lip with her tongue. "Take the rest of your clothes off."

He did as she commanded, toeing off his shoes, pulling off his socks, and shucking his jeans and briefs until he was in the buff and there was no disguising his desire for her. He dug through the front pockets of his pants, tossed a handful of condoms on the nightstand,

and discarded the jeans somewhere on the floor with the rest of his clothes.

She looked from the prophylactics and back to him. "Five of them?" she asked incredulously.

He winked at her, and grinned. "Don't ever underestimate how much I want you. What we don't use tonight, I'm sure we'll put to good use later."

He reclined back on the chaise, one leg outstretched and the other draped over the side of the chair—giving her just as intimate a view as he had of her. He settled in more comfortably, liking the way the cool, velvety material felt against his skin. Liked, too, the way her wide-eyed gaze was taking in the long, thick length of his erection in rapt fascination.

Resting one hand behind his head, he flattened his other palm on his belly in a pose that was more casual than he felt. "This is your show," he murmured, wanting her to take the lead. "You start and give me an incentive to follow."

She understood his insinuation, that he wanted her to tempt and tease him. Her palms came up and fondled her breasts, and her thumbs rasped across the rigid tips. Her movements were hesitant at first, then gradually she relaxed and gave in to her body's explicit demands. She rolled the pearls over her nipples and moaned softly as her other hand drifted lower, caressing the soft, smooth skin of her stomach and played with the satin strap of her garter belt.

She was so damned sexy she made his insides ache and his palms sweat. Anticipation gripped him, and his jaw clenched hard as those long, slender fingers of hers delved between her splayed thighs, traced the opening of her panties, then glided over her wet, swollen flesh in a series of slow, languid caresses. She closed her eyes, her head fell back on a groan, and she shuddered with need.

Eric knew she was lost in her own little world where gratification was the ultimate goal, and she was heading toward her own climax fast. No way was he going to let her go there without taking him along for the ride.

Wrapping his fingers around the base of his shaft, he began a slow, squeezing upward stroke. His hand enveloped the head of his cock, his thumb grazed over the sensitive tip, and his entire body vibrated as his own orgasm beckoned. "Watch me, too, Jill," he rasped, his voice as dark as the night, as raw as the hunger welling within him.

Her lashes fluttered open to half-mast. But it was enough for her to watch him pump the rigid length of his penis in a tight grip while her hips undulated sinuously against her fingers. Knowing she was as close to coming as he was, he gauged her response, the quick rise and fall of her chest, the sensual haze clouding her eyes, and the flush rising on her cheeks. Her moist lips parted, and a low, throaty moan erupted from her throat as she lost herself in wild sensation.

He watched her take her pleasure for as long as he could, but there was no denying the familiar tightening between his legs, and the way his stomach muscles constricted in warning. Exhaling a hissing breath, he erupted in a gut-wrenching release, the sheer primal heat of his climax radiating outward in scalding, pulsating waves that seemed to go on and on.

With a quivering, replete sigh, Jill fell back on the mattress to recover while he grabbed a tissue from the box on the nightstand. He was still semi-erect, and there was no doubt that by the time he was done with the foreplay he still had in mind, he'd be raring to go again.

Jill ran a shaky hand through her hair, unable to believe what she'd just done . . . that she'd just brought herself to an incredibly intense orgasm in front of a man, something she'd never done before. And she'd liked doing it, as much as she'd enjoyed witnessing Eric's own loss of control. She felt light-headed, drunk on passion and power and the thrill of the forbidden.

"Move to the center of the bed," Eric said, his voice a soft, sexy rumble that reawakened her senses.

Too sated to move, she forced her eyes open and rolled her head to the side to get a better view of him. He stood at the edge of the bed, between her spread legs, his pitch-black hair falling haphazardly over his forehead. He was amazingly aroused all over again and she would have been just as happy if he pulled her thighs over his hips and drove into her just as they were.

But it was the wide sash from her robe that he was running through his fingers that caught her attention, as did the wicked gleam in his eyes. He wasn't done with her, and her heartbeat accelerated.

"Did you not understand my request?" His tone was clipped and impatient, his entire demeanor weaving a dark, dangerous kind of fantasy.

His abrupt change startled and confused her, because she wasn't sure if they were segueing into another fantasy. "Yes. I heard you."

The muscles in his arms flexed as he tightened the long, silk tether between his two fists. "As your owner, keep in mind that I don't like to ask for anything twice, and I won't tolerate disobedience from you."

Her owner? It took an extra moment for understanding to dawn in her sluggish brain. "Which makes me your sex slave?"

His gaze raked down the length of her possessively, visually branding her as his. "You're mine, bought and paid for, to do with as I please."

A slow, curling warmth pervaded her body, and she was feeling reckless enough to follow his lead and slip into whatever role he wanted her to play, do anything he asked, because she knew she'd be rewarded with exquisite pleasure. She moved to the center of the bed and stretched out, shivering as the cool pearls glided around her neck and gathered at her throat. He first took off her heels, then knelt between her thighs. Dropping the sash to the side, he unfastened one of her stockings from the garter belt and slowly, leisurely rolled the garment down her long leg and let his fingers trail along the smooth skin he exposed. He repeated the process with the other pale stocking and removed the garter belt itself, but left her provocative panties in place.

Then he straddled her waist, and his wide shoulders seemed so massive, his hips so lean, his thighs so hard and strong. He was all male, as dominant and aggressive as he claimed to be. His heavy sacs rested against her stomach, and his penis was impressively hard once again. He was a man who could easily overpower her in such a position, yet she felt no threat and trusted him implicitly with her body. It was her heart she had to protect from him, she feared, because he drew her like no other man ever had.

He unclasped her bra, barely grazing the undersides of the plump flesh with his fingers in the process, but the fleeting contact set off an instantaneous response. Her freed breasts swelled and peaked, aching to be fondled, caressed, suckled, but he did none of those things, much to her frustration.

He picked up one of her discarded stockings and tested the durability with a strong tug. "Give me your hands."

Remembering his earlier words about not asking twice, she submitted obediently to his request. She extended her hands, and he bound her wrists with the sheer silk, then tied them securely to the wooden headboard with the other stocking.

He reached for the sash he'd left on the bed beside her and wrapped the three inches of fabric over her eyes, blocking her vision, and tied the ends at the back of her head. She was completely at his mercy and every whim. She wondered how something so utterly barbaric could be so tantalizing. So stimulating.

"Why do I need to be tied up *and* blindfolded?" she asked.

"When you can't see, all your other senses are heightened." Lazily, he trailed his fingers from the pearls around her neck, down her chest and over her ribs as a demonstration.

She trembled and gooseflesh rose on her skin. "My senses are heightened just fine, and I feel at a complete disadvantage."

"Umm, that you are," he murmured huskily. "Which is all the better for me to have my way with you."

He leaned over her and kissed her lips, softly, sweetly, and she automatically opened her mouth to him, inviting him deeper. He slanted his mouth across hers, and their tongues tangled and mated insatiably. The kiss was deliciously unhurried, designed to make her melt beneath his sensual assault, which she did.

What seemed like minutes later, he lifted his lips

from hers, his hot, damp breath feathering across her cheek. "See, all you have to do is lie there and enjoy yourself," he said.

She heard the wicked timbre of his voice, and knew he was wearing a grin that matched. Tentatively, she tugged on her restraints to test them, but they were secure, allowing her no escape unless she begged for it, which she suspected Eric would have no qualms making her do.

A frisson of excitement shot through her, and she waited for the illicit fantasy to begin.

Eric stood by the side of Jill's bed for long minutes, letting the anticipation build as he stared at the beautiful woman secured to the bedpost for his sole pleasure and enjoyment—a woman who'd extended him so much trust with her body. Now, he wanted that same faith with her emotions, which was what tonight was all about. Trust, and honesty, too.

He'd never wanted those things with any other women, but he found he needed that intimacy and bond from Jill. Their relationship might have started out based on sex and a temporary affair, but there was no denying there was so much more at risk now.

Such as his own emotions, possibly even his heart.

The lamplight gave her curvaceous body a warm, golden sheen and enhanced the highlights in her auburn hair. She shifted anxiously on the mattress and her thighs rubbed sinuously. He licked his dry lips, wondering if he'd ever seen such perfection. Wondering, too, if what he was about to do to her would bring them closer, or shatter any chance at a relationship with her beyond tonight.

It was a gamble he was willing to take. His plan was risky, and certainly recklessly erotic, but he had little to lose, and so much to gain.

Picking up the lavender rose from the nightstand, he touched the bud to her nose, allowing her to inhale the sweet, drugging fragrance. Lightly, he dragged the flower down her neck and over the rapid pulse at the base of her throat. He circled the breasts that had firmed and swelled the closer he glided the satiny petals toward their taut crests.

Tugging on the bonds holding her arms above her head, she moaned in frustration and arched her back, bringing her nipples into direct contact with the velvet textured petals.

"Please," she breathed, the one word holding a wealth of meaning.

"Oh, I plan to," he drawled in low, hushed tones. Sweeping the delicate rose over her belly, he dipped into her navel, and traced her thighs down to her feet, causing her entire body to quiver in expectation. There was only one place left untouched, and as he trailed the flower back up the inside of her legs she eagerly parted them for his caress. Her breathing deepened the closer he came to the treasure nestled between her thighs, and a gasp caught in her throat when he twirled the tip of the rose against the swollen nub of flesh, rewarding her for her submissiveness and heightening her need.

When he finally lifted the flower, the lavender petals glistened with her moisture. Plucking a petal, he let it flutter to her flat stomach. "She wants me . . . she wants me not," he recited playfully as each satiny petal drifted to her skin, until the last one settled on her mound and he finished with, "She wants me."

He splayed his hand on her belly and rubbed the fragrant petals over her skin, then leisurely moved upward to knead each breast. "Do you want me?" he asked.

"Yes." She moaned raggedly, and bit her bottom lip when he rolled an erect nipple between his fingers.

"I assure you, the feeling is mutual, but I'm not through playing yet." Unclasping the pearls from around her neck, he followed the same path he'd just taken with the rose, rolling the beads around her breasts and over her hard, straining nipples. "Do you like the way that feels?"

She nodded and whispered, "Yes."

He dragged the gleaming pearls over her soft belly. "Do you want more?"

Her hips lifted in an intimate dance of desire and need. "Yes. *Please.*"

"So polite." He let the pearls slither over her stomach and arranged a strand so it fell between her parted thighs and teased her plump outer lips with the slightest movement she made. "No need to be proper, love, because I'll give you anything you want, and more, if you'll let me."

"Yes." The word escaped on a croak, and she tried again, *"Yes."*

"Good girl." Walking to the end of the bed, he moved up onto the mattress and knelt between her thighs. Hooking his fingers along the underside of her knees, he drew her legs up and lowered his head. At the first touch of his lips on her skin she groaned and quivered. He skimmed his open mouth up her thigh, making a trail of hot, damp kisses that had her writhing and the pearls he'd so artfully arranged flickering against her feminine folds. The scent of her arousal teased his nostrils, making him impossibly harder and thicker than he already was. Her passion pleased him and her response fired his blood.

He upped the stakes on their game of fulfillment.

Knowing what he was about to do would undoubtedly shock her, he moved up and over the length of her, buried one hand into her hair at the back of her head to hold her steady, and crushed his mouth to hers. Her lips parted on a gasp, and he slipped his tongue deep into the sweet recesses of her mouth. She kissed him back, matching the wet, silken glide of his tongue while his free hand skimmed down her body, found the pearls, and rolled the smooth beads along her soft, wet cleft.

She tensed. With a confused whimper, she attempted to clamp her legs together. He was stronger, more determined, and he had the advantage since her hands were secured. Holding her legs spread with his thigh wedged between, and deepening his kisses, he gently pushed the pearls into her sheath, one by one. Her body bucked frantically beneath his and he swallowed her soft moans. The two strands were long, filling her until the clasp, and about a dozen pearls remained as a catch.

She wrenched her mouth from his, panting. "What are you doing?" She yanked on the silk wrapped around her wrists and thrashed wildly. "This can't be normal!"

"Normal? Definitely not," he agreed, plucking one, two, three pearls from her and watching her chest rise and fall and her nipples tighten. Lowering his head, he flicked his tongue along the sensitive spot just below her ear. "Sexy, naughty, and erotic, *absolutely.*"

"Take them out," she said primly, though there was an unmistakable quiver of excitement in her voice.

"Oh, I will," he promised, nuzzling her neck. "As soon as you admit you're turned on, and that you like the way those silky pearls feel against your inner walls."

Her skin warmed with a full body blush, but her jaw clamped shut.

He chuckled, amused by her stubborn display. "If you won't admit it, then I guess it's up to me to do my best to make sure that you *are* turned on." He nipped her jaw and dragged his teeth along her throat, drawing a ragged groan from her.

"That's it, love," he coaxed in a low, gentle tone as his hand charted a heated path along her shoulder, down her waist, and over her hip, stroking her and pulling the tension from her body. "Relax and let go . . ."

He was grateful for her bound wrists, because it gave him the freedom to explore and take his time, and savor every inch of her without any interruptions. Slowly, he inched his way down, until his lips closed over a straining nipple. His hands shaped her breasts, and he suckled her strong and deep, his mouth and tongue inflicting sensations that had her softening, relaxing, melting.

He settled between her thighs once again, using the width of his shoulders to keep her legs apart while his finger traced the lace panties framing her femininity. "So pretty," he said, and dipped his head for a taste.

At the first touch of his mouth on her mound she stiffened and attempted to move away, but he anchored his arms around her thighs and ruthlessly demanded her total surrender. He lapped at her leisurely, and spent an infinite amount of time pleasuring her, drinking in her honeyed essence, lost in the taste of her and reveling in her wispy sighs of total acquiescence. With every soft, slow stroke of his tongue, she slid deeper into his spell, and he into hers.

He built her climax gradually, waiting until he had her on the precipice before he tugged on the pearls. The strand shimmered out, tickling, teasing, cajoling her sensitive flesh.

"Oh, God," she groaned, husky and deep. Her head

rolled to the side, her hands clenched into fists, and with a low cry and a convulsive shudder she came, sobbing, begging him for *more*.

He obliged. Another gentle tug and the last of the pearls spilled out of her. He played her exquisitely with his mouth and tongue, lifting her higher and letting her soar over the edge once more.

He reared up, grabbed a condom from the nightstand, and sheathed his penis, needing her with a desperation that defied anything he'd ever felt or done before. Sliding the smooth tip of his shaft along her dewy, slick flesh, he eased over her body and drove into her, riding her hard and fast, his thrusts untamed and frenzied as he strained toward his own completion.

His heart hammered in his chest, his frantic pulse matching the throbbing in his erection. His muscles grew taut, and his lips sought hers in a searing, open-mouthed kiss, completely possessing her. Their tongues touched, tangled, as sweet and welcoming as the legs wrapping around his waist and holding him tight as his hips pistoned relentlessly against her, creating a hot, slick friction neither of them could deny.

She wrenched her mouth from his and screamed as another orgasm ripped through her, her back arching up off the bed to take him even deeper. With one last powerful thrust he came on a wild, guttural groan. When the last of the pleasurable shudders were wrung from his body, he collapsed on top of her. Trembling and spent, he buried his face against her neck as he waited for his world to right itself again, though he was beginning to accept that his world, his life, would never be the same again.

He was falling in love with Jill Richardson.

Chapter Five

Still blindfolded and tied up, Jill surfaced from the sensual haze enveloping her by slow degrees after sharing such an earth-shattering climax with Eric. Her body was still intimately joined with his, their skin damp with perspiration, and her senses drugged with the heat and musky scent of the man draped along the length of her.

After long, silent moments passed, he finally stirred, lifting up enough to take the heaviest weight off her. Warm fingers tenderly brushed damp tendrils of hair away from her face, then he pressed his lips to her throat. "Are you okay?" he asked, his tone rough with spent passion.

His concern made her smile. Despite her earlier struggles, he'd been ruthless in his conquest, but infinitely gentle in his taking. She was certain he would have stopped at any time—*if* she'd really wanted him too. But she hadn't, and he'd known.

"I'm fine, but I think I'm ready for you to untie me." She tugged on the silk binding her wrists, aching to touch him and explore his body as thoroughly as he'd consumed hers. She didn't question her total abandon, only knew it felt so good, so right with him. "And take the blindfold off, too, please."

He removed the sash covering her eyes, then worked on the knot that had tightened around her hands every time she'd pulled on the restraint. She lay there as he gently tended to her, and when the tie finally fell free, he brought her wrists to his mouth. Holding her gaze, he kissed the chafed skin, soothing it with his lips and the soft touch of his tongue.

"Did you like what I did to you?" he asked, his warm breath fanning across the erratic pulse in her wrist.

Another fire started within her, this one tiny, licking flames that ignited in her belly and spread outward. "It was . . . different."

An amused smiled curved his lips. "Yes, but did you like it?"

She couldn't deny the rippling effects those pearls had on her entire body. And she had to admit that she liked everything he'd done to her. Even the pearls. Especially the pearls—the way they'd filled her with a provocative heaviness, and how they'd slid out of her in a sensuous inner caress.

"Yes," she replied, giving him the answer she knew he was waiting for. "It was very erotic, and sexy."

His eyes turned a smoky shade of blue. "*You're* sexy."

With him she felt beautiful, and yes, alluring. "Did *you* like it?" she asked tentatively.

"Oh, yeah." His gaze held hers steadily, and his expression changed, turned more serious. "I liked the way you ultimately trusted me and at the end gave yourself so openly. And I loved watching you unravel and come apart for me."

She swallowed hard. She'd never bared herself to a man in such an uninhibited way. Emotionally and physically, she'd held nothing back with Eric. Then again, he'd given her no choice, and she would have given him anything to experience the exquisite sensations he'd woven throughout her body. The thought was a little thrilling, and frightening.

He stood up, went to the bathroom, and a few minutes later returned to the bed. He snuggled up behind her, pulled her back to his chest, and wrapped an arm around her waist. She couldn't bring herself to resist his affectionate cuddling.

"I've been meaning to tell you, I really like your house," he murmured into her ear.

His intimate comment surprised her, especially since they'd never indulged in personal conversation after their fantasies. For that matter, he didn't usually linger, either, but at the moment she didn't want him to go, and she wasn't ready for the warmth and closeness to end. Not just yet.

"You haven't seen much of the house," she pointed out, a wry smile touching the corners of her mouth. "Just the master bedroom."

He laughed, the sexy sound vibrating along her spine. "I've seen enough to know the house is well cared for. It shows in this room with the floral wallpaper and matching pale shade of paint on the walls, and even the antique furniture. Your bedroom reveals a lot about you."

She tried to see her choice of decorating style through his eyes, and wondered what he'd learned about her. "You think so?"

"Yeah, I do. I think you're a romantic, and a bit old-fashioned, despite trying to be a tough cookie at work."

It shocked her that he'd been so observant during their sexual encounters, and equally perceptive when it came to her personality. And so accurate. They'd conducted a hot, illicit affair in this room and shared many carnal fantasies, yet he'd taken the time to discover more about her than just what turned her on in bed. She wasn't sure what to make of that, nor was she ready to delve too deeply into why he'd paid so much attention to her surroundings and what they revealed about her.

His hand idly stroked over her bare hip, soothing her from the inside out. "I've also been up close and personal with the landscaping while sneaking through the backyard," he went on, humor infusing his voice. "They don't build the kind of stone walls surrounding this house anymore, so I'm guessing the wall was constructed thirty or forty years ago. And most of the plants, shrubs, and trees look like they've been here a very long time and are well tended to. All that landscaping adds a lot to the character of the house."

She was amazed that once again he'd noticed so much more than superficial details. "My parents moved into this house when it was brand-new and before I was born. My mother loved to plant flowers and shrubs, so many are the original ones she planted. I used to help her when I was a little girl, and I still enjoy gardening." That was more than she'd intended to reveal, but the words came easily with him.

He buried his nose in her hair and she heard him take a deep breath of the fragrant strands. "So, the house belongs to your parents?" he asked.

"Technically, it's mine now." She closed her eyes, her body pliant against his, and her mind just as mellow. "A few years ago they moved to Florida to live near my mother's sister, and they put the house in my name. This place is all I've ever known and these walls hold a lot of fond memories for me. I hope to raise my own children in this house one day." The secret she'd always held in her heart slipped out before she could stop the words, as if she were talking to a close friend rather than a man who was in her life for only a few more nights.

He was quiet for a few moments, then said, "I can understand why it's such a special place for you. Do you have any brothers or sisters?"

"No. I'm an only child." Feeling as though there was too much focus on her, she turned in his arms, glanced up at him, and put him in the spotlight instead. "What about you? Any siblings?" she asked, admittedly curious to know more about him, too.

They were face-to-face, with his head resting on her spare pillow and his hair rumpled so enticingly around his head. He looked all male and as though he belonged there in her bed. His gaze held hers, warm and inviting, and the awareness between them increased. "I have two older brothers. There's Steve, who's a private detective, and then there's Adrian, who the family has dubbed 'The Wilde One'."

She laughed, amused by the cute play on words that included their last name. "I think the title fits *you* just as well." She playfully poked him in the chest with a finger.

He grabbed her hand and placed a lingering kiss in the center of her palm. "Not as much as it fits Adrian. Trust me, I'm tame in comparison."

She lifted a skeptical brow. After her firsthand experience with just how *untamed* Eric could be, she found that hard to believe.

"Adrian has always been wild and reckless, and is always pulling crazy stunts and doing dangerous things." His lips and tongue skimmed the pulse at the base of her wrist, then he flattened her hand on his chest. "He loves extreme sports and recently started up an extreme sporting event business. My parents swear Adrian is the reason they have so much gray hair."

She was all too aware of his rapidly beating heart, and struggled to keep their conversation light. "And you didn't help to contribute to those gray hairs?"

A wicked light shone in his eyes, matching the grin that appeared. "I might have been a bad boy a time or two, but I just never got caught like Adrian did."

She laughed, enjoying herself, and him. "Now *that* I believe." She leaned down, meaning to give him a quick, frisky kiss on the lips, but as soon as her mouth touched his he slipped his fingers around the back of her head and held her in place for a deeper exploration.

She expected something fast and frenzied, but he threw her off-kilter with a soft, unhurried kind of kiss filled with a languid sensuality and a hunger that went beyond the physical. His mouth made slow, sweet love to hers, his teeth nibbling, his tongue licking and seducing. She moaned and sank deeper into his sensuous embrace.

Long minutes later, he ended the kiss and brushed his damp lips across her cheek, then settled her body against him again, spoon fashion. "Rest for a little bit," he murmured.

She felt his rigid shaft pressing against her bottom, and wondered why he didn't just take her again and ease his arousal. Instead, his actions were selfless and tender. Intimate in a way that defied the physical "fantasy world" they'd agreed upon. Then again, so had their conversation about their families.

Recognizing the subtle shift in their relationship, she swallowed hard, wishing she had the strength to tell him it was time for him to leave. But she couldn't do it. She was quickly learning that Eric Wilde was one of her biggest weaknesses. While she reminded herself that there were only a few nights left before their affair was over, for the moment, in her mind, in her heart, she pretended they were more than temporary lovers.

When she woke a few hours later and reached for Eric, he was gone. Abruptly, she sat up and glanced around the empty room, noticing that her French doors were closed. She found the silk stockings and sash he'd used to enhance their earlier fantasy, and she touched those items, remembering everything. The arousing scent of roses and the musky fragrance of sex filled her senses, evidence that he'd indeed been there tonight.

She couldn't stop the acute disappointment filling her, or the "what ifs" she didn't have the answers for. A hot, memorable tryst with Eric was exactly what she wanted from him, and him from her. It was the only way it could be between them, she told herself for the umpteenth time, despite the fact that she was coming to realize that she was losing an integral part of her heart to Eric in the process.

Four days and numerous fantasies later, Jill was still trying to come to terms with the fact that she'd some-how, some way, allowed Eric to become more than a fleeting plaything. Ever since the night with the pearls, he'd made a point of indulging in pillow talk after their fantasies, and seemed to draw things from her she'd never intended to share with him.

She'd also come to the conclusion that her current emotional upheaval was all his fault, because she never expected that beneath that rebel personality of his was a man so tender, sensitive, and intuitive. One who'd genuinely cared about her feelings and insecurities and seemed to cater to them—in bed and out.

He'd been labeled as a bad boy, and rumor around the office had it that he was a known playboy, but she had to wonder how much of all that gossip was true. While she'd been the recipient of Eric's bad boy image, she'd also seen so many facets to the man over the past week and a half. Intriguing, honorable traits that had managed to penetrate the emotional barriers she'd sworn he'd never touch during their brief affair.

Oh, yeah, she was definitely in over her head with Eric. And she had to find a way to keep herself from completely drowning so she wasn't a total emotional wreck when their nightly fantasies ended.

"So, tell me, how did the big presentation go today?" her best friend, Renee Brooks, asked from her seat across from Jill at The Daily Grind, a hip coffeehouse in downtown Chicago they frequented, especially when girl talk was in order. Like tonight. "I hope we're here to celebrate your new success with the cruise line account."

And to discuss her turbulent love life, she thought silently. She needed to hear a voice of reason, along with a good dose of practical advice and hard-nosed reminders of her past relationship gone bad that would finally put her emotions into better perspective so far as Eric was concerned.

But first, she'd share her good news with Renee. "As a matter of fact, we are celebrating," Jill said, unable to keep the pride from her voice. "The Enchanted Cruise Line loved the presentation, and other than a few modifications to the marketing plan, they signed on with Massey."

"That's fabulous!" Renee said, knowing how much this account meant to Jill, and how far that bonus would go in terms of making her agency solvent. "Congratulations. Here's a toast to you."

Jill lifted her iced mocha and clicked her plastic glass to Renee's. "Here's to independence and financial freedom. Sort of," she added with an impish grin.

"Here, here!" Renee agreed, and they both laughed and drank to the big bonus coming Jill's way.

"So, other than this big account, what's been going on with you lately?" Renee settled into the comfortable corner and propped her feet up onto the mismatched coffee table that was part of the café's charm and decor. "We haven't really talked in a couple of weeks."

Jill grew quiet, trying to figure out the best way to tell her friend the predicament she'd gotten herself into. It was just enough hesitancy for Renee to jump to her own conclusions.

"Ohmigod, you're seeing someone, aren't you?" she guessed accurately, having learned long ago to read Jill's shift in moods. "Why didn't you tell me?"

An attempt at a casual shrug lifted Jill's shoulder. "Because it's just a temporary thing."

Renee's brown eyes widened. "Temporary? As in a hot, wild affair for the sake of great sex?"

A warm flush spread across Jill's face, and she took a sip of her drink to cool off. "Oh, it's definitely that."

"Woo-hoo! You go, girl," Renee cheered enthusiastically. "It's about time you got back into the sexual swing of things after your relationship with Jeremy."

Jill inwardly cringed. "It's a bit more complicated. The guy I'm seeing is essentially my boss at Massey. And if I'm not careful, I could really fall hard for him." *Boy, that certainly was an understatement.*

Renee's excitement visibly dwindled and concern

settled in. "All right, spill the details. *All* of them, and then we'll assess the situation."

Jill curled her legs beneath her on the big, over-stuffed armchair she was sitting in, immensely grateful to have Renee in her life. The two of them had met during their sophomore year in college, and seven years later they were still the best of friends who confided in each other and shared their deepest secrets. Honesty and trust were the cornerstones of their friendship, and it was times like this that Jill both treasured and appreciated Renee's presence in her life.

With a deep breath for fortitude, Jill told Renee everything about her proposition with Eric, but left out the more explicit details of their fantasies. She even confided her true feelings for Eric to Renee, and her fears of repeating past mistakes. By the time she was done, Renee was uncharacteristically quiet.

Jill bit her bottom lip uncertainly. "It's bad, isn't it?" she asked, certain her friend was about to berate her for being such a fool.

Renee's expression turned thoughtful. "The relationship could end up really hurting you, if you let it. But I think you can still save yourself."

Undeniably curious, Jill asked, "How so?"

Renee took a drink of her blended caramel latte. "How many more times do you anticipate being with Eric before the affair ends?"

Jill considered her friend's question, realizing with a start just how little time she had left with Eric. Her heart gave a painful twist in her chest she tried to dismiss, and failed. "Well, we won't be seeing each other tonight, because he's working late to wrap up the modifications to the marketing plan so accounting can get started on the contract procedures." She swallowed the unexpected lump that rose in her throat. "Actually, now that the project is completed, I only need to go into the office tomorrow to wrap up any lingering presentation details, so tomorrow night, Thursday, will probably be our last night together."

Renee's look turned pointed. "Judging by everything you've told me, it sounds as though he's controlled most of the fantasies, yes?"

Jill replayed those arousing memories in her mind, from her first encounter with Eric up until last night, when he'd instigated a hot, erotic game of hide-and-seek in the darkened shadows of her backyard. He'd stalked her, heightening her awareness and excitement of the forbidden until he'd finally caught her, ripped off her clothes, and had his wicked way with her.

She was surprised to realize that Eric *had* initiated and dominated all their fantasies in one way or another—not that she'd ever complained about being the recipient of his fierce passion and carnal desires. But it was definitely an eye-opener to see just how much influence this man held over her.

"Yes, I guess he has been the one in control," she admitted reluctantly. He'd even been the one to instigate their after-sex conversations.

A savvy grin lifted the corners of Renee's lips. "Then it's time to turn the tables on him this last time you're together, and go out with *you* in control and on top, literally and figuratively." She bobbed her eyebrows for emphasis.

Jill laughed. Her friend's idea certainly had merit. If her sole focus was on pleasure and Eric being *her* love slave, she'd be able to keep her emotions in check. This time, she'd be the seducer, the dominant, aggressive one, and there would be no small talk or shared intimacy after sex. She'd end the affair with dignity, and no regrets.

For her heart's sake, she prayed she could pull it off.

Something was up with Jill. Throughout the day Eric was aware of the fact that she was deliberately avoiding him, and during the times when they had to discuss final business details on the Enchanted project, she kept her replies direct, curt, and to the point. He hated the fact that she was already withdrawing from him when it was the last thing he wanted from her.

His stomach was in knots, and he felt anxious and edgy, knowing that his time with Jill was limited. Tomorrow, Friday, she was due to come in to collect her bonus check and clear out her office, which meant they only had tonight left together . . . one last fantasy for Eric to convince Jill that they ought to take a chance and go public with their relationship and see where their attraction and the emotional connection he'd established over the past few nights led them.

Unfortunately, with her past and insecurities standing in their way, he was up against some huge odds. But he'd never been a quitter, and he loved a challenge, even if it meant putting his own feelings on the line.

Snapping the locks shut on his briefcase, he left the office and rode the elevator down to the parking garage. Jill had snuck out an hour earlier without saying good-bye, but he wasn't going to let her off so easy. And the last thing he wanted to hear from her lips was a farewell. No, if he had his way, she'd be begging him to stay.

Oh, yeah, what a true fantasy that was, he thought, giving his head a rueful shake.

As he approached his car, a piece of pink paper on

his windshield caught his attention. He withdrew the scrap of stationery and read the note, written in Jill's familiar feminine handwriting: *You're mine tonight. I'll be at your place 8 P.M. sharp.*

A slow grin curved his lips, and his mood lightened considerably. This unique woman would never cease to amaze and surprise him, which was all part of her allure, he knew. She managed to keep him guessing and anticipating—something no other woman had managed to capture with him.

Over the course of the past two weeks, he'd discovered that Jill was one of a kind, and he was more than willing to be hers tonight, and every night into the future if she'd let him.

Jill approached the front door to Eric's house and wiped her damp palms down the black cotton stretch pants encasing her thighs and legs. She was dressed all in black, from the long-sleeved turtleneck to her leggings and the enclosed sandals on her feet. Her stomach tumbled nervously, and she felt like a thief sneaking through the night, which added a certain excitement to her fantasy, she had to admit.

Now she knew how Eric had felt moving stealthily through her backyard in the dark of night, but she wasn't brave enough to scale his fence to find a way into his house. No, her approach tonight was going to be straightforward and fast, a whirlwind of pleasure that would leave her in control and Eric totally wasted and wondering what the hell had happened to him once she was gone. One final fantasy to recall and savor in those lonely nights ahead, when work wasn't enough to satisfy the emptiness in her heart and soul.

As for tonight, she didn't want to think. She just

wanted to *feel,* and Eric was certainly great at making her body come alive with just a look, a touch. She might be the one seducing him for this final fantasy, but she knew his excitement would only heighten her own. Already, she was damp and slick with arousal, and tingling with anticipation.

Lifting her hand, she knocked on the front door, and seconds later it opened with Eric filling the threshold. His velvet blue eyes appraised her from head to toe, and a slow, lazy grin curved his lips.

She didn't wait for a greeting or an invitation. Talk was unnecessary for what she had in mind for tonight. Splaying a hand on his chest, she guided him back into the house, shut the door behind her, and pressed him up against the wall in the darkened entryway—a perfect place to begin her seduction.

His eyes widened in surprise, and she leaned into him, aligning their bodies from her unbound breasts to their thighs. He was already hard, and she gyrated her hips against his erection, loving the way his body responded so eagerly to hers.

He clamped his hands on the curve of her waist, holding her still. "Jill—"

"Don't say a word," she breathed into his ear. "Like the note said, you're *mine* tonight, and my fantasy is to have hot, mindless sex with *you,* a man I just met in a bar. I'm not looking for conversation, stranger, just a willing body. If you can't give me what I need, I'll leave."

Eric had no idea what to expect from Jill, but he couldn't deny that he was curious to see how she played out her erotic fantasy. Yet he wasn't used to relinquishing control to a woman, especially during sex. Ever. But for as much as his instincts rebelled against being the one to submit, he couldn't bring himself to balk at her rules and risk her ending the fantasy before it even began.

He loosened his hold on her waist, silently surrendering to her tempting proposition. With a triumphant smile, she skimmed her cool hands under his T-shirt, and he lifted his arms for her to pull it up and over his head. Wanting her just as bare, he reached for the hem of her turtleneck, but she pushed his hands aside, took a step back, and stripped it off herself.

He caught only a quick glimpse of her gorgeous breasts, and then she was back, her fingers exploring the contours of his chest, and her soft, damp lips nuzzling the side of his neck. Her full, lush breasts branded his flesh as she leisurely licked and bit her way down his throat to his nipples. He groaned when her teeth scraped across the erect disks, but her tongue was quick to soothe the sting. That talented mouth of hers traveled lower and she knelt in front of him, scattering moist, openmouthed kisses on his taut belly while her fingers eagerly ripped open the buttons on his fly. His erection sprang free, and hooking her fingers into the waistband of his jeans, she yanked the faded denim down his long legs and off, leaving him completely naked.

She gazed at his jutting penis in rapt fascination, and licked her lips hungrily, causing his insides to coil tight. Dampening the tip of her finger with her tongue, she rubbed the slick wetness over the head of his shaft, then blew a gust of warm breath on the moist spot. Sensation shot through him like a streak of lightning. His stomach muscles bunched, and his cock twitched and thickened, eager for more of her brazen attention.

She merely smiled, then flattened her hands on his hair-roughened thighs and slid her palms upward until her thumbs grazed the heavy sacs between his legs.

Soft fingers explored and cupped his testicles, while her other hand wrapped snug around the base of his shaft. With long, wet strokes of her tongue she measured the length of him, and used her hand to pump his solid erection in a slow, squeezing caress that made his eyes roll back in his head and his breath hiss out between his clenched teeth. Leisurely, she licked the sensitive tip of his cock, lapping up the essence she'd drawn from his body, and swirled her tongue over the swollen head in an unbelievably erotic way. Unable to take much more of her sensual, teasing torment, he tangled his hands in her long, silky hair, and muttered a raw, earthly expletive of exactly what he wanted to do with that warm, wet mouth of hers.

She looked up at him, and with her eyes gleaming with sinful intent, she parted her lips and obliged his request, taking him slow and deep, enveloping him in the exquisite sensation of liquid heat and velvet softness. Her moan of genuine pleasure vibrated along his aching shaft, and then she *sucked,* hard and strong, and he went wild. His fingers fisted tighter in her hair, his head rolled back against the wall, and his hips began to thrust, matching the rhythmic strokes of her mouth. She took him to the brink, and just as his climax beckoned she pulled back, releasing him, leaving him dazed and his body trembling with the need to relieve the pressure she'd so exquisitely built.

She stood up, her breathing as labored as his own. "Take me to your bedroom," she demanded huskily.

Grabbing her hand, he led the way into his masculine domain, his desire for her so strong he could deny her nothing. She kicked off her shoes and removed a single condom from the waistband of her stretch pants, tossed it on the bed, and shimmied out of her leggings. He recognized the significance of that single foil packet—

she only intended for them to have one encounter tonight, a final fantasy between them that *she* orchestrated from beginning to end.

She stood before him, gloriously naked, and before he could truly appreciate, admire, or caress her sleek curves, she pushed him down onto the center of the mattress and climbed on top of him, the dominant position not escaping his notice. She sheathed his erection, and without further foreplay she straddled his hips and impaled herself to the hilt.

They shuddered simultaneously, and their gazes met ever so briefly in the darkened room. He caught a glimpse of emotion glistening in the depth of her eyes before her lashes fluttered closed and she rocked her pelvis against him. Lifting her hands, she cupped and kneaded her breasts and rolled her tight nipples between her fingers. Her head fell back as she arched, and her fingers fluttered along her belly and dipped between her thighs, right where they were joined.

While his mind screamed at him to thrust and follow her into the sweet oblivion her body promised, something within him rebelled. She was going too fast, her actions too detached, and as ridiculous as it seemed, he felt used, alone, and separate from this woman who was physically a part of him. She was intent on giving herself her own orgasm, the intimate connection he wanted and needed from her was nonexistent, and he knew it was all deliberate on her part.

The fantasy she'd created, of picking up a stranger in a bar, allowed for no sentiments or anything remotely emotional. They hadn't even kissed, which was one of the most intimate expressions of a physical joining. To her, this was all about sex. Or so she was trying to convince herself in her attempt to take charge of the fantasy, and her response to him.

As she continued to touch herself and ride him in an increasing tempo, he realized exactly what she was doing. Just as he'd always insisted on being in control during sex to maintain an emotional distance during his past affairs, Jill was using the same technique to keep *her* true feelings from him. The irony of the situation didn't escape him, and he realized he didn't like being on the receiving end. Not when Jill had come to mean more to him than a casual, temporary affair.

Refusing to let their relationship end so superficially, he gripped her waist to hold her still so he could redirect the fantasy. But she was so caught up in her own personal pleasure that there was nothing he could do to stop the orgasm rippling through her except hold on to his own restraint for all he was worth and wait for her climax to end, which nearly killed him.

With a sated sigh, she collapsed on top of him, her soft breasts crushing against his chest, and her hot, panting breath fanning his neck. Taking advantage of her pliable state, he wrapped one arm tight around her back, secured another beneath her bottom, and rolled them both so that she was pinned beneath the weight of his body, putting *him* back in control.

Their bodies were still intimately joined, and he widened her thighs with his own and flexed his hips, lodging his throbbing cock deep inside her. After her self-induced orgasm she was snug, gripping the length of him like a slick fist. He resisted the instinctive urge to drive mindlessly into her.

She sucked in a quick, startled breath, and there was no disguising the panic that flared to life in her eyes. "Eric . . ." Her voice trembled, and her hands shoved at his shoulders in an attempt to dislodge him, all to no avail.

He brushed a gentle kiss across her cheek. "Shhh,"

he soothed, understanding her fear, but knowing she'd given him little choice in how to handle the ending of tonight's final fantasy. Grabbing the hands digging into his muscled flesh, he placed them at the side of her head and entwined their fingers. "I'm not done yet, and neither are you," he murmured.

And then he began to move inside her, his thrusts strong and sure, matching the uncharacteristic hammering of his pulse. Jill turned her head to the side and closed her eyes, trying to protect her emotions, he knew, and he refused to let her shut him out that way. She remained stubborn and defiant, a challenge he wasn't about to lose. Not here. Not now. Not tonight.

As he continued to pump into her, he lowered his head, nuzzled her neck, and whispered in her ear how good she felt around him, how perfectly they fit together. He told her he wanted to watch her come for him, with him, and how much he ached to feel her inner muscles milking him to completion.

A soft whimper escaped her, and his heart gave a strange twist in his chest. He kissed her jaw, the corner of her mouth, needing so much more than she was giving him. "Look at me, Jill. *Please.*"

Much to his surprise, she turned her head and her long lashes lifted, revealing the sheen of moisture filling her eyes. His gut clenched, and he knew her tears weren't designed to manipulate a man. No, hers were genuine and told of her confusion, her fears and insecurities. She blinked, and a tear escaped. He kissed it away, then pressed his mouth softly, gently, to hers.

Her lips parted, her tongue sought his, and her tentative surrender nearly undid him. He accepted her invitation to deepen the kiss, as well as lengthen his thrusts and build the delicious friction between them. He knew her body well, and used everything he'd learned about pleasing her to increase her pleasure. In time, she softened beneath him, hooked her legs over his hips, and gave herself to him with abandon. He recognized the soft, mewling sounds she made in the back of her throat, felt those wondrous contractions clamping around him, squeezing his shaft, and another stroke later he lost himself in the sea of wild sensation he'd held at bay just for her.

He circled his hips, grinding against her sex, and she came with him, her soft cries intensifying the orgasm spearing through him. He groaned into her mouth, a deep, resonant, soulful sound that no other woman had ever pulled from him in the throes of passion. In that moment, he knew Jill was *the one*. In every way.

And he didn't want her to leave tonight, because it would signify the end to *them*.

Dragging his lips from hers, he stared into her brilliant green eyes, and took a huge risk. "Stay the night with me."

The light in her eyes faded, and he felt her withdraw from him and his request. She didn't verbally answer him, but his hopes dwindled anyway. He wouldn't try to coerce her any further; she had to stay on her own accord, because *she* wanted to.

He moved off her. "I'll be back in a few minutes," he said, and disappeared into the bathroom, shutting the door behind him. He took care of business, but didn't rush back out. Instead, he splashed cool water on his face, giving Jill extra time to make her decision, even though he knew what choice she'd already made and that she would be gone when he returned to his room.

For once, he hated being right.

Chapter Six

Coming into work Friday morning to pack up her things was one of the hardest things Jill ever had to do. Especially since it meant facing Eric and the cowardly way she'd snuck out on him the night before. But staying beyond the fantasy meant confronting her greatest fears and insecurities, of getting involved with a man and letting her emotions interfere with the goals she'd set for herself and her agency. Eric presented a conflict to both, and she'd accepted the rules of their fantasy world for a reason, so it would make walking away easier, without any expectations or promises to complicate the issue.

She just wished she was one of those sophisticated women who could have an affair, enjoy the physical aspect of the relationship and carnal, erotic pleasures, and leave her heart out of the matter.

Obviously, she was not.

"No regrets," she muttered to herself as she placed her coffee mug into her small packing box. She'd chanted those words a hundred times since she'd crawled into her own bed last night, battling an onslaught of emotions and tears. Regrets were good for nothing, and she'd never been one to wallow in self-pity. She wouldn't do so now.

A brisk knock sounded at her office door—or what had temporarily been her office at Massey and Associates—and she glanced up, locking gazes with the man who'd consumed her thoughts for the past twelve hours. He strolled into her office, looking sexy and gorgeous in a neatly pressed button-down shirt and creased khakis, and his hair tousled around his head. She was grateful to see that there wasn't so much as a glimmer of accusation in his eyes for the way she'd left him last night.

"I have something for you," he said, stopping on the other side of her desk.

Her heart picked up its beat, much too hopeful for her liking, until she realized he was holding a window envelope out to her and she could see her name imprinted on a company check. Her bonus money. Of course.

"Thank you." Reaching out, she retrieved her check, which represented financial breathing room for her own agency, along with the end of her freelance job with Massey, and her relationship with Eric.

Pushing his hands into the front pockets of his pants, he tipped his head, his grin charming and boyish. "Are you sure I can't change your mind about staying?"

His double meaning was shrewd and unmistakable, combining the offer from Massey to remain with the firm, and his own desires to extend their affair. While she recognized his dual question for what it was, he didn't cross any of those boundaries they'd agreed upon about not bringing their affair up at work. To keep business and pleasure separate. Not unless *she* chose to do so.

She glanced away from his compelling eyes that could weaken her resolve if she let them, and tucked the envelope into her purse. "I'm sure," she said, her answer encompassing both requests. She wasn't changing her mind about either.

Disappointment passed over his features, but he gave a short nod of understanding and turned to go. Halfway to the door, he stopped and turned back around. "Would you like to go out sometime?"

Startled by his question, she stammered, "On . . . on a date?"

"There seems to be a certain chemistry between us," he said, speaking as though they'd never discovered just how combustible the two of them were together. That the last two weeks of incredible pleasure hadn't existed. "So, I thought a date would be a good place to start. We could go out to dinner and get to know one another better."

A casual date. His way of making it clear that he wanted to pursue their relationship—*out* of the bedroom. She shook her head, and tried to speak around the knot of fear tightening her throat. "I'm sorry, but no." She'd learned more about him, his life and family, than she'd ever intended to. Any more, and she might not be able to walk away.

He accepted her reply gracefully, and without further prompting. "I guess I'll see you at the celebratory party for the Enchanted Cruise Line next Saturday, then?"

She'd debated about declining the invitation from Massey to welcome their new client into the firm's fold, but in the end couldn't bring herself to say no. She wanted to leave the company in good standing, and since she'd been such a big part of the campaign and she'd pitched the presentation, she also knew that Enchanted would expect her to be at the celebratory bash.

"Yes, I'll be there," she told him, even knowing it would be sheer torture being in the same room with him for those few hours, watching him mingle and flash that sexy grin of his, and make small talk with her.

"Great. I'll see you there."

And then he was gone, leaving her to finish packing up her things, along with her aching heart.

"What has you so down in the dumps, little brother?" Steve asked, scrutinizing Eric's mood from across the patio table at their parents' house, where the family was gathered for a Sunday afternoon barbecue. "I don't think I've ever seen our happy-go-lucky brother so distracted before."

Adrian eyed Eric speculatively, as well, as he popped the top off his second bottle of beer. "I have to agree. Even Mom mentioned that you're unusually quiet today, and she's worried about you."

Eric resisted the urge to tell his brothers to back off and stop with the third degree, but knew that would just make them more determined to discover the cause of his mood. Steve, being a private detective, loved analyzing the slightest enigma until he finally figured out the source of the problem. And Adrian was just plain nosy and didn't need much of an excuse to give their youngest sibling a hard time.

"There's nothing for anyone to worry about." He scooped up a handful of the pretzels his mother had put on the table for them to snack on while their father barbecued the steaks on the grill. "I just have a lot on my mind."

A sly grin lifted the corners of Adrian's mouth. "It's that same woman that had you so on edge the night we played racquetball, isn't it?" Knowing he'd guessed accurately, he shook his head in disgust. "No woman is worth all this grief and misery you're putting yourself through."

Yes, she was. And Eric proved it. "Her name is Jill Richardson."

Steve's brows rose in surprise. "Wow, we actually get a name?"

Adrian sputtered on the drink of beer he was swallowing and coughed a few times to clear his throat. "Holy shit," he exclaimed once he recovered. "We *never* get a name! This must be serious."

"Watch your mouth over there, Adrian," their father, Paul, piped up from his position at the grill a few yards away. "You know how your mother feels about you boys cussing."

Adrian winced at being caught, but appeared grateful that their mother was in the house preparing the side dishes. "Sorry," he muttered.

Steve snickered, and Eric hid a grin, too.

Even though they were all grown men, a "potty mouth" was something their mother still didn't tolerate from her sons. At least not in her presence. Adrian was fortunate that only their father had heard him, or else Angela Wilde would be serving them all a lecture along with dinner about how no respectable woman liked a man who cursed all the time. Not that Adrian, or even Steve, were in the market for a respectable woman.

As for Eric, he'd finally found a woman *he* respected,

intellectually and physically, only to find himself on the receiving end of a brush-off. When he'd given Jill her check Friday afternoon, he'd attempted to pursue their relationship, only to have his invitation for a real date turned down. He figured that Jill was still in denial, still clinging to fears and insecurities, and hoped that it was just a matter of time before she trusted in what they'd shared together.

Then again, time was his biggest enemy, he knew. The more days that passed, the easier it would be for the emotional distance between them to grow, until their affair was nothing more than a distant memory. Unfortunately, he didn't know what else he could do to change Jill's mind.

Adrian leaned across the table and lowered his voice. "Jesus, Eric, if you're not careful, the next thing you know you'll be bringing her home to meet Mom and Dad and the family." Adrian shuddered at the thought.

He would have enjoyed bringing Jill to his parents and sharing his big family with her. "You all would've liked her."

"Would've?" Steve asked pointedly. "As in past tense?"

Eric tried for a casual shrug, and knew he failed. "Her choice, not mine."

"*She* dumped *you*?" Adrian asked incredulously. "And now *you're* mourning the loss?"

Eric frowned at his brother's cynical tone. "The split was amicable, and I'm not mourning anything. I just would've liked to have seen where the relationship could have gone."

"Man, the sex must have been really hot to have you so whipped." Adrian tipped his beer at Eric in a masculine salute before taking a drink.

Eric wasn't about to share the details of the private,

erotic fantasies he and Jill had enacted. Besides, their affair had traversed past the physical, and it was the intimacy that they'd established in the aftermath of their encounters that remained so vivid in his mind.

"Believe it or not, it's more than the great sex that has me hooked," he admitted, deciding to lay his feelings bare. "She's smart and amusing and beautiful, and I genuinely enjoy being with her. For the first time, I feel as though I've met a woman who's my equal."

Adrian rocked back on the hind legs of his chair and placed a dramatic hand over the left side of his chest. "Oh, be still my heart."

Steve's expression turned big-brother stern. "Knock it off, doofus." Beneath the glass-topped table, Steve shoved the edge of Adrian's seat with his foot, knocking his brother off balance and nearly sending him flipping backward to the wooden deck, which earned him a glare from Adrian. "I'd like to think at least one of us can be lucky at love and happy with a woman. Just because the two of us were burned and have no interest in a permanent relationship doesn't mean that Eric can't make things work with a woman he cares about."

"Yeah, well, it takes two to make a relationship work," Eric said, wiping the condensation off his bottle with his fingers.

"That it does," Steve agreed. "And I've never known you to not go after something you wanted."

And that's exactly what he'd done two weeks ago when he'd issued Jill the mutually satisfying proposition. He'd wanted her, and he'd gone after her. Little did he know he'd crave more than a brief tryst.

Exhaling a deep breath, he absently pushed his fingers through his hair, watching as his mother exited the house and walked over to his father to give him a clean platter for the steaks. The two of them talked, and his mother smiled at something he said. There was no mistaking the affection in her gaze, or the love and respect between the two of them. His brothers' relationships might have failed for whatever reasons, but his parents were a perfect example of everything that was good and right in a relationship.

Commitment. Trust. Honesty. Being equal partners in all things and the willingness to compromise through good times, and bad. He wanted that with Jill, but how could he expect her to put her heart and emotions on the line when he hadn't done that for her?

He owed it to Jill, and himself, to tell her how he felt about her. To let her know she was special and unique, a woman who complemented him in all ways, and he needed her in his life.

He'd been aggressive in his initial pursuit of Jill and had gotten exactly what he wanted. This time would be no different.

The following Saturday, Eric stood in the midst of the celebratory party for the Enchanted Cruise Line, watching Jill mingle with the president of the company and other important guests. Feeling anxious to be alone with her, and knowing it might be hours before that happened, he took a sip of his Jack and coke to bide his time.

She'd arrived minutes before the party started, giving them only enough time to exchange polite hellos before her presence was demanded elsewhere and she was whisked away to the other side of the banquet room. During the cocktail hour she kept herself in the thick of things, deliberately keeping her distance, though that didn't stop her gaze from seeking him out when she thought he wouldn't notice. More than a few times he'd caught her looking his way, had even seen glimpses of longing and desire in her eyes before she realized he'd witnessed those emotions and quickly glanced away again.

Knowing she still harbored some kind of feelings for him kept him optimistic, but it was what she'd worn to tonight's party that snagged his attention. Accenting her powder blue skirt suit and cream-colored silk blouse was the double strand of pearls he'd given her, and her long, slender legs were encased in familiar pale stockings that made his groin tighten with vivid memories of how she looked wearing nothing but the provocative lingerie he'd purchased for her. Her choice of undergarments spoke louder than words ever could—that he was still on her mind.

The opportunity to finally seek out Jill presented itself after dinner, when most of the guests flocked out to the dance floor to enjoy the rock music the DJ played. He started toward her, but she saw his approach and managed to exit the room before he reached her and disappeared down the long corridor leading to the ladies' room. Undeterred by her attempt to avoid him, and determined to reach her emotionally this time, he waited a few minutes to make sure no one else headed in the same direction. Then he discreetly slipped inside the women's rest room.

He was surprised to find himself in a huge, lavishly decorated lounge with a couch, chairs, and a fancy gold-framed vanity. That's where Jill stood, and seeing his reflection behind her in the mirror, she whirled around, her eyes wide in incredulity and her mouth gaped open in astonishment. He'd obviously rendered her speechless by his bold, shameless intrusion.

Taking advantage of her shock, he twisted the lock on the main entrance door and strolled into the adjoining room, doing a quick check of the stalls to make sure they didn't have company. Satisfied that they were alone, he returned to the lounge area and slowly, purposely, approached her.

Jill stared at the confident, sexual man heading her way, his eyes dark and hot with intent, and forcibly shook herself from her stunned state of disbelief. A heady, undeniable excitement quickened her pulse, her stomach fluttered in acute awareness, and a liquid heat pooled between her legs.

And he hadn't even touched her yet . . .

She'd escaped to the rest room when she'd seen him coming her way in the banquet room, because she couldn't bear to make small talk with him when she still wanted him so badly. But what made her think she'd be safe from him here in the women's lounge? He was a rebel, a bad boy who made up his own rules to suit himself, consequences be damned. He didn't seem concerned about getting caught, and at the moment, she was too overwhelmed by his presence to worry about that, either.

He stopped inches away, and her entire body responded to the familiar, masculine scent of him. "Just in case you didn't notice, this is the ladies' room," she managed to say in a normal tone of voice, even while her insides trembled. "I think you made a wrong turn somewhere."

One of those devastating smiles of his made an appearance. "Sweetheart, I'm right where I want to be," he drawled in a low, husky timbre.

His softly spoken declaration made her knees buckle, and she curled her fingers around the edge of the counter by her hips for support. "Eric . . . what are you doing in here?"

Leisurely, he stroked the shorter strand of pearls

where they rested on the full swells of her breasts. "I'm fulfilling one last fantasy." His finger caught on the top button securing her silk blouse, and he unfastened the first one, then the second, his gaze never leaving hers. "I'm going to make love to you."

Make love. In all their shared fantasies, neither of them had ever used those profound words, and she was both entranced and terrified by what was happening between them. "You can't . . . we can't do that in here."

"Sure we can." His expression turned gentle, reassuring, that aggression and dominance she was so used to tempered by a softness she didn't fully understand yet. "And I promise it'll be an experience you'll never forget."

When he pushed open the sides of her blouse and touched her, she couldn't bring herself to object, not when her heart ached for him and her body was already his. Dipping his fingers into her stretch lace bra, he lifted and cupped both of her breasts in his big hands, then bent his head, his warm, damp breath wafting across her nipples before he suckled one tight crest deep into his mouth, and then did the same to the other.

A soft, purring sound rose from the back of her throat, and she pushed her fingers through his hair to hold him close and gave herself over to the sweetest sensations she'd ever known.

His movements were slow and unhurried, as if they had all the time in the world. Slowly, he bunched the hem of her skirt to her waist, then lifted her up so she was sitting on the vanity counter. Hooking his thumbs into the waistband of the white panties she wore, he dragged them down her legs, and tucked them into his suit jacket pocket. Pushing her knees apart, he skimmed his fingers along the creamy flesh just above the lacy band of her stockings, then grazed his knuckles through the thatch of curls between her thighs. He delved deeper, stroked along the swollen folds of her sex, and found her already wet and ready for him.

With unsteady hands, he unbuckled his belt, unzipped his fly, and sheathed his straining shaft with a condom. Moving back between her spread thighs and lifting her legs high around his waist, he slid into her in one long, sleek, heavy glide. His big body shuddered against hers, and she wrapped her arms around his neck as she struggled to catch her own breath.

"God, I've missed you," he groaned against her cheek, and she heard the honest need in his voice.

She'd missed him, too.

All thought ceased as he buried a hand in her hair, brought her lips to his, and kissed her long and slow and deep. His hips picked up the same seductive rhythm, and there was no denying that this time between them was different. Their lovemaking was erotic yet tender, and there was no struggle for Eric to maintain control of the act or her response. He was giving all of the control to her, like a man who trusted her with his heart. Like a man who wanted everything a relationship between a man and a woman offered.

In that moment, his generosity and selflessness outdistanced all her misgivings and uncertainties. All she felt was this man and the emotions he evoked in her. Need and desire. Tenderness and hope. And yes, the sweet beginnings of love.

Clinging to him, she clenched her thighs tight around his waist and tilted her hips. The position brought their bodies into a more intimate contact that built the slow, simmering heat between them into a burst of flame that tumbled them both over the edge of a stunning climax.

With his mouth still on hers, he swallowed her soft cries, and his own low growl vibrated against her lips.

He brought her back down with soft, lush kisses, and it seemed an eternity had passed before either of them could breathe normally again.

Untangling his fingers from her hair, he met her heavy-lidded gaze. His eyes were a subdued shade of blue, his features just as serious. "Thank you for sharing my fantasy world with me. It was more than I ever anticipated, and making love to you was the best of all," he said, feathering his thumb along her jaw. "But reality is yours if you're willing to take a chance on us."

His words swirled through the passion-induced fog still consuming her mind, and her heart pounded hard in her chest. But before she could form a response, the door behind them rattled, causing her to jump in startled surprise, which also brought her surroundings immediately back into focus. Her cheeks burned with mortification at being caught *making love* in the rest room. No doubt within minutes the rest of the Massey employees would know what had transpired between her and Eric, too.

One of her greatest fears had just been realized.

"Is someone in there?" a feminine voice asked.

"We'll be done in a minute," Eric replied, and adjusted his clothes, then Jill's, though he didn't give back her panties.

Once they were both decent again, he headed for the entrance, unlocked and opened the door, then stopped and glanced back at her. His eyes were gentle as they met hers, his voice soft when he spoke. "By the way, I want you to know that I'm falling in love with you, but I won't settle for a temporary affair or keeping our relationship a secret. I want you to be a part of my life, in all ways."

All or nothing. The choice was hers to make. She reeled from his candid declaration, paralyzed where she stood and unable to say a word because she was so afraid to *believe.*

Eric apologized to their coworker, Carol, for keeping the bathroom occupied, then he stepped around her and was gone.

Carol strolled into the lounge, her expression bemused. "I had no idea that you and Eric were, well, *you know.*"

Sleeping together. Having an affair. Fulfilling erotic fantasies. All applied, yet Eric had just elevated their relationship by *making love* to her and expressing his feelings for her. Privately and publicly.

Carol fluffed her hair and pulled a tube of lipstick from her purse. "What a lucky girl you are. Eric is quite a catch," she mused, a wistful note to her voice as she applied a slash of pink to her lips. "But it's nice to know that the baddest of boys can fall hard when it's the right woman."

And he'd fallen for her. In ways she'd never imagined or expected. He wanted her like no man had ever desired her before—heart, body, and soul. Not as a temporary plaything, but a long-term lover. And she was tired of being alone, of fighting herself and what she wanted. So weary of letting fears rule her emotions.

The other woman slanted her an incredulous look. "Good Lord, Jill, what are you still doing standing in here? Are you just going to let him walk away after he just told you he's falling in love with you and he wants a commitment?"

"No, I'm not." He'd just taken such a huge emotional gamble for her. She trusted Eric, and that meant it was time to take a few risks of her own, as well.

She ran from the lounge and back into the banquet room, her stomach twisting into a knot of nerves as her gaze searched for a certain dark-haired, blue-eyed, sexy bad boy. Her bad boy. She found him shaking hands with the president of Enchanted and saying his farewells for the evening to the Massey partners. Then he headed for the double doors to leave.

Panic welled within her, that she'd possibly hesitated too long to go after him. "Eric, wait!" she called as she hurried toward him.

He turned to look at her, as did at least two dozen nearby guests—including a good portion of the employees and partners she'd worked with at Massey. She felt their curious eyes on her as she closed the distance between her and Eric, no doubt speculating what was between the two of them.

She realized she didn't care. If her relationship with Eric meant never getting another freelance project with Massey, then so be it. He was all that mattered.

Lifting her chin high, she welcomed the liberating feeling setting her free and giving her the courage to be herself, to let this man bring out the very best in her. Including the love filling her heart.

Everything that needed to be said between them had already been spoken. With words and with their bodies. There was only one thing left to tell him. "I'm taking a chance on us."

He tipped his head, but there was no mistaking the relief and satisfaction etching his features. "You're taking a lot of chances tonight."

The pride in his voice warmed her. He knew how difficult this moment would be for her, and understood what it had taken for her to be so bold in front of so many witnesses. "You're worth it."

His sensual lips curved into a teasing grin. "You sure about that?"

"Absolutely." Then she proved it. Circling her arms

around his neck, she pulled his mouth to hers and kissed him in front of everyone. Much to her surprise, the crowd broke out into applause, whistles, and cheers.

She laughed, welcoming the happiness that bubbled through her, and knew everything would work out just fine. "Take me home, Eric," she whispered in his ear, needing to be alone with him. "I'm in the mood for something Wilde."

He grinned at her play on words, and swept her up into his strong arms. "Now that's a request I'd be more than happy to accommodate."

Touch Me

Shannon McKenna

Chapter One

Tomorrow at four, tomorrow at four. Jonah's appointment was tomorrow at four. The thought looped through Tess Langley's mind with the annoying persistence of a commercial jingle, the only diffcrence being the jangling, feverish edge to the tune.

Mrs. Vailstock had canceled, leaving her a blessed free hour, so there was no need to rush as she ticked off the points on her checklist: heating pad, fresh sheets, adjust the massage table for her next client, blankets, towels. She rummaged through the tape box until she found the whale songs, and lit a pink Love Dreams candle. Irene's favorites.

The busier she kept herself, the less liable she was to start mooning over Jonah Markham's storm gray eyes, his sensual lips, his unimaginably perfect body. Or writhing over the effect he had upon her. He left her tongue-tied, practically blithering. Thank God the service she provided for him didn't require her to speak much.

It wasn't just that he was gorgeous and built. Sports

massage was one of her specialties, and she had many pro athlete clients with incredible bodies. Kneading their muscles was interesting from an aesthetic point of view, but had never thrown her into a tizzy of speechless lust before. No, Jonah Markham was special. Whenever she touched him, something magical happened. A tingling rush of enhanced sensory awareness, as if someone had slipped an aphrodisiac into her mug of organic green tea. For heaven's sake, he wasn't even due in today. It was stupid and unprofessional to fixate on a client. Particularly not a guy who ought to have "trouble" tattooed on his forehead. It had taken all her courage to get where she was right now, and would take another quantum leap to get where she wanted to go. What she did *not* need in her life was an arrogant, brooding, drop-dead gorgeous sex god who probably went through women the way he went through socks.

Concentrate, she told herself. She was so tired, and Irene Huppert was coming in at six, the compulsive talker with sciatica. Yay, hurray. She squirted grape seed oil into a bottle and personalized it with lemongrass and lavender essential oils, her mind racing. A guy like him could never be interested in her, at least not for long, and really, it was just as well, she told herself desperately. She didn't even have the energy to keep a cat, let alone invest in the care and feeding of a hungry male ego. And Jonah Markham was bound to have . . . a big one. So to speak.

So why couldn't she stop thinking about him?

Because he asked you out last week, airhead, whispered the little devil on her shoulder. Wonder of wonders. And the week before, and the week before that. At the beginning of his session, he'd turned his close-cropped dark head, and fixed his gaze upon her face like a hot gray tractor beam. "You married?"

Her mouth flapped uselessly for a moment. "Uh, no."

He didn't even blink. "Boyfriend?"

She fully intended to roll out her well-rehearsed, friendly-but-not-too-friendly "I'm not available" routine. It jammed, and all that escaped her was a strangled little "No." He gave a short, satisfied nod, and laid his head down, closing his eyes. At which point, she had seen the claw marks on his shoulders. Long and red and angry looking.

She'd stared in horrified fascination for almost a minute before she'd finally worked up the nerve to begin, very carefully. Those gouges had to hurt. Finally, she'd just shut her eyes to block them out.

As always, she'd been swept away by the spell of touching him, which left her woefully unprepared when she lifted her hands off his body, still soaring on a thunderous rush of unfamiliar endorphins, and heard, "Will you have dinner with me?"

She had to be dreaming. Hallucinating. She was speechless, rattled, blushing . . . and so incredibly tempted. Even if she ended up getting used and tossed away, she was willing to bet that being used by Jonah Markham would be one hell of a memorable experience.

So would the tossing away part, unfortunately.

She let out the trapped air in her lungs. "No," she said quietly.

His dark brows snapped together. "Why not?"

She fished around for a good brush-off, polite and yet forceful. Nothing floated to the surface of her brain but the raw, uncensored truth. *Because you've obviously just had wild crazy sex with a woman who's way more responsive and uninhibited in bed than I am.*

"I'm sorry, Mr. Markham, but we've run overtime,

and Mr. Stillman is waiting." Her words sounded lame and flat. A pitiable evasion.

She was convinced that she would never see him again, but the next week he was back, right on time. And at the end of his massage, he asked the same question. The claw marks had faded away, but her memory of them had not. She refused again. Last week, he was back again, with dogged persistence in his eyes. Same question, same answer, same long, searching look that probed her motives, challenged her fears. She wondered if he would ask again tomorrow.

Which must mean, God help her, that she was actually beginning to consider it. She'd been depressed for days after seeing those claw marks, but she'd also lain awake nights wondering what exactly he'd done to that woman to make her react like that. Which led to a whole host of other fantasies, as uncontrollable as they were inappropriate.

Like, what might happen if she just bent over one day and kissed the supple, velvety skin at the curve of his neck, right where his hair was razored off in a sleek line. His neck was so thick and strong. Tense, badly in need of soothing, stroking.

The neck-kissing impulse was sparked by not just lust, but something that felt almost like tenderness. The alarming thought made her squirm. Tenderness? She didn't even know the guy. How pathetic and absurd to project her lonesome, love-starved fancies onto him. But the back of his neck still called to her. So deliciously . . . kissable.

He had surrendered the rigid armature of his muscles to her with such perfect trust, she had been startled and moved. Such a thing occurred more often with dancers, or practitioners of massage, yoga, or other bodywork. People who were used to exploring other dimensions of sensory awareness, who were accustomed to profound relaxation and trance states. It never happened with men like him. High-powered, cutthroat businessmen without a fanciful bone in their bodies. Men who never let down their guard, or dared to be vulnerable.

Vulnerable, my butt, she told herself. The only vulnerable one around here was Tess Langley, starry-eyed idiot, and the only thing she should allow herself to obsess about was saving up the money to open her studio. She didn't have the looks, the legs, or the wardrobe to be part of that guy's harem. She knew better than to try to be something she was not. Been there, done that, crashed and burned to a blackened hulk. From here on out, it was no-frills, no makeup, sensible shoes, what-you-see-is-what-you-get Tess.

She repeated that sobering resolution to herself, forcing herself to picture the kind of woman Jonah Markham usually dated. Tall and leggy, not like her shrimpy five foot two. Gym-toned, hard-bodied, not round and over-full in the chest and rear. Perfectly dressed and styled, like she'd tried so hard to be for Larry. All that effort. All in vain.

Forget it. Just say no. She knew how this movie would end. He would take what he could get and bore very quickly—but not quickly enough. Not before the damage was done. She'd just barely succeeded in piecing herself back together after the Larry debacle, and here she was, contemplating hurling all that carefully reconstructed self-esteem right through the plate glass window that was Jonah Markham.

Bet he's good in bed . . . The red-clad devil waggled her pitchfork as she chirped that thought into Tess's ear. *Good like Larry wasn't. Good like you've never imagined. Looks like he's had loads of practice.*

She was startled out of that disturbing but highly stimulating line of thought by a commotion up front. Lacey, the receptionist, was yelling. Someone was shouting back. A deep, resonant male voice.

Dear God. It was him. But he was Thursday, not Wednesday. This wasn't possible. She wasn't constitutionally capable of confusing that particular appointment. She hustled out of the back rooms, and sure enough, there he was, glaring down at Lacey over the receptionist's counter. His eyes flicked up to her, like chips of gray ice.

"What's wrong?" Tess demanded. "Did I make a mistake in the scheduling?" They both started to talk at once. Tess clapped. The explosive sound cut them off into a startled silence.

"People are getting massages! Keep your voices down! What is going on?" She jerked her chin at Lacey. "You first."

Lacey flounced her hair with her usual self-importance. "Mr. Markham wants an emergency appointment! I explained to him that you're booked up, and he can wait till six if he wants Elsa, and he—"

"All I asked was if it would be possible to reschedule another one of your clients today," Jonah broke in icily. "Offer a free massage to whoever you reschedule, and I'll pay for it. Hell, offer them two."

"But she's *booked,* I already *told* you, and it's not our *policy* to—"

"Stop, Lacey!" Tess held up her hand and studied his face.

He looked tense and strained, his eyes hollow, his mouth white about the lips. He was hanging on by a thread. She knew that feeling all too well. She wished she knew him well enough to ask what was wrong.

Jonah let out a long, controlled sigh. "At the end of

the day?" There was a tight, pleading edge to his voice. "After your last client?"

"No way am I staying late to lock up after you!" Lacey piped up. "And no way would Jeanette let a therapist stay in the center all alone with a client! I'll just call Jeanette right now, and she can deal with—"

"No," Tess said quietly. "Don't call Jeanette."

She knew how that would play. Jeanette would come thundering out of the back office. She would throw her weight around until Jonah was completely affronted. He would storm off and never come back.

She couldn't bear the thought of it.

Besides, she wanted to comfort him, soothe him, pet him until he felt better. Until the tension melted out of his face and body, until he purred with bliss. She was a pushover, a softie, a blithering idiot, but she was nudging Lacey out of the way and dialing Irene's number.

Lacey's painted eyes grew wide with outrage. "You're actually going to let him get away with bullying me?"

Tess waved her down. "Hello? Irene? It's Tess, at the Multnomah Massage Center, and I . . . yes, I'm so glad I caught you at home. I just wanted to . . ." It took two minutes of false tries to trample on Irene's prattling monologue. "Irene, please let me finish. I've had an emergency . . . nothing terrible, but would you be kind enough to let me reschedule you for tomorrow at four? Oh, thanks . . . no. Chloe isn't the one who's going to be looking at that stenciling every day. You are. Tell me about it tomorrow, OK? Bye." She hung up, and shot a quick, guilty look at Lacey.

"That is, like, so totally unprofessional," Lacey hissed. "Jeanette is gonna have kittens when she finds out."

"Jeanette can fire me if she likes," Tess said, with forced bravado. She turned to Jonah. "You—" she sternly indicated a seat, "—wait quietly while I prepare the room. And Lacey, please pretend he's not there. No more yelling or rudeness. Is that clear?"

Lacey flipped her hair and pouted. Jonah sat and lifted his big shoulders in a meek little "who, me?" shrug.

The room was ready, but she went down her checklist, just to calm herself. She adjusted the table. Lavender and lemongrass weren't right for Jonah. She filled a bottle with almond oil, and added some sandalwood oil and just a touch of coriander. Her heart had to slow down before she marched out there, all calm and businesslike, and—

"You ready?"

She spun around and dropped the oil. "You scared me!"

"Sorry." He scooped up the bottle that was rolling toward him. "The receptionist from hell was making personal phone calls, so I—"

"Lacey is not a receptionist from hell." Tess snatched the oil out of his hand. "She is a very good receptionist. When treated nicely."

"I was perfectly nice," he growled. "I even offered her a big tip. What's with the candle?"

She remembered the hot pink, embarrassingly phallic candle, with "Love Dreams" scripted on it in pale, glowing wax. She lunged to blow it out. "Um . . . nothing. It was for Irene. My six o'clock."

"You could've left it burning." His deep voice made the fine hairs prickle on her neck. "I like love dreams as much as the next guy."

The room seemed breathlessly warm. "Go ahead and get ready," Tess murmured, sidling past him. "I'll be back in a few minutes."

When she stole back into the room a few minutes

later, he was laid out between the sheets. No claw marks today, thank goodness.

She put oil on her hands, and smoothed them over his back, tracing ropy knots of tension with her fingers. He hissed in pain, his muscles twitching. "You're very tense," she said. "Did you get a chance to do those stretching exercises I recommended last week?"

"Too busy. Crazy week."

"Try to make the time," she urged. "They really will help."

"You're always scolding me." He twisted around, and his gaze swept over her as if that hideous white dress that Jeanette mandated was actually sexy. "But that's OK. I kind of like it."

She gaped at him. "I do not scold!"

"Next you'll tell me I'm a very bad boy and need to be punished. I'm already laid out on the table, ass-up. Go ahead. Smack me one."

Tess drew in a shaky breath. Suggestive comments were wildly inappropriate in the context of a therapeutic massage. She would be within her rights to stop the session.

It was the very last thing she wanted to do.

She cast around for the perfect response in their gentle game of deflect and evade. Something to keep him at arm's length, and yet not threaten their delicate equilibrium. She didn't want to drive him away. She desperately needed something sparkling and effervescent in her life, even if it were just a faraway fantasy. Life without weekly doses of Jonah would be intolerably drab and savorless.

She placed her hand between his shoulder blades and pushed him gently down. "I think you've had a very stressful day," she said softly. "And we are both going to forget that you just said that."

He was quiet as she spread oil across the quivering muscles in his shoulders with broad, circular strokes. "Sorry," he muttered.

"Shhh," she whispered.

It took longer than usual for him to calm down, but eventually the door between them opened up like Aladdin's cave. Everything she'd ever learned in massage school or technique workshops melted away, along with every other conscious thought. His body was a vast landscape for her to wander through, following pure instinct, raw feeling. Horizon upon horizon, wild and exotic and unknown.

She wanted to map them all.

Her voice floated to him from so far away that the words had no meaning. All he caught was the caressing tone in her husky alto voice. He had to hold the words in a containing cell in his blissed-out mind until he woke up enough to process the data.

He fished the words out of the containing cell when the fog cleared. It was just what she always said. *"Take a few minutes to come back before you get dressed. I'll be out front."*

How could such an innocuous statement sound so sexy? He swung his legs down from the table, sat up, and dropped his face into his hands. Massive boner, of course, but he was used to that by now.

He rubbed his face, and bit by bit, the painful details of his monumentally horrible day floated back to him. The early morning call about the heart attack. Granddad with an oxygen mask and tubes stuck in him, sniping at him from his hospital bed, telling him to get lost. His cousins John and Steve, staring at him from across the room with blatant loathing. And as if that wasn't enough, the apocalyptic scene in the restaurant with Cynthia three weeks ago had to come floating back, too. He'd have been better off not remembering.

Too bad he couldn't maintain the floating high that Tess's massages gave him, but he would have to abuse controlled substances to maintain that kind of buzz. Not his scene. He was doomed to keep both feet flat on the concrete. A chip off old Granddad's block.

The up side, of course, was that if the old bastard had enough energy to kick Jonah's ass out of his hospital room, then he must not be ready to die yet. Even if Granddad wouldn't speak to him or forgive him, he was still roaring like a steam engine, making noise, dominating his world. He allowed himself to be comforted by that.

He put his watch back on. She'd massaged him for almost an hour and a half. Yeah, she liked him for sure. He grinned as he pulled on his clothes, remembering how tense and awkward he'd been the first time he'd walked into the place. He'd only done it because his office staff had gotten together and bought him a six-massage package at the Multnomah Massage Center, and though they'd laughed it off as a gag gift, it was a pretty damn costly gag gift. It had gotten his attention, conscious as he was of exactly how much he paid them all. Besides, Eileen, his assistant, had seen to it that he got the real message, which was *"Dude, you are losing it, and you need to chill. Right now."*

Then his doctor told him that the headaches were due to muscle tension and the stomachaches were from the painkillers he took for the headaches. Yo, bozo. You're creating the perfect conditions for an ulcer.

Fine. Message received; everybody could stop beating the dead horse, already. He would get some freaking massages.

Then Tess had walked into the waiting room and called out his name. Shaken his hand with her small, capable-looking hand. Looked him over with those big, tilted gold-green eyes. Asked him brisk, businesslike questions about his medical history, his headaches, his back pain. What a turn-on. Who'd have thought.

She was so pretty, in a subtle and yet luscious sort of way. With those generous tits, tightly constrained in the white dress that was clearly designed to discourage sensual thoughts while utterly failing to do so. Her Jennifer Lopez-esque ass, which he checked out thoroughly as he followed her into the back room. A few massages from that bodacious little number suddenly seemed like a very good idea.

It had taken him the entire first session just to get used to the concept of someone touching him for any reason other than to make him hot. Hah. Tell that to his cock. It had no clue.

Truth was, just lusting after his massage therapist wouldn't have been such a big deal. So what? He would just keep his boxers on and stay rigorously face down. It was what happened during the massages that blew his mind. She put her hands on him and *zing,* the world turned upside down. Since Granddad's business troubles, and the subsequent series of heart attacks, Jonah's stomach had been in knots, his lungs tight and constricted, his mind racing day and night. But when Tess touched him, his mind slipped loose of that frantically spinning hamster's wheel of anger and regret, frustration and guilt. It floated unexpectedly free, into a vast open space that he exhaled his whole self into, with a rush of relief so intense it almost made him want to cry. Though thank God, it had never come to that.

He was strung out on her. Look at him, running straight from the hospital to the massage center like a toddler running to his mommy to get his owie kissed. Throwing a goddamn tantrum in the waiting room, for Christ's sake. His out-of-control desperation was kind of freaky.

And his crush on Tess had gotten way out of hand, too. When he was all loosey goosey and dazzled from one of her massages, she looked like she was lit from within. Resplendent. The luminous, delicate flush on her lovely face, devoid of makeup. The wavy chestnut hair, wound into a braided bun so tight that he could never get a good sense of how long it was. Today, adorable fuzzy bits corkscrewed around her slender neck. Soft and tousled and sensual. Yum.

She kept blowing him off when he asked her out, but he couldn't seem to stop trying. To hell with dignity. The words just popped out of him. Whenever she leaned over him, he caught whiffs of her scent. Not like the nose-tickling, knock-you-on-your-ass Eau de Whatever that Cynthia drenched herself in. More like rain on a spring night. Cool, leafy. Lemon and mint, wood and water. Vanishing before he could pull enough into his lungs to satisfy himself, leaving him gasping for more.

And then there was the sweep of her eyebrows, with the little swirling snarl of darker hair marking the crest of the arch. The black, curling lashes. And her lips. Damn. His cock had just started to calm down to socially acceptable proportions, and he'd ruined it by picturing the crease down the middle of her plump lower lip, dividing it into two succulent, kissable pink cushions. He'd have to drape his jacket carefully over his crotch when he marched out front. As usual.

She was standing next to the Devil Receptionist from Mars, who was giving him the death-ray look. Time to bump back into reality.

The receptionist flipped her big hair and opened the appointment book. "Same time? Or do you anticipate any more *emergencies?*"

"Could I schedule an appointment for this weekend?"

"No way." Lacey was clearly delighted to thwart him. "Elsa could—"

"I am not interested in an appointment with Elsa," he snarled. He turned to Tess with the most coaxing, soulful puppy-dog look he could muster. "Couldn't you rearrange your schedule again? Like today?"

A rueful smile activated the little dimples at the corners of Tess's mouth. "It was a mistake, letting you get away with this. I've spoiled you rotten. Now there'll be no reasoning with you."

"Yeah," he agreed swiftly. "I'm completely ruined. So can you?"

She shook her head. "Not a chance. I won't even be here this weekend. I'll be working up at Cedar Hills Resort."

"All weekend? How much do they pay you for that?"

Lacey bristled in outrage. "None of your business!"

"Shall we put you down for the usual time?" Tess asked gently.

He nodded as he wrote out the check. Nothing more to be gained from talking to her while that extraterrestrial harpy looked on, but the thought of Tess giving massages at a resort planted an idea in his head.

He wandered out onto the street and turned it over in his head. Her car was parked across the street in front of a Starbucks. He would get a decaf, in honor of the fact that he'd just spent eighty bucks trying to relax, and let his plan develop while he waited for her to come out.

He got his coffee and checked out the surreal art that hung by his table. A painting of a floating, naked transparent guy with clouds inside him. New Age fluff, but it reminded him of himself during one of Tess's massages. Maybe she put him in a hypnotic trance. Some brain wave thing. He'd read articles about stuff like that, in health magazines that he found in the bathrooms of other people's beach houses. He imagined his body as a revolving galaxy of light, visited by a benevolent feminine entity with small, strong hands that glowed with life-giving heat. Yikes. He'd been catching too many late-night *Star Trek* reruns lately.

But being a relatively normal guy, and as such, having an appropriately dirty mind, the next obvious question was, what would sex be like under such conditions?

Sexually, he was very skilled and aggressive. It was a game of conquest, a hot, sweaty duel, and orgasms were points he scored in the game. He liked to make his lovers have lots of them. That was how he won. And he wanted to win with Tess Langley. He wanted to kiss that luscious mouth, pop open the buttons on that kinky white dress, stroke and lick and suckle her until she screamed with pleasure. But as he stared at the naked floating guy, a suspicion began to form inside him.

The rules of the game as he knew it would be null and void in that magic landscape where he went with Tess. He would be brand-new, a bumbling beginner. Vulnerable and helpless.

The idea intrigued him as much as it alarmed him.

"Excuse me."

Tess stifled a squeak as she spun around. Her nerves

couldn't take much more of this overstimulation. "Were you following me?"

"Just waiting." His voice was defensive. "That doesn't count as following. I have a business proposition, and I couldn't talk about it in front of your colleague. Let me buy you a drink. I'll tell you about it."

He waited patiently while she made repeated attempts to access that part of her brain that governed speech. Seconds ticked by. He frowned. "Got other plans? A date?" His eyes swept over her, taking note of the hideous white uniform under her jacket, the white shoes.

Date, hah. Just a half-formed plan to flop openmouthed on the couch and watch *Frasier,* or *Xena,* or whatever else she found channel surfing. Hardly a reason to not have a drink with the sexiest man she'd ever seen in real life. She shook her head. "No date."

"Great. There's a restaurant at the end of the block."

He got right to the point as soon as they were seated in the bar, and lucky for her, since she was too tonguetied to handle chitchat.

"When you said you were working at a resort all weekend, it gave me an idea," he told her. "I want you to come up to my house at Cougar Lake, and do the same thing for me. Friday night."

"This Friday? For . . . you? But—"

"For my house party," he clarified. "I'm having people up this weekend, and I'd like to surprise them with something special."

She covered her confusion taking a nervous sip of her Dos Equis. "It doesn't sound very ethical," she said. "The MMC—"

"The MMC would never know. And it would be lucrative. I pay eighty bucks for a massage here. What percentage of that do you get?"

She hesitated, biting her lip.

He nodded, looking satisfied. "Exactly. I'll give you twenty-five hundred. A thousand a day, and five hundred for Friday night."

She was dumbfounded at the sum. "But that's . . ." She choked off the words *too much*. Such words didn't belong in the vocabulary of a future entrepreneur. "But I'm already scheduled to—"

"Get someone to cover for you," he cut in. "Get this famous Elsa who's so monumentally available to do it for you."

She set down her beer with a decisive thud. "Elsa is an excellent massage therapist," she said crisply. "Come to think of it, you might call her for your party. You would have no complaints if—"

"No. I want you." There was a bright, steely glint in his eyes.

Yeah, that's the problem, right there, she almost blurted. "I don't think it would be a good idea," she said hesitantly. "I really don't like the idea of going behind my employer's back, and furthermore—"

"Four thousand." He gave her a winning smile.

She gasped. "But I . . . I wasn't bargaining with you! I can't—"

"I'll write you a check for two thousand now." He pulled out his checkbook. "I'll give you the rest when you get there on Friday night."

Her spine stiffened up, ramrod straight. "Money is not the point!"

He glanced up from the checkbook. "Money is always the point." His tone suggested that he was stating something painfully obvious.

Her chin lifted. "Not with me, it isn't."

And it wasn't. That was one of the vows she'd made when she left her old life behind. She'd left her old values, too. Or rather, the values that others had imposed upon her. Money would never rule her again.

Jonah studied her for a moment. He signed the check, ripped it out, and laid it on the bar, equidistant between their two beers. "So what is the point, then?" He sounded genuinely curious.

She stared at his jagged black signature. Two thousand dollars. Another two on Friday. With what she'd already saved, and a couple of loans, she'd be able to quit the MMC and open her studio right now.

She swallowed, and looked away. "I do strictly therapeutic massage," she said stiffly. "Going to the private home of a man I don't know seems to invite misunderstanding. You must know what I mean."

His sensual mouth curved. "Of course I know what you mean. I just get a kick out of watching you blush."

She leaped off the bar stool and backed away. "You know what? It's just exactly that sort of flirtatious, inappropriate comment that makes me nervous."

"Sorry, sorry," he said hastily. "Relax. My guests know what a professional massage therapist does and doesn't do. And so do I. I'm not inviting you to an orgy. Bring a friend, if it makes you feel better. Bring a squad of Ninja bodyguards. There's plenty of room." His expression was so winsome and contrite that her face ached to smile back. He put his finger on the check and pushed it toward her. Slowly. Inch by inch.

She looked away, flustered. "I have to think. And I have see if someone can cover for me at Cedar Hills."

He fished a card out of his wallet and wrote two numbers on the back. "Home phone and cell phone. Call me anytime." He leaned forward and tucked his card and his check into the breast pocket of her denim jacket, ignoring the flinch and tremor that his touch provoked. "Take the check, too. Meditate on it." His eyes flicked down over her body. "I'm hungry. Can I buy you some dinner?"

She backed up another step, holding her purse in front of her.

His eyes gleamed with silent amusement. "Oh, yeah, I forgot. You've got something against having dinner with me. Wish I knew why."

"I don't have anything against you," she babbled, taking another step back. "I'm just not dressed for dinner, and I have to go. Right now."

"Hey. Tess."

The quiet force in his voice stopped her. She shot a nervous glance over her shoulder. "Yes?"

"I'm harmless," he said. "Really. I swear. A great big pussycat."

Pussycat. She imagined petting him, making him purr and stretch. Sinuous and sensual . . . and predatory.

"Yeah, right," she muttered. "Totally harmless."

She turned, and fled.

Chapter Two

"Yo, Tess. I just found your purse in the fridge. You going to tell your good buddy Trish what's up, or am I gonna have to nag?"

Tess looked up from her tepid mug of tea, and took the purse that Trish held out. The leather was clammy. "It's cold," she mumbled.

"Duh." Trish popped open her Diet Coke and sat down, fixing her roommate with an eagle-eyed stare. "So?"

Tess let the purse drop. "I got a business proposition today."

"So far, so good." Trish gave her an encouraging nod.

"From Jonah Markham. Remember the guy I told you about?"

"Oh, my God. The to-die-for handsome one who melts your brain?"

"The very one," Tess admitted.

Trish whistled. "How titillating. What's the proposition?"

Tess squeezed her eyes shut and braced herself for Trish's reaction. "That I go out to his house on Cougar Lake this weekend and give massages to his house-guests. For four thousand dollars."

Trish's cornflower-blue eyes widened. "Whoa! For four thousand bucks, I hope you're gonna give him a blow job, too."

Tess leaped up as if she'd been stung. "Trish! That's not funny!"

"So who's kidding?" Trish asked in a plaintive voice. "Come on, Tess, not even a hand job? With some of that perfumed oil you use? I can see it now, Mr. Pecs-R-Us with bedroom eyes, all tousled and ripped and bulging, just begging you to rub on his big, stiff—"

"You are incorrigible." Tess stomped into the kitchen and dumped the cooled tea into the sink.

Trish followed her in, undaunted. "That can't possibly sting you. You live like a nun, chica. It's high time you got some decent nooky. I'd pay four thousand bucks myself to get you some, if I could afford it."

Ignoring her was clearly not going to work. "Wasn't Tyler supposed to take you out on a dinner cruise tonight?"

"Not for another hour or so," Trish said cheerfully. "You're stuck with me, sweet pea. Let's discuss your outfit, shall we? You aren't going to wear the Vee Have Vays To Make You Talk monstrosity Jeanette makes you wear. Tell me that you're not."

Tess marched past her into the living room. "I haven't even decided if I'm going," she said stiffly. "And if I do, I'd better stick with the Vee Have Vays dress. It'll help me keep some professional distance and authority."

"Screw distance and authority. How about that flame-red stretch lace teddy that I got you for Christmas?"

"Trish." She gritted her teeth. "Read my lips. I am not going out there to have sex. No sex. None. Got it? If I go, it'll be for the money."

"Money's great, but money *and* sex are better," Trish pointed out.

Tess pretended not to hear. "With that four thousand, I could open my studio without making any . . . unacceptable compromises."

"Like asking your folks for help?"

Tess winced. "I'd only rather be dipped in boiling lead."

The phone rang. They stared at it, then at each other. "Speak of the devil," Trish said. "Whenever your family is mentioned, she calls."

"I wasn't the one who brought them up," Tess snapped. "Thanks a lot, Trish." She sighed and picked up the phone. "Hello?"

"Well, well, well. This is my youngest daughter, isn't it? I'm not quite sure, you see. I've forgotten what your voice sounds like."

Tess rolled her eyes at Trish. "Hello, Mom. How's everybody?"

"Oh, so so. We miss you terribly. Daddy wants you to know that your job is still open, honey bunch. Anytime you come to your senses."

Tess's stomach knotted with an old, familiar pain. "I'm not coming back, Mom."

"Oh, Tessie, honey, when are you going to grow up? My headaches are terrible since you left, and Larry's just pining away—"

"Oh, please. He can't possibly be pining, since he never cared about me in the first place. I was just the boss's daughter, that's all."

"Tess! That is unkind, and untrue! I know Larry as

well as I know my own children! He's putting a brave face on it, but everybody knows you broke his heart, running off like you did. But know what I think, hon? I think there's still hope. If you came back, Larry would—"

"You don't get it, Mom." The weariness that Jonah's massage had dispelled crashed down upon her. She flopped onto the couch.

"What I don't get, darling, is why you're being so obstinate. What am I supposed to tell my friends? That my smart little girl, who did so well in business school and had such a lucrative career ahead of her, to say nothing of a dream of a fiancé, just threw it all away to work in a massage parlor? It's barely respectable! What's that, Bill? . . . oh, that's funny. Daddy says next you'll be reading Tarot cards!"

"Nothing wrong with that." Tess's words cut off her mother's tinkling laughter. "Some of my friends make a nice living reading Tarot."

Tess squeezed her eyes shut as she waited out the cold silence.

"You are deliberately missing my point, Tessie," her mother said.

"Therapeutic massage takes talent and training. And I'm very good at it." Tess felt like she was running a scratchy, worn-out promo tape for some unwanted product. "It's a very respectable career choice."

"Maybe for some people, but not for a Langley! You should be working in the family firm, like you planned ever since you were little!"

"Like *you* planned," Tess said, though she knew it was futile.

"You're just doing this to upset me, aren't you? You should get therapy, dear, really you should. Because the person you're actually punishing is yourself. You're barely scraping by. You work so hard you didn't even have time to come home for Melissa's birthday party!"

"Did she get the present I sent?" Tess tried to deflect her mother's relentless trajectory, to no avail.

"The point is that your current profession is a financial dead end compared to working for Daddy. Oh, Daddy just made Larry CEO, by the way. And if you come home, Daddy will give you a raise of—"

"I'm opening my own massage studio," Tess blurted.

There was another gelid silence. "I beg your pardon?"

"I've already got a client base," Tess said desperately. "I get lots of referrals. I'm very confident that it'll go well."

"Opening your own studio?" Her mother repeated the words as if she couldn't quite grasp them. "And where did you get the capital?"

"I've been scrimping and saving," Tess said, crossing her fingers.

Trish made a questioning gesture, asking if Tess wanted her to leave the room. Tess shook her head and waved her back down onto the couch. "This is something I've wanted for a long time, Mom."

The silence on the other end of the line made her want to scream.

"Well," her mother said. "I suppose there's nothing more to say."

"You could wish me luck," Tess suggested softly.

"I'm sure you'll need it. Good-bye, dear."

The line went dead. Tess lay the phone down, chin quivering.

All teasing was gone from Trish's face. "You've boxed yourself into a corner, chica. You're gonna need that gig out on the lake, now. She's for sure gonna check up on you to see if it's true. She never lets up."

Tess let the phone drop to her lap. "It'll be true," she said in a small voice. "With that money, I can do this on my own. I know it."

"Of course you can." Trish got up and rummaged through the clutter on the phone table until she found Tess's address book. She sat down next to Tess, plucked the phone off her lap and dialed.

"What are you doing?" she asked suspiciously.

"Helping you. You're too rattled to do this by yourself. You, like, just refrigerated your purse. Oh, hi, Elsa? Yeah, this is Trish, Tess's roommate. I'm her personal secretary tonight. Are you free to cover for her at Cedar Hills this weekend? . . . Yeah? Really? Oh, awesome. I'll tell her. Yeah, she really owes you one. Thanks, Elsa."

Trish hung up, her face glowing with triumphant satisfaction. "The coast is clear! Now you've just gotta call up Mr. Deltoids and tell him you'd be thrilled to get paid four thousand big ones for the privilege of running your hands all over his gorgeous bod."

Tess fished Jonah's card and check out of her pocket, and stared at them. She picked up the phone with cold, shaky fingers. "I need privacy for this call," she said faintly. "I'm going into the bedroom."

Trish bounced with glee. "Take all the privacy you need, cupcake!"

"Oh, stop it," she said halfheartedly. "This is a business thing."

Trish's voice followed her into the bedroom. "Sure it is, chica. Hey. Promise me you'll at least pack the red lace teddy. Pretty please?"

"Enough!" She slammed the door, and stood for a

moment in the dark room, clutching the cordless phone. She fingered Jonah's card as she sank down onto her bed. Weak in the knees. Scared to death.

But it wasn't Jonah she was afraid of. Not really. All alone in the darkness, it was easier to admit to that what really terrified her was her own aching hunger for magic, for sensuality, for something real and shining. A real life. Maybe even . . . a real love.

That was why she'd run away from Larry, the picture perfect fiancé who had made her feel so small, she'd almost disappeared. It was why she had run from her suffocating family, and the lucrative job that she hated. She had been running toward a romantic dream of joy and fulfilment. It was that dream that made her so vulnerable. Jonah Markham shocked all of her intense romantic longings to life, along with knee-trembling physical desire. A devastating combination.

She wandered over to her dresser and flipped on the light, unbuttoning the white dress with a sigh of relief. The cheap synthetic fabric did not breathe. She gave her body a long, critical look in the mirror, and rummaged through her top drawer until she found the gift box that held the red lace teddy Trish had given her. It had been a while since she'd tried it on. It was time for another look.

She struggled out of the rest of her clothes, and pulled the fragile thing on, looking at herself from all angles. Wow. It barely covered her nipples with scalloped red lace, leaving the entire bulging top of her bosom bare. She struck a pose, and tried to look sultry. She looked almost aggressively sexy. It made her think of—oh, no. Please, no.

She tried to shake away the memory, but it had a will of its own. It rose up in minute, painful detail. That day in the department store fitting room, when her

mother had tried to persuade her to consider breast re-
duction surgery. *"Really, hon, D cup breasts are ridiculous for a girl your size. They look disproportionate.
Like you're trying to draw attention to yourself. Larry
agrees with me, you know. And such a big bosom gives
the impression that you're overweight, when you're really not. Not that much, at least."*

She put her hands on her breasts, covering them,
and willed the memory away with all her strength. She
was a different person from that luckless, stomped-
upon, past Tess. She had recreated herself. And her
bosom was just fine exactly the way it was, thank you
very much.

She peeled the teddy off, carefully avoiding the sight
of her own naked body. She yanked on an old, wilted
flannel nightshirt, but sensual images kept creeping
back into her mind. Herself in the red lace teddy, thrusting out her boobs as if she were fiercely proud of them.
An arch in her back worthy of a Playboy bunny. And
Jonah, on his knees, all bulging muscles and bedroom
eyes, begging her to rub on his big, stiff . . . hold it.
Don't do it, don't go there, don't lift that towel, her rational self pleaded. But the red-clad devil just used her
little pitchfork to snag the edge of Jonah's imaginary
towel, and flung it off him with a shrill cackle.

She imagined him stark naked. Staring up at her
with that hot, dark, no-turning-back look in his eyes.
His body, hers to please herself with. A heaving ocean
of pleasure and danger. She wanted to fling herself into
it. Her lower body tightened with a restless ache that
stole her breath, that made her want to whimper and
squirm and press her legs together. This feeling was
unfamiliar, almost frightening.

She had to keep in mind that she was no red-hot love
goddess in bed. Larry had made that very clear. She

was a good listener, she baked great brownies, and she gave unbeatable backrubs, but sex with her was like trying to light a fire with a wet match. She had counted herself lucky if she could get through it without too much discomfort.

And she would just die if she had to see that look of polite disappointment on Jonah Markham's face. Better a lifetime of celibacy.

She needed to think positive, to concentrate on her strengths, not her weaknesses. To remember how great it would be to open her own studio, to achieve autonomy, independence, success. To follow through on her own dreams and plans, and no one else's. To prove to her family, once and for all, that she was capable of making it on her own.

Nothing was going to stop her. Certainly not a silly spasm of lust.

Braced by that hopeful thought, she picked up the phone.

Four thousand bucks. Ouch. He'd officially lost his mind.

Jonah let himself into his apartment and dropped the takeout Chinese on the table. It wasn't that he couldn't afford it. He had plenty of money. He was just appalled at his own reckless extravagance. Just one more example of the unnerving desperation that Tess inspired.

Then again, the weekend with Cynthia at Lake Tahoe had cost a lot more than that, and he hadn't even come home relaxed. He winced, imagining what Granddad would've said if he'd seen the Lake Tahoe credit card bill. Granddad believed that frugality was a virtue. Too bad Jonah's cousins Steve and John, who were driving

Granddad's company into the ground, didn't adhere to that philosophy. Dickheads.

Oh, fuck 'em. Why ruin his mood thinking about those brain-dead bozos when he could think about Tess instead? Her white dress had haunted him all the way home. The way it strained across her chest made him want to rip open those buttons, rub his face against that bulging cleavage, licking and kissing like his life depended on it.

She was so self-contained and mysterious, he couldn't predict what she'd be like in bed. His fantasies morphed and changed so often that he'd run the entire gamut. Maybe beneath that shy, subtle exterior, she was a hot little nympho sex fiend. What a concept; Tess astride him and riding hard, her flushed, beautiful face flung back, moaning in a rising tempest of pleasure, her wet opening clutching his cock with each stroke. Or maybe she was the sweet, mellow, earth mother type, hugging him tenderly and making soft, encouraging sounds as he rocked his hips, sliding lazily in and out. Relaxing and delicious.

The phone rang, and he knew with every cell in his body that it was Tess. He lunged for it, and stopped. Forced himself to wait, like a teenage girl afraid to seem too eager. Two rings. Three, and he couldn't take it anymore. He snatched it up. "Hello?"

"Hello. Is this Mr. Markham?"

A wave of anticipation made him dizzy. "Hi, Tess. Call me Jonah."

"Oh. Hi. How did you know it was me?"

"I've memorized your voice." What an understatement. Her low, golden voice brushed over his nerve endings like her hair would brush over his body if it were loose. Feathery, silky, sliding, soft. Like a kiss.

She hesitated, and he forced himself to wait. He didn't dare rush her. So far, the eager, panting puppy routine had gained him nothing.

"I just wanted to tell you that I'd, uh, like to take you up on your offer. If it's still open," she said hesitantly.

"Oh, excellent." He wanted to whoop with triumph. "It's about an hour and a half from the city. What time can you be there Friday?"

"Well, my final appointment is three o'clock, since I was planning to head up to Cedar Hills, so—"

"So you could be there by six." Excitement roughened his voice.

He sensed her sudden caution in her long pause. *Chill out, bonehead.*

"If you like," she murmured.

If he liked. Hah. If she only knew. "Let me give you directions."

He managed to dictate directions to his place and say good night without blurting out anything inappropriate or otherwise making an ass of himself. He had to keep reminding himself that she hadn't agreed to wild and crazy sex. She hadn't even agreed to a date. He had no reason to hope that he might get lucky.

Of course, he almost always did, but Tess Langley was unlike any woman he knew. The usual statistical norms didn't apply with her.

He knew that she was attracted to him. He'd seen it in her eyes. She got flustered and confused, she blushed often, she forgot what she was saying, all the signs were there. But she never flirted. He didn't know how long it had been since a woman had completely stonewalled him. He threw out lure after lure, and she just brushed them aside with her shy, mysterious smile, making him feel foolish and needy and obvious. And then she put her hot, strong, sorceress's hands on him and whisked him off to never-never land.

Weird. The massages weren't sexual, but they were so much more intimate than the sex he'd had lately with Cynthia. Sex with Cynthia was sweaty and pounding and highly athletic, but not particularly intimate. He always finished feeling like he'd played a really demanding set of racquetball. To say nothing of those fucking nails. He had to hold her down on the bed at all times to keep from getting hurt. Having to apply antiseptic ointment after sex got old really fast.

Tess's nails were short, buffed to a delicate pink glow. He wanted to kiss each one. And her lips, that same soft blush pink. She had him thinking about romance, enchantment. Not racquetball. Or Bactine.

Time to get that excess oil off his skin. He wandered into the bathroom and turned on the shower. He tossed away his clothes and got underneath the hot, pounding spray, speculating about the hidden details of her stunning body as he sudsed up with shower gel. He'd seen the perfect slender ankles, graceful, rounded calves, and cute, dimpled knees. Then the skirt defeated him. He bet her thighs were sweet and soft and rounded, like her phenomenal ass. And she had a great belly, plump and Marilyn Monroe-ish. He would love to see her in low-slung jeans with a too-short tank top straining over her breasts, and that cute belly pooching out a little, just begging to be nuzzled.

Oh, hell, if he was going that way, he might as well go to the end of the line. He scooped up some lather and took himself in hand with a sigh of surrender. A guy had to do what a guy had to do if he wanted a hope in hell of sleeping tonight.

Forget the top, the jeans, the kinky white dress. He

wanted her stark naked, standing in front of him. He would lounge in a chair, throbbing cock in hand, pumping himself slowly as she turned, arching and undulating. Showing him all the dips and curves and sweet mysteries of her body. Plump breasts that would be so soft and heavy in his hands. Nipples puckered and hard, aching for his mouth.

He would tell her to change position. Widen her legs, arch her back, lift her arms, toss her hair. Put her leg up on the chair, bend over and show him that sweet, round ass, all open and ready for him. The shadowy cleft, the crimson lips of her sex. He beckoned her closer, and the fantasy split into Version A and Version B. He couldn't decide between them. In Version A, she sank to her knees, green-gold eyes glinting flirtatiously up through long dark lashes, and gripped his cock in her strong, slender hands. Then she took him into her mouth, sucking him, taking all of him, deep and hot and wet. Fantastic. The image blurred and segued seamlessly into Version B, seconded by his pumping hand, his ragged breathing. She straddled his legs and very slowly sank down until the head of his cock nudged delicately into her wet, swollen folds, probing deeper and deeper, sinking lower until he was buried inside her. He would grip her hips, right on the lush curve, and cut loose, pounding himself heavily into her moist depths. Deep and hot and faster, faster . . . oh, God. The orgasm pulsed through him. He stood there for a long time, head flung back under the stream of water. Weak-kneed, sucking air, sputtering out water.

He turned off the water, hoping only that this exercise in self-indulgence had cleared his head enough to start coming up with a plan.

Damn. A house party. It was going to be tricky, to make his lie into a truth at such short notice.

To hell with it. A solution would come to him. That was his genius, finding solutions to problems. More important, and more fun, was to plan the menu. He had to schedule a trip to the gourmet grocery. Order the pastry from that kick-ass fabulous bakery next to his office. And he had to give some serious thought to the wines, too.

It all had to be perfect for her.

The sky was streaked with sunset pink when Tess peered for the last time at the directions taped to her dashboard, and made the turnoff into the driveway. She drove down a narrow road through towering pines and firs. She saw the glimmer of lake water, then the house, and was abruptly sure she'd gotten the right place.

It was a simple, angular place that blended harmoniously with its surroundings. Larger than it appeared, a subtle, weathered color like the rocks at the lakeside, it had a deep terrace and picture windows looking out at the lake and Mt. Hood. The only vehicle was a black Ford pickup, which seemed odd. Maybe his guests were late.

She got out and looked around, enchanted. The trees that framed the lake seemed at first glance to be an impenetrable dark wall, but when she looked deeper, she glimpsed vaulted depths, vast inner spaces. A fragrant mystery, redolent with tree resin, wood, and water.

The lake lapped tenderly against pebbles and tree roots that descended right down into the water. She saw no neighbors, no powerboats. The slosh and gurgle of the little waves was sensual, almost hypnotic. She gazed at the perfect reflection of the mountain in the lake water, blazing with wild colors and rippling in the soft breeze.

It was so beautiful, her throat tightened and her eyes

stung. Nature beckoned to her with its savage allure. It didn't pretend to be anything. It had nothing to prove. It had no need to impress or placate or convince. It just was what it was, with serene indifference. Complete unto itself. Dear God, how she wished she could be like that.

The screen door squeaked. Usually when she was awestruck and torn open by the beauty and mystery of the ocean, or a sunset, or the stars, the feeling diminished when another person walked into it.

Jonah didn't diminish it. He deepened it.

She turned, composing herself. He stood on the porch, dressed in jeans and boots and a dark gray sweatshirt. They stared at each other.

"Hi," she said.

He nodded. "Glad you made it OK. Any problems?"

She shook her head. Social custom now dictated that she climb the steps, shake his hand, say polite, formulaic things, but the program wouldn't run. The screen in her mind stayed blank, cursor blinking.

He was so handsome. The sharp, austere planes of his face were warmed by the sunset's fiery glow. The jutting cheekbones, the shadows beneath his eyes. He looked wary. Apprehensive.

The place was silent but for the immense rustling of wind in the trees. Too silent. No laughter or talking from inside. No music.

"Have the rest of your guests not arrived yet?" she asked.

His eyes flicked away. He looked up at the sky, down at his feet, and came down the porch stairs, seizing her massage table and suitcase. He carried them up to the door, beckoning her to follow with a jerk of his chin. "Come on in. Let me get you something to drink."

The front room was dominated by picture windows

and a flagstone fireplace. It segued into the kitchen at the back, with a rustic table dividing the two spaces. Delicious food smells wafted out of it.

No sign of anyone, no purses, suitcases, coats, voices. Nothing.

"Where are your guests?" she demanded.

His face looked tense with apprehension. "Uh, that's something I have to discuss with you. They, uh . . . canceled on me."

"Canceled?" Her jaw sagged.

"Yeah. Something came up."

She was bewildered. "But you should've called me. Obviously you'll want to reschedule if they couldn't—"

"No." He shook his head slowly.

"No?" Her voice rose to a terrified squeak.

"Nothing's changed. It's just that instead of giving massages to a whole bunch of people, you'll give them all to me."

She backed toward the door, pulling against the palpable tug of his hungry, possessive gaze. "You lied to me," she accused.

He scooted in front of her, blocking her flight to the door. "No, I didn't. I just—"

"I can't possibly stay here alone with you!"

"Don't worry about the money," he said. "The deal stands. I prefer not to share you anyway. As far as I'm concerned, it's for the best."

"I don't give a damn about the money. I'm not comfortable with this at all." She hated the way her voice quivered, the color rising in her face. She yanked open her purse and rummaged for her wallet. "I *hate* being lied to. Here, take back your goddamn check—"

Condoms exploded out of her purse and scattered across the floor. Over a dozen of them. All different brands and colors.

Jonah stared down at them, back up at her. A grin lit up his face as he crouched down and started gathering them up. "Wow. Talk about high expectations."

Tess dropped to her knees and wrenched the condoms out of his hands, shoving them into her purse. "These are not mine," she hissed. "My roommate plays practical jokes. I'm going to kill her, I swear to God."

Jonah plucked one off the floor and examined it. "This one glows in the dark," he remarked. "Very cool."

She snatched it from him. "Trish dies. And I am out of here."

She lunged for the door, yelping as his arms closed around her from behind in a gentle but implacable embrace. "Wait, Tess. Please."

"Let go of me." Her whole body vibrated with the electrical charge of contact with his body. It was such a hot, shivery rush, she almost burst into tears. She fought against a surge of blind panic.

"I will, I swear, in just a second. Calm down and listen. Please."

She twisted until she could see his eyes. So pale and penetrating. They saw too much. She couldn't bear it. "Talk fast," she whispered.

"First, let me apologize. I really wanted this, and I put it together at the last minute. That's why my guests fell through—"

"So you admit it," she challenged him. "You lied. When you lured me up here, there was no house party. You made it all up, didn't you?"

"There was a firm intention to organize one," he protested. "It just turned out that my friends had plans. I didn't mean to mislead you. I'm sorry if the situation is other than you anticipated, but I'll do everything in my power to make you feel comfortable. I swear, I'll be so good."

She glanced down at the thick, steely forearms that were wrapped across her chest. "Then why are you manhandling me?"

"To keep you from running, of course," he said patiently. "At least stay for dinner. I cooked this whole elaborate meal, just for you."

"You can cook?" She twisted to look at him again, startled.

"Yes. I'm a very good cook. And I've got a bottle of Chianti breathing on the table." His voice was soft with pleading. "Call your roommate, tell her the phone number, give her directions, have her call you every hour on the hour to make sure your virtue's still intact. Call your mother, call whoever you want. Please, Tess. You're safe here."

"You can let go of me now," she said quietly. "I won't bolt."

He released her with obvious reluctance, but he didn't step back. His body remained in contact, his heat kissing the surface of her body.

"You know, my colleagues warned me about you today," she said. "They say you're trouble. Too intense. That you've fixated on me."

"Maybe." His voice was elaborately light. "But you don't need them to tell you what to do. You can decide for yourself, right, Tess?"

She couldn't help but smile at his craftiness. That wily bastard instinctively knew just what buttons to push.

He smiled back, his eyes still wary. "You'll stay for dinner?"

"Just dinner," she murmured. "Then I'll see how I feel."

His face lit up with relief. He poured her a glass of wine and pressed it into her hand. "I'll go finish up the food, then. Call your roommate, like I said. It'll make us both feel better." He indicated the phone table near the door.

Trish picked up on the first ring. "Chez d'Amour."

"Trish, I suggest you enjoy your evening, because it's going to be your last," she hissed.

"Well, if it isn't the love goddess herself. How's it going, chica?"

"There is no house party! It's just him and me and a bottle of wine! And what on earth possessed you to fill my purse with condoms?"

Trish clucked. "As if! No way would I let my precious Tess go off on a provocative weekend massage-a-thon with a hot sexy love god without stocking you up with latex! I mean, like, duh!"

"Trish, damn it, I—"

"Friends don't let friends have unsafe sex, Tess," Trish lectured.

"But I'm not here for sex!" she shouted.

There was a stifled snort of laughter from the kitchen behind her.

She slammed the phone down and marched toward Jonah, her arms folded across her chest. She glared at him until he turned around with a nervous, what-have-I-done-now? look on his face.

"Why is it that every single person in my life assumes that I don't know what's best for me?" she demanded.

Jonah stirred something bubbling in a gleaming pot. "I'm not touching that one with a ten-foot pole."

"That's the smartest thing you've said so far," she observed.

His eyes gleamed with sly humor. "That's just because I don't know you well enough yet," he amended. "As soon as I do, I'll let you know what's best for you. In great detail. You can count on it."

She tried not to smile, but it was a losing battle. "You just had to ruin it, didn't you? Just couldn't resist, huh?"

"Nobody's perfect." An answering smile spread over his face; something fluttered inside her. His warmth pulled at her.

He felt it, too. His smile faded, and he took a step toward her. Something sizzled and popped in the pan behind him. He spun with a muttered curse and did something with the spatula.

"You're distracting me," he said. "Why don't you take that glass of wine and go out and watch the sunset fade off the mountain? By the time the colors are gone, dinner will be ready."

She looked out the window. The mountain had faded from pink to orange. She took another sip of wine. "OK," she murmured.

Jonah stirred the polenta with one hand, and roasted the sweet red pepper over the gas flame with the other. He felt off balance and weird. The only way to keep her here was to assure her that he had no lustful designs on her luscious bod, and lying made him nervous. He wasn't the devious type. Usually disarming honesty mixed with beguiling charm was his winning formula. But he'd never encountered so much resistance before, and he'd never wanted anything so badly.

How strange, to listen to himself promising so earnestly to be good, while the rest of him stood by laughing its head off at the load of bullshit he was shoveling. He couldn't wait to get his hands on her.

She was drinking her first glass of wine, at least, the horny bastard inside him noted. A great first step.

The fucking polenta was lumping up because he didn't have enough hands to stir it constantly. Like an idiot, trying to do three things at once so he could get on with the business of seducing her. He craned his neck as he stirred, struggling to see if she was still on the porch. He wished he could go watch the sunset with her, but this meal was too important. The mushrooms were ready, the parm was under the broiler, the cream for the chocolate soufflé needed whipping.

This grasping intensity wasn't like him. It dismayed him, but there wasn't a damn thing he could do about it. A beast had reared up out of the black lagoon of his subconscious, puffing out its chest and demanding its way, a thing with no manners, no self-control, no scruples. It wanted what it wanted, and since it wasn't acquainted with the concept of delayed gratification, it was therefore capable of fucking his chances of getting a massage or getting laid, either one.

He peeled the blackened skin carefully off the peppers, his mind considering and abandoning various half-formed strategies for controlling the situation. A delicious meal was the best he could come up with. He resolved to project an air of total harmlessness. A goofy, sort of feckless vibe. He had to seem awkward, anxious. It shouldn't be too damn hard. Put her off her guard, make her think, oh, yeah, I can handle this clown with one hand tied behind my back.

The blackened skin peeled smoothly away from the brightly colored flesh of the roasted pepper beneath. It had rendered up its crunchy stiffness to the searing flame, had gone voluptuously soft and lax. He sliced it into strips, dropped them onto the pool of olive oil and slivered garlic waiting on the plate. Swirled them till they were coated with oil, soft and moist and glistening. Some shredded basil on top, and that part of his seduction spell would be good to go.

Tess sipped her wine as she strolled down the twisting path that led into the forest. It was utterly dark. If she ventured inside, she could lose herself. The thought of a forest big enough, wild enough to lose herself in sent a thrill of excitement through her.

It stirred a buried memory. That trip, to see the redwoods with her parents, when she was ten. Long-forgotten details spread out like ripples through her mind. She had stared up at the enormity of those ancient, kingly trees, awestruck, and then tried to slip out of earshot of her mother's constant, anxious harping. Just far enough so she could hear the huge silence that embraced an infinity of tiny, harmonious sounds; rustling and quivering and chittering. Her ears strained for it.

She'd sneaked almost far enough to hear it when all hell broke loose, and she was hauled back to shrill, hysterical lecturing. *Stinging bugs and snakes . . . lost in the woods and wander for days . . . broken leg and starve to death . . . my poor nerves, where's my medicine. Look through my purse, my hands are trembling!*

Then it was back to the car, to look at the redwoods safely ensconsed behind childproof auto-lock windows. *Sit straight in your seat and get your nose off the window, Tessie, there are* germs!

But she had never forgotten that moment of almost breaking free. That was how she felt right now. Something inside her was struggling to emerge, gasping for breath, for life. She drifted closer to the darkness of the trees. No one was here to shove her into a car with childproof windows. Nothing could hold her back, no one could save her, no one could stop her. She could do anything. The hugeness of her freedom crashed over her like a wave. Terrifying and wonderful.

Time was measured only by gradations of fiery light on the mountain. It faded slowly to softer and softer shades of mauve, dusty pink, violet. The dream of violet faded. The colorless shadows of twilight embraced her. The screen door squeaked. Tess turned away from the mystery of the trees and watched his dark silhouette move toward her. She sensed that he was nervous. Wary.

As well he should be. He had lied to her and manipulated her, and she did not owe him a damn thing. She could always throw his check back in his face. She didn't need to worry about pleasing him, or be anxious about offending him. Let him sweat to please her. Let him fret about not offending her.

She couldn't see his eyes in the dark. He was as impenetrable as the dark trees, yet she knew his beautiful body by heart. Muscle and sinew and bone and skin. She had absorbed him through her hands. In a way, he was already hers, and she wanted what was hers. A longing as sharp and urgent as the cry of an eagle in a vast, empty sky.

"Dinner is, uh, ready," he said hesitantly.

She took a deep breath of the fragrant evening air. The old Tess would have said something grateful and appreciative about him going to the trouble of cooking just for her.

The new Tess just took a leisurely sip of wine, and smiled.

"Good," she said. "I'm hungry."

Chapter Three

The dinner table left her speechless.

Candles illuminated a lavish culinary array that was ridiculous for two people. An earthenware crock of polenta with exotic sautéed mushrooms on top. Eggplant parmigiana, the golden mozzarella that topped it still bubbling. Roasted peppers adorned with fragrant shreds of basil. Crusty Italian bread, three different kinds of cheeses. Tender salad greens, baby spinach, watercress, endive. A heap of artichoke hearts, with a ramekin of melted butter nestled among them. Tantalizing odors made her head swim, her mouth water, her knees weak. It had been eight hours since she'd eaten a cheese sandwich.

"It looks incredible," she said. "It makes me want to cry."

"It's all simple stuff, really. Quickie recipes, except for the parm, and I put that together last night."

His casual tone was belied by the gleam of satisfaction in his eyes. She laughed at him, pointing an accusing finger. "You're patting yourself on the back for scoring points, aren't you?"

His lips twitched. "Maybe. We'll see. You haven't tasted it yet."

"Go ahead," she conceded. "Fifty bonus points for Jonah."

He made a move to refill her wineglass, and she put her hand over it, stopping him. "Do you want a massage tonight?" she asked.

His eyes flashed hungrily. "God, yes, if I can get one."

"Then I shouldn't have any more wine."

He frowned. "Don't be ridiculous. If you're too buzzed to give me a massage, I'll have only myself to blame. Let's be informal, OK? Otherwise I'll get tense and crabby, and the massages will be useless."

She lifted her chin. "You're a fine one to be making pronouncements and setting conditions."

The frown faded from his face. He looked uncertain. "True. But you're hungry, and we're celebrating. Have some wine, Tess. Please."

Slowly, she took her hand off the glass. The low gurgle of the liquid swirling into the gleaming bulb of glass was as tender and intimate as a kiss. He poured himself a glass, and set the bottle down.

They stared at each other in mutual shyness. "I've never met a man who can cook like this," she told him.

He swirled his wine around in his glass and took a sip. "I decided a few years ago that I needed a hobby, or I was going to turn into my grandfather. A workaholic steam engine with no life. I like food, so cooking was the obvious choice. And like you said, it earns me points."

"You made all this food just for me?"

He looked away from her, embarrassed. "Yeah," he said gruffly.

She fought the feeling, but everything he did, every word he said drew her deeper into his net. How sweet of him, to try so hard to please, with such attention to detail. She was utterly charmed.

"I decided to play it safe tonight, just in case you were a vegetarian, but I've got fresh steaks and fresh salmon fillets in the fridge. I brought along my kitchen pots of fresh herbs, and I've got pasta, and veggies, and six different kinds of cheese. I'll plan the menu around your preferences, of course. Whatever, you know, turns you on." He looked suddenly awkward, and shot her a crooked, apologetic smile. "So? Any dietary restrictions that I should know about?"

She was dazed by the variety, accustomed as she was to a diet of sandwiches, toast, fruit, yogurt, and Lean Cuisines. "No restrictions," she said. "It all sounds wonderful. I'll eat anything." The tense, meaningful silence that followed her words made them seem provocative, and she rushed on, blushing. "I do try not to eat too much chocolate, even thought I love it. But that's my only restriction."

His eyes slid over her appreciatively. "You don't look like you need to restrict anything. You look perfect. And lucky for you, because there's a hot chocolate soufflé with fresh whipped cream for dessert."

"Oh, God," she said weakly.

"I didn't make it," he hastened to admit. "I bought it at the Sensual Gourmet Bakery. I haven't mastered pastry yet. Here, start with some peppers. They're good spooned over bread . . . like this."

She was a goner at the first bite. The peppers melted in her mouth, their sweetness set off by the spicy tang of the fine olive oil, the sensual hint of garlic, all soaked into the savory hot bread. She closed her eyes to savor it with a moan of pleasure, abandoning herself.

When she opened her eyes, his eyes were glowing with hot excitement. "God, I love it when you do that."

"Do what?" she asked nervously.

"Give in to pleasure. Wow. Here, have some more. Do it again."

She tried not to giggle and blush and slide under his spell, but she was failing, she was falling. The wine was making her giddy. Every new flavor, every succulent bite made her moan.

Jonah watched her decimate her loaded plate with evident satisfaction. "Tell me something," he said, dipping a chunk of steamed artichoke heart in butter. "That thing that happens when you give me a massage, does that happen with everyone? Here, try this."

She accepted the succulent morsel off the end of his fork and savored it with a murmur of appreciation. "What thing?"

"You know. That magic thing, like your hands are talking to my back. You do feel it, don't you? Or is it just me?"

"Yes, I feel it," she admitted softly. "And no, it doesn't happen very often. It depends on how receptive the person—"

"I've never been particularly receptive," he cut in. "Just ask any of my ex-girlfriends."

The claw marks flashed through her mind. She toyed with the salad greens on her plate. "I'd, uh, rather not," she murmured. "What you're feeling is probably just a light trance state. When you achieve deep levels of relaxation, your brain produces—"

"Don't spoil it for me by explaining it away."

Her mouth closed with a snap. "You know, you have a really bad habit of interrupting."

"Sorry. I'll try not to do it, if it bugs you."

"It's jarring," she said sternly. "Like having bad shocks in a car."

He looked abashed. "Ouch. Sorry. I'm kind of, uh, nervous."

She tried not to smile. "I thought that men liked scientific, logical explanations for things."

"Yeah. Usually I do like them. Just not when it comes to you."

Suddenly, there wasn't quite enough air in the room to breathe. It was hot, immensely silent. Candles hissed and popped.

He got up and went into the kitchen, pulling something divinely chocolatey and fragrant out of the oven. He spooned steaming helpings of chocolate soufflé onto dessert plates and adorned them with towering mountains of whipped cream. He carried them to the table and laid them down, grinning. Immensely pleased with himself.

She giggled again, melting. "You've got to stop flirting with me."

"Do I?" His eyes took on a predatory gleam.

"Yes. You do. This whole situation is getting out of hand." She made a sweeping gesture with her hand, and almost knocked over her wine. Jonah's hand shot out, just in time, and gently put it in its place. "The food, the wine, the candles, the chocolate soufflé. It's over the top."

He shook his head. "No, Tess. This is normal for me. I like to treat myself well, and I have the means to do so. That's why you're here."

An image flooded through her mind. Herself, naked. Decked out in jewels and a sheer veil. Summoned to pleasure the lusty, sensual pasha. Commanded to fulfill his every erotic whim.

The image left her speechless. Her face felt damp and hot.

His glittering eyes seemed to read every thought that passed through her mind. "I like the way you massage me," he said softly. "I want to indulge myself, for hours. Is that so terrible? What's the crime? I'm willing to pay for my fun. I'm not stealing from anyone."

The harem maiden in her dream image threw off the sheer veil, and drew closer to the beautiful, naked pasha. Eager to prove herself. Desire sharpened to a dagger point that pierced through fear.

Nervous tension made her voice sharper than usual. "You're spoiled, Jonah. You're used to getting exactly what you want."

He smiled lazily. "I do favor that scenario. Who could blame me?"

The arrogant, casual entitlement in his voice made her angry. "I could," she snapped. "The world's not like that, you know."

"It's not?" He picked up her dessert spoon and scooped up a mouthful of chocolate soufflé. He dunked it until it was heaped with whipped cream and leaned closer, holding the morsel out to her.

"Try this," he said softly. "Let yourself go. Open up."

She hesitated. He was projecting an intoxicating cloud of seductive energy. Pulling her effortlessly into his trap.

She opened her mouth, as if hypnotized, and accepted a mouthful of perfect bliss. Rich, creamy sweetness exploded through her senses.

"Welcome to my world, Tess," he said softly.

* * *

She sipped the espresso that Jonah insisted on making for her, but it did nothing to bring her back to earth. She was mellow and goofy from the wine, and trying very hard not to think about where this was almost certainly leading. If she thought about it, she would clench up and ruin it. She didn't want to ruin it. She was having too much fun.

He wasn't even coming on to her, just lounging his long, graceful self at the far end of the couch with a relaxed, lazy grin on his face, laying on the foolish flattery, exerting himself to make her laugh. It was working, too. She was giggling and snorting like a teenager.

She laid the espresso cup on the coffee table. "I'm a little tipsy, but I could still give you a back rub," she offered shyly. "It won't be one of those intense, mystical massages you like so much, though. Our stomachs are too full."

His eyes lit up. "Great. Fine. I'll take whatever I can get."

She set up the table and draped one of her flannel sheets across it, carefully keeping her back to him as he undressed. When she dared to turn around, she was surprised to see his jeans still on.

"You're going to leave on your jeans? I can drape a towel—"

"It's my back that needs work. Believe me . . . it's best."

She squirted oil into her hands and stared down at him. She'd never been the target of a strategic seduction before. She'd been tempted by food and wine and chocolate, mountain and forest and moonlight. Now the choicest bait of all was stretched out on the table in front of her, eyes closed in anticipatory pleasure. He couldn't wait to be touched. And she couldn't resist for another second.

She placed her hands against his hot, smooth skin. A shock of awareness went through them both. He drew in a sharp breath, his eyelids fluttering. Far from relaxed. She could feel his tense, coiled eagerness. He was waiting, with the patience of a seasoned hunter for . . . what? What did he want from her? What did he expect?

She ran her hands over his powerful back, leaning low enough to smell his subtle, unique scent beneath the perfume of scented oil. Clearly, he was either leaving it to her to make the first move or simply biding his time. She appreciated his delicacy and restraint, but she didn't have a clue how to begin. If only she could take a little time-out and call Trish for a quickie consultation. Should she follow her neck-kissing fantasy and find out where that led? Her heart pounded with excitement. Maybe she would hyperventilate. It would be so awful to flub this, to embarrass herself. To have him, God forbid, *pity* her.

She was monumentally untalented in the bedroom, after all. Larry's voice floated out of her memories, snappish and tense. "Can't you please at least *try* to concentrate?" She'd tried and tried to be less ticklish and tense, keep herself from floating out of her body and noticing odd, comical things that made her want to giggle—like the way Larry's skinny shoulder blades stuck out like wings.

Jonah's shoulder blades did not stick out like wings. He had the most beautiful, powerful back she'd ever seen. And she didn't feel ticklish or tense. She felt hot. Inflamed. Her hands were sliding over him purely for their own pleasure, not for his. She didn't have a therapeutic thought in her head.

She put both hands on his shoulders. She was leaning over, like she was actually going to do it, to just up and kiss that beautiful place on the nape of his neck that was so vulnerable and tender it just broke her heart and made her toes curl. She was inches away from the point of no return and drawing closer. Her breath came quick and fast and audible. He could probably feel it against his skin by now. The sense of anticipation, of waiting, swelled, like a wave about to crest.

She jerked back, and lifted off her hands. *Damn* lily-livered, scaredy-cat chicken. "What's going on, Jonah?" she whispered.

His eyes opened. He looked unsurprised at the question. "A back rub?" he ventured, clearly just for the hell of it.

She shook her head. "I'm not buying it."

He rolled onto his side and sat up, his legs dangling over the table. His erection strained prominently against his jeans. "Are we being truthful here?" he asked. "Totally honest and sincere?"

"I think . . . that's best," she faltered.

He reached out, very slowly, and seized her wrists, pulling her toward him. He lifted her glistening hands and held them up, close to his face, breathing in deeply. "What smells so good?"

"Almond oil." She stared at the size of his graceful hands. "With a few drops of essential oil. I change the oil according to the client."

"And what's my oil?"

"Sandalwood and coriander." She let out a silent gasp as he pressed her hands against his hot chest, splaying them out. Covering them with his own, sliding them around until his broad chest gleamed.

The clear purpose in his eyes made her breathless and giddy. "Jonah," she said, almost inaudibly. "What are you—"

"It's your own fault. You're the one who blew the

whistle. I was going to be such a good boy. I was going to play it cool, all polite and refined. Get my massage, and then show you to a guest room with a lock on the door. But no. You had to unmask me. So here we are, Tess. Now you have to deal with naked reality. Whether you're ready or not."

"Jeans," she murmured. "Reality is wearing a pair of jeans."

He pulled her hands away from his chest and cupped them inside his own, dropping a kiss on her knuckles. "Your hands are so much stronger than they look. You're small, but I bet you're pure dynamite."

Larry's disappointed face flashed through her mind. She tugged at her hands with a pained, nervous laugh, but he would not relinquish them. "Uh, wrong. Sorry, but I'm not. Don't go building castles in the air about me. You'll just be disillusioned."

"How do you figure?"

She pulled again at her hands. "Past experience."

"Forget the past. I want you. And you want me, too. I can feel it."

It would be untruthful and undignified to deny it. "It doesn't matter," she said in a tiny voice. "It isn't part of the bargain."

"God." He rubbed his hand across his face. "This is driving me nuts. Can we change the bargain? What would it take?"

She straightened up to her full five foot two. "Some things can't be bargained for. Some things aren't for sale."

"Ah. Now we're getting someplace," he said, relieved. "I would never in a million years think that you were for sale, Tess. Why won't you let me get close to you? I'm trying so hard. I'm being so good. I'm being so charming and patient and goddamn careful, it's driving me insane. And I know that you want me. What is it about me that scares you so much?"

"You don't scare me. And it's none of your business."

"It is now," he said. He pulled her until she toppled against him, and trapped her between his thighs. "Nothing has ever been more completely my business. It's just you and me, Tess, and this thing we have between us. Our mutual business."

"We don't have anything between us," she protested weakly.

"We could. We could have something incredibly special."

She longed so badly to believe him, but it would be so much worse for her this time, if she let herself fall. She could really care about Jonah. She could fall wildly in love with him. She was teetering on the brink already. And when he got bored and moved on, it would sting and sear like the very fires of hell. It would make her feel so small.

She wrenched her hands away. "I don't need another rich, spoiled playboy walking all over me," she blurted.

His face froze. He dropped her hands. "Rich, spoiled playboy?" She stumbled back, unnerved by the controlled anger that smoldered in his eyes. He advanced upon her. "Where the fuck did that come from?"

"Uh, s-sorry," she stammered. "I shouldn't have said that."

"Sorry's not good enough. I did not deserve that, Tess."

"You're absolutely right. You didn't deserve it. Forget that I—"

"You can't erase what comes out of your mouth," he cut in. "Not in the real world. You have to face up to it."

She swallowed and pressed her trembling lips together.

"Rich, yeah. That I'll admit to. But I swear to you, I worked my ass off for it. Nobody handed it to me. Spoiled? I don't know. If I see something I want, I take it. But I pay full price. And I never whine. And I never for one second thought that the world owed me a goddamn thing."

"Jonah, I—"

"But playboy? What, do I come across like some pampered fop with a Ferrari and a pinkie ring? I work twelve fucking hours a day! I don't have time to be a playboy!"

"Oh, you find the time somehow," she lashed back. "I've seen the marks your lovers leave on your body. It wouldn't do my self-esteem any good to be part of your harem."

He looked bewildered for a moment, and then his eyes widened in dismayed comprehension. "Oh, God," he muttered. He closed his eyes, and opened them again, looking chastened. "You mean to tell me that the day I asked you out, I had, uh . . . claw marks on me?"

"They looked quite painful, actually. I tried not to get oil in them."

"Shit." He dropped his face into his hands and shook his head. "I should have canceled my appointment. No wonder you blew me off." He looked up at her, his face a dull red. "This may sound lame, but please believe me, I'd already ended that affair before I asked you out. I don't juggle women. My life is stressful enough as it is."

"You don't have to excuse yourself to me," she said hastily. "And I don't think there's anything morally wrong with seeing more than one person at a time, if everyone's aware and consenting. I'm just not wired that way myself. It would destroy me to be a notch in someone's belt."

He winced. "Ouch. Admitted, the timing and the claw marks make me look really bad, but that's still not fair, Tess."

"I'm just saying what pops into my head," she said. "I don't mean to hurt your feelings."

He didn't reply, just looked at her quietly. She became increasingly more aware of the crackling of the fire, the wind sighing in the treetops outside. Shadows played across the planes and hollows of his face. She didn't even see him move, but suddenly his warm fingers were wrapped around her wrists, and he was tugging her closer again.

"Let's take this from another angle," he said. "You said you don't need another rich, spoiled playboy, which implies that there have been other spoiled playboys in your past. Right?"

She remained stubbornly silent. He tugged on her wrist. "So?"

She sighed. "Just one. But I'd rather not talk about him. It just makes me depressed."

He nodded. His thumb moved against his her palm in a tiny, soothing caress. "OK, foiled again. One last try. The playboy in question walked all over you, meaning he was an egotistic, selfish, oblivious asshole. Guess what, Tess? I'm not like that. I was brought up better. I would treat you like the queen of the universe."

"Oh, please." An unexpected giggle burst out of her.

His grin of relief was radiant. "Oh, yeah. Ever been treated like the queen of the universe before?"

A dull ache of old sadness pulled at her from below, and her smile faded. "I most certainly have not."

Jonah lifted her hand to his lips. "If you stay with me tonight, I promise you won't regret it. It'll be all about you. Your call, your rules, your pleasure, Your Exalted Majesty. You don't have to worry about anything. Just let me please you."

"Oh, my God," she murmured. Her hand tingled, shimmered with the heat, the tenderness of his soft lips.

"I won't do anything unless you say I can," he assured her. "Which is not to say that I won't make plenty of suggestions."

The teasing humor in his face warmed and reassured her. "How do I know you'll keep your word?"

He lifted his shoulders, let them drop. "You can't know," he said quietly. "You just have to trust me. Life's like that."

His calm, direct gaze, his warm hands, his gentle words, made something that had been tight and pinched in her chest relax and soften. She took a deep breath and for the first time, she let herself really look at him. Not through the lens of Larry or any of her past disappointments and heartbreaks and fears. Just at Jonah.

What she saw dazzled her. He was so solid. Beautiful and sensual, yes, but there was something fair and honest and stubborn in his eyes that was even more alluring to her.

He endured her long scrutiny with quiet patience.

"Do you really mean it, the queen thing?" she whispered.

He touched her cheek. "Is it so hard to believe?"

"For me, it is," she admitted.

He slid off the table and sank to his knees. "Oh, my queen. I am at your command." He smooched up the length of her arm until she shook with nervous laughter.

He pressed a hot kiss against her palm. His teasing grin faded, supplanted by naked desire. Her laughter abruptly stopped.

"Let me kiss you," he said hoarsely. "Then you'll understand exactly how it'll be tonight between us. Please, Tess. Can I kiss you?"

He rose slowly to his feet. His face was inches above hers, his eyes hot and pleading. She drifted closer and closer with the slow inevitability of clasped hands on the planchette of a Ouija board. The waiting, the breathless curiosity, and then the gasp of delighted terror when the oracle yielded its answer. Yes, or no? Yes, or no?

She drifted closer. Closer. *Yes.*

She touched his hot face as she had longed to do for weeks, running her fingertips over his skin, his high, elegant cheekbones. Tracing the strong, dark slash of his eyebrows, the faint rasp of beard shadow, the sharp line of his jaw.

The hot, thrilling, pulsing life of him beneath her hands.

She pulled his face hungrily toward hers.

Chapter Four

Her lips trembled beneath the light, brushing contact, which was all that he dared to allow himself. She was still poised for flight, and if he lost her now he would implode, self-destruct, disappear out of sheer frustration. He was as tormented by lust as if he were a young boy, everything brash and raw and unmoderated. No veils of hard-won self-control or calm experience to overlay the roar of need.

He tasted her lips, shaking with exultant eagerness. They were just as he had dreamed they would be, full and unimaginably soft. As fine-textured as a dream of silk or suede. Pansies, poppies, butterfly wings. Things too delicate to touch.

She was kissing him back now, praise God, and the sweet, liquid contact of her lips made him wild, crazy; first the pull, then the slide, then the tiny wet pop as her lips disengaged, panting for breath, and then another hungry, tender assault upon his mouth. One brush of her hot, eager tongue blotted out his ambitious promises. Her small, fragrant hands stole around his body with eager curiosity, stroking across his ribs, his back. He pressed the throbbing heat of his hard-on against her, hoping it wasn't too rude, too soon.

But it didn't seem to alarm her. She just stroked and petted and soothed him, opening to his kiss. Her response emboldened him to put his arms around her. He marveled at how small and deliciously curvy she was, her narrow rib cage with the pillowy softness of her bosom pressing against his chest. He clasped his legs around her, a grasping, possessive gesture that he couldn't control. His body spoke a language that needed no translating. *Mine, all mine.*

She murmured against his hungry, marauding mouth, and he forced himself to pull away. "I want—" He stopped, panting and unsure of himself. "I want to kiss you deeper, but I don't want to scare you." He barely recognized his voice, it was so shaky.

She smiled her mysterious smile that never failed to turn him inside out. Pure Tess, warm and unforced and achingly sweet.

"You're not scaring me, Jonah."

She let her head drop back trustingly into his cupped hand, going soft and pliant against him. Her response was like a match to gasoline, a heavy *whump,* and then flames roaring up. Careful, careful, pleaded the tiny voice in the back of his mind. This is the queen of the universe he was dealing with. He had promised to control himself, to indulge her utterly. But she was pressing her plump breasts against him, so lush and soft and tempting. He couldn't stop to ask, he couldn't help himself; he slid his hands over her, cupped her abundant curves through all those layers of clothing. He wanted to rub some of that scented oil on her breasts and bury his face between them. His mind was a mass of roiling sensual images. His mouth roved over her slender throat, fumbling desperately for buttons, zippers, anything. He became dimly aware that she was saying his name, over and over.

"Huh?" He lifted his mouth reluctantly from the hollow of her throat, groping for the curve of her ass through her voluminous skirt. That Little House on the Prairie outfit was pretty weird, but she could wear a burlap sack and he would be on his knees, salivating for her.

"I've decided my first royal command." Her tone was hesitant, but her green-gold eyes sparkled with challenge.

He tried not to pant like an animal. "Let's hear it."

"I want you to rub my feet," she announced.

He blinked at her.

She looked slightly defensive. "This might come as a shock to you, Jonah, but I've been on my feet all day long. And after a day like that, the most erotic, luxurious thing I can imagine is to have a big handsome guy kneeling in front of me, rubbing my feet."

He started to grin as the sensual potential of the situation dawned on him. Touching her delicate little feet until she purred and relaxed, and then moving slowly, inexorably upward. What an awesome lead-in.

She reached for the bottle of oil and smoothed some onto her hands, smiling up through her eyelashes as she rubbed them over his shoulders and chest. "Fantasy detail," she explained. "My love slave should be oiled up and gleaming."

He stared at her small, strong hands as they rubbed him all over with casual skill. His cock throbbed so hard it was a wonder there was enough blood going up to his brain to keep him on his feet. His tongue seemed to have dried out and adhered to the roof of his mouth.

"There," she said, with an approving pat. "You look

perfect." She put the bottle of oil in his hands and raised her eyebrows. "Well?"

"Want me to be stark naked?" he suggested hoarsely. "You could oil up the rest of me, too."

Her cheeks flushed even pinker at the bold suggestion. "Let's take this one step at a time, shall we?" she said primly.

"As my queen commands."

She could hardly believe her luck. By some trick of amazing intuition, Jonah had come up with the one scenario that might not make her clench up and botch the whole thing. By declaring her queen of the universe, he had taken all the responsibility for the success of the evening upon his own broad, capable shoulders. She didn't have to worry about being skillful or responsive or creative enough. He had given her permission to be pampered and indulged, to think only of her own pleasure. And she was going to take him at his word.

Besides, he was tough. He was so supremely confident that she could bounce him around like a rubber ball, and he would never break. And such a sweetie, too, grinning at her like the idea of rubbing her tired feet thrilled him no end. It was adorable.

She watched him pull the couch closer to the fire, hypnotized by the beauty of his lean torso. He crouched, silhouetted against the flames, and set another oak log on it. She took advantage of the moment to dart behind the couch to unlace her shoes. White rubber-soled sneakers did not belong in a sensual fantasy of the queen of the universe being pampered by her brawny love slave.

He was looking at her now. There was no graceful

way to reach beneath the long skirt of her dress and tug down the black wool tights. She had to just do it.

Her fingers brushed across the scalloped lace of the red teddy. Dear God. She had forgotten all about the teddy. She had put it on this morning, just to give herself a jolt of confidence and have a naughty little secret against her skin. Now he would deduce that she had come up here intending to go to bed with him all along, and—

Or had she? Was this what she had wanted all along?

She didn't know, she couldn't tell. She felt like her body had been taken over by a mysterious stranger.

Oh, well. Too late to worry about it now. She peeled the tights down, striving to perform the graceless act with queenly panache. Jonah indicated the couch with a gracious, sweeping gesture of his arm, and she settled into the soft cushions.

He sat down cross-legged in front of her and squirted some of her oil into his hand. "Any particular way you want me to do this? You're the expert, after all."

"Just follow your instincts," she said.

He cupped her foot tenderly in his big palm, and closed his fingers around it—and a heavenly chorus burst into song.

Oh, he was good. His hands were wise and warm and knowing. Strong when she needed him to be strong, gentle where she needed gentleness. Exquisitely slow and thorough. Her head fell back against the sofa cushions, her eyes closed. She abandoned herself to the feeling of being pampered and caressed. Almost . . . loved.

The foot that he wasn't massaging was resting on his thigh. A very hot, hard, long something was beginning to nudge against it. Then more than nudge. She could feel the heat, the pulsing energy.

Her eyes popped open. She remembered that the source of this sweet, heady bliss was a big, powerful, extremely aroused man.

"I read once in a health magazine that every part of the body corresponds to a point on the foot," he said. "Some kind of Chinese medicine thing, right?"

"Yes," she said. "Reflexology. Shiatsu and acupuncture are based on . . . ah . . . the same principles, as well."

He laid the foot he was working on tenderly on his other thigh, and rescued her other foot, his fingers sliding intimately around her arch. "So you know all these pressure points?"

"Of course. Oh, God, that's so wonderful, Jonah. You're incredibly good at this. You could be a masseur."

"Great. Nice to know that if the bottom ever falls out of my consulting business, I've got one more card to play."

She almost hummed with pleasure. "Don't be snide. A guy who looks like you could make a fortune rubbing women's feet."

"Yeah, right. How about you tell me what part of the body this corresponds to?" He rubbed the pad of her big toe, then tenderly manipulated the other four.

"Ah, the pads of the little toes correspond to the sinuses."

"So if I do this"—he lifted her foot and kissed each of her toes—"then it's like I'm kissing your nose and eyebrows, right?"

She laughed at his foolishness. "I suppose you could say that, if you wanted to be fanciful."

"Oh, but I do. And the big toe?"

Her brain was so swamped with pleasure, it was hard to concentrate. "The tip is the brain, and the inner side is . . . is the side of the neck. And the fullest point in the middle are the eyes and ears."

He kissed her big toe, sides, tip, pad, his mouth warm and soft. His hot breath tickled the delicate skin of her arch, and sensation shivered up her legs. He pressed hot, seductive kisses against the ball of her foot. "How about this part?"

"Lungs. Shoulders. Heart," she whispered.

"Yes. Heaving lungs, kissable shoulders, pounding heart. I love it." He kissed her foot repeatedly.

She giggled and tugged her foot, but his hand wrapped around her ankle. "Jonah, I—"

"How about this foot? I don't want to neglect it. How about this part right here?" He kissed the tender arch near the outside.

"That's, ah, the sciatic nerve, I think. And the appendix. And that should be . . . the ileocecal valve."

He covered the spot with tender little kisses and grinned at her. "You lost me there, sweetheart. I missed that day in eighth grade biology. But I'm sure yours is the cutest little ileocecal valve ever."

His butterfly kisses made her shake with laughter. "Jonah, you're tickling me. Stop!" She pushed at his chest with her other foot, and he grabbed that one too, wrestling with her playfully.

Suddenly he let go. Both her feet shot out past his shoulders.

She froze. Her legs were wide open and draped over his hot, naked shoulders. And the look in his eyes was so purposeful. As if she were about to let him—oh, God. She scrambled back against the cushions, twisting and flailing.

"Hey, hey, hey. Don't panic," he urged. "You're still the queen."

She tried to breathe, to relax, to stop struggling. He was kissing her knee, making soothing noises, but she didn't feel soothed. She felt like she was going to fly apart in his hands, do something disgraceful and un-controlled. It was scaring her to death.

"I love these dimples on your knees," he told her. "They're so cute. Hold still, let me put more oil on my hands. I want to massage your legs, too." He stopped, and looked doubtful. "That's OK, right?"

"Yes," she whispered. He pushed her skirt up. She jumped when his hands closed around her knee, and tension left her body in a long, shuddering exhalation. She closed her eyes, wanting, needing to trust him. His big, oiled hands crept higher, gentle and mesmerizing. He stopped and waited, motionless, until she opened her eyes. He stared into them for a moment, silently asking her permission, and pushed very gently against her inner thighs.

She opened for him with a soft, trembling sigh.

"I love the red lace panties," he said appreciatively. "They make your skin look pearly white." She gasped as he pushed her back against the cushions. "Shhh," he murmured. "I'm just going to touch these lacy under-pants with the tips of my fingers. Like this."

The light, teasing circles against the dampening silk of her panties were sweet little flames licking against her. A heavy, aching desperation began to grow out of the pleasure. For the first time, she actually understood why people were willing to do dangerous, self-destructive, even immoral things in order to follow this impulse.

She invited him with her eyes to touch her wherever he pleased. She couldn't say it with words, but when he deepened the pressure and circled his thumb around her clitoris, she reached down and pressed his hand against her harder, with a pleading, wordless murmur.

He pinned her against the couch with his weight, his own breathing ragged and audible in the silent room, and she moved against his hand, her head thrashing back and forth, striving for something unknown and yet so seductively close, beckoning her.

When the hot oblivion pulsed through her body, she was so surprised, she actually fainted.

She floated back, dazed and limp. That was nothing like any orgasm she'd ever had—or rather, thought she'd had. She'd never understood what the big deal was about orgasms; to her they seemed no more than a sudden dissipation of whatever mild tension she had managed to build, a deflated sense that there was no point in continuing. Sort of like watching water swirl down a bathtub drain.

This had been . . . mind-shattering.

Jonah's arms were wrapped around her waist, the side of his face pressed against her belly. His breath had warmed her skirt. She put her hand in his hair and stroked it. Damp and silky and springy beneath her fingers. He was sweating, too.

He lifted his face, his eyes dark with wonder. "I've never felt anything like that," he said.

She licked her lips. "I think that's my line," she whispered.

"I felt it go right through me. Like a hot wind. You are incredible."

She tried to smile, but her muscle coordination was not yet up to such a complex task. "Of course you have to say that," she teased. "It's in the script. Queens have to be flattered and adored."

He scowled. "Fuck the script. That was for real. And so am I. Don't you get that yet?"

She was startled at his harsh tone. "Um, yes," she conceded softly. "I think I get that."

"Good." He pressed his face against her belly again, his big, naked shoulders rubbing against her thighs. She clasped her arms around his neck, pulling him closer with a soft murmur.

He lifted his head, his eyes hungry. "And? So?"

"And what? So what?"

"I'm waiting patiently for you to command me to take the next logical step, and the waiting's killing me," he said.

"What step?" she hedged.

He shook his head. "You have to articulate your desires. The queen of the universe knows exactly what she wants. So go on. Instruct your eager servant."

She opened her mouth, but nothing came out. She swallowed. "I can't," she whispered.

He lifted his eyebrow. "You have to, Tess. Otherwise, we can't proceed."

She gathered her wits. "That's 'Your Exalted Majesty' to you. Don't you dare presume to tell me what I have to do, Mr. Love Slave, or I'll have you punished for your insolence."

"Ah. That's better," he said softly. He bent down to lick her thigh. She caught her breath at the warm, wet intimacy of the caress. "So? What does my queen command?"

She reached down and ran her fingers across the rasp of beard stubble that covered his jaw. She knew what she wanted, but the words were stuck in her throat, pounding against a brick wall. She bit her lip in frustration. "What do you want to do?" she asked.

"Everything," he said promptly. "But for starters, I want to pull those panties off and lick you between your legs until you come again."

Heat pulsed through her at the image his words invoked: a tangle of lips and tongues and limbs, of kisses and caresses. Her breath jerked into her lungs, shallow and fast. "That sounds, um, interesting," she said. "My royal command is to . . . do what you want."

His eyes gleamed. "Whatever I want? You're sure?"

"Within reason," she amended swiftly.

He shook his head. "Can't have it both ways, sweetheart. If you give control to me, I'll take it and run with it. And I'm so turned on that I'm probably going to run long and hard and fast."

She let out a breathless laugh. "Are you trying to scare me?"

He shrugged. "Just being honest. If you can't tell me what you want, then I'm just going to have to show you what I want."

"Oh," she whispered.

"I'll let you off the hook now, but eventually, I'm going to get it out of you," he went on, kissing her thighs. "What you want, what you like, what you fantasize about. I want to hear the words. In explicit detail."

"I don't know how to talk about it," she said desperately.

"Then you'll learn." He lifted his head and gave her a slow, implacable smile. "Because I'll teach you." His hands moved over her, bold and skillful. "I'm going to make you come again now, Tess. Over and over, with my mouth and my fingers and my cock. Until you're begging me to let you rest. Until you've forgotten what it feels like to be shy or embarrassed. Do you want that?"

She nodded. She couldn't stop her lips from trembling.

"So, I'm taking over, then?" he said insistently. "You're sure?"

She pressed her lips together and nodded again.

He rose up with smooth grace, and pulled her to her feet. "My first act as an emancipated love slave is to get these clothes off you."

Alarm went through her like an electrical shock. She clenched her teeth and tried to let it go. "OK," she whispered.

She tried to help him, but her hands were clumsy and ineffectual, just getting in the way of his swift, strategic assault on her clothes. Finally she just held her hands out, as stiff and passive as a doll, hoping desperately that he wouldn't be disappointed by what he found.

He got rid of the dress first, shoving it down off her shoulders. Then her loose fleece shirt, his deft hands making short work of her buttons. Her silk knit chemise sailed up and over her head into the shadows.

And there she stood, in nothing but the flame-red lace teddy. She squeezed her eyes tightly shut. She could not breathe.

He was silent for an agonizingly long time.

"My God," he whispered. "Did you wear that thing for me?"

She licked her lips, tried to speak. Tried again. "I . . . I guess I did," she admitted in a tiny voice.

Another maddening silence. She clenched her fists and waited.

"Thank you," he said simply.

She finally dared to open her eyes, and she was shocked by the look on his face. He looked moved, his eyes soft, dazzled.

He lifted his eyes to her face. "You're so fucking beautiful," he whispered. "You blow my mind. I'm afraid to touch you."

She let out a hitching little laugh that threatened to turn into tears. "Well, you better get over it."

They both laughed. He lifted trembling hands and placed them on her shoulders. Brushed them tenderly down her arms. He slid his fingers around her lace-covered waist. Splayed them over her hips with a sigh of approval, then cupped her bottom. She nudged herself closer, breathing in shallow little gasps.

One of his hands slid up to touch her breast. She nestled in his warmth as his fingers traced the pattern of the scalloped lace, brushing over her lace-covered nipple, making her heart pound. He pushed the stretchy fabric down over her breasts, until her nipples peeked over the edge of the fabric. She pressed herself against him, hiding her face against his shoulder.

"I hate to take it off you," he said shakily.

"I can always put it back on for you later."

"Promise?"

When she nodded, he began to inch the fabric down over her torso. He freed her breasts and peeled it down over her thighs. Gently lifted one foot, then the other. He smoothed the little garment in his hands and lifted it to his face, taking a hungry whiff. "Delicious."

She was laughing at his silliness when she suddenly realized that he was staring at her naked breasts. She made a move to cover them with her arms, and at the same moment realized how stupid that was.

She forced herself to drop her arms, closed her eyes, and tried to breathe. It had been so long since she'd been naked in front of anyone, and it wasn't as if she'd ever gotten very comfortable with it.

She jumped nervously as he reached around her

shoulders, feeling for the thick knot of hair at her nape. His long fingers searched delicately for the pins, and he flung them away to join the rest of her discarded clothes and he let the knot unravel. It spiraled down to the small of her back. "I've been fantasizing about seeing your hair down since the first moment I saw you," he said, draping it across her shoulders like a shawl. "It's even more beautiful than I imagined."

He pushed her back, gently, until the backs of her knees hit the couch, and kept pushing until she fell into the cushions, staring up at him. Wide-eyed. He stroked her thighs, staring hungrily at every detail. He tucked a pillow behind her, and pulled her until her bottom was at the end of the couch cushion. "Your breasts are amazing," he said. "I wish my mouth could be everyplace at once, but the night's still young." And he pushed her legs wide open.

She tried to squirm, but she was pinned. "Jonah, wait—"

"What for?"

His mouth was on her, his tongue sliding boldly along her most intimate flesh. She was transfixed with pleasure.

Never. Never like this. She'd always been far too tense and self-conscious to enjoy this the few times that she had attempted it. This was utterly different. All she could do was stare at his dark head, her breath coming in harsh, audible gasps. His hands held her wide open as his tongue fluttered across the exposed, swollen bud of her clitoris. It rasped tenderly across the glistening folds of her labia, slowly up and down, lapping and licking with hungry abandon. He slid one long finger slowly inside her while suckling her clitoris, and looked up at her as he slid it slowly out. It glistened.

He thrust it again, harder. "You're so wet and tight," he muttered. "Clinging to my finger like you're sucking on it."

She barely understood what he said. Her body was lit up like a torch. Everything he touched was melting. Shimmering hot, liquid, lost. The center of the universe was the agonizing pleasure of his lips and tongue and clever hands. He brought her almost to the brink, and then drew back. Wave after wave, closer and closer, till she wanted to scream with frustration.

She clutched as much of his short, silky hair as she could grab. "Damn it, Jonah," she gasped. "Do it!"

His laughter vibrated through her sex. His tongue probing, teasing. "Trust me."

"Please," she begged. "Please, do it now."

"Soon," he promised.

"Now!" She swatted his shoulder, hard.

He thrust with his hand, bold and forceful. It almost hurt, but then he was pressing tenderly against the hot, shivering sweet spot deep inside her sheath that she had never known existed, while his tongue circled the swollen bud of her clitoris. He drove two fingers into her flushed, swollen opening, and it all came crashing down. A throbbing explosion of rippling pleasure, widening out. A pulsating red glow that spread to every part of her body.

When she opened her eyes, he was on his feet, shoving his jeans down. She stared at the erection bobbing in front of her and suddenly remembered that she had ceded all control of their tryst to him.

He was impressive. Much longer and thicker than Larry. Rising out of a rich thatch of dark hair, thick and blunt, flushed to a deep, purplish red. Veins pulsing. He stood there and let her get used to the sight of him. He was so tempting and powerful and perfect.

He stepped closer. "Touch me there," he said quietly. "Please."

She put her hand against him, startled at how hot and smooth he was, how delicately soft the skin that covered his hardness. "Harder," he said. His hand closed over hers, squeezing and pulling, rougher than she would ever have dared to touch him on her own.

The pressure milked a gleaming drop of pearly moisture from the slit in the tip. She didn't stop to think, she just pressed her mouth against it, licking it away. Sweet and salty, heat and bursting pressure. She could get used to this feeling of power, the helpless groan of pleasure she dragged from him. She could learn to love it.

She gripped him, taking the whole tip of him into her mouth. It was big and blunt, and barely fit. She swirled her tongue around, moistening him, and was just about to suck him deeper when she felt his hands cupping her face, holding her in place.

"No, please," he said in a strangled voice. "I'll come in two seconds if you do that."

He pushed her back, and she stared at the thick hard shaft bobbing next to her face, radiating heat. Her eyes traveled slowly up his big, powerful body, saw his flushed face and dilated eyes.

Long and hard and fast, he had said. His size and strength were suddenly disconcerting. But she'd been so wanton, so selfish and eager and willing so far, there was no way she could draw back now. It was his turn, and she had to just relax and try to not be nervous and silly. It wasn't like she was a terrified virgin. She was twenty-nine years old. And the man clearly knew what he was doing.

Jonah was moving briskly ahead, unaware of her spasm of doubt. He had already produced a condom out of thin air, and had rolled it purposefully over himself. His eyes dragged slowly, hotly over her body.

"I'm too big for the couch," he said. "Let's take this to the rug in front of the fire. It's nice and soft."

She was frozen in place, mute. He grabbed the fluffy afghan from the back of the couch and flung it out over the rug. He scattered a couple of the thick, fleece covered pillows onto the afghan, and held out his hand, a swift, imperious gesture. "Come on."

He was so overwhelming, she couldn't control her primitive hesitation, but Jonah had no intention of letting her pull back. He scooped her into his arms.

She protested, wiggling. "Jonah, you'll hurt yourself!"

He snorted. "Get into the moment. Do you think Scarlett said that to Rhett while he was carrying her up the stairs?"

She was startled into giggling as he lay her against the cushions. "So men fantasize about that scene, too? I thought that was a girl thing."

"You mean about what he does to her once he gets her into that bedroom? Hell, yes. At least I did. To start with, I think he throws her on the bed and rips open her dress, and goes like this—"

He lunged over her, covering her with his body, and pressed her breasts together, burying his face between them. He kissed and swirled his tongue against her curves, leaving a trail of wet, pulsing pleasure in his wake.

He looked up at her face as he suckled her nipple, and dragged his teeth gently across the sensitive flesh. The rasp of his teeth made her cry out, clutching his head to her chest. He lifted his eyebrows and hummed the theme to *Gone With the Wind*. She dissolved into giggles.

He lifted his head. "Then he rips open her bloomers or petticoats or whatever the hell else women wore back then, and he fucks her brains out. He tries to show her who's boss. Never works worth a damn, but it's fun while it lasts."

Her laughter cut off abruptly. She stared, transfixed, into his burning eyes as he pushed her legs wide, settling himself between them. The hot, powerful bulk of him was poised over her. No wiggling away, no second thoughts. Her fingertips dug into his upper arms.

He leaned down, covering her face with coaxing kisses. "Relax. I'm not going to hurt you. You're ready for me. I made sure of it."

"I'm sorry." She squeezed her eyes shut as she felt the smooth, blunt head of his penis sliding tenderly against her labia, probing, pressing. Then insisting.

"Open your eyes," he said. "I'm Jonah, and you're Tess, and this is no fantasy. This is for real. Right here, right now. Keep your eyes open, Tess. Look at me."

"I can't," she said tightly.

He cupped her face in his hands. "You have to," he said. "Now."

And such was the force of his will that her eyes actually did pop open. She stared into his face, lost and overwhelmed. A certainty was growing inside her, that opening herself up to this man was going to change her in ways she could not yet imagine. But there was no going back. She dug her hands into his shoulders and tried to relax. It had been three or four years since she last tried this, and he was so big and solid, stretching her tender opening to the point of pain.

"Stay with me, Tess." His voice was tense and strained. He stared into her eyes so intensely, she felt as if she were chained to him. His muscles flexed, and she cried out as he thrust all the way inside.

It was too much. She felt pinned, immobile. Stifled by his size, the force radiating out of him. The deep, aching pressure of his shaft inside her was a painful intrusion. She turned her face away, her breath getting short and strangled and panicky.

She felt his hands on her face again, wrenching her face back toward his. "Damn it. Look at me."

The steely anger in his voice stung her own anger to life. "What the hell do you want from me?" she spat out.

He shook his head, his eyes full of angry confusion. "I don't know! Be there for me! Meet me halfway! Tell me to fuck off, whatever the hell you want, but just be strong for me. Don't you dare slip away and leave me alone, like you're scared of me. I can't take that!"

She tried to wiggle beneath him, in vain. "Aren't you happy now?" she flung at him. "Isn't this what you wanted?"

He drew back and thrust slowly inside her again, holding her gaze. "No. I want more. I want everything."

"Great. Well, spell it out for me, then," she snapped. "Because I don't know just exactly what everything entails."

He cut off her words with a deep, plundering kiss that left her breathless. "I'm sorry I pissed you off, but I'd rather have you mad at me than slipping through my fingers like sand."

"This is your lucky day, then, Jonah, because I'm furious! I don't know why, but I am. You're too big, and too heavy, and you're making me nervous. Let . . . me . . . *breathe.*" She wrestled her arms between them and shoved at his chest.

He arched himself up so his weight lifted off her, and trapped her wrists and pinned them over her head. She could breathe, but having her arms stretched out over her head made her feel helpless and maddened.

She heaved and bucked beneath him, but he wouldn't dislodge himself. He just thrust in again with a voluptuous surge that made her gasp.

Despite her furious tension, she was slicker and wetter and softer than she'd ever been. He sensed the exact moment that her body found the right angle to clasp him, move with him. The moment that the pressure of his thick penis sliding along the length of her humid sheath made a flush of excitement race like a grass fire across the entire surface of her skin.

She was burning up. Crazed and feverish. She tried to free her hands, but he was immensely strong. "Let go, God damn it," she panted.

He slowly shook his head. "No way. Be mad, Tess, if that works better for you."

"You bastard," she hissed. "It doesn't!"

"Liar," he said softly. "You're opening up to me, now. All wet and soft and scalding hot. You like it. Feel this." He drove himself deep inside her, a heavy lunge that shocked a wail of pleasure out of her throat. "See? Go on, spit some more venom at me. It turns me on, too."

"Damn you," she said shakily. Her face was crimson, and she couldn't stop her legs from twining around his, her sex from tightening around his thick, hard shaft. She couldn't control her own body, jerking up to meet his plunging hips.

He thrust again. "You're gorgeous when you're mad." He slid his arms beneath her shoulders, scooping her up to kiss her again. His tongue slid into her mouth, following the same slow, plunging, sensual rhythm as his hips.

She had been poised to tell him to stop, but the words wouldn't come. They receded, slipping back into the swirling pool of emotions, anger blending with desire and confusion, in a hopeless, muddled mix. "Jonah, please."

He kissed her face, her jaw, her ear. "Don't worry, sweetheart," he whispered. "I've got everything under control."

"Including me?" she snapped.

He grinned, delighted. "That's the spirit. Keep your eyes on me." And then he began to move.

She'd never felt anything like this before. Totally new sensations bloomed, one out of the other, and he watched it all, studying her face with heated fascination. The tension in her trapped arms, in her straining body, just sharpened her exitement, heating the volatile blend of feelings closer and closer to the edge. He reached down with a murmur of encouragement, toying with her clitoris while his hips pulsed and ground against her. Silently demanding that she take that blind leap, again.

His cry of triumph was the last thing she heard as she flew off the edge and lost herself.

He waited, motionless, for her to come back, while the aftershocks of her orgasm clenched him rhythmically. When she opened her eyes, he began again, and this time she sensed that he had given himself leave to seek his own completion. He was rougher, more urgent. The deep, slamming thrusts would have frightened and intimidated her before, but not now. She was changed. The wild, rebellious part of her, dormant for so long, had roared to life and found its equal. She wanted to lose control, to bite and scratch, to be taken deep and hard. She didn't even notice when he let go of her hands. She just found herself clutching his waist, holding herself up so she could see his thick penis, gleaming as he thrust and withdrew, his hard, ridged belly, his muscles flexing. She dug her fingers into him greedily, demanding without words for everything he had to give.

He shoved her down onto her back and rose up onto his knees, folding her legs up until she was spread as wide as she could go. "Is this what you want?" He lunged into her, deep and hard.

She grabbed his butt and dragged him closer. "Please."

"You'd better not punish me for this later," he warned.

Passion had changed her body, lengthening her shcath to accommodate him, waking up millions of nerve endings she had never known existed. She was made for this sweet, savage rhythm. Made for him, desperate for the sliding friction, and the deep, sweet pressure against the mouth of her womb.

Then pleasure burst, rushing over them and through them both, fusing them together like molten gold.

Chapter Five

He lay trembling on top of her, till he became aware of how hard she had to struggle to breathe beneath his weight. He lifted himself out of her tight, clinging depths, flopping onto his back.

"Jesus," he muttered. "I think you practically killed me."

He let his head flop to the side towards her. She licked her lips.

"That doesn't sound very complimentary," she whispered.

"Believe me, it is," he said solemnly. "Right from the heart."

"Not very poetic, either." Her voice was barely audible.

He would've laughed if he hadn't been so limp. "So you want mind-blowing sex, and then you want me to be poetic, too? Let me recover, OK? As soon as I can breathe, I'll be a perfect gentleman."

She rolled up onto her side. "You're not gentle," she said quietly. "I'm never buying that perfect gentleman line of yours, ever again."

A pang of guilt assailed him. "You didn't need gentleness," he said defensively. "I'd already done the gentleness bit. It did its job. If I'd kept on being gentle, you would have gotten bored."

She snickered. "Bored? With you? Hardly. So now you're the expert about what I need?"

He knew he was skating on thin ice here, but he had nothing to follow but his instincts. "Yeah, Tess. I think I am," he said simply.

She propped herself up on her elbow, her eyes shot through with gold from the firelight, wide with fascination. "So it was all calculated, then? Don't get mad, please. I just need to—to understand how this works. I didn't know sex could be like that."

His stomach clenched with apprehension. "Like what?"

"That it could go so far," she said softly. "Make me feel so strongly. It was scary."

"I didn't mean to scare you," he said roughly. "In fact, I hated it when you were scared."

"I know you did." She reached out and patted his chest, an unconscious, soothing gesture. "So you were deliberately trying to—"

"No. Nothing was deliberate. I didn't think, I didn't try, I didn't calculate. It just happened."

Her hair tumbled forward over her chest as she sat up, her eyes full of thoughtful speculation. "So you just lost control, then?"

His hand slammed down hard against the afghan. "Yes, I did," he snapped. "I lost control. I admit it. Sorry, OK? Are we done, now? Do we have to keep hashing this out? Can we please move on?"

She leaned over and touched his cheek gently. "I wasn't criticizing," she assured him. "I'm glad I wasn't the only one who lost control. It makes me feel less self-conscious."

Her eyes were soft, completely sincere. She really wasn't blaming him. She wasn't even angry. The look in her eyes was so sweet, he felt himself stirring again. He took her hand in his and pressed a kiss against it. "You really are innocent, aren't you?"

"Not anymore," she said primly. "You made like you were all harmless and docile. Pussycat, my butt. You're Attila the Hun."

The gleam of humor in her eyes reassured him. "It worked for you, though, right? I made you come, what, four times?"

"Don't be cocky," she reproved. "It's unbecoming."

He pulled off the condom, grinning. "Speaking of which. Anytime you want to try oral sex, I'm at the ready. Now that I've taken the edge off, I think I can risk it."

"Edge? I'm totally destroyed, and you've just taken the edge off?"

He got to his feet and held out his hand. "You didn't think we were done, did you?" he asked in mock horror. "Please, please, please, tell me you didn't think that."

She linked hands with him and let him pull her to her feet. "Are you a sex maniac?" she asked. "Or is this normal?"

"I don't know," he admitted.

They stared at each other, speechless and shy. He kissed her hand again, wondering how long this shaky, off balance feeling was going to torment him. "We'll see how you feel after a midnight snack," he told her. "Come on, let's go have some leftovers."

It was definitely time to lighten up, take a step back, he told himself. He'd shocked himself. He'd never meant to let things get so intense. He'd intended to be gentle, careful, endlessly patient. Not a sweating, pounding, screaming madman.

Even so, here she was, holding his hand, and padding stark naked and trusting alongside him into the kitchen. His erection bumped up another notch. Well over a forty-five degree angle, and heading up to ninety. She noticed it, her eyes skittering away. So cute and shy.

"I didn't know men could recover so quickly," she observed.

He washed his hands, waited while she did the same. "You make me so hot, I can't see straight," he said, opening up the fridge. "I've been fantasizing about that white dress of yours for months."

"Oh, please." She covered her smile with her hand. "You mean the Vee Have Vays to Make You Talk dress?"

"Is that what you call it? Grab some forks out of that drawer."

She handed him the forks. "My roommate Trish named it. The most un-sexy garment ever created."

He snickered as he pulled plastic wrap off the eggplant. "Not."

"A guy would have to have a truly dirty mind to find that dress a turn-on."

"That's me," he said cheerfully. He stuck the bread in the toaster oven. "I can already see myself, flat on my back, and you in that dress, standing over me. Legs spread. No underwear. Interrogating me."

She giggled, wrapping her arms across her breasts. He gently peeled them away, pushing them down to her sides. "You cold?"

"Not really," she murmured. "Just not used to being naked."

He touched her breasts with the tips of his fingers, light, tender strokes. "You're gorgeous," he told her.

She reacted to his touch with a little tremor, and a flush swept up over her chest, her neck. "It's sweet of you to say so."

He realized, with horrified dismay, that she didn't believe him. "I'm not particularly sweet," he said. "I don't give false compliments. And you're not just gorgeous, you're drop-dead gorgeous."

"Please, Jonah. Don't push it." She backed away from the intensity in his voice. He followed her, trapping her against the counter.

"It just gets me going, when you tell me not to push it. Did you know that I've been obsessing about every detail of you for months, now? I'm crazy about your hair, you know. I love all those little fuzzy bits that curl around your neck at the end of the day. I've been dying to unwind that bun and see how long it was. To put my face in it and just inhale your smell. God, what a rush."

Her face was tight with discomfort. "Jonah, you don't have to—"

"And your tits," he forged on. "God. You can't imagine how many times I thought about popping open the buttons on that white dress, one by one, and seeing those unbelievable breasts pop out—"

"I wear a T-shirt under the dress," she said, giggling.

He cupped her breasts in his hands and leaned down, kissing them. "Don't trample all over my favorite fantasy," he protested.

And before he even realized what he was doing, she was arched back over the counter, gasping, saying something in a pleading voice, but he was too swept up in a flare of unexpected lust to hear it. He licked and suckled her, reveling in her abundance, his erection pressing against her soft belly. He was rock hard, as urgently aroused as if he hadn't just had wild, wonderful sex on the living room rug, and her clutching hands, her flushed, shivering eagerness just egged him on.

She was so small, it would be easy to just push her up against the wall, spread her wide, and pin her into place with his thrusting body. And she was still soft from the last time, more than ready to—

"Jonah! The toast!"

He lifted his head and wiped his mouth, dazed. "Huh?"

"The bread! It's starting to burn! Don't you smell the smoke?"

"Damn." He let go of her and lunged for the toaster. "God damn automatic timer's broken." He sneaked a guilty look at her. "I, uh, thought the smoke was coming out of my ears."

Nothing was going as smoothly as he had hoped, though it was a thousand times more interesting than he had imagined. Too interesting. Of all the sex scenarios he had envisioned, jagged, scary, on-the-edge-of-disaster sex was not one of them. The primal instinct to conquer and subdue. Caveman stuff. Wild. The woman really did it to him.

He fished the bread out of the toaster. Tess was staring down at his erection again. She made a nervous little gesture toward it.

"Wow. Are you always . . . I mean, do you already want to—"

"It can wait while you have something to eat," he said, with what he hoped was a reassuring smile. "This erection isn't going anywhere. Not while you're walking around my kitchen naked." He piled a tangle of roasted pepper onto a chunk of bread. "Come here," he urged. "It drips."

Her smile as she chewed made his chest practically

puff out with self-satisfaction. He hand-fed her until she was laughing and begging for mercy—his cue for the coup de grâce. More chocolate soufflé. And he oh-so-clumsily let a big glop of whipped cream slide off the spoon and down over her breasts, leaving a creamy white trail for him to follow with his tongue. There were drops on her belly, and some slid lower to tangle in the luxurious nest of dark ringlets at her crotch.

And that was it. He had to taste her again, right here, right now. He shoved her up against the kitchen cabinets. Her small hands clutched his head, her thighs trembled as he forced his hand between them and opened her, sliding his tongue into her damp curls and seeking the delicious, delicate little bud of pure sensation. Loving it, worshiping it with his tongue. He lapped up her sweet, copious juice, sliding his tongue voluptuously up and down the slick, delicious folds of her tender cleft until she cried out and clenched around his thrusting finger.

She went limp. He caught her before she could fall to the floor, and swept her up into his arms. Time to take this to the bedroom. He didn't want to do anything creative or playful or fun, didn't want to show her the hot tub, didn't want to try any tricks. He just wanted to pin her down on his bed and bury himself in her, face to face, hips grinding, eyes locked. All his.

Staking his claim.

Jonah carried Tess up the staircase and down a corridor, into a large, moonlit bedroom. He laid her on the antique four-poster bed, shoving aside the thick down coverlet. He flicked on a bedside lamp, staring down at her, his eyes hot with predatory hunger.

When he had that look on his face, he made her very nervous.

He pulled a condom out of the bedside stand, rolling it over his erection with casual skill, and climbed into bed, pushing her down onto her back. "You're shivering," he said. "I'll warm you up."

"I just bet you will," she said with false bravado. "You're burning up."

She stiffened against him as he pushed her legs wide, but he had already gained entrance; there was no shutting him out. He shoved the smooth, blunt tip of himself into her and surged inside, in one smooth, seamless thrust. The wind tossed the trees outside. They sighed and moaned uneasily around the house. She splayed her hands against his chest. "Jonah," she said breathlessly. "What are you doing?"

"God. If you have to ask."

He thrust into her, hard enough to make her gasp. She shoved against his chest, suspicious. "Hey. Are you trying to show me who's boss?"

"Now why would I do a stupid, futile thing like that? I know better. Besides, I already know who's boss. I am, because that's how you need it to be. When you want that to change, let me know."

"You arrogant bastard." She writhed, and he responded with a deeper thrust. "You're doing it again. Making me angry on purpose."

"Yeah." His voice was matter-of-fact. "You were getting scared again. What am I supposed to do? Sing you a lullaby?"

"Are you challenging me?" she demanded.

"Do you need to be challenged? How's this for a challenge?" He reached down, hooking her knees with his arms. Spreading her wide.

She tried to gather her wits, but it was hard when he had that dark, volcanic look in his eyes. "Don't answer a question with another question," she said shakily. "It was OK the first time, to trick me out of being nervous, but now you're just pissing me off for the fun of it."

"Why are you afraid of me?" he demanded. "What did I do?"

"I am not afraid of you!"

He swooped down on her with a fierce, hungry kiss, as if he wanted to devour her whole. He lifted his head, panting. "Yes, you are. That's why you're angry. Because it's better than being scared. But there's something on the other side of your anger. I want to know what it is."

"You won't get to it by forcing me," she said sharply.

"Oh, I don't think I'm forcing you." He pushed both her legs to the side, and stared down at where his penis was squeezed between her trapped legs, hot and tight. He slowly pushed himself deeper. Pulled back. The intense friction made her whimper with terrified pleasure.

He found just the angle and pressure she needed. Everything he did was calculated to drive her wild. He was as skillful at manipulating her emotions as he was with her body. She hated him for playing her like an instrument. She loved him for being a virtuoso.

She flew apart around him, sobbing with yet another bursting rush of pleasure, but she felt him holding back his own release. His face was a grimace of concentration. He wasn't done with her yet.

He smoothed the damp curls off her forehead, his own breath shuddering with reaction to the little convulsions pulsing through her body. "You're fine," he said. "I'm not forcing you. Am I?"

She shook her head, her eyes squeezed shut.

"What is it?" he demanded. "Am I hurting you?"

She shook her head, helpless to explain. "Not exactly."

His face was rigid. "What do you mean, not exactly?"

"I don't know what I mean!" she said desperately.

He drove into her, letting her feel his anger. "So figure it out."

She didn't know why he pushed her, where he wanted to take her, what he was trying to force her to admit. But passion overpowered him, too, sweeping away his arrogance and rendering him as helpless, as desperate as she. They gripped each other, and the momentum of their explosion hurtled them unimaginably far. To the far side of fear or anger. Beyond words, beyond thought.

He gathered her into his arms afterward, wordless and trembling. They stared into each other's eyes. Tess tried to speak. An infinitesimal shake of Jonah's head stopped her.

Much later, he disentangled himself, just long enough to dispose of the condom. He slid promptly back into bed and grasped her tightly, as if he needed to assure himself that she was real.

Tess lay in his arms, wide awake, watching the moonlight shimmer on the lake, marveling at this new self that was emerging. Everything she had always taken for granted about herself had been thrown into question. Anything seemed possible.

Jonah's sleeping face seemed younger, innocent and vulnerable. His hand was tucked under his face like a little boy. She lifted the comforter to look at his body. He murmured in protest and rolled onto his back, seeking the lost warmth. She lifted it higher.

He was so beautiful, his broad chest tapering down

to a lean, muscular abdomen. The dip and curves and hollows in the muscles of his flanks enticed her. She wanted to stroke them, explore them with her fingers and lips. This was the first time she had seen his penis soft. It was dark and curled up on its nest of hair. She touched it with the tip of her finger. Velvety soft, tender, and vulnerable. She touched the bulge of his scrotum, tracing a barely there caress, as soft as a kiss. Relaxed and vulnerable like this, he didn't intimidate her at all. Nothing stood between her and the impulse to lean forward and take his penis in her hands.

She caressed his balls, following the delicate tracery of veins, marveling at the unexpected fragility of his body. She stroked the graceful lines of his groin, his muscular thighs. Leaned forward to inhale his scent, musky and male, mixed with the smell of sex, of herself. He was already swelling, thickening. Fuller, longer. Quickening in her hand.

He jerked awake with a sharp exclamation, his body rigid with surprise, and stared at her, dazed with sleep. She smiled, and closed her hand around his penis, pulling slowly. "Oh, God," he said thickly.

She put her finger over her lips. "Shh."

He reached for her, but she shoved him down without ceremony.

He had woken up in the middle of one of his favorite adolescent wet dreams. She was a fantasy princess, gorgeous and stacked. All she needed was a little metal armored bikini, like Red Sonja. No, scratch that. To hell with the bikini. She didn't need a damned thing. She was naked. She was perfect. She was heaven.

She slid down his body with voluptuous slowness, licking and kissing him everywhere. She rubbed his cock gently against her silky soft, flushed cheek, kissed him with her lush lips, and then pulled him into her mouth, a warm, liquid, sliding, suckling bliss. She slid her clever little tongue all over the seething tension at the tip of his cock, making him sob with pleasure.

She pushed his legs apart and cuddled up between them, her eyes mysterious pools in the moonlight. She gripped him, a hard, strong grasp as he had shown her, and drew him deep into her mouth.

It was the sweetest, most delicious, explosively exciting thing he had ever felt. Heavenly torture. She lapped at him like a kitten lapping cream, sliding and swirling her tongue. He arched off the bed and cried out, begging her not to stop. But she wasn't stopping. She tried everything that came into her head—deep and slow, hard and fast. Exploring him, putting him through his paces, finding out what made him weep with pleasure, what made him scream.

She settled into a lazy rhythm of suckling bliss. Her other hand crept around his waist and caressed his ass, pulling him even deeper into her mouth. He flung his head back and stared up at the moon, his eyes filling with white light as his orgasm rushed through him, huge and uncontrollable. She let out a surprised sound at the long, wrenching spasm of pleasure. There was an astonished silence.

"Sorry," he muttered, as soon as he could speak.

She wiped her mouth and kissed his thigh. "What for?"

"I didn't ask if it would be OK. To come in your mouth, I mean. It just, uh, happened," he said cautiously.

"Don't worry about it," she murmured. "I think I communicated nonverbally that I had no problem with that."

He was still panting, dizzy with pleasure. "Do you want me to, uh, get you a glass of water?" he offered.

She reflected for a moment. "That would be nice."

He scrambled to his feet and stumbled, weak-kneed, to the bathroom. Ran her a glass of water and brought it back to her. "That was amazing," he said as she drank. "A fantasy come true. Thank you."

"I liked it," she said.

"Anytime," he assured her. "I swear. Anytime."

He waited until he was sure she was asleep before he dared to close his eyes, but even then, they wouldn't close. He was too dazzled by the blazing moonlight to sleep now. Too astonished by the sweet passion of the mysterious woman in his arms.

He held her close against him and let the shape of the moon burn itself into his sleepless eyes.

Chapter Six

She woke up disoriented. Her body felt different. Sore, glowing, strangely alive. The air on her face was cold, but her body was incredibly, wonderfully warm, tangled up in the sleek, powerful limbs of— -oh, God. It wasn't a dream. It was Jonah, holding her tightly against him. His muscular chest rose and fell beneath her cheek.

Memories flooded back, of what he had done to her, what she had done in return. She didn't even recognize the woman she had been; wild and desperate, out of control. At his mercy, body and soul. She had never been like that with anyone. Jonah had pried open doors she never knew were there. He had moved her to the core. And if Larry had been able to wreak such havoc with her feelings and her self-esteem, she could not even bear to imagine the damage that Jonah could do.

The mountain was glowing pink with dawn, and the spectacular beauty of it just scared her all the more. Her eyes were wide and hot, and her stomach ached with nameless dread. She jumped nervously as Jonah stirred beneath her and lifted his head. "What?" he said sleepily.

"How did you know I was awake?" she whispered.

"I heard you thinking," he said grumpily. "What's wrong?"

"Nothing." She wiggled out of his arms.

"Bullshit." He wrapped his arms around her and pulled until her back was sealed against the delicious heat of his torso. "You're upset."

She struggled away from him and sat up. The drawer of the little nightstand was open, a box of condoms torn open, used wrappers discarded on the surface. She covered her hot face with her hands and let out a harsh little laugh. "Condoms everywhere, huh? Living room, dining room, bedroom; do you keep them in every room in the house?"

"What the hell? You're upset because I have condoms?"

"It's not the condoms. It's the thought of being one of a crowd. Do you bring a different woman here every weekend?" She knew she was being bitchy and unreasonable, but the words just flew out.

His body stiffened. "Stop it. That's not fair. I told you that I'm not seeing anyone else, and my past is none of your goddamn business."

"You are so right." She scrambled out of bed. "I'll just grab my clothes and be on my way." She looked around. "Where are my clothes?"

"Scattered all over the living room floor." He lunged for her, hauling her back against him, and dropped down onto the bed, pulling her onto his lap, against his hot, prominent erection. He grabbed her arms and wrapped them around her waist, clasping her wrists and holding her in a breathless clinch. He pressed his face against the side of her neck. "What the fuck is the matter with you?"

She struggled against his tight embrace. "You," she spat out. "You're the matter with me, Jonah Markham. I want to go, and you're holding onto me like a vise. Let me go, and I'll be fine."

"No way," he said. "You're not going anywhere. Not in this mood."

She twisted around, staring up into his furious eyes. "You can't keep me here against my will."

"Watch me."

She went very still in his grasp, appalled. "But that's—"

She squeaked in alarm as he flung himself onto his back, taking her with him. He rolled over so that she was flat on her belly and he was on top of her, covering her. His erection pressed against her bottom, hard and urgent. If he dared, if he even so much as *thought* that he could—panic exploded inside her. She wriggled frantically.

"Jonah," she said breathlessly. "This isn't right."

"I've already tried to do the right thing. I did everything you said. I obeyed you to the letter—"

"Oh, sure! Like hell! You totally ravished me. I was not in control for one second," she said furiously.

"Only when you gave me permission," he pointed out.

She craned her neck up at him, glaring. "And when did I do that? I do not recall doing that!"

"Bullshit," he said impatiently. "Sex is messy and complicated. At least good sex. Good sex doesn't follow rules, it follows instinct. And the sex was more than good. It was incredible. I made you come till you fainted. And now you're acting like I'm Jack the Ripper."

She gasped in outrage. "I did not—"

"So fuck it. If following the rules doesn't earn me any points, then fuck the rules. No more rules, Tess, except for mine."

She froze beneath him. "You're scaring me now, Jonah."

He let out a snort of disgust. "Don't be stupid. I would never hurt you. I'm just not going to let you run out on me. I *will . . . not . . . allow it.*"

"Damn it, Jonah—"

"This is just a spasm. It'll pass, and you'll thank me later."

The calm certainty in his tone sparked a burst of furious strength, and she made one more wrenching effort to throw him off. He shifted, trapping her legs between his and burying his face against her hair.

"Damn, but you're difficult," he muttered. "All I want to do is kiss you and pet you and tell you how gorgeous you are. I want to make you come again. Then I want to cook you an incredible breakfast. Why won't you just go with it and let me make you feel good?"

She couldn't think of a coherent answer to that. There was no good answer. The pleading tone in his voice confused her, made her heart ache and burn. She was so sick of the constant effort of staying clenched up like a fist. Exhausted from struggling to make it all alone, tired of the constricted feeling in her chest. Jonah was the antithesis of that, with his big, gorgeous body and his voluptuous appetite for pleasure, for laughter, and spontaneous delight. He had sneaked through her guard, and now he utterly refused to yield the ground he had gained. But the real problem was the burning ache of longing.

The real problem was her own reckless, treacherous heart.

To her embarrassment, she dissolved into tears. She pressed her face against the sheet to hide the silent scream of frustration, and sobs tore through her, out of control. A cynical voice in her mind pointed out that if she wanted to definitively scare him away, a good crying jag ought to do the trick. Heaven knew it always worked with Larry.

But Jonah just curled himself over her, nuzzling his face into the curve of her neck and shoulder. Breathing with her.

She cried for everything: for the shame of having disappointed her family, for the embarrassment of disappointing Larry. For how small and inadequate she had come to feel before she'd finally realized that she would never, ever satisfy them, no matter how hard she tried. For the desperation that had spurred her to run away, for the loneliness and the doubts, the hard work and penny-pinching, the effort of trying to build a life on her own, against all advice. It swept through her like a storm, thunder and lightning and a hot rain of tears.

Sometime later, she realized that she had stopped crying. A while ago. Maybe she had even slept for a while. She had cried herself to sleep with a big, live, warm Jonah blanket on top of her. She would have giggled if she had the energy.

Jonah dropped tiny questioning kisses on her neck, like he was afraid of scaring her. His breath was so warm and soft. He took the shell of her ear gently between his teeth and tugged at it. A soft, animal gesture, demanding, insisting, coaxing.

She felt renewed, reborn. Clear and light, but shivering, like she could melt into tears again at any moment. Full of light that flickered and changed with every breath, every thought. Her face buzzed with energy, as if electricity were running through it. She pressed her damp face on the sheet. "I need a Kleenex," she said soggily.

He reached out, and presented her with a Kleenex.

"I need my hand," she informed him. "To blow my nose."

They gazed at each other for a long, doubtful moment, and he let go of one of her hands, and watched her blow her nose.

"Are you OK now?" he ventured.

She made a little jerking motion that would have been a shrug if she hadn't been pinned to the bed. "I think so," she murmured.

He slid some of his weight to the side and stroked his hand very slowly, very tenderly over her hip. "So it wouldn't be a profound insult to your person if I did . . . this?" His fingers tangled tenderly into the thatch of ringlets between her legs.

She felt so shaky and melted and soft that her body was almost unbearably sensitive, but his touch was tender and unerring. She made a tiny, whispery little sound in the back of her throat and slowly parted her legs for him, letting him seek her pleasure.

And he found it. The rush of liquid heat was almost immediate. She clenched her trembling thighs around his hand. "You're taking advantage of my shaky emotional state," she accused him.

"With you, I'd better take every advantage I can get."

She laughed at him, and closed her eyes, squeezing her face against the crumpled sheets when the laughter started to blend into tears. She was so shaky and vulnerable, she felt like she were inside out. Every brushing touch, every kiss had a shocking, crackling intensity that shot through her whole body, jacking up the heavy yearning between her thighs into something hot and desperate.

She arched her back for him, opening wider and moving against his hand in silent pleading as he prepared her, spreading her slick juices across her vulva. She heard the tiny rip of the condom packet he was opening, the time it took to roll it over himself, and he slid his arm below her hips, raising her bottom. And then the relentless push and surge of his heat and hardness, sliding into her. Part of her.

He slowed down at the breathless sound she made, but he couldn't stop. He knew instinctively that if she bolted now, he would never pin her down again. And everything depended on keeping her here with him. He hoped he hadn't misjudged everything, ruined everything, but his sleep-fuddled wit failed him to think of any way other than seduction to soothe and persuade her.

The dawn revealed a whole array of new little perfect details, the pattern of scattered moles that set off the opalescent paleness of her skin, the sweet little dimples at the top of her buttocks. His breath caught in his lungs. She was the sexiest thing he had ever seen, the sensual curve and arch of her back, that round, rosy, gorgeous ass all spread out for him, the tight, glistening pink lips of her cunt clasping him, caressing him. Arching silently up, asking for more.

He settled into a deep, pounding rhythm, following the cues she gave him, the pulsing of her bottom as she jerked up to meet him, the rough sobbing of her breath. He curved himself over her so he could kiss her shoulders, her back, nuzzle her hair as he surged into her.

She twisted around, her eyes dewy and huge. "Jonah, wait."

Icy panic sped through his veins. He'd read the cues wrong, he'd committed the unforgivable sin, he was an unredeemable jerk.

He clasped her bottom in his hands and withdrew from her immediately. "What? Did I hurt you?"

She twisted around, and shook her head. "I just want to be able to move a little more. Can we change positions?"

Relief made him dizzy. "Hell, yes. Any position you want."

She scrambled up onto her knees. She had him right where she wanted him, if she only knew it. A panting puppy, desperate to please, terrified of making a mistake. She pushed him down onto his back and straddled him. He blinked, astonished, up into her cautious little smile.

"I'd like to try it this way," she said. "Is that OK with you?"

"Are you kidding? Anything is OK with me. Anything at all," he said shakily. From his position below, her luscious tits were full and enticing. He cupped them in his hands with a moan of delight. The plump heft of them, the tickle of her puckered nipples against his palms. Heaven.

He tried to be patient and let her figure out the mechanics of it, but she was adorably awkward and slow to find the right angle. It was driving him crazy. He gripped her hips, lifting her until he could nudge his stiff cock slowly inside her. He groaned in an agony of pleasure at the resistance of her tight, hot sheath as it clasped him, accepting him with tantalizing slowness. She slid down the length of his shaft, inch by delicious inch, eyes wide with discovery.

She braced her hands against his chest and began hesitantly to move, and he soon saw the realization dawning in her eyes, the hot flush of excitement as she shifted herself, rubbing against him with a purring moan of pleasure. She closed her eyes and flung her head back, and her hips pulsed faster and faster against him. It was so beautiful, and it squeezed his heart; it made everything inside him shake apart into a rushing torrent that swept them both away.

When he opened his eyes, he realized that she was crying again. But he could hardly object, since he was trembling on the brink of it himself. His throat was quivering, and his lungs hitched and shuddered dangerously when he tried to pull in a deep breath. He cuddled her and stared at the ceiling. "This is not normal," he blurted.

She snuggled against his neck. "Hmm? What's not normal?"

"For sex to be this good," he admitted. "I don't know about you, but this is not normal for me. I mean, I always like it fine. What's not to like? But it doesn't usually—" He stopped and shook his head, wishing he'd kept his big mouth shut.

She pushed herself up onto her elbow. "Doesn't what?"

"Blow my mind. Leave me all scared and humble and shaky."

She smiled. Her eyes were full of perfect understanding. "Like you've been run over by a herd of stampeding buffalo?"

He winced. "Ouch. I wasn't that rough, was I?"

"I meant that in a good way," she assured him.

He scowled. "What's good about being trampled by buffalo?"

"Oh, don't be so sensitive," she murmured. "You know exactly what I mean."

He yanked her back down against his chest and hid

his face against her hair. She was laughing at him. The sound vibrated through his body. It was disturbing, to feel so doubtful and awkward and raw.

"Maybe I'm supposed to apologize for having been all macho and controlling just now," he said carefully. "But being as how it had the desired effect of keeping you in my bed, I'm not going to. You're still here, so I must be doing something right. I hope."

Tess extricated herself from his arms and gave him a slow, solemn nod. "So, uh . . . now what happens?" she asked.

He sensed that her question was fraught with importance, but he was too shaky to deal with anything heavy after being trampled by a herd of buffalo. He kissed the tip of her nose. "Now we go down to the kitchen, where I proceed to make you buttermilk pancakes. Fluffy and golden, with real butter and maple syrup. Bacon, or ham, or eggs if you want them. Fresh squeezed orange juice. Strawberries. Fresh ground French roast coffee with half and half."

"Oh, my God," she said weakly. "That's not fair, Jonah."

"My secret weapon," he said smugly. "The way straight to your heart. I'll keep you here with me in my seductive trap, baited with whipped cream and wild sex. You'll never want to leave."

"Hmm." She sat up and cocked her head to the side, studying him with eyes that were too solemn. "If I tried to leave, would you stop me?"

Tension gripped him. He tried to keep his voice light. "I'll use every resource I've got. Including maple syrup and whipped cream."

"And brute force?" She wrapped her arms around her knees and studied him intently.

He took her hand, pulling it up to his lips and kissing her knuckles. "Let's just say that I really, really hope that you won't put me to the test."

And thanks be to God, she let it go at that.

Breakfast was a resounding success, judging from the approving moans of pleasure and the amount that she tucked in. She tried to do the dishes, but he was adamant. "Nah. Forget it. You're a guest."

She giggled and stuck another perfect ripe strawberry in her mouth. "But I was supposed to work this weekend."

"So things change. Now you're a guest. Which reminds me. We have to think about dinner. Do you like steak?"

"How can you already think about dinner? Of course I like steak!"

"With herbed baby red potatoes? Stuffed mushrooms and grilled eggplant? Ceasar salad? Strawberry shortcake? Or should we go with the Dutch apple pie with the whipped cream and caramel sauce?"

She shook her head, laughing. "Are you trying to impress me?"

"Yes," he admitted baldly.

She sat on his lap, wrapping her arms around his neck. "It worked," she admitted. "I'm impressed. I'm charmed, my defenses are in ruins. You can relax. You don't have to go to such ridiculous lengths."

His cock started swelling beneath the sweet pressure of her ass. "Don't encourage me," he said. "I'll feel compelled to do my filet mignon with caramelized onions, so I can conquer you utterly."

"You always conquer me utterly," she said quietly. "Every time you touch me."

In a heartbeat, he found himself kissing her desperately. Hints of coffee, of cream and strawberries clung to her soft lips. He was on the verge of just lifting her up onto the table, shoving down his jeans and thrusting into her. He could already imagine every scalding, pounding detail: her soft thighs locked around his waist, her tender little cunt gripping him all the way to the screaming finish.

No condom. He hadn't put one in his pocket. God. He pulled back, panting and speechless, and hid his face against her chest.

She slid off his lap. "I'll just, um, run and take a shower."

He managed a speechless nod, his heart still thudding.

He was wiping down the counters when she came downstairs, a cloud of moist, perfumed air clinging to her. She was wearing the Little House on the Prarie dress again. It almost succeeded in hiding how sexy she was, but then again, he hadn't been fooled from the start.

"You shouldn't hide behind your clothes," he said.

Her face went so pale and stiff that he barely recognized her. "I didn't ask for your opinion of my wardrobe."

He cursed his own idiocy and searched for a remedy in the frigid silence that followed. "Uh, I wasn't criticizing. I only meant that—"

"I know perfectly well what you meant. *Let . . . it . . . go.*"

"Sorry, sorry," he said hastily. "Look, do you, uh, want to go for a walk in the woods? It's raining, and your shoes and clothes aren't great for it. They'll get muddy. But I think it's worth it."

Her face lit up like a torch, his gaffe forgotten. He was pathetically grateful for the distraction.

* * *

The dress got damp around the hem almost instantly, and the pristine white tennis shoes she wore with the Vee Have Vays dress would never be white again. In fact, at this point, they were barely recognizable as shoes. Thorny branches snagged the skirt as they pushed through the underbrush, and before long her face was beaded with rain, she was soaked from the waist down, and slimed with mud up to her ankles. She'd been let loose in a mythical fantasy world, pulsing with mystery and magic. She had never been so happy in her life.

Huge trees disappeared into the mist above them, their branches tipped with the bright, lambent new growth of spring. Pale yellow glacier lilies poked up out of the pine needles, jewel-like drops of rain clinging to their drooping heads. The earthy sweetness of the air made her dizzy. They could've been Adam and Eve in the garden, wandering through the breathless, vaulted hush of a forest cathedral, speechless with awe.

She stared at Jonah's tight, muscular butt from behind and finally understood what moved people to grope and grab and fondle, an instinct that had always struck her as vulgar. Hah. What a humbling surprise. She was so far beyond vulgar, she couldn't even remember what the far side of it looked like. She wanted to grab his butt, pet it, sink her teeth into it. Yank those jeans down and run her hands all over his big body, to feel every dip and curve, every muscle. The graceful way his sweater draped his torso, the long, clean, elegant lines of him made her so breathless with lust, it was impossible to think.

He smiled at her over his shoulder, and her knees almost buckled at his beauty—every delicious detail: the good-natured crinkles around his beautiful gray eyes, the sexy grooves that bracketed his mouth. He turned to go on. She lunged toward him. "Jonah. Wait."

"Hmm?"

"Hold still." She slogged heedlessly through the soggy undergrowth until she reached him, and laid a hand on his chest, feeling his warmth, the rise and fall of his breath through the damp fabric. She put her other hand against his face, smoothing the elegant planes and hollows with her fingertips. She ran her fingers through his glossy dark hair, along his strong neck, his broad shoulders.

Wordless comprehension dawned in his eyes. He understood the impulse that moved her. He waited quietly, letting her have her fill of touching him. Reassuring her of his warm, solid reality. Being there for her. Silently communicating his readiness.

He placed his hands over hers. "All yours," he said softly. "Anytime, anywhere, any way you like. Just tell me what you want."

She slid her hands around his waist, under his shirt. Gripped his lean waist, slid around to feel the taut muscles in his back. Then his butt, with a low, humming sound of approval. He drew in a harsh breath as she ran her hand over the bulge in his jeans, measuring the heat and length and hardness of him.

"I like this place," she told him. "It makes me feel primeval."

A hot flush burned itself high onto his cheekbones. "You're different today," he said. "You've changed. You take up more space."

"Yes," she agreed. "I do. I feel it, too."

He shoved her up against a tree, his hands moving eagerly over the sodden dress. "I like it," he said. "It turns me on."

She snickered. "Yeah, and what doesn't?"

He yanked up the waterlogged dress. "Primeval, huh? I guess that means you want me to be all macho and masterful and Neanderthal?"

She challenged him with her smile. "You really go for that, don't you?"

"With you, I go for anything." He plucked at the barrier of the wool tights with an exclamation of disgust. "Layers upon layers. Jesus. You do like to present a guy with a challenge, don't you?"

"So easily discouraged, Jonah?"

She abruptly regretted taunting him when he grabbed the wool knit fabric and ripped it open with one sharp wrench. "Wrong answer."

"Jonah! You're wrecking my—"

"Too bad," he said. Another sharp tug, and her panties gave way. Her most intimate flesh was open to the cool, damp breeze. "My primeval woman is always ready for me to tear open her fur robes, pin her up against a tree, and go for it."

She tried to steady herself by grabbing handfuls of his sweater. "It's dangerous to challenge you," she said shakily.

"You get off on it, though, don't you?" He parted the folds of her sex and caressed her tenderly with his finger, dipping into her liquid heat with a low growl of hunger. "You like pushing me to the edge."

He seized her mouth in a conquering kiss that did not coax or wheedle or charm. He claimed what was rightfully his. His savage ruthlessness was no game, and they both knew it. It was the truth between them, at its most elemental. He drew back, his eyes glowing with primal heat. "You want me to fuck you right here, don't you?"

She licked her lips. "Yes," she whispered.

"Say it. Say the words," he demanded. "I need to hear them."

Such a thing would have been impossible yesterday. But not anymore. She squeezed her eyes shut and took a deep breath.

"I want you to fuck me right here," she said clearly.

She was almost afraid to open her eyes and see the triumph on his face, but he didn't look triumphant. His face was a taut mask of need. "I love it when you talk dirty," he said hoarsely.

He shoved her back against the tree and plunged her back into the chaos of his kiss. She was pinned and breathless, her toes barely touching the ground, whimpering against his mouth, rubbing herself against his hard body. Reaching with every instinct for something shining just beyond her reach. He tantalized her until she couldn't take anymore. She groped for his belt, the buttons on his jeans. He hadn't bothered with underwear. His penis sprang out, turgid and ready, into her eager hands.

He had to set her down to retrieve the condom, and she took the opportunity to stroke and caress his engorged shaft, making him gasp and curse under his breath. He pushed her hands away just long enough to roll the condom on, and then scooped one of her legs up high, pressing his thick, blunt flesh against her labia, pushing slowly inside. She was tender from the unaccustomed sex, but so aroused that the sting was just a sharp definition around a hot, demanding ache of pleasure.

He forged inside until he had sheathed himself completely, and leaned against her, breathing hard. She could feel his heart pounding, his breath feathering her hair, his body trembling, his fingers digging into her bare bottom.

He stared into her eyes, holding her in a tight, speechless communion, and began to move. He withdrew with agonizing slowness, and surged in again, making her feel the sweet, licking caress of each stroke, inch by inch. It went on and on like that, until she began to pant. She was a live flame writhing against the tree, desperate for the plunge and slide of his thick shaft. She needed . . . she needed—

"Jonah," she gasped. "Please. More."

"More what?" His voice was as harsh and shaky as hers.

She clawed at his sweater, at his naked waist. "More everything! Move, damn it!"

He laughed triumphantly, and gave her what she needed. The power he had awakened swelled, bursting hot and golden in her chest and belly, surging like a fountain of molten liquid pleasure between her legs. Everything gave way to that blinding rush.

He waited for her orgasm to subside, nuzzling her neck, petting her bottom, murmuring against her hair. Then he eased himself out of her and let her slide down until her feet hit the ground. He caught her when her knees gave way, holding her until she found her balance.

And even then, he wouldn't let go. He held her tight against him, warm and panting and damp. Chest heaving against hers. He pushed her hair aside with his face and kissed the side of her neck as he arranged himself, zipping his jeans and buckling his belt. "You OK?"

She nodded, unable to speak. Her knees were weak, her legs still tangled in her ruined tights, her voice tangled in her throat.

He pushed back her hair, his eyes worried. "Sure?"

She didn't know how to express how she felt. She didn't even recognize the feelings roaring through her. Needs that could not be denied, emotions that blazed up like fires rushed through her like a flash floods, changing the landscape of her inner self in an instant, carving out canyons, mudslides, unexpected chasms.

She flung back her head. Drops of rain shed by the trees fell onto her face, pale sunlight pressed against her closed eyelids. She breathed in the heat, the light, the wild freedom of this new, changing self.

When she finally dared to open her eyes, he was staring at her face, fascinated. He didn't think she was crazy or hysterical or overwrought. His face was alight with triumph.

He knew exactly what was happening to her, and he liked it.

He pulled her close and sank his teeth gently into her throat with a fierce growl of approval. "You're fine," he whispered. "More than fine."

"I'm flying," she whispered back.

She abandoned the sodden dress and put on one of Jonah's T-shirts when they got back to the house.

When she came downstairs, he was building a fire. "Want me to make you some lunch?" he asked.

"How about a massage?" she suggested.

His eyes lit up. "Hell, yes. But only if you feel like it."

She gave him a misty smile, still euphoric from the forest. "I feel like it. I like pleasing you. But lie down on the rug this time, not the table. Otherwise it'll be too much like work, and I'll get confused."

He stripped and lay down with a sigh of blissful anticipation. She laid her oiled hands against him, and the strength of the charge between them ran all the way up her arms, made her shiver. She didn't have to soothe or calm him this time. His barriers were already flung wide. Her hot, tingling hands moved over him of their own volition. She had never felt so powerful. She would have floated right up into the air but for the immense gravitational force of his beautiful body.

She had no idea how long she touched him. It could have been hours. She would never have stopped if he hadn't rolled over with a sigh of pure delight and reached for her. "Please," he said simply.

He pulled the loose shirt over her head, flung it away, and pulled her into his arms, pressing his face against her hair. He squirted some of her oil onto his hands began to explore her body with the same reverent attention to detail that she had just given his. His hands slid slowly over her skin, as if he wanted to memorize every inch of her. He kneaded her shoulders and arms, hands, fingertips. He traced every vertebra in her back, brushed his fingertips across her ribs in soft, feathery circular strokes. He explored the hollows of her collarbone, the muscles and tendons in her neck. Her touched her face, tracing every feature, following his caresses with kisses like a hot, soft rain.

She huddled against him, lost in ever-widening ripples of pleasure. She sighed as his hands moved lovingly over her breasts, but he was just as fascinated with her belly button, her throat. His touch soothed her into a state of perfect trust, amazed by the luminous tenderness between them. His generosity made her want to offer him the best of herself. Everything that was good and kind and true.

They were melted into one shining being when they groped for the condom. Four trembling hands fumbled together, gleaming with scented oil and clumsy with eagerness as they smoothed it over him. A sweet confusion of arranging limbs, kisses and sighs, and finally he settled her into place, straddling him, her legs around his waist. The whole length of their torsos were in hot, kissing contact. Her nipples brushed against his chest. She wiggled carefully, reaching below herself to grasp him, seeking the angle that would permit him to nudge inside her soft opening. She let gravity do the rest, sinking down and enveloping him.

Joy swelled inside her, almost painful, but she welcomed the pain. He was so beautiful, it hurt to look at him. She hugged him close, leaning her forehead against his as they rocked together—sometimes almost motionless, locked together in a circle of shimmering perfection where neither dared to breathe, then melting seamlessly into pulsing, surging movement once again. She didn't want it to ever end.

The fire died down to embers, untended and forgotten. Light faded, but they stayed clasped together, afraid to break the spell.

But the room grew cold. Rain slanted down, gusting against the windows. She began to shiver, both inside and out, as she realized what she had done. She had flung herself wide open, held out body, heart, and soul in front of her like a sacrificial offering, and he had swooped down like a hungry bird of prey and taken them all.

If it had only been her body, that would have been perilous enough. But he had laid claim to all of it. He had devoured her, pleasured her beyond any fantasy with his sweet, ravishing tenderness.

He stirred against her neck. "No sunset tonight," he said with soft regret. "I should've grabbed my chance last night."

"Chance for what?"

"To look at you in the sunset. But that's OK. You're beautiful in any kind of light. Hey, you're getting cold. Wrap this around yourself."

She accepted the blanket without protest, but he sensed every shift in her mood, even in the darkness. He turned her face to what little light still glowed from the windows. "What?" he demanded.

She forced out a laugh. "Nothing," she said. "Hungry, I guess."

The tiny frown between his brows did not fade. "I'll make dinner."

"I'll help." She held up her hand, forestalling his protests. "Just let me chop veggies, set the table. I promise I won't get in your way."

Doing something mundane and practical might help this dull, scared ache taking hold inside her. At least she hoped it would.

Chapter Seven

They worked together silently. She washed salad greens, he prepared the steaks, put the potatoes on to boil, and stuck the stuffed mushrooms in the toaster oven. He opened a bottle of wine and poured her a glass.

"Tell me about yourself," he blurted out.

She was thrown off balance by the demand. "Tell you what?"

He shrugged. "Anything, everything. Hopes, dreams, plans. I've been so focused on getting you into my bed that I've gone about this whole thing backward. If you'd gone out to dinner with me when I wanted, I would've had all these facts straight by now. But no. You had to blow me off, string me along. Make me wait."

She relaxed a little and sipped her wine. "OK. I come from San Francisco, and I just moved to Portland three years ago and enrolled in massage school. I got my license last year."

"Last year?" He looked incredulous. "But you're

amazing. I would have thought you'd been doing it for years."

She sighed. "I should've been, but I was too busy trying to make my parents approve of me. A losing battle if ever there was one, which culminated in my dropping out of my last term in business school. They still haven't recovered from that."

"Business school? You?"

She laughed at his expression. "Yeah, it's a concept, isn't it?"

He turned the steaks that sizzled on the grill. "So, to be a massage therapist, that's what you've always wanted, then?"

"I've always liked it. I was always good at giving massages, and it's something I never get tired of. The more I learn about the body, the more I like it. I'm opening my own studio, as soon as I can scrape the money together. I want to create a perfect environment for therapeutic massage. Maybe eventually expanding into a sort of mini spa."

He nodded his approval, and turned to the sink to drain the potatoes. "And?" he said expectantly.

She lifted her eyebrows. "And what?"

"I was hoping you would tell me about the playboy who trampled all over you," he said.

Her stomach knotted up. "Let's not and say we did, shall we?"

The potatoes sizzled as he tossed them into the hot pot with melted butter and fresh herbs. "Please, Tess," he said quietly. "Just the bare bones."

She sighed. "Larry," she said finally. "My ex-fiancé. The CEO of my dad's investment banking firm, which I was being groomed to join. And he wasn't really a playboy, to be honest. He worked very hard, and he's good at what he does. It's just that he has really high standards."

Jonah paused in the task of transferring the steaks onto plates, his face baffled. "Meaning?" he asked. "You're a goddess. Beautiful, smart, fascinating, sexy. What was his problem?"

She laughed at his gallant flattery, blinking away a rush of tears. "You are so sweet."

He frowned. "I am not sweet. High standards for what?"

"Larry felt that he deserved the best in everything," she explained wearily. "He wanted top quality, especially in his wife. He picked me out mainly because I possessed the sterling attribute of being the boss's daughter, but to do him credit, he truly did think that he could train me into being good enough. He told me once I was great raw material."

Jonah drizzled olive oil on the salad, waiting patiently for more. "And?" he prompted.

She shrugged. The memory of Larry's disapproval made her queasy and depressed. "I wasn't trainable," she said flatly. "In fact, I was a hopeless case. I was the wrong shape, I dressed wrong, I didn't laugh at the right places in the conversation, I wasn't witty enough, I couldn't—"

The wooden spoon froze in the act of tossing salad. "He didn't like your *shape?*" Jonah looked horrified. "What planet was he from?"

Trust Jonah to fixate on that. She was touched by his dismay.

"He wanted me to be more, uh, contained," she explained. "Larry was into control. Finally I just couldn't take anymore. I ran away. Like a coward, I guess."

"Like hell!"

She flinched back, startled by his tone.

"He didn't appreciate you because he was a brain-dead asshole! And you ran away because you're brave, and smart, and no matter what he said, you know your own worth deep inside."

She blinked at him, utterly taken aback. "Uh, well . . . thank you for defending me, Jonah. You are really—"

"Sweet, yeah. Right." He thumped the wooden salad bowl down onto the counter with such force that greens flipped into the air. Chunks of radicchio and arugula flopped over the sides.

She crossed her arms over her chest and studied his rigid face. "You're angry," she whispered.

"Sure I am. It pisses me off that people put you down. It pisses me off even more that you bought into their bullshit. And you still do."

She closed her mouth with a snap and crossed her arms over her chest. "Oh. I see. How about if you tell me some intimate, painful details about your past now, so I can criticize you and judge you? Go on."

He opened his mouth to respond, but the cell phone on the counter rang, cutting him off. He checked the number on the display, and his face suddenly went blank of all expression. "I have to take this call," he said. "Stir the potatoes, would you?"

He walked out onto the covered side porch. Tess craned her neck to watch him as she stirred the sizzling potatoes and herbs. It was none of her business, but she couldn't help peeking. His face was grim and tense, and he listened more than he talked. Bad news.

After a few minutes, he came back inside and dropped the phone back onto the counter. He met her questioning gaze. "Work," he said.

She turned back to the potatoes without a word.

Jonah slipped his arms around her waist and took the spatula from her hand. He stirred the potatoes, turned off the flame, and kissed her shoulder where the neck of his T-shirt had slipped off, leaving it bare. "I'm sorry," he said. "It was none of my business."

"It's OK," she whispered.

"No, it's not. We were in a really fine place together, and I wrecked it somehow. I don't know what I said or did, but I—"

"It's not you." She spun around and hugged him hard, pressing her hand against his mouth when he tried to speak again.

His chest heaved in a heavy sigh. He kissed her fingers, and his arms tightened around her. She squeezed as hard as she could. Larry would have been horrified by her intensity, but Jonah seemed unfazed.

After a long while, he lifted his head. "Food's getting cold."

They smiled at each other carefully. "So let's eat," she said.

He'd broken the spell somehow. He could've kicked himself.

Good food was always a point in his favor, but it wasn't enough to bring back that perfect, shimmering intimacy of their magic afternoon. Now that he'd had a taste of it, he would forever be pining for more.

Half of his mind was reeling over the news Dr. Morrison had called to deliver. Triple bypass surgery for Granddad on Wednesday.

Ever ready to multitask, the rest of his brain churned right along, speculating on what the hell he might have said or done to pitch them into this awful downward spiral. They ate, chatting inanely. Both trying so hard to be neutral and nice that he wanted to scream. It was like a big, dark animal was sitting on the dining room table blocking their view of each other, and they were trying to pretend it didn't exist.

There had to be some way to dispel it.

He dished up the hot Dutch apple pie, scooped ice cream over it, and drizzled it with hot caramel sauce, and when he turned around she was cupping her stubborn pointed chin in her hands, looking stern.

"OK, Jonah. Your turn," she announced.

"For what?" He was pathetically relieved to see the sparkle back in her eyes. He preferred a difficult spitfire to a timid, careful mouse.

"Now you tell me something about you." She sat back in her chair, looking expectant.

He set her heaping dish of pie and ice cream before her. "OK," he said obediently. "I'm thirty-five. I have my own consulting business, specializing in problem solving and brainstorming techniques."

She rolled her eyes. "Blah, blah, blah. I read all that in your profile in *Northwest Business*. I was thinking a bit more personal, please."

"Personal?" He eyed her suspiciously. "What do you want to know about, my ex-girlfriends?"

She took a bite of her pie. "I was thinking more along the lines of family," she said loftily. "Basic historical detail. Are you a dog person or a cat person? Do you resemble your mother or your father?"

"No parents," he said. "They were killed in a plane crash in Chile. My dad was an archaeologist. I was eleven."

Tess's spoon froze in the air near her mouth. She slowly lowered it. "Oh, God, Jonah. I'm sorry. I didn't mean to—"

"It's OK," he assured her. "It was a long time ago. And I got through it. I had Granddad. He was the one who raised me. He was great. Strict, but great."

"He's still alive?" she asked cautiously.

"Yeah." *God willing and the creek don't rise,* he thought, silently willing her to change the subject.

They ate their dessert silently for a minute or two, both of them afraid of making another wrong move.

Finally Tess lay down her spoon and took a deep, audible breath. She touched his hand. "Jonah. That phone call. Was it bad news?"

He stared down at her hand. His throat tightened. He didn't want to talk about it. His stomach was knotted enough as it was, thinking about Granddad's chances. And then there were John and Steve, trying like hell to keep him out of the loop. Worried about their cut in the fucking will, as if he gave a shit about Granddad's money. He'd made plenty of his own, but that didn't help matters. His very success showed up their own lack of ability and made them hate him all the more.

It was all so raw that even at the thought of her gentle sympathy, the questions she would ask, made him flinch. He would shove her away by reflex if she tried to comfort him, and that would cook his goose for sure. That was no way to get back to their magical union.

He took a deep breath and did what he had to do. He plastered on a bright, ain't-life-grand smile. "Work stuff. Nothing I can't handle."

Disappointment flashed across her expressive face. He felt guilty and stupid for lying, but he didn't want to burden her with the embarrassing truth. He wasn't on top of the world. He was scared to death of Granddad dying and leaving him all alone again. He remembered that empty, falling away feeling all too well, from when he was a kid. The awful, aching finality of it.

And no good-byes this time, either, since Granddad wouldn't talk to him. The stubborn old geezer was still furious with his grandson for turning down the chance to head up Markham Savings & Loan.

Oh, fuck it. He was just about to open his mouth and lay it all out there for her when the shifting play of emotions in her luminous eyes abruptly receded, as if she had closed a door in his face.

It was replaced by a dazzling, utterly impenetrable smile.

"Well. That's good, then," she said.

"Uh, yeah." He blinked at her, puzzled. "It is?"

She stood up and very slowly pulled his T-shirt up over her astounding tits. She tossed it behind herself. "I'm so glad for you, Jonah. Not a care in the world. It must be awfully nice for you."

"Uh, yeah," he said hoarsely. "It's . . . great."

There was a trap here, a bad one, and he was headed right for it, but with those perfect, puckered brown nipples right at eye level, his IQ was drooping in direct inverse proportion to the swelling in his cock. He would so, *so* much rather do this than talk about his deepest fears.

She stuck her finger into the soupy vanilla ice cream that was melted together with caramel sauce. She began to paint designs on her plump, full breasts with it. Deliberately glazing her nipples with creamy caramel goo. Loops and swirls, until she was wet and gleaming. She licked her fingers, one by one, and smiled. Not the shy, glowing smile, with all of her sweetness shining out of it. This smile taunted him, guarding its secrets. Provocative and bold.

Unreal, that after all the unbelievable sex he'd been having that he was ready to go at it again.

"You wanted me to articulate my desires," she said.

He tried not to pant. "Uh, so I did."

"Lick me clean, Jonah," she commanded.

He didn't have time to marvel over the sharp edge of command in her voice before he leaped to obey her. He was gone, lost, all over her, devouring her. She was sexy and syrupy and delicious, and if this was a trap, all he wanted to do was to dive into it headfirst, and stay in it.

For as long as he possibly could.

She had no idea what she was doing, or even why she was doing it. A powerful impulse had risen up out of the churning chaos inside her, and she had grappled onto it blindly. She wanted to be a goddess with the power to bestow pleasure or agony at her whim—a dark, tangled impulse, mixed with hurt and anger and fierce, animal need.

She wanted to make him beg.

It was going to be tricky. She had a tiger by the tail. He had pulled her onto his lap, licking the caramel and ice cream off her breasts with passionate thoroughness. Her panties had already sailed off into limbo, and his hand was between her legs, pressing with delicate skill against her clitoris. He shifted her so that he could shove his jeans down, and his penis sprang out, heavy and hot and straining.

He was going to be hard to master.

She reached down and wrapped her hand around his hot shaft—and squeezed. Hard enough to make him drag in a startled breath.

"Whoa," he said. "Go easy with that."

"Slow down, Jonah. I'm running this one."

His eyes widened at the cool command in her voice. He lifted his hands in mock surrender.

"Kick off those jeans," she said. "You won't be needing them."

He did as he was told, his eyes locked on hers.

"Let's go to the bedroom," she said.

His head jerked in agreement. She suffered a stab of doubt at the foot of the stairs, reluctant to walk in front of him and wave her big naked bottom right in his face, in all its full-blown glory. But she couldn't think that way, even for a second, or she would lose the tenuous upper hand that she barely knew how to maintain.

She started up the stairs, back straight, hips swaying. He sighed with pleasure behind her, and then his big, warm hands were on her hips. His breath was hot against her skin. His mouth pressed against her backside. She spun around to tell him to stop, but before she could speak, he pressed his face against her mound, making her stumble back, almost falling onto the steps behind her.

"Give me a taste," he said. "Just one little sip from the fountain of life, to get me up the stairs. Or I'll fall down and expire right here."

She stared down into his pale eyes. The house was silent, and the staircase was dark, just the sigh of the wind and the lash of the rain against the windows. She clutched the banister and let her thighs unlock, widening her stance. A guttural exclamation of triumph vibrated against her sensitive flesh, and he parted the folds of her sex, pressing his face against her, his tongue thrusting.

He knew instinctively what she needed, the perfect, voluptuous blend of licking and suckling. His tongue fluttered and swirled against her clitoris, his teeth rasping, tugging, sucking her, bathing her in the hot cloud of his breath. He grasped her hips and devoured her as if he were starving. She was suspended in darkness and empty space, wind and rain swirling around her, and Jonah at the center, his mouth a hot vortex that claimed everything she had. She heard only the sounds of his mouth, saw only his broad shoulders, his dark head. She had no memory of sitting or falling, but she found herself sprawled on the stairs, legs draped over his shoulders, moving helplessly, eagerly against his face.

He knew her so well now, better than she had ever known herself. He could do what he pleased with her, and he damn well knew it.

No. The thought came from a cool, remote place inside her head that stood and watched her helpless pleasure, unmoved. If she let him unravel her, then the night would be his. The upper hand would be lost, and so would she. Undone, unglued. Conquered.

It went against every instinct, but she reached down and pushed his face away from her. He murmured in fierce protest.

"No," she whispered. "This is my show. I have to tell you when."

She couldn't see his expression in the dark, but she could picure the cool speculation on his face. He released her slowly, wiping his face on his arm, and let her struggle to her feet without offering to help.

They stared at each other in the gloom. He made an impatient, questioning gesture toward the head of the stairs.

She turned, trying to be dignified as she continued up the stairs.

Upper hand. Think upper hand, she repeated to herself as she led him into the bedroom. The upper hand really had less to do with physical strength than it did with confidence, inner power. Poise.

With Jonah, it was like walking a tightrope in a hurricane wind.

She flipped on the bedside lamp and made an imperious gesture toward the bed. "Lie down, Jonah," she said.

"What game are you playing, Tess?" he asked.

"You'll see." She flung open the closet and saw what she had hoped to see. Silk ties. Not a lot of them, but enough for her purposes. She pulled a handful off their rack.

His eyes narrowed in deep suspicion. "What's this?"

"Lie down, Jonah," she said coolly. "You've been very bad, luring me up here. Lying to me, seducing me, breaking our bargain."

"You drove me to it," he protested.

"No excuses," her voice snapped out. "You have to be punished."

He looked like he was trying not to smile. "You really . . . ?"

"Oh, yes. Really. Lie down. *Now.*"

He sat down slowly on the bed, his eyes fixed on hers. "I really, really hope I won't regret this," he said.

"Arms up, please."

He presented his arms, and she tied them to the posts of the old-fashioned bed. She knelt with her backside to him, and tied his feet.

"I don't know quite how I feel about this," he muttered.

"You will in a minute or two," she informed him.

"You're so unpredictable," he said. "Not like I expected."

"Expected?" Her voice was falsely sweet as she swung her leg over him and straddled his belly. "So you planned this all along, hmm?"

He scowled. "I didn't plan. I hoped. Are you going to punish me for that, too?"

She dragged her fingernails over his chest. "I'll punish you for whatever I feel like punishing you for. We'll see what comes to me."

He drew in a sharp breath, his eyes guarded. "You're in a dangerous mood," he murmured.

She reached for a condom, tossing it onto the rumpled coverlet. Then she scooted down the length of his body and began to play.

She fondled his balls, and traced the veins that throbbed on the surface of his penis lightly with her fingertip. It lay against his belly, stiff and hard and twitching with every ragged breath he took. He hissed at her teasing, tickling touch.

"Tess," he growled. "Are you going to—"

"Shhh," she murmured. "Suffer in silence . . ." she leaned over, brushing his lips with her fingertip, ". . . or I'll gag you."

His face tightened. "Hey. Wait a minute. You really are mad at me, aren't you? This is no game. I can feel it. You're messing with my mind."

She didn't answer, just straddled his chest and shimmied down until her labia pressed against his stiff shaft, and began to slowly, deliberately slide her wet cleft up and down the length of him. She pleasured herself with the contact with his heat and power. Smiling at him, pitiless, as the realization of his plight grew in his eyes.

He struggled to nudge inside her, but she just rose up onto her knees, evading him easily. She reached down, holding his penis right where she wanted it. Rubbing against him. Hot, slick, slow torture.

He flung his head back, the tendons standing out on his neck. "Damn it. What did I do to piss you off this time? I thought we were a million miles past all that tedious crap this afternoon."

She smiled at him through her eyelashes and

scooted lower. Licked his belly. Breathed softly against the thick, gleaming head of his penis, and then dropped the very lightest of maddening butterfly kisses on the tip. "You didn't think it was so tedious last night," she told him. "You liked it just fine, playing me like an instrument. Keeping all the control. Not risking anything."

He flailed beneath her, almost bucking her off. "What the hell do you know what I risked?" he snarled.

"Less than me," she said. "Way, way less than me."

He jerked as far up as his bonds would allow. "That's not fair. It's not true, either. And you are seriously pissing me off."

She gripped his penis, milking him as roughly as she dared. He arched beneath her again, lifting her right up off the bed. "That's the spirit," she taunted him. "Go ahead, Jonah. Be pissed off. You did this to me deliberately last night. Try a taste of your own medicine. See how it feels to be spread out and naked and helpless while somebody has her way with you."

She scrambled down over his tense, rigid body and bent low, flicking her tongue across the head of his penis and licking up the gleaming drop that had formed there. Just one teasing swipe of her tongue was all she offered him, then she drew back and gave him only the warmth of her breath, the slow drag of her hair as she brushed the heavy mass back and forth over his penis, his balls.

She straddled his chest again and gazed down with a secret little smile. She lifted up onto her knees, face flushed, showing him how wet, how soft and excited she was. Deliberately stoking the volcanic energy that was building up between them.

She undulated, parting the folds of her sex so that her clitoris poked out from the top of her cleft, flushed and crimson. She laid two fingers on either side of it and began to move them slowly up and down.

His eyes were locked onto her stroking hand. He panted, his face as flushed and damp as her own. "You're trying to drive me insane, aren't you?" he said. "You manipulative bitch."

She ignored him, caught up in her own pleasure. She caressed the undersides of her breasts, trailed her fingertips around stiff, taut nipples. She pulsed her hips against her hand, dragging in harsh little gasps of air. "Watch me come, Jonah," she whispered.

It was his eyes upon her, dilated with anger and desire, as much as her own hand, that catapulted her into climax. It was long and violent, different than the others. A wrenching blast of red and pounding black. She jerked back, mouth open in a soundless scream.

She opened her eyes, gasping for air. The fury on his face made her go very still. She had teased him mercilessly, given him no outlet at all. His stiff, empurpled shaft jerked with unfulfilled excitement. Long, glistening strands of fluid from the tip gleamed against his belly.

It occurred to her that she had to untie him sometime.

She didn't dare do so if he had that look on his face. She fell forward, catching herself against his damp chest, and searched the rumpled bed for the condom. She ripped it open with trembling fingers and smoothed it over his rigid penis and poised herself over him.

"Beg me, Jonah," she said. "I want to hear you plead."

His breath hissed through his teeth, his neck and arms corded with strain. "Stop fucking around, Tess. Do it. Now. Or else."

She guided the tip of his penis into her swollen wetness. Sinking lower with a gasp at the blunt size of him. She lifted up again, leaving just the tip of him kissing her opening. "Beg," she insisted.

"What the fuck do you want from me?" he exploded.

"Everything," she said rashly. "Everything you've got."

His face changed, as if she had flipped a switch. "Done," he said.

He wrenched at the ties, and yanked the knots loose with a few quick, violent jerks. He surged up off the bed, holding her against himself as he freed his ankles. He'd been able to free himself all along.

He had chosen not to. Now that restraint was swept away.

He flung her onto her back with a speed that left her breathless and disoriented. He shoved her thighs apart, and prodded roughly until he was lodged inside her, not bothering to remove the silk ties still clinging to his wrists. He shot them a quick, contemptuous glance.

"Girl knots," he said succinctly.

"I'm going to learn to tie knots you can't pull out of," she snapped.

He let out a harsh laugh. "You're not going to learn it from me."

He thrust himself deeply inside her and held her immobile. His face was rigid, mouth sealed, as if he didn't trust himself to speak.

She gathered her tattered bravado. "Don't be so huffy. You had all that coming. But go ahead. Tie me up, if it makes you feel better."

"I don't have to tie you," he said. "I can just hold you down."

Her nerve ebbed away. "Jonah, don't—"

"You said everything. You wanted it all. You didn't specify what that means, though, so I'll interpret it however I want. Anything, everything, anyhow, anywhere, as much as I want. I'm going to take you for everything you've got. Does that turn you on?"

She shoved against his chest, chilled. "Hey. I never said—"

"Or are you going to chicken out? Again?" he taunted. "You keep pushing me, Tess. If you push me right over the top, I have to assume that's right where you want me to be. Over the top. Out of control. Right? Go on, tell me that I'm right."

She swallowed. "Within reason," she whispered.

He laughed. "There is no reason out there in no-man's land. You push me farther away from reason with every breath you take."

She glared at him. "Stop trying to scare me."

"I'm not. I'm being absolutely straight with you. It's you who's fucking with my head. You betrayed my trust."

"Oh, please. Don't be silly and melodramatic," she snapped. "I didn't do anything to you that you didn't do to me last night."

"Bullshit. I might have teased you, but I was never cold," he said furiously. "Why were you cold to me, after what we shared this afternoon? What did I do to deserve that? Why, Tess?"

She winced away from the fury in his voice. A long moment ticked by. "I don't know," she said in a tiny voice.

He was silent, waiting for more, but she could think of nothing more to say that might satisfy him. She finally dared to look up.

The anger on his face was mixed with pain and baffled hurt.

"So figure it out, Tess," he said quietly.

He hid his face against her neck. When he lifted his head, it was a stark mask of pain. "If you don't want me, I won't force you," he said. "But decide, real quick. Because I'm right on the edge."

The rough, trembling honesty in his voice went straight to her heart, and her heart took over in an instant. Needing him, wanting him. All of him: his strength, his his confusion, his anger. His unknown past, his untold secrets, whatever they were. Hers, damn it. All hers.

She wrapped herself around him. Squeezed him. "No," she whispered. "Don't leave me."

His breath escaped in a sob of relief. "Then stop playing games with me. I can't take it. Deal with me straight."

"That goes for you, too," she said.

They gave each other one last searching look. He nodded. "Deal."

He gathered her close and breathlessly tight into his arms, nudging and arranging her until her her legs were twined around his. The look in his eyes made her want to cry. He kissed her, with heartbreaking intensity as his body surged into hers, and she accepted him.

All her tricks and games and efforts to protect herself seemed so vain and foolish now. Her heart was laid bare. There was no hiding from the fierce attention in his penetrating eyes. No denying the power he wielded over her. His very existence excited and moved her. His beautiful body, his strength, his restless intelligence, his sensitivity.

And his passion was like a key to a lock, opening up a whole new secret world inside her. A tidal wave began to gather, building higher and higher. They cried out together as it broke. It swept her under, and she felt him following her. Joined with her.

Reality crept back slowly. They were glued together by sweat, hearts pounding. He had gotten what he wanted. There was no going back. Too late now to put up walls or close doors. She'd taken her chances coming up here. She'd rolled her dice.

And she'd lost everything to him.

She dissolved into silent tears, her face against his chest.

He clutched her, alarmed. "God. What is it now? Did I hurt you?"

"Just shut up and just hold me," she snapped.

His arms tightened fiercely. "OK," he said. "That I can do."

Chapter Eight

A small eternity later she calmed down, and Jonah disentangled himself. He went out on the deck, tossed the plastic cover off the hot tub, and checked the water. Nice and hot against the evening chill. He flipped on the deck light to its lowest setting, a dim golden glow no more obtrusive than candlelight, and went back inside.

Tess was a lump under the covers and two shadowy eyes that regarded him solemnly.

"You OK?" How embarrassing that he should have to bleat out his insecurity by asking her that question, over and over.

"I don't know," she said. "I don't even know myself around you. All my demons wake up and go nuts."

"Oh." He could think of nothing comforting or cheerful to say to that. It didn't sound very goddamn promising. "Uh, sorry."

"It's not your fault," she told him.

"I guess that's a relief." He twitched the comforter

off her and tugged on her hand. "Come try out my hot tub."

She sat up. "Oh, please. Is this another one of your tricks? Next you're going to show me your etchings."

He pulled her up off the bed. "Actually, no. To be honest, I'm kind of freaked out myself. I want to just sit in hot water and mellow out for a while."

Tendrils of steam rose up, illuminated by the underwater lights. They sank slowly down into the hot water, and silence spread out between them, becoming more vast and heavy with each passing minute. He took a deep breath, and forced himself to break it.

"It was perfect between us. Why are you so upset?"

She twisted her hair up into a knot, her eyes downcast. "Perfection is impossible," she said quietly. "No one knows that better than me. I want to hang on, but I know that I can't."

Vague, restless anger churned in his gut. "Why not?"

She looked away. "Because I can't. Things end. It's the nature of life."

Her bleak word foretold doom for this fragile, beautiful thing budding between them. She was jinxing it. It made him feel panicked.

"It doesn't have to end," he said. "I certainly don't want it to."

Her gaze snapped up to him. "Don't you dare dangle that in front of me, like all the other bait," she said, her eyes blazing with unexpected anger. "The foot rub, the chocolate soufflé, the queen of the universe. I won't bite this time. I may be stupid, but I'm not *that* stupid."

"Do not ever let me hear you call yourself stupid again," he said.

She sat up, her nipples just clearing the waterline. "Do not scold me," she said, enunciating very clearly.

They stared at each other, at a blind impasse. He'd never felt so baffled, so helpless. "What's happening, Tess?" he asked. "Tell me what I'm doing wrong. Tell me what you want from me."

Her eyes squeezed shut. "I don't know," she whispered.

He stared at her beautiful, averted face, praying to find the right formula not to fuck this up. He was starting to need her. Her sweetness, her sharpness, her beauty. She made him feel so alive. And the more he wanted her, the more she seemed determined to slip away.

"Well, I know exactly what I want from you," he said rashly. "I already know what I want to cook for you, what I want to show you, how I want to touch you. I want to help you open your studio, too. I'll do a business plan for you—"

"Jonah—"

"Let me finish. I can give you double the money I was planning to give you this weekend right away. If that's not enough, then I can—"

"Don't be ridiculous!" She jerked back, horrified. "I can't take money from you! What would that make me?"

"Get real. You turned down paying work to come up here. I was the one who seduced you and turned everything upside down. You're entitled to that money. Call it a start-up loan if you insist, but—"

"Jonah. Not one more word."

The coldness of her voice stopped him. *Shit.* He'd bombed again.

"I can do this on my own," she said. "I don't need anybody to rescue me. I am not a child. Or an idiot."

He pushed his hair back off his forehead with a silent groan. Everything he said came out wrong, everything he did flew back in his face. It was like a bad dream. "I never meant to imply otherwise," he said stiffly. "Please don't be offended."

She hunched down in the tub, her arms wrapped across her chest. She looked so lost that his heart thudded painfully. He would offer her anything to make her smile again, anything. He stretched out his arms. "Please, Tess. Come here."

She drifted toward him, her chin lifted. He ached to soothe the proud hurt in her eyes. "Come home with me tomorrow," he urged. "Move into my apartment. I've got plenty of space. I want you in my bed. You can even have your own bathroom, if you want. I've got two."

Her eyes went wide and startled. "Wow. That's bold."

"Bold. Yeah. That's me," he said. "Will you? Pretty please?"

She opened and closed her mouth. "But I . . . my roommate will be expecting . . . and I'll need my clothes—"

"To hell with your clothes," he broke in. "I'm going to buy you a new wardrobe, anyhow. Enough of those ugly burlap dresses you wear, particularly if you're opening a business. You need stuff that—"

She sprang to her feet. Water sloshed into his mouth, blocking off the rest of his phrase, *"shows off how sexy and beautiful you are."*

She clambered out of the tub. "No way." Her voice shook with anger. "I dress the way I dress, Jonah Markham. I am what I am, and to hell with you if it's not good enough."

Oh, hell. He should have remembered. The clothes were a hot button, and he'd stomped all over it. He reached for her, but she wrenched her wet arm away from him with such desperate violence that he shrank back. "Tess, I'm sorry. I—"

"I mean it, Jonah. Don't touch me."

He stared at her trembling back. "I can't believe this. Dealing with you is like walking through a fucking minefield. I can see what your ex's problem with you was, if you were always this hysterical and unreasonable. I guess I've got some goddamn high standards of my own."

His shot met its mark, but the devastated look she shot back over her shoulder gave him no satisfaction at all.

In fact, it made him feel like five different kinds of shit.

Her clothes were scattered all over the house. She searched for them feverishly, pulling them on as she found them. This was worse than she had ever dreamed. Painful memories crowded through her mind: Larry gently suggesting a fitness trainer, to "help get rid of that puppy fat." An image consultant, for her clothes. A makeup expert, to teach her to compensate for her beauty problems. A wine-tasting course. Diction classes, to get rid of that lingering California college girl flavor in her accent. Larry believed in investing time, money, and effort in one's greatest personal resource: oneself; and Tess's mother had applauded his efforts. *"It's good that you have someone who pushes you to be the best that you can be, honey. A mother can only do so much."*

Well, wasn't that the truth, and thank God for it.

She had to get out of here, before she started to sink into the cracks in the floorboards, the incredible shrinking Tess. Embarrassed to take up space, apologizing for the very air she breathed. She thought she had worked through these awful feelings and left them behind, but here they were, stronger than ever, and it was

Jonah's face, Jonah's voice superimposed over Larry's. And that was a thousand times worse.

Jonah appeared at the foot of the stairs, watching as she broke down her massage table. He hadn't bothered to dry himself. He just stood there, naked, a puddle forming around his feet. The silent reproach in his shadowy eyes tore at her. She had to get away before she shrank too small to even see over the dashboard of her VW Bug. There seemed to be no end to how bad she could feel about this.

"Sorry," she whispered.

He did not reply for a long moment. "Me, too," he said finally.

It took over two and a half hours in the rain to get home, sniffling all the way. Trish turned away from the TV and regarded her with blank astonishment when she stumbled in the door.

"What are you doing back already?"

"It didn't work out." Her voice was dull and flat.

Trish switched off the TV and stared at Tess with big, worried blue eyes. "Are you, um, OK?" she asked cautiously.

"Let me give you the short version, because I can't handle a full-scale debriefing right now. Did I earn four thousand bucks? No. Did I have sex? Yes. Was it good? Yes, it was so unbelievably good that it practically destroyed me. Do I want to jump off a bridge? Maybe."

"Oh, dear." Trish bit her lip. "No money, hmm? How about the start-up? What are you going to tell your mom?"

Trish let the massage table fall to the ground with a rattling thud. "I'll tell her what I should've told her all along. That it's none of her goddamn business. I'll find the money some other way, in my own good time. And I am never, ever going to let anybody push me around, ever again. Not my parents, not Jonah, not Jeanette, not even you, Trish."

Trish blinked. "Not even me? That is some serious stuff, chica. I'm not sure whether to break out the champagne or dial 911."

Tess's chin started to shake. "How about you just give me a hug?"

Trish almost fell over her feet rushing to her.

It was a damn good thing he had more important things to occupy his mind, he kept telling himself.

Uh-huh. Yeah. Right. The fuck-up with Tess looped endlessly through his mind, whenever he wasn't worrying about Granddad.

It was driving him nuts. He didn't need a woman like that in his life. Too much trouble, too oversensitive, too quick to take offense. Life was too short to spend it tiptoeing around her tender little feelings.

But she was so sweet, and funny, and sensual. He'd never had sex like that in his life. He was ruined for normal women.

His office staff were whispering and circling around him like he was a rabid animal. He kept calling the MMC, and slamming the phone down before it started to ring. He would have called her at home, if he had her number, but she wasn't in the book, and he didn't know the roommate's last name, and besides, why bother? She had his number. If she wanted to talk to him, she could call him anytime.

But she hadn't. She wouldn't. He had to get that through his thick skull, and let it go, and that left Granddad to worry about.

Sunday, Monday, Tuesday. Days ticked into nights that ticked relentlessly back into days again.

Wednesday morning dawned. The day stretched out ahead of him, long and bleak. He had to sit through the surgery sharing the waiting room with his asshole cousins and their bitchy wives. Oh, it wasn't that big of a deal. He'd survive. Those clowns didn't make his life bad, they just made it stupid. He didn't have the energy to deal with stupidity.

Hah. Then why did he keep dialing the goddamn MMC?

Maybe he could just drop by today, and ask her to wish him luck. There wouldn't be any other friendly face to pat him on the back today, and he was going to sit in a hard plastic chair in a hospital waiting room, clutching an outdated *Field & Stream* magazine, facing his deepest fears today for God alone knew how many hours. It would be really nice to get a hug first. Just to have those strong, warm hands on him for a minute would soothe that jittery ache inside him. He had just enough time to go down to the MMC on the hour and catch her between clients before he headed to the hospital.

He had to get over himself. Granddad was an old man; he had to go sometime. Everyone did. Just not quite yet. Please, not yet.

He got there five minutes early, and was doomed to deal with the Martian receptionist. Great. As if he weren't going to get enough hostile glares from his cousins at the hospital today.

"She's booked all day. And she's with a client now," the receptionist informed him, with a sugary, fuck-you smile. "And she can't bag somebody else's appointment for you, because Jeanette chewed her out for that last week. Big time. So don't even think it."

He glanced at his watch, exercising all the self-

control at his command. "Just tell her I'm here,
please," he said, rigidly polite.

The receptionist rolled her eyes and flounced into
the back rooms. She came back moments later, with a
long-suffering look. He grinned at her with all his
teeth. She got very busy with her appointment book.

Tess came out a few moments later. Her hair was
screwed into the most severe knot he had ever seen,
and her face was pale, washed out by the white dress.
Her rubber-soled shoes squeaked with every step. He
glanced down at them. She'd either done a superhuman
job getting the mud off, or she had more than one pair.
They were snow white. As if the primeval sex in the
forest had never happened.

Her face was just like her shoes. She had an it-
never-happened expression: cool, polite, ever so slightly
strained. With a professional, can-I-help-you-you-
pathetic-bastard smile.

Dread gathered in his gut like an ice-cold stone.
"Can I, uh, speak to you for a few minutes?"

"I have a client, Jonah."

He clenched his teeth and he swallowed, resolved to
see this through, one way or the other. "Please," he
said. "It's important."

She sighed and circled the receptionist's desk. The
squeak-squeak-squeak of her shoes was driving him
nuts. She stood in front of him in the waiting room, in
front of everyone. Arms crossed over her chest. Waiting. Her foot would tap, if she weren't so fucking polite.

"Can we go someplace more private?" he asked.

Her sensual mouth tightened to a thin line. "I have a
client in the back room," she said. "And if you want an
emergency appointment, I'm very sorry, but I can't ac-

commodate you. Welcome to the real world. I'm sure it must be a rude shock, but sometimes mundane reality just can't conform to Jonah Markham's whims."

Shields up, shields up. The red alert went off in his head, but it was too late. The torpedo had already gone speeding straight in, dead on the mark, completely trashing his main reactor. He had no way of knowing what expression he had on his face as he backed away. All that was important was getting out that door.

He jerked back as if she'd slapped him, his face going pale and stiff, and a horrible realization yawned open inside her, as if she had just stepped over a cliff. She was hurtling down, down, with a sick, scared falling feeling in her stomach. She had made a terrible mistake.

She lunged for him in a panic. "Oh, God. I didn't mean that. I'm sorry, Jonah. I just—"

He wrenched his arm from her, backing away faster. "Never mind. I'm out of here. Sorry I bothered you."

She scrambled to intercept him at the door. "No. Please, tell me what's wrong. Why—"

"Never mind. I got my answer. Out of my way. I'm in a hurry."

She watched him run down the stairs and stride away, as utterly wretched as if she'd just killed something beautiful, out of pure, blind stupidity. Her body exploded into movement, pure instinct taking over. It knew what it wanted, knew what was right. It could not be reasoned with, or cowed. She raced after him, legs pumping, and tackled him from behind. She clung to his slippery canvas coat like a monkey.

He cursed and tried to shake her off. "I don't have time for your weird mind trips today, Tess."

"I said I was sorry. I was a heinous bitch for saying that. You didn't deserve it, and I'll make it up to you somehow. And you are not getting away from me until you tell me what you came here for."

He tried halfheartedly to detach her clinging hands. "You're strangling me, Tess," he said wearily.

She tightened her arms, pressing her wrist hard against his windpipe on purpose. "Tough titties."

His shoulders shook with silent laughter. He grabbed her forearms and pulled them down so that he could breathe. "My Granddad's getting open-heart surgery today. I was just going to . . . oh, shit, I don't know. Maybe ask you to come by the hospital later, if you have time. To sit with me while I wait. But you're super busy, I can see that, so whatever. I didn't have any reason to think you would want to. Just thought I'd ask."

"Oh, Jonah—"

"Let go of me, for Christ's sake. I feel bad enough as it is. And I want to get over there before they put him under."

"But Jonah, I didn't mean to—"

"No big deal." His voice cut across hers. "Get on back to your client. Let go, Tess. I really don't want to have to be rough with you."

She swung herself around, still clutching his arm. His face was like graven stone, turned resolutely away from her.

"Can you wait a minute?" she pleaded. "Just long enough for me to grab my purse and tell my boss what happened?"

"You don't have to feel sorry for me," he said. "I was an idiot to come here. I should have learned my lesson back at the lake."

She clung to his arm with all her strength. "Believe me, Jonah, there is nothing on earth I would rather do than go and wait at the hospital with you. Wait for me. *Please.*"

The anguished doubt in his eyes tore at her. He had always seemed so strong, vital, and confident. It hurt like hell to see him in pain. What a thick-skulled idiot she'd been; so intent on protecting her own heart that it never occurred to her that she actually had the power to wound his.

And the more jealously she guarded her heart, the more barren and cramped and arid it would be. At this rate, it wouldn't be long until there was nothing left in there to protect.

She raised his hand to her lips, dropping a supplicating kiss onto his knuckles. "Please," she whispered.

He closed his eyes. "I'll wait two minutes. Then I'm out of here."

She didn't even remember what she said in that mad flurry of explanations and apologies. Thank God she'd been lying about the client in the back room, and a quick glance at the schedule assured her that there was enough staff to cover her clients for the rest of the day. She grabbed her purse and ran, heedless of the protests that Lacey and Jeanette shouted after her. To hell with that stupid job. She'd been bullied, taken advantage of, overworked, and underpaid for too long, and she was sick to death of that ghastly white dress. She would find another job if her bridges burned this afternoon.

Jonah was more important.

She had to scurry to keep up with him as he strode through the corridors of the hospital. She clutched his rigid forearm and let him tow her along beside him. He beckoned her through a pair of big automatic doors, and finally they entered a room where a very pale elderly man with bushy white eyebrows and a hawklike nose lay on a gurney. His gray eyes glinted with anger, like a trapped animal. He saw Jonah, and his brows snapped together in a thunderous frown.

Jonah pulled Tess until she stood next to him, in the old man's line of sight. "Hi, Granddad," Jonah said, in a cautious voice. "This is my girlfriend, Tess. We just wanted to wish you luck."

The old man's eyes shot back to Tess, scrutinizing her with fierce concentration. She smiled at him. "Good to meet you, Mr. Markham."

His grizzled brows shot up, and his gaze dropped appreciatively down the length of her body. She could have sworn that he winked at her, but a nurse hustled into the room, clucking with disapproval.

"Authorized surgical personnel only, at this point," she said sternly. "Out you go."

"Sorry," Jonah muttered to Tess as the nurse herded them out.

"For what?" she asked.

"For calling you my girlfriend. It just popped out."

She slid her arm around his waist. "I liked it," she whispered.

A flash of a smile crossed his pale face. "He likes you."

"How can you tell? He didn't say a word."

"Yeah, he's still pissed with me. I wouldn't take over for him at Markham Savings & Loan, so he still won't speak to me. Stubborn old bastard. But he likes you. Believe me, I can tell."

Shortly afterward, the waiting room began to fill. Two middle-aged men, one paunchy, the other thin and balding, and two women of the same age filed into the room, all talking in loud voices and staring at Jonah and her with what could only be described as pure hostility.

It was disconcerting. She glanced at Jonah, but he either hadn't noticed them or was pretending not to.

His eyes were closed. She leaned closer to him. "Who are those rude, horrible people?" she whispered.

Jonah opened his eyes and shot them a weary glance. "My cousins, John and Steve, and their wives, Marilyn and Sandra. They're jealous of me, because I was Granddad's first choice to head up his company. Even though I turned it down and went my own way. They hate my guts. Long, boring story. Try to ignore them. That's what I do."

She slid a protective arm around his shoulder as one of the women came over, a well-dressed, strained-looking blond with a stringy neck. "Jonah, it's really very selfish of you to insist on being here when you know perfectly well that it upsets Frank to see you."

The woman's voice had the studied forcefulness that comes from assertiveness training workshops. Tess should know, since Larry had insisted that she take one "to increase her confidence and personal effectiveness." Tess tightened her arm around Jonah's shoulders and decided to put everything she had learned in that workshop to use.

"Why don't you just piss off?" she asked, in a calm, well-modulated voice. She gave the blond woman a dazzling smile.

The blond's mouth dangled open for a moment. It snapped shut. The nostrils of her pinched, narrow nose flared unpleasantly.

She glared down at Jonah. "Who is this person?"

Jonah looked at Tess. His weary, drawn face relaxed into a smile so radiant and beautiful that she almost burst into tears.

"Sandra, meet my girlfriend, Tess Langley," he said. "And she's just made a truly excellent suggestion. Piss off."

His arms wrapped around Tess, sealing them into a

private space where the shrill, hostile voices squawking across the room were less important than the sound of faraway cars honking.

Time passed differently in their hushed, magical intimacy. She held his hand and contemplated the huge tenderness she felt for him, amazed that she had not allowed herself to acknowledge it until now. She wanted to protect, to heal, to comfort him. She couldn't fight against it, and she didn't want to. All she could do was hang on to his hand and try to breathe around the soft, melting feeling in her heart that kept getting bigger with each passing minute. She kept reminding herself that to cry would be self-indulgent and inappropriate. She had to keep it together, for Jonah's sake.

Hours went by. Cups of coffee, hushed conversation. Jonah's relatives looked glum and stressed, sniping at each other.

Jonah straightened up when the surgeon came out, relaxing visibly when he saw the smile on the man's face. Frank was doing well, the surgeon told them. The procedure had gone smoothly, his vital signs were stable, and they didn't expect any complications.

Jonah pressed his face against her shoulder, and her eyes overflowed. She couldn't hold it back any longer. The soft feeling in her chest made her feel strong. No more incredible shrinking Tess. She finally understood the puzzle that had confounded her for so long.

Her love for Jonah made her bigger, stronger. More of everything that was right and good and real.

She shifted, anxious not to let him think even for a fleeting second that she was pushing him away, and slid herself onto his lap. She fit his head under her chin, inhaling his warm scent. Delicious and satisfying.

He smelled like home.

* * *

He was out there, in orbit. Way beyond civilized, normal conversation. Emotions roared through him: relief at having the fear of losing Granddad lifted, and jagged, edgy exultation at having Tess in his grip again. She was looking at him with those glowing eyes that made him want to fling himself at her feet and clutch at her ankles.

He should be charming her, thanking her, he thought dimly. She'd been really sweet to him, sticking by him, defending him from Sandra and the rest. He should be making nice, thinking of something impressive to cook for her, being witty and urbane. Earning points.

It wasn't happening. All he could do was bundle her into his car, sweep her away to his lair, and use every trick that came to him to keep her there. Whatever it took to persuade her that she belonged with him.

He heard her ask where he was taking her, through the roaring in his ears. He snapped out "home," in a voice brusque enough to discourage any further attempts at conversation. So much for his boyish charm. And his converted warehouse apartment in the Pearl District, furnished with the sleek, postmodern chill of a well-to-do bachelor pad, was not homey. At least the fridge was full. He wished he could take her back to the lake, but it was too far away. He needed her now. So bad that it scared him.

The car alarm and door lock chirped behind him as he pulled her up the battered warehouse staircase that he hadn't had a chance to renovate yet. It was spooky-looking, but if he pulled her into the apartment really fast, she wouldn't have time to be creeped out.

The door swung shut behind them with an ominous, resounding, Dracula's Castle type of thud. At this rate, he was going to end up scaring her to death. He cast around helplessly for something normal, soothing, welcoming to say to her. No words came to him.

He gave in to brute necessity, and wrapped his fingers around her slender wrist, pulling her through the apartment. He couldn't be bothered to turn on the lights, to take her coat, to lay down her purse, or offer her a drink. He headed straight for the bedroom.

He shoved her coat off, letting it fall to the floor, and seized her. Kissing her like he was dying of thirst, and she was an oasis in the desert, full of sweet, life-giving water. She didn't recoil from his intensity at all. She pressed herself against him and opened for him, freely offering him all the springlike freshness of her soft mouth, her fragrant breath. The tender, wet assay of her tongue against his made him shudder with need. He didn't want to spoil this by being clumsy or rough, groping and pawing like a gorilla, but his hands had a will of their own. He couldn't stop touching her, cupping her lush curves.

She pulled away, and he was about to howl in frustration until he realized that she was just pulling loose the laces of her sneakers. She kicked them off and reached under her skirt to peel off the white hose. He couldn't wait to feel her pansy-soft skin sliding beneath his hands, the sexy swell of her ass. Every tiny detail thrilled him.

She shook with soft laughter as he wrenched her hose down to her ankles, and shoved the skirt up to her waist. Just what he was dying for—Tess all naked and soft and open. He could smell the humid warmth of her femaleness. It made him dizzy. He could barely make out the soft dark curls between her thighs, the graceful female curves in the dim room, but he couldn't bear to stop even long enough to turn on the light. He explored her with his hands, his face, his nose, his mouth, nuzzling and kissing her with desperate appeal. Assuring himself that she was real, she was here, she was his.

She grabbed his shoulders to steady herself against him, but he didn't want her steady. He wanted her flat on her back beneath him, wide open. With one well-placed push, he sent her pitching backward with a cry of alarm onto his bed, legs sprawled. He lunged to cover her before she could draw breath or protest.

Her eyes were wide, breath coming soft and shallow as he wrenched open the buttons of the dress. They yielded with a soft popping noise. No T-shirt under it, just a silk bra of indeterminate color, cupping the luminously pale bulges of her stunning breasts. She glowed like moonlight on his bed. Her fingers slid through his hair, touched his face. Cool and soft and caressing.

He buried his face against her bosom, rubbing it against the incredible softness and scent of her. Drinking it in, big greedy gulps.

She petted his hair as he nuzzled her cleavage. "You seem so desperate," she murmured.

Her thighs tightened around him as he licked the shadowy cleft between her tits, and his cock hardened even more, if that were possible. "I feel desperate," he admitted.

"You don't have to be," she assured him. "You've got me right where you want me." She stroked his hot cheek, soothing him, like he were some pitiable, maddened animal. He hated it and loved it, felt shamed and eager, like a trembling puppy grateful for every little pat.

He lifted his head, trying to calm down his ragged breathing, and noticed that her bra was the front-clasp type. He could have wept with appreciation for the convenience, but there was something he had to tell her, if his damn throat would stop vibrating long enough for him to use his voice. He swallowed over and over to make his larynx descend.

"I won't hurt you," he said.

She cupped her face in her hands, smiling at him. "Of course you won't," she told him. "I trust you."

His breath froze in his throat. "You didn't before," he said.

She kissed his jaw. "Give me credit for learning," she said softly. "I won't hurt you, either. You can trust me, too."

She squirmed beneath him until he realized that she was reaching back to undo the knot of hair—an enterprise he was absolutely willing to second and support. He plucked out hairpins and tossed them away with a disdain that bordered on hostility.

"You should wear your hair down all the time," he said.

A spasm of dread froze his insides. She was going to freak out on him for critizicing her hairdo. He'd fucked up again.

But she just laughed. "I will, if you like it that way. But you'd better get good at combing out my tangles."

"I'll be great," he promised her rashly. "I'll spend hours, naked, combing your hair. My new career. Naked hairdressing."

She looked like a pagan goddess with all that long, amazing curly hair spread over his pillow. He buried his face in it, letting tears leak out of his eyes and soak into her hair. He had to distract himself, quick. Sex and tears did not mix, at least not with him, and he wanted the sex.

So did she, thank God, if the focused attention she was giving to his shirt buttons was any indication. He undid the clasp of her bra and rubbed his face against her breasts with a moan of appreciation. He stroked the rich full undercurve with the soft, fluttering fingertip caresses that she loved, and pressed them together, kissing and licking until she writhed and moaned.

He unbuckled his belt, undid his jeans. She slid her hands eagerly inside the waistband of his underwear and gripped his cock, with the tight, slow pull that she knew he loved. He tried to keep his weight poised above her without going boneless with pleasure. Then it hit him. He collapsed against her, limp with dismay. "Oh, God, no."

"What?" Her eyes were wide with alarm.

"The fucking condoms," he groaned. "I left them at the lake. This is it. The final insult. I'm going to die right here, in your arms. Get ready for the tragic, tender moment. Move over, Scarlett and Rhett."

She started to laugh. "You're not going to die," she teased. "I've still got that stash that Trish put in my purse, remember? We can use the glow-in-the-dark one if you want. We'll probably have to expose it to light first, though, if we want it to work."

"Forget it. It'll take too long," he snapped.

"OK," she said cheerfully. "We'll save the glow-in-the-dark one for the third or fourth time. I'll get the chocolate and raspberry flavored one, instead. Just let me figure out where I dropped my purse, and—"

"Stay right where you are," he ordered. "I'll get them."

She lay back, apparently submissive, but he knew her too well to be fooled, particularly when she had that smile on her face. She opened her legs wider, the white skirt still crumpled around her waist, the bodice gaping open, her plump tits spilling out of it. Taunting him.

She put her hand against the dark tangle of hair on

her mound. "It wouldn't make any difference if we had no condoms," she said huskily. "I'd just suck on you. Make you explode in my mouth. As many times as you want."

He was wide-eyed, frozen, and as stiff as a railroad spike. Hypnotized by the sensual pulse of her hips against his bed. "Are you pushing me again?" he demanded. "Playing games with me?"

She shook her head. "Oh, no. I just love the feel of your eyes on me. They press on me, burn me. It turns me on. And I love the feel of your, um . . . your cock. In my mouth. So hard, and yet so soft and velvety. Strong and sensitive. Delicious."

He dumped the contents of her purse heedlessly onto the bed, pawing through the assorted female paraphernalia until he found what he needed. He ripped open the condom and rolled it over himself. "I'm going to hold you to that," he warned. "For the third or fourth time."

He mounted her, guiding himself to her tender opening. It was too soon, experience and instinct all screamed at him that it was too soon, but he couldn't wait. He could only drive himself into her, deep and hard. The sound that jerked out of her throat as her body slowly yielded to him was not unmixed pleasure, but he pushed deeper, clenching his jaw. And withdrew, and drove in again, harder than he meant to. Her fingers dug sharply into his upper arms.

"I'm sorry," he said, his voice shaking. "I'm too—I can't—"

"Shhh." Her arms and legs closed around him tightly. "It's OK. I love you. I feel it, too. I love you."

Nothing but that hot blaze of joy and disbelief could have shocked him into stillness. "You do?"

She pressed her damp face against his. "Yes. I've never felt like this before. It's so huge, I'm lost in it."

He marveled at her words for another frozen, breathless moment. "So am I," he said. "But—the other night—"

She shook her head. "You have to forgive me for the other night," she said. "My whole universe was falling apart to make space for you. It felt like dying. I just panicked."

He pried his face away. "And now?" he demanded.

Her smile was luminous with joy. "Now I'm bigger," she said simply. "Now there's space. I finally figured it out today. I know I'm good enough, because I'm the best I've ever been, loving you."

He was so moved, he had to fight to speak. "I'm lost in it, too," he whispered. "I love you, Tess."

The triumphant joy inside him melted away every last vestige of his self-control.

Tess dug her fingers into the muscles in his shoulders and hung on. It didn't hurt at all anymore, after that first rough moment. Almost instantly she had softened to him, and now she was lost in bliss. Nothing was more perfect than this voluptuous give and take, the sweet, hot friction. He followed cues she didn't even know she gave him, shifting his weight up and pressing the length of his fingers on either side of her clitoris. Sliding them slowly up and down her slick cleft, exactly as she had shown him when she had tied him down and touched herself. His face was tense with concentration, eyes locked with hers. The power rose between them, higher and higher. It broke, and they collapsed into a sweaty, trembling knot of desperate tenderness.

They stayed clenched together, for a long time.

Jonah flung himself onto his back beside her and covered his face with his hand. "Don't run away from me again, Tess."

She rolled up onto her elbow. "Jonah—"

"I wanted to come see you at the MMC, but I was afraid I would creep you out if I dragged my tongue around on the ground after you. So I tried to play it cool, you know? Stay away. But it didn't work. I can't be cool. I just can't do it. I'm madly in love with you."

"Oh, Jonah." Tears made her voice quiver. "I'm so sorry about the other night. I thought that you were . . . that you were trying to—"

"To what?" His hand dropped. He stared at her.

She plucked at the duvet. "I thought you wanted to . . . make me good enough to fit into your gourmet lifestyle," she confessed. "To bring me up to standard."

His face was expressionless. "Like the other guy did."

She sighed, and nodded.

He grabbed her wrist, tugging her until she was eye to eye with him. "Can we make a pact, here and now, to never, ever—"

"Oh, God, yes," she said fervently. "I'm so embarrassed. I will never compare you to him, ever again. You are nothing like him, Jonah, nothing. He was just a hollow shell. You're for real."

He gave her a pleased, baffled smile. "Thank you," he said. He stroked his knuckle with reverent gentleness over her cheekbone. "And just for the record, I don't think you need fixing. I think you're perfect. But if we're going to be together, you're going to have to deal with me buying you clothes and jewelry without getting all huffy about it. Because I'm not going to be able to help myself."

She kissed his hand as it touched her face and snuggled closer to him. "I, um, think I'll learn to cope somehow."

"I can't wait to really introduce you to Granddad. He'll be out of his mind with curiosity about you. That'll motivate him to forgive me, if anything will. Granddad never could resist the ladies. And you're his type."

"What type is that?" she asked.

"*My* type," he said forcefully. "Strong, smart, sexy, sweet, fascinating. Challenging, complicated. And absolutely for real."

"Like you," she said. "For real."

His lips met hers, with reverent tenderness. "And forever."